PRAISE
FOR

The Girl in the Corn

"[An] unholy mash-up of creepy, high-body-count paranormal
thrills . . . Readers will find themselves well sated before the end."
—**Publishers Weekly**

"*The Girl in the Corn* is a haunting, unsettling, gripping novel.
I will have nightmares of circles filled with needle teeth for years
to come. In these cornfields are such original, disturbing beasts—
I was hypnotized by their presence on the page."
—**Richard Thomas, Bram Stoker and Shirley Jackson nominee**

"Norse mythology gives this story . . . a unique touch [with] an
exhilarating conclusion." —**Booklist**

THE BOY FROM TWO WORLDS

THE BOY FROM TWO WORLDS

JASON OFFUTT

CamCat
Books

CamCat Publishing, LLC
Fort Collins, Colorado 80524
camcatpublishing.com

Hardcover ISBN 9780744308242
Paperback ISBN 9780744308259
Large-Print Paperback ISBN 9780744308273
eBook ISBN 9780744308266
Audiobook ISBN 9780744308280

Library of Congress Control Number: 2023947345

Book and cover design by Maryann Appel

Interior artwork by A-Digit, Bitter, Bortonia, Oksancia

5   3   1   2   4

For AC⚡DC.

*You boys have pulled me out of more than one
writing rut over the years.
And that ain't noise pollution, man.* ✌

2016

ST. JOE
ANGEL OF DEATH
IDENTIFIED

By CHAD CLAYTON

News-Press Staff Writer

ST. JOSEPH, Mo., Dec. 26— Through DNA tests, authorities have identified the orchestrator of the domestic terrorist attack that killed 462 people in St. Joseph, Missouri, just before Christmas, mostly patients and staff at St. Joseph Children's Hospital. St. Joseph native Robert Patrick Garrett rigged the chain of explosions, which involved many underground gasoline tanks at downtown convenience stores, that injured more than 1,500 others and resulted in $3.2 billion in property damage.

Garrett, dubbed the "St. Joe Angel of Death" by bloggers and true-crime podcasters, murdered 16-year-old camper Ronald Henry Johnson at Smithville Lake in 1990, and spent four years in the Missouri Juvenile Detention Facility in Cameron before being committed to psychiatric care for two more years at Sisters of Mercy Hospital in St. Joseph.

Searching the ruins of the Garrett home in South St. Joseph—that exploded around midnight Dec. 21 with homemade C-4, which killed Buchanan County Sheriff Boyd Donally and Emily Kristiansen—authorities discovered the remains of Garrett's parents, Todd and Vera Garrett, along with those of Karen Novák and her daughter, Millie. The Nováks went missing in 2005 while selling Girl Scout cookies.

ST. JOE ANGEL OF DEATH IDENTIFIED

Apart from Donally and Kristiansen, Garrett's victims bore blunt trauma to their heads, St. Joseph Police Chief Emery Trumble said.

"The explosion scattered the house across a two-block area," he said. "But the bodies were stored by Garrett in the basement and were protected by concrete and brick. We identified the victims' remains through DNA and dental records. The skulls of the Garretts and Nováks showed signs of being struck repeatedly with a heavy object."

Investigators from the FBI discovered parts for homemade timers along with ingredients for C-4 in the debris. They also determined Garrett repeatedly searched online for news reports of the Rolling Meadows Mall ricin attack, as well as the arson of the Mid-Buchannan High School that occurred during a basketball game, claiming 60 lives, and the destruction of the Missouri River bridge at Atchison, Kansas, with thermite that resulted in 27 more. Prior to each attack, Garrett used his St. Joseph Public Library card to access the internet under the name Jack Torrence, the antagonist of the Stephen King book, "The Shining," FBI Special Agent Garnett Renfro told the Associated Press.

"His research foreshadowed each attack," Renfro said.

Garrett died in the explosion that destroyed the children's hospital where he worked as a custodian. Co-worker Connie Dunwoodie said Garrett came to the hospital the night of the bombing, although he wasn't scheduled to work.

"Bobby told our manager, Randolph (Blythe), I'd asked him to work for me," she said. "I never did. I was at work like always. I went outside for a smoke when the bombs went off." Dunwoodie shook her head. "I'm so lucky."

Authorities still investigating "The Day St. Joseph Died" are not sure if Garrett acted alone.

ST. JOE ANGEL OF DEATH IDENTIFIED

Found at the center of the attacks were Marguerite Jenkins of Savannah, Missouri, whom Garrett kidnapped after the ricin attack, and Thomas Cavanaugh and Jillian Robertson, a couple from rural Buchanan County. All were injured during the explosions; Jenkins was pregnant with Garrett's child at the time.

All were questioned by the St. Joseph Police Department and the FBI.

Inquiries for interviews with Jenkins, Cavanaugh and Robertson have been unanswered.

THE
BEGINNING
OF THE
END

2017

PROLOGUE

SNOW PAINTED THE bleak landscape white as Kurt Russell, Keith David, and a band of Antarctic scientists and explorers faced a screaming Norwegian helicopter pilot brandishing a West German Heckler and Koch assault rifle. The pilot squeezed off a few rounds at a fleeing dog (a wolf-Alaskan malamute hybrid, Marguerite once read) before shooting an American scientist in the leg, finishing a screaming tirade in Norwegian with, "*Kom dere vekk, idioter!*"

The pilot jerked backward, falling to the snow, when Antarctic Outpost 31 Commander M. T. Garry shot him in the eye. Not one of the Americans realized the Norwegian was actually yelling, "Get the hell away! It's not a dog, it's some sort of thing! It's imitating a dog, it isn't real! Get away, you idiots!"

Marguerite Jenkins sat on the couch in her mother's house, her sore legs up on a footstool, a bowl of popcorn resting on her swollen belly as she watched *John Carpenter Weekend* on TMC.

"Americans are so stupid," she said through a full mouth, kernel shrapnel scattering down her turquoise maternity blouse.

As if Baby Jenkins heard her, he rolled in her uterus, like a human body was built for this kind of torture.

Dear God, nature was the worst.

"Do you need anything, honey?" her mother asked from the kitchen.

After her father died when she was young, Linda Jenkins turned into the mom Marguerite had grown up envying on black-and-white sitcom reruns. She felt guilty now that she couldn't move without hurting, but it was nice when—

A dull ache pushed through her lower abdomen; if her pelvis had a mouth it would have screamed.

"Oh," she said, wrapping her arms around her belly. A warm wetness soaked through her panties and sweatpants onto the couch, then ran down both legs.

"You all right?" Linda said, poking her head around the corner.

Marguerite grabbed another handful of popcorn and stuffed it into her mouth.

"I really wanna finish *The Thing*," she said, "but I think I need to go to the hospital. Can you TiVo the rest?"

[2]

Fireflies streaked through the darkness on Carlyle Street like tiny comets dancing in the night. The insects Glenn chased on his parents' farm as a child, and the net of silence cast over the dead street, drew broad strokes of peace over the evil that once lived in the house at 4244.

Not all the evil had gone.

A red face stared at Glenn Kirkhoff—Sheriff Glenn Kirkhoff—in the flashlight beam he shone on the old foundation. A simple face as if it had been painted by the hand of a child—round, with a wide, smiling, triangular mouth—but what sent a chill through Kirkhoff's already tight shoulders were the teeth. Long, sharp, pointed, like one of those freaky-looking deep-sea fish they show on Animal Planet.

Kirkhoff stood with his thumbs in his big black belt like he'd seen Boyd do countless times. The flames, the smoke, the explosion were long gone from this address. So was Boyd. What connected Boyd to this hole in the ground that once held up the house where he and his girlfriend died six months ago was that face. That creepy goddamn face once painted in blood on walls in Elvin Miller's house and Carrie Mc-Masters's house, places where a spouse had butchered their significant other with a bladed object: Miller an ax, McMasters a butcher knife.

And the thing was here.

"What were you into, Boyd?" Kirkhoff whispered, the far-off grumble of a car engine the only sound in this old, lonely neighborhood.

He swung by Carlyle Street whenever he came to this part of St. Joe, drawn by that painted face. Somebody, probably the city, cleaned out the wreckage of the old Victorian home, mowed the lawn, and prepared the property for auction.

The sooner this puckered butthole of the world was buried in dirt or garbage, or the foundation destroyed and hauled off, the better. The destruction Robert Garrett had rained over St. Joseph, Missouri, needed to be buried in the past. The city had erased the many downtown scars, only one replaced with a memorial. The plaque read: "St. Joseph Children's Hospital. Two-Hundred Forty-Three Innocent Lives Lost. May We Never Forget."

Innocent. No one was ever innocent. A career in law enforcement had taught him that.

His mobile phone buzzed in the front pants pocket of his uniform. He pulled it out. Linda. Margie's mom. The one good thing to come from the explosions and fires that raged in this city: Marguerite Jenkins got free from that psycho Bobby Garrett.

Kirkhoff swiped his thumb toward the green button and answered: "Hello?"

"Glenn," Linda said, her voice high and tight as a military haircut.

"Linda?" he said, his own voice calm. Hostage negotiation training worked in so many situations. "Try to speak calmly and tell me what's the matter."

Linda's phone crackled as she shifted it. The horn honk came through to Kirkhoff muted. "Pull over, you son of a bitch," she shouted. Linda was inside a car.

"Mom." It was Margie, her voice subdued, away from the phone.

"I'm sorry, Glenn, honey," Linda said. "Some jerk swerved into our lane."

Great. Exactly what I need. "What's wrong? Where are you going?"

"Oh, my," Linda mumbled before answering. "Eastside Hospital. Glenn, it's Marguerite. She's having the baby. You got anyone between Savannah and St. Joe that can give us an escort?"

Kirkhoff's spine shot him up straight. He'd known Margie since high school. She's a great kid. Kid. Hell, she's in her thirties and having a baby. She's no kid. His jaw muscles tightened. She was having Bobby Garrett's baby.

"I'll come myself." Kirkhoff moved away from the empty, blackened foundation, taking one more look at the horror of a child's painting. "It's important for you to take a few deep breaths. It takes a while for a baby to come, especially if it's the first one."

The door to the cruiser opened in silence, and Kirkhoff slid behind the wheel. "I'll meet you on the highway," he said. "What are you driving?"

Linda's exhale, loud as the smoker she was, came through the phone: "A 2015 white Ford Escape." The panic in her voice nearly gone. "You were always such a good boy."

[3]

The phone dropped into the seat between Marguerite and Linda, Marguerite scooping it up before her mother made another whackadoo danger call to Glenn or Thomas or anyone else. Thomas Cavanaugh. A constant thought between each of the growing contractions was she wanted him to be in the Ford Escape with her, driving her to the hospital instead of her mother. Thomas was strong and gentle and wouldn't scream "Pull over, you son of a bitch" at oncoming traffic. Linda's definition of "our lane" probably differed from other drivers', or law enforcement's. A voice, small but powerful, said, *Slow down.* Marguerite looked around the cab of the car, but she and her mother were the only ones there.

And the voice, it—it—

Was it a voice, she wondered, if it came from inside my head?

"You can slow down, Mom," Marguerite said, the words calm. "My contractions are still pretty far apart. We don't have to hurry."

Actually, the intensity of her contractions had decreased since the first powerful pull when her water broke. If that hadn't happened, she thought she'd probably blame the slight twinges on Braxton-Hicks, or Flamin' Hot Cheetos.

"You don't know that," Linda barked.

Oh, Mom was in a tizzy, all right.

Marguerite pushed herself back in her seat to stretch out her belly. That kid didn't leave much room for anything. "I do, Mom. I went to all those classes. They told me what to expect, and although they didn't specifically tell me to expect my mother to kill me in a car accident on the way to the hospital, I'm sure it was implied."

"But—" Linda started.

Now, the voice said flatly, plainly.

"Now!"

Linda backed her foot off the accelerator and braked until they reached the speed limit of the rural highway just as an old Chevy pickup careened around a sharp curve into their lane. The pickup's horn blared as it cut through the spot of the road where Linda's Escape would have been if she hadn't slowed. Linda screamed as the truck swerved around them, hit the ditch, and popped back onto the blacktop, never slowing.

That was you, wasn't it? Marguerite thought. You told me that, Jakie.

"That goddammed lunatic almost killed us!" Linda shouted, her knuckles white on the steering wheel.

"Don't worry about it, Mom," Marguerite said, smiling as she rubbed her belly. A wave of calm drifted through the car. "Everything's going to be fine."

[4]

Glenn sat in his Crown Vic cruiser on a gravel access road in the median between US 71 North and US 71 South. Some jerk-off in a four-by-four GMC—with stacks behind the cab, going at least 80 mph in a 65 zone—hit his brakes once he saw the sheriff's car pointed in his direction. Today was that redneck's lucky day; Glenn had something more important to worry about.

The child's drawing of the bloody, toothy face slapped onto the basement wall of the missing house stuck with him. It had since December. Merry freaking Christmas; here's a nightmare—oh, and let's kill your friend to really drive the message home. The face came to him in his sleep. It came to him when he fried an egg too round. Then there was Dakota.

Dear Lord. Two months ago, Glenn had been sitting at his sister's table drinking coffee when his niece danced into the kitchen and flopped into the chair next to his.

"Hey, Uncle Sheriff," she said, the suppressed giggle pulling her face into every adorable shape possible.

Glenn leaned forward and spoke, coffee on his breath. "Hey, Niece Gigglemonster."

A laugh, as true as only a four-year-old can make, erupted from her. "Wanna see the picture I drawed?"

"Drew," Kirkhoff's sister Kathy said from where she was speaking on her mobile phone; their mom was on the other end, and Mom was in a snit.

Dakota pulled a sheet of printer paper from behind her back and slapped it onto the table in front of Glenn. His stomach fell in a steep roller-coaster drop. A red crayon in his niece Dakota's hand had drawn a circle with a huge triangular mouth and rows of sharp needle teeth. A spot of blood hung at the edge of the paper.

"Do you like it?" she asked, looking up at him.

When his eyes met hers, all he saw were black wells.

"No," he mumbled, his feet fighting for purchase on the linoleum as his legs churned to push him back, away from this—

"Glenn!" Kathy snapped.

Glenn's chair tipped and clattered to the floor, spilling him next to the refrigerator, plenty of Dakota's drawings over his head held in place by magnets.

His sister stood, a hand over the phone. "What's wrong with you?"

He shook his head and looked up at Dakota. She sat, silent, tears welling in her eyes; the drawing in her hands was of her family done in brown, yellow, blue, and green crayons. There was no circle, no teeth, no red, no blood. But I saw it. I *saw* it.

Kathy stood over him. "Are you all right?"

No. I am not.

"I don't feel so good, all of a sudden," he said. "I should probably go home."

He pushed himself to his feet, kissed Dakota on top of the head, and left. As he sat in the cruiser now, his mind on Dakota's drawing, he nearly missed the white Escape blast past him on its way to the hospital.

[5]

Lights, red and blue, flashed in the mirrors of the Escape, Marguerite smiling as the sheriff's cruiser moved into the left lane and passed them. She waved at Glenn, who couldn't see her, before he pulled in front of them and escorted them toward St. Joseph. The official law-enforcement escort made her feel like a dignitary, or a celebrity, or a drug lord.

"You're going to be fine, honey," Linda said, her voice still tight as a lug nut. "Glenn'll get us there safely."

Marguerite smiled because she already knew that. A warmth spread through her like the first time she had a shot of whiskey. No, that wasn't right. It was the warmth that radiated from her chest to her face, through her arms and loins. The warmth she felt whenever Thomas came to visit. But Thomas always brought Jillian, so Marguerite kept her distance and held her tongue, although sometimes she couldn't keep her gaze; it landed on Thomas's and both lingered a bit too long.

A flutter danced inside her; the contractions were coming faster, she guessed.

"Is having a baby supposed to tickle?"

Linda's head turned, her face momentarily frozen in a grimace. "No," she said, the word coming out in more seconds than two letters should allow. "It hurts like hell. Do your contractions tickle?"

A long exhale forced its way through pursed lips as Marguerite squirmed in her seat.

"Uh, no way. Oh my. It. Ow. OW. It hurts. A lot."

"That's normal," Linda said, her eyes on Glenn's bumper. "You felt like I was trying to pass a bowling ball. I never thought I'd be able to walk again."

A giggle welled up inside Marguerite. She slapped her hands over her mouth, but it came out anyway.

"What's so funny?" Linda asked.

Nothing. Nothing was funny, but the next contraction tickled her again, and Marguerite laughed out loud, the sound an explosion in the car.

"Honey?"

The sheriff's cruiser signaled, and then pulled onto the off-ramp, the hospital growing in the distance. The contractions grew stronger and Marguerite bit her bottom lip, simply hoping her nurse was nice and would keep her mom out of the delivery room.

[6]

Elizabeth Condon stood at the head of the birthing bed, and the patient, a woman in her thirties, lay beneath a white blanket, her legs in the stirrups making a tent. Elizabeth had been a nurse for twenty-five years: four on the floor, ten in the ER, the rest helping babies into the world. She'd seen nothing like Marguerite Jenkins.

Marguerite's cervix had dilated from six to nine centimeters in the twenty minutes since she arrived at the hospital. From Elizabeth's experience, that sort of dilation for a first-time mother would take five to six hours at minimum, and that would be coupled with the moans from contractions and the inevitable "I can't do this" tears. But Marguerite lay in the birthing bed, her eyes bright, her smile big, clean, and white.

Elizabeth had seen a lot of strange things come through hospital doors, but Marguerite Jenkins was the strangest.

"How are you feeling, Ms. Jenkins?" Elizabeth asked, shifting her weight to get a look at the cardiotocograph. Another contraction, but the patient didn't even flinch.

"Ope," Marguerite said. "There's another one."

Was that a laugh in her voice?

"How close am I, nurse?" the woman asked. "Can I have my baby now?"

Elizabeth had never felt so unprepared to answer a question in her career. All she wanted was to help deliver this baby, pray to God it was healthy, finish her shift, go home, and have a drink, or two, or three, and forget this night ever happened.

"It's hard to tell," Elizabeth said, poking buttons on her pager. "But I think we're close enough to ring the doctor."

Marguerite clapped. She freaking clapped before she giggled again.

"Whoa. There's another contraction," Marguerite said, twisting her shoulders to look at Elizabeth full-on. A smile decorated the woman's face. Her skin, bronzed by the sun, glowed with health; there wasn't a bead of sweat on her. "I've heard so many horror stories, but my contractions tickle."

Something's seriously wrong here.

The door to Marguerite's private room soundlessly slid open and Dr. Morrigan swept in, a new nurse in his wake. Elizabeth couldn't remember her name, but she was young, cute, and blond, which meant she was going places.

"Ms. Jenkins," the doctor said, grinning his thousand-dollar teeth at the expectant mother, his breath smelling of spearmint Mentos, his blood flowing with low-dose amphetamines. "And how are we feeling?"

Elizabeth hated working with Dr. Phil "Golf is My Life" Morrigan, but it was his night.

"Um, Dr. Morrigan," Elizabeth started, but he waved her off. Prick.

"I feel great," Marguerite chirped in a cheerleader sort of way. "Can I have this baby now? Jake's telling me he's ready."

Dr. Morrigan settled himself on a stool at the end of the birthing table and looked up the leg tent, right into the Action Zone. He leaned back enough to see Marguerite over her wide-open legs, his forehead creased.

"Dear Lord," he said, his voice nearly a whisper. "The baby's crowning." Dr. Morrigan looked up at Elizabeth. "Nurse. Why didn't you page me sooner?"

That drink sounded better and better.

Marguerite tried to sit up; Elizabeth slapped hands onto the woman's shoulders and held her down. She tried to shake off Elizabeth's hands, but the strength from too many years of dealing with patients, heavy medical equipment, and a drunken ex-husband kept Marguerite pinned to the bed.

"What's happening?" Marguerite asked as calmly as if she'd asked the time.

Elizabeth didn't flinch. This woman should be screaming.

The Mentos smile pulled at the doctor's lips. "Oh, nothing. Nothing at all. Everything's fine here." He pushed the sheet higher on Marguerite's thighs and settled in. Seconds later, he held a silent baby, its head full of black hair.

"Well, Ms. Jenkins," he said calmly, although Elizabeth caught the waver in his voice. "You have a perfectly, um, perfectly healthy baby boy."

Dr. Morrigan stood and stepped toward the head of the birthing bed. The baby lay in his arms, its eyes wide, chest rising and falling steadily. It didn't blink, it didn't cry—the umbilical cord was gone, the belly button a hole in the infant's pudgy tummy.

Jesus Christ.

"Uh, Doctor," Elizabeth began, but a hard flash of Dr. Morrigan's eyes cut her off.

His smile returned and his eyes softened as he lowered Jacob Jenkins onto his mother's now-bare chest. The baby immediately began to nurse.

Marguerite laughed. "He's an eager little guy, isn't he?"

He was. Most babies Elizabeth had seen took coaxing to feed. She stood still in her Oofos clogs, staring into the baby's eyes. Its black irises stared back into hers. It never blinked.

"Nurse," Elizabeth thought she heard, her eyes trapped by the baby's. The silent, sucking baby. Darkness pulled a frigid line across the room. The Mentos doctor, the mother, and the young blond nurse were all bathed in shadow. Elizabeth's breath rose in white dragon huffs.

A hand fell on her shoulder. "Nurse."

Elizabeth broke eye contact with the quiet infant feeding from his mother's breast. Dr. Morrigan stood next to her, his face white. A line of sweat ran down his temple. The room suddenly became bright again, the temperature its normal 73 degrees Fahrenheit.

"I'm sorry, Doctor," Elizabeth said, trying to swallow the vile thoughts inside her. The baby. Something was wrong with the baby.

"Please take"—he paused to look at Marguerite—"Jacob, is it?"

Marguerite's effortless smile was nothing Elizabeth had ever seen on a mother who had just given birth.

"Yes. I'm going to call him Jake."

"Then," Dr. Morrigan said to Elizabeth, "when Jake's finished feeding, please clean him up, check his vitals, and take him to the nursery." He motioned to the young blond nurse, who wanted to be anywhere else but here. "Madison will help ease Ms. Jenkins into postpartum recovery."

"Doc—Doctor?" Madison stuttered.

"Get her ready," Dr. Morrigan said through clenched teeth, then walked through the door, leaving the nurses alone in a small room with a mother who felt no pain during birth and a baby who didn't have an umbilical cord.

Elizabeth coughed before speaking. "May I?" she asked, stepping to the side of the birthing bed and holding out hands snapped inside latex gloves.

What the hell is this? shot through her head. The room felt different from any delivery room Elizabeth had ever been in—including her own. It should stink. Body odor, urine, feces, the sweet stench of amniotic fluid, but the room smelled of, smelled of—

What?

A childhood memory from growing up on a farm crept into her thoughts. Corn. The smell of the birthing room was like a cornfield.

Jacob's head turned from his mother's breast, the pink nipple popping from his mouth. His eyes found Elizabeth's; they weren't blue like most of the newborns she'd welcomed to the outside world. These were black pools of iris in the stark white of clean sclera. Her hand caught the bed rail to keep her from spilling onto the floor. The eyes. Dear God, the eyes. Those eyes knew something.

"I guess I could use a nap," Marguerite said. "Or maybe dinner and some TV. The thought of raising a kid is exhausting." She looked at Elizabeth, the woman's simple grin seemingly alien to her. "You know what I mean?"

The room swam.

"Oooh," shot from Elizabeth as she dropped to the floor. Her elbow cracked the bed frame as she fell, collapsing in a ball. Pain shot through her arm.

"Hey," Marguerite said, turning toward the side of the bed and looking over; her swollen breast stuck between the bed and the rail. Milk dripped onto Elizabeth's forehead.

Elizabeth turned and looked up at the woman who was still her patient. The baby in Marguerite's arms smiled at her. It smiled. The fucking baby smiled.

"Are you okay?" Marguerite asked.

Elizabeth nodded, her head uncomfortably slow. It hurt.

"Yes," she said, wiping breast milk from her face. "I just slipped, that's all."

She inhaled through the nose and exhaled through the mouth, like she was supposed to teach mothers during childbirth, mothers who weren't Marguerite Jenkins.

"Madison," Elizabeth said from the floor. The young nurse unfroze and hurried toward her; there was panic in her face. "Please take Jacob and do his readings, then bathe him and get him a bed in the nursery."

A flash of shock crossed her face. "But—"

"Do it!" Elizabeth barked.

Madison glared down at her but turned toward the bed and took Jacob from his mother. The young nurse's arms shook—that didn't escape Elizabeth. She rolled and pushed herself off the floor, stopping just a moment by Madison, who was weighing tiny Jake, with his adult eyes.

On the drive home, those eyes lingered in her rearview mirror, and she screamed, and screamed, and screamed.

PART 1

2021

CHAPTER ONE

"DAMN IT."

Thomas Cavanaugh yanked his hand from under the hydraulic hose assembly of the old John Deere 4630, blood glistening on his skinned knuckles. His wrist caught a hose; it popped free from the gauge adapter and golden-brown fluid gushed onto his already sweat- and oil-stained T-shirt. His dad, Kyle, grabbed the hose and pushed it onto the nipple, clamping off the spray.

Kyle grinned at Thomas and clapped his shoulder. "All those times you helped me work on the truck, the combine, this tractor, and you never paid attention. Did you?"

"I had more important things on my mind," Thomas said, wiping the blood onto his shirt.

Kyle's hand dropped back to his side and he turned toward his rusty, battered toolbox.

That dig was uncalled for. Thomas knew it before it came out of his mouth. He died as a child, spent time in a mental ward, and failed to stop Bobby Garrett, a maniac, a mass murderer, from destroying a hospital. He remembered the fight with Bobby, he remembered the hospital—a children's hospital the news said was near capacity—leaning to one side as homemade explosives took out its support pylons and dropped the tall building into the parking lot. Then, it was Jillian hovering over his bed at the hospital, her smile wide but her eyes red, her cheeks wet with tears. He didn't remember much else, but the horror of that moment would stay in his mind forever. I had more important things. He knew his father didn't deserve that.

"Hey." Thomas wrapped his knuckles in his shirt tail, red bleeding through. "I didn't mean it that way."

Kyle shook his head, the toolbox lid clanking as he shut the latch. "That's okay, son," he said. "All that was years ago for me. I'm sure it still feels like yesterday to you."

Thomas looked at Kyle. Yes, years. The gray on Kyle's temples that once amused Thomas had spread throughout his dad's hair. Thomas's girlfriend, Jillian, said she'd taken him somewhere, somewhere apparently magical, and he hadn't aged a bit while everyone around him grew ten years older.

"It's not—" he started, but Kyle raised a greasy, wrinkled hand, quieting his son, his eyes as soft as Thomas had ever seen.

"I'm sorry, boy," Kyle said. "Accept it, and let's move on." He pointed toward the house. "The next thing is to get to the house and clean up those knuckles." He patted Thomas's shoulder. "Come on. I'll get you a beer."

Kyle clamped onto that shoulder, his hands still strong as a young man's. He started walking his son toward the house.

"I'm going to have a Dr Pepper or some iced tea, if you've got either." Thomas unwrapped his bloody knuckles, the skin ripped, blood still oozing. "I'm trying to cut back."

"Good, good. I'm proud of you." He stuck his hands in his pockets as he approached the next subject gently. "How's Jillian?"

As if on cue, the mobile phone in Thomas's pocket played the Doors' "The End."

"Well—" Thomas began, but stopped himself from saying more.

"That's a pretty brutal ringtone," Kyle said. "Everything okay at home, son?"

Thomas pulled out the phone. As he knew it would, it read "Jillian."

"She's gotten really on edge, like, all the time," he said, sliding the phone app to "ignore" and dropping it back into his jeans pocket. "She's wanted to babysit Marguerite's boy ever since he was born. He's four now and Marguerite hasn't called her to do it once." He raised his hand to his mouth to stifle a cough. Marguerite. The farther Jillian pushed him away, the more Marguerite crept into his thoughts. "I think Jillian wants to have a baby."

Kyle's laugh echoed off the house as they walked up the yard.

"It's not funny. That thought scares me to death."

Kyle wrapped an arm around Thomas and squeezed. "You think your mom and I were ready for you? Nobody's ever ready. But maybe you could delay it a while if you told her you had to get married first."

Thomas let himself be smothered in his father's embrace. "I'm not ready for that either."

"You think I was?" Kyle resumed walking toward the house. "Take your boots off before you hit the porch. With that rain last night, if we track mud anywhere, your mother's going to have a fit."

Mud. Porch. Thomas had seen mud on that porch before; it went through the kitchen and up the stairs. Tiny footprints that grew and grew, and the voice: "I'm upstairs. Come play with me."

By the time Thomas reached the porch, nervous sweat beaded his face.

[2]

The cinnamon schnapps burned as it went down; it always did for the first couple of shots. By the end of her shift, Elizabeth knew it would go down like water. She popped similar-smelling cinnamon mints and slid open the lock to the bathroom stall, slipping outside. She'd never drunk at work before. The concept was wrong, inexcusable, irresponsible, but that baby, that monster of a baby. It didn't give her a choice. The damnable thing with the dark eyes and the belly button—and the smile. Newborns didn't smile—it forced her, shoved her to the edge of sanity until she needed a nip or two, just enough to keep her from falling over the edge of a psychological cliff into an abyss she knew there was no way back from. The schnapps calmed her nerves enough to step into another birthing room. But nobody knew. How could they? The cinnamon mints covered everything.

Dr. Morrigan. Dr. Mentos. That bastard. He refused to talk about the demon baby. Refused to admit there was anything wrong with it, or the mother, or the birth. She didn't like him to begin with, but his willful ignorance made her hate him.

She stepped into the hall, blinking at the bright white that surrounded her. The birthing hall was quiet—only three mothers in labor, and only one who would probably give birth during her shift. Elizabeth approached the door as Dr. Mentos opened it and stepped out. She stopped and let him pass.

"Doctor," she said, taking care to enunciate both syllables.

"Yes, nurse." His eyes avoided hers as they had for the past four years, since that Jenkins woman. He coughed into his hand and said, "Mrs. Tolbertson is dilated to seven centimeters. This is her third child, so please keep a close eye on her. Page me when she's ready."

Then he left. No, he didn't just leave, he scampered down the hall. Elizabeth had a feeling Dr. Mentos's amphetamine habit had grown into something more.

[3]

Kyle Cavanaugh drained his second noon beer and dropped the can in the recycling bin. Thomas sat at the same table where his mother had served meals his whole life.

"You know, Dad," Thomas said, dishing spoonfuls of mashed cauliflower from a bowl. "You could cook every once in a while. It's not the 1950s."

His mom laughed through a mouthful of chicken. She held up a hand in front of her mouth until she swallowed.

"Your father tried to cook, to erase some of the . . . what did you call it, honey? The inequitable burden of spousal stereotypes?"

Dad nodded. "Something like that, yeah."

"It lasted for a week," Mom continued. "I'd have had better meals eating out of the hamper."

A knock came from the screen door and Jillian stepped in wearing Thomas's Quiet Riot T-shirt, her fiery hair pulled back in a ponytail. A laugh that formed inside Thomas died before it could erupt. He'd known Jillian for a long time, had been in love with her for a long time, but she wasn't the person he once knew. The feelings between them had changed, on both sides.

"Jillian," Mom said, waving for her to come in. "Get yourself a plate."

Jillian crossed the scuffed black-and-white-tiled kitchen floor and sat at the table. "No, thanks. I'm not hungry," she said before shooting back up and skipping to the fridge. "I will take a beer though." She turned to Thomas's dad. "Kyle?"

He nodded, and she grabbed two.

"So," Dad said, pulling back the tab. It opened with a crack. "Thomas says you want to have a baby."

Beer spit across the table. "What?"

Dad laughed hard enough he slapped his thigh.

"No." She glanced at Thomas, her brows pinched. "For the record, I told Thomas I wanted to babysit Jake. There's a difference."

"I would like a grandchild," Mom said as calmly as if she'd said, "I'd like a sandwich." "Eventually."

Jillian slid her hand over Thomas's, her touch cold; a shudder ran through him.

"I've talked about Jake so much because I like children, especially babies, and he's the only kid in our . . . circle? Triangle? Straight line of friends." She squeezed. "Did you know, when we're at the store, and there's a young mom with a baby in front of us in the checkout line, I want to ask her if I can smell its head."

"That's weird," Thomas said.

"No," Mom said, glancing from Jillian to Thomas, a hazy look in her eyes. "It's not. You must have never smelled a baby's head, hon. It's heaven. I want to smell babies' heads too."

"You see." Jillian's face suddenly looked different. Harder. More angular. The pink rash she sometimes got spread across her cheek. "Your mom gets it." She took a drink of beer and glanced at Thomas's mom. "And what's better is their toes."

The grin across Thomas's mom's face looked like she was the one drinking. "Yes. Yes."

"Don't you just want to eat their toes?"

"Oh, yes, yes, yes. They're like little bits of popcorn chicken."

Thomas glanced at his dad. He'd fallen asleep in his chair, a forkful of potatoes suspended above his plate.

Thomas's stomach grew taut. What's happening?

"I know, Debbie," Jillian said, a giggle in her words. "And their fingers. Oh, yes. I love to eat their fingers. They're like little—"

Debbie's face dropped slack; seemed to lose its hold on the conversation. Her next words came out in a whisper: "popcorn chicken."

Thomas pulled his hand out from beneath Jillian's.

"Jillian?" he asked, his mouth thick, like it was full of peanut butter. The kitchen sank into darkness, and thick fog formed over the table. A wave of exhaustion tilted Thomas's head backward in his chair.

"And their succulent little thighs—"

Thomas's head fell forward, and he jerked awake, the fog (Fog? In the house?), the exhaustion, the heavy, thick air gone. Jillian sat next to him holding a can of Miller Lite. Mom stared at him with her glassy four-vodkas-in smile, though she never drank before lunch. Dad shook his head and ate the forkful of potatoes as if he hadn't fallen asleep at the table.

Jillian smiled at Thomas as if everything was fine.

[4]

A yawn pulled at Elizabeth Condon in between Mrs. Lilith Tolbertson's four millionth contraction and her four million and first. Or fifth. Whatever.

Come on, Elizabeth thought. Have this baby already.

Elizabeth had another tug or two by this point. Dr. "Mentos" Morrigan didn't seem much better, not that Mrs. Tolbertson or her husband—Elizabeth called him Mr. Lilith—could tell, but Elizabeth could; his hands shook as if he were on a carnival ride. The Liliths had more to worry about than her having a snootful.

"You're at ten centimeters, Mrs. Tolbertson," Dr. Mentos said, parked on the stool between her spread knees, squatting like a baseball catcher. "I want you to concentrate on breathing, and when I tell you to push, you need to push."

Her head crushed back into the pillow; her hair, soaked with sweat, stuck to the white pillowcase, stringy and limp. The cardiotocograph jumped and scratched.

"Another contraction, Doctor," Elizabeth said. She was close. Contractions meant the baby was one second closer to appearing from beneath the sheet, bloody and cheesy in the doctor's latex-gloved hands. For the past four years, this moment had made her skin crawl, panic always waiting just beneath her thin film of calm patience. Inside, Elizabeth screamed.

"I can't do this," Mrs. Tolbertson whimpered.

"Oh, yes you can." Dr. Mentos pulled the blanket higher up on her thighs. "The baby's already on its way."

A moan dragged itself from her.

"Just breathe, honey," Mr. Lilith said. "Just like the birthing coach said. In through the no—"

Her hand shot out and latched on to her husband's forearm. The man winced. "Shut up, Chad," she hissed, sucking in three sharp breaths.

"Now, push, Mrs. Tolbertson," the doctor said, his voice calm, and steadier than his hands. "Push."

"I can't." Her voice nothing more than a whimper.

"Now. You have to push *now*."

Dear God, Elizabeth prayed. Please make this baby normal.

The prayer caught her off guard. After the Jenkins birth, Elizabeth no longer believed in God. What god would curse the world with the Jenkins monster?

"Yaaaaaaaaaa!" Lilith Tolbertson screamed, pushing, her body tense. Seconds passed and she relaxed. Dr. Mentos stood, a baby girl in his arms.

"Congratulations," he said. "She's beautiful."

Monster.

Elizabeth hated looking at babies, fearing black eyes and a belly button, an unnatural smile on their toothless faces. But this baby was pink, spotted with vernix caseosa, the umbilical cord intact.

The other nurse in the room—Zoe, or Chloe, or something—was new, blond, and cute, just like Dr. Mentos liked them. She sucked clean the newborn's mouth and nostrils. It cried out, and Elizabeth let loose the breath she held. Another normal baby.

Mr. Lilith—Chad—cut the umbilical cord; Elizabeth instructed Zoe to wash and prep the little girl, and she left the room.

The doctor joined her in the empty hallway. He stopped next to her.

"Got any more schnapps?" he asked.

The question. Elizabeth had expected it. She was a good nurse, a damn good nurse, for years. No complaints, no arguments, and plenty of "she was so nice to us." The drinking tugged at Elizabeth, just at the hem of her nursing scrubs. It didn't affect her job. No. The schnapps was relaxing, just the thing to keep her from screaming her lungs out if a baby like the Jenkins kid ever squeezed out of another mother's fetid crotch.

Jesus.

She dropped a hand into the deep pocket of her scrubs and relaxed her shoulders, pressing them into the wall. The half pint of cinnamon liqueur lay neatly at the bottom of the pocket, covered by a handful of Kleenex and a Snickers bar.

Dr. Morrigan leaned into the wall next to her.

"I know we haven't talked about this, Elizabeth," he began.

Her head snapped toward him, although he never stopped looking down the long, dim hall. He'd never called her by her first name before.

"But that Jenkins birth a few years ago seriously messed me up." The doctor looked over at her. "How have you been?"

Elizabeth exhaled slowly. Why now, Dr. Mentos?

"I have been on a razor's edge of freaking out every time I assist a birth." She removed her hand from her pocket and sucked sterilized hospital air in through her nose, then let it out. Even when she went home, she could still smell that antiseptic odor. "I'm afraid another one of those things will pop out."

Dr. Morrigan met her gaze for a few moments before dropping his. "Me too." He stepped away from the wall and held out a thick white hand. "Hey, schnapps. You got any more?"

She dropped her hand back into the pocket and pulled out the bottle, handing it to the doctor. He unscrewed the cap and drained the rest.

"Thanks," he said, handing the empty bottle back to her. "I don't know how much longer I can do this." Then he walked away, pulling out his pager and thumbing a switch before clicking it back into its cradle.

He turned it off. Jerk.

Elizabeth went back to the nurses station to pick up her bag. It was 3 p.m. Her shift was over. Zoe/Chloe/whatever was on her own.

[5]

The rain kicked back up around 4 p.m., and Dad sent Thomas home. Mom spent the afternoon in her art studio, which used to be his bedroom, then the guest room the decade his girlfriend had spirited him off to wherever. Jillian hung around the house, reading *People* magazine and napping on the couch. His childhood home was home, but it really wasn't. Not anymore. He and Jillian lived in Uncle Boyd's house, but that wasn't home either. Boyd, the former Buchanan County sheriff, had been dead four years, he and his girlfriend Emily murdered by Bobby Garrett. Thomas moved in sometime after, although he couldn't get it straight in his head when. His memories had gotten foggy.

Thomas pulled his pickup under the tree where Uncle Boyd had always parked his patrol car and got out, the steady mist beaded in his hair; Jillian's old Camry was parked closer to the house. She'd beaten him home—again. She always got home before him, even when he left first.

His live-in girlfriend was lounging on the couch when he walked through the door, their laptop open on her knees, sitting like she'd been there for hours. Thomas used to ask how long she'd been home; he didn't do that anymore. Jillian seemed to live in a different world from his, a place where time moved strangely, a place he didn't like visiting. Thomas went into the open kitchen and grabbed a soda, the can crack loud in the quiet house.

"What do you want for dinner?" he asked, feet apart, butt resting against the cabinet.

Her gaze never left the computer screen. "I got an email from Marguerite," she said, waving a hand toward him. "She sent pictures of Jakie. Come see."

Marguerite.

Pink colored his cheeks. They'd all remained close since Jillian comforted her after the hospital explosion. Marguerite named them the godparents, but with none of the benefits. They never watched the boy. Considering how they'd all met, Thomas couldn't blame her a bit.

He sat next to Jillian but not close enough to touch her, the soda can shoved between his legs. The first photo of the boy staring at the camera would have been haunting in black and white, his dark eyes like chunks of coal. The second, probably taken by Marguerite's mother Linda, showed Marguerite in a T-shirt and shorts, her hair held back in a clip, four-year-old Jacob in her arms. Neither smiled, and dark smudges stained the skin beneath Marguerite's eyes.

"Isn't he just so cute?" Jillian nearly squealed.

He was, Thomas couldn't deny it. But his face, a face mostly his father's, seemed hard, joyless. And Marguerite? She was still lovely, but tired. Too tired. The Marguerite in the photo begged for help.

"Have you talked with her lately?" he asked.

"I just want to snuggle that little man forever," Jillian said, not registering Thomas's words.

He shook his head. "What do you want for dinner?" he asked again.

"I ordered Chinese delivery from that place we like," she said, pushing the thin laptop lid closed and setting it on the coffee table. Jillian turned toward him, her eyes bright, nearly glowing in the golden-hour light pouring in from between the breaking clouds and through the great front window. Her legs dropped into his lap, nearly sending the can of soda to the floor.

"They don't deliver this far out."

She nuzzled her face into Thomas's neck and kissed him; the touch of her lips sent a cold wave of revulsion through him. Her kisses did that more and more.

"They do for me," she whispered, her voice airy, "baby cakes."

"I, uh, was going to bake chicken tonight with"—she kissed him again, pulling his T-shirt tail up and slipping a frigid hand onto the skin of his belly—"lemon, rosemary, and garlic."

"Sounds delicious, for tomorrow."

Her hand moved on to his chest; his face tightened.

"I thought"—his words shaky—"I thought you said you didn't want a baby."

Her hand came up through the neck hole and turned his face toward her. "I don't, but I didn't say we shouldn't practice."

"I don't really feel like—" Thomas said but never finished. A damp cloth of fog wiped across his thoughts and he lay back on the couch as Jillian unbuckled his belt.

[6]

Sheriff Glenn Kirkhoff looked up from a report Deputy Glines submitted that morning. His corner of the world had been quiet for the past few years. A string of rural robberies, mostly lumber and copper wire from new construction, a couple of hunters from the city trespassing on private land. That was about the worst of it, and the rural crimes gave him no problem, but he needed to get Maddy Glines a dictionary. She was a good, smart officer and had the makings of a sheriff on down the line, but her spelling was awful.

Tap.

Tap.

Tap.

He looked up to find Sergeant Shanks at his open door.

"Come on in, Aaron," Glenn said. "What can I do for you?"

Aaron, brown felt hat in his hands, stepped in and sat in one of the hard wooden seats across the desk from the sheriff. He'd once suggested padded seats, back when Boyd Donally was sheriff, but Boyd filled Aaron in on a little secret. Most people the sheriff had in his office were criminals, crying victims, county commissioners, or the press, and he didn't want any one of them to get too comfortable.

"I read Glines's report."

Glenn lifted the papers off his desk and sat them back down. "I'm just now getting to it myself. More lumber missing?"

Aaron shifted in his chair. "No. A dead heifer on Hiram Southwick's farm, the grazing land just south of Cosby."

The small stack of paper rustled as Glenn flipped over the first sheet. "Mutilated?"

Aaron nodded, his thinning hair trapped in place by . . . spray? Gel? Glenn didn't know; Glenn didn't care.

"Yes, sir."

Glenn flipped over another page. "So why'd you come in? Maddy too busy?"

The sergeant shook his head. "She's back up at Hiram's place."

A low whistle escaped Glenn when he pulled out the photos. The heifer lay in mud, the young bovine's throat ripped open, the cut all the way down to its udder; slick, blue-gray intestines spilled onto the muddy ground.

The sheriff looked up. "Dear God. What did this? Not coyotes, that's for sure."

"No, it wasn't coyotes," Aaron said. "We've got a vet out there with Maddy, and the new guy with the conservation department. They're trying to figure out what did this."

"Flamank," Glenn said. "John, I think. That's good, but you must have some guess. What kind of prints were out there?"

The sergeant sucked in a deep breath and held it before he spoke. "Not many, Sheriff. Not counting the hoof marks of the cattle, there was only one set of prints."

The old wooden office chair creaked as Glenn sat back.

"One? One thing did this to a . . . what? Seven hundred, seven hundred fifty-pound animal?" He leaned forward again.

"More like twelve hundred, sir."

Okay, okay. "Quit dragging this out, Aaron. What kind of tracks were they?"

Aaron stood, and flipped over the next photo in Maddy's report. Glenn's hand moved in slow motion before lifting it from the stack.

"Is this a joke?"

"No, sir. These prints were the only ones other than the cattle's."

Among the blood, the intestines, and the mud left from the rain mingled with animal waste, were two prints, side by side with what Glenn figured was Maddy's boot for size comparison.

"These prints are from a little kid," Glenn said, the words sharp, heavy. "Where'd the kid come from?"

Aaron shook his head, that hair not moving a millimeter. "Nowhere, Sheriff." His finger landed on the small footprints in the photo. "Those prints were it. The only ones there."

Glenn flipped through the rest of the pictures. Nothing. Those footprints from probably a kindergarten-aged kid were it, standing right in front of the rip through the heifer's midsection.

"Bullshit."

Aaron silently sat back onto the chair, perching himself on the edge.

"That's what Maddy, Dr. B, and Agent Flamank are out there to determine," he said, his voice soft. "I don't know what to tell you, Sheriff. Hiram thinks—"

Glenn's hard, cold eyes kept the words in his throat.

"What does Hiram think?" He pointed an index finger at Aaron. A grimace slid over the sergeant. "No." Glenn dropped the open pages and leaned forward, elbows on the big, old desk. "Do not. I repeat, do NOT say space aliens."

"But that *is* what he thinks."

Glenn shot from his chair and took cautious steps to the coffee machine. He'd made the coffee early this morning, so it was going to taste like it had been drained from an engine block, but he poured himself a cup anyway.

"Little green men. Next thing somebody's going to tell me it was fairies."

Aaron exhaled, the sound louder than it should have been. "Things have been pretty quiet since, well, since—"

"I know," Glenn cut him off. "And that's how I want to keep it. Send Maddy in here when she gets back."

Something was seriously wrong.

CHAPTER TWO

THE WET GROUND kept Thomas and his father out of the fields. Kyle shooed Thomas away from the tractor, unless he "wanted to tear up his other knuckles for a matched set."

"Well," Dad said, the ratchet wrench twisting *tic-tic-tic* in his hand. "You could always go home and have a day off."

Home? Thomas felt himself deflate, a Bobo doll left ignored in a corner. Jillian was home. A feeling of dread accompanied the thought of driving the few miles to what was once the residence of Boyd Donally, thirty-year sheriff of Buchanan County. Over the past four years, it didn't feel more like Thomas's home, it still felt like Boyd's; the furniture was the same, so were the appliances and plates. His uncle had just begun to date Emily, a woman Thomas hadn't gotten the chance to know past a family meeting in his parents' kitchen when, when, when . . . what? What did we talk about? People shouted, someone cried, Emily accused Jillian of something, and they all drank beer. Lots and lots of beer. But what happened?

That night had been tense and nearly violent, but Thomas couldn't remember anything that occurred, except Jillian that remained calm through it all, even though every finger pointed to her.

"No. I'll find something to do."

The *tic-tic-tic* stopped, and Thomas's father turned to face him, a streak of grease across his cheek. "Then there *is* something going sour at home," he said, setting the wrench onto an arm of the three-point hitch and pushing himself straight. "What?"

The exhale seemed to take an hour.

"Yes. There's something wrong with Jillian." Thomas looked off toward the old milking barn, the once-red paint now mostly flaked off, revealing the gray wood beneath. "Or not. I don't know. It's just that something feels, it feels . . . off."

Kyle leaned into the big back tire of the tractor, his working-man arms crossed over his chest. "Like what? You think she's cheating on you or something?"

"Cheating? No, Dad. That's not it. That's not it at all." Thomas ran a hand through his hair; a still-thick shock stood straight up. "It's just. It's—" He couldn't look at his father. He fixed his eyes on the machine shop. "She's keeping something from me. I know. Dad, I *know* more happened in St. Joe than what I was told. I *know* there are events in my life, especially when I was a kid, that are just, they're just . . . gone."

Kyle picked up the open Miller Lite from the top of his tool chest and took a sip. When he lowered the can, he looked at Thomas from under pinched brows.

"What does that have to do with Jillian?" he asked. "That sounds like you two need to work something out."

A harsh laugh broke from Thomas. "Work something out. Seriously, Dad? You watching *The Drew Barrymore Show* now?"

Kyle pointed a finger at him, but Thomas cut him off before he could speak.

"Do you remember the night four years ago when Jillian and I came home after being gone for years?" he asked. "We were covered in dust and drove some random meth head's car? You asked Uncle

Boyd to come over, and I was mad because I felt you called the cops on me. He brought Emily; it was the first and only time I met her. We sat around the kitchen table and talked. It got pretty tense. You remember that?"

Kyle Cavanaugh's face fell blank. "No, son. I don't remember that at all."

But it happened. It really happened.

Thomas shook his head; the spike of hair had mostly fallen back home. "You're right," he lied. "I must be misremembering." Thomas nudged his head toward the machine shop. "I'll clean up in there, then I'll go home."

Kyle laughed. "I've been meaning to do that for the past twenty years. Good luck."

Thomas stepped inside the pole barn walled with corrugated tin, the floor oil-stained concrete. A weight fell onto him and his knees nearly buckled.

When he pulled his head up, light streamed through filthy windows, dust mites danced through the rays. The memory of this setting no more than poison.

"You were here," snuck from his lips, although he didn't know who he was talking to. "I heard you. You giggled."

The drill press, air compressor, band saw, and old Case tractor engine were where they'd always been. But something was missing. When he was a child, his father put a cooler in the middle of the floor. A cooler with beer and a Dr Pepper. A memory from deep inside broke free and slammed into him.

"Cake," he whispered. "There was chocolate cake on the cooler."

A cake he knew wasn't chocolate, not really. It was a turd left by a little red-haired girl. A girl who had terrorized his childhood. This sliver of a memory wiggled in the bonds that held it buried deep in Thomas's mind, and broke free.

"Good Lord," he whispered. "That really happened?"

A cloud of steam swirled behind Rebekka Marshall as she walked from the bathroom, a towel wrapped around her mop of wet hair. Her feet left watery prints on the bedroom's hardwood floor. She paused and rested her hands on her swollen belly decorated with stretch marks—tiger stripes, she called them. The tight skin she held rolled under her palms.

"Whoa," she said, trying to push the foot of her unborn child away from her ribs. "Calm down, little man. We'll eat in a minute."

Taking a step toward the king-sized bed she shared with her husband, Todd, she stopped before she could grab her bathrobe. A noise came from the living room; she was the only one home.

"Todd?" she called.

Her husband didn't respond.

"Honey?" she said again. The house sounded empty, except the light sounds of conversation.

Todd's pistol, a Springfield Hell Raiser or some other stupid name, lay beneath a magazine in the night-table drawer. Todd was big on the Second Amendment, big on home defense. He'd taken Bekka to the shooting range once or twice despite the fact that there was no way she wanted to touch the thing. "Bekka, baby," he'd said the first day he convinced her to go with him. "We have money now. There's a chance somebody is going to break into our house to try to take *our* money. If you're home alone, you'll need to know how to use this thing." Then he stopped, gently grasped her shoulders, and looked her in the eye. "And what if we have a baby that day?"

A baby? That's exactly what they were having.

She slid across her side of the bed when Todd Jr. crammed his heel into her ribs again and she lurched forward, falling palms-first onto the floral-print comforter. A wince pulled at her face because, gosh darn it, being eight months pregnant hurt. A breath in slowly through her nose, and out through her mouth like she was extinguishing a candle—as the doula showed her—didn't calm her one bit.

A few more breaths, and Todd Jr.'s foot moved. She reached her bedside table, where Todd made sure to put the Taser she hadn't wanted him to buy either, but at that moment, the handle felt natural. She caressed the firing stud with her thumb and turned toward the open door to the hallway, praying to God Todd Jr. found something else to do.

"Todd?" she called again, her heart beat in her ear.

Am I having a stroke?

The conversation in the other room never stopped. Bekka took three silent, naked steps toward the center of the house, the Taser in front of her like she held a flyswatter.

Then the studio audience laughed.

"Are you kidding me?"

The seventy-inch television flickered with images of Ellen DeGeneres joking with Ryan Gosling. Gosling responded, and the studio audience laughed again.

"I'm an idiot," Bekka wheezed, dropping her shoulder into the wall. Her eyes rolled to the ceiling.

"So," Ellen said over the surround sound Todd had insisted on installing. "Do you call the shit you do acting? Or did you suck somebody's dick to get famous?"

Bekka froze, and a chill, like electricity, ran down her back. She watched Ellen's show, she watched it most every day, and Ellen would never say that.

"Hey, fatty," Ellen said. Bekka didn't move. "You. Yeah, you, Bekka, baby, look at me."

What?

Bekka's knees wobbled, and she leaned fully into the wall as Todd Jr. beat her up from the inside. The television dominated the room, just like Todd wanted for NFL games. Ellen DeGeneres stared right at her.

"Hey, Ryan," Ellen said, thumping Gosling on the shoulder. "You ever see a knocked-up skank like this too stupid to know when she was on TV?"

Gosling laughed into his hand, pointing through the screen directly at Bekka. "And she didn't have the decency to get dressed. She's clean, though."

The shot changed to the studio audience clapping and laughing like Gosling was Robin Williams.

Disbelief froze her where she stood. "Are they talking to *me*?"

Ellen smiled, her mouth full of razor-sharp teeth. "You bet your ass, Bekka, honey."

Bekka lurched from the hallway and stumbled into the living room, Todd Jr. rolling in her uterus. She leaned against the back of the couch and fired the Taser at the television. Two darts struck the screen; anger flared across Ellen's and Ryan's faces before smoke rose from the TV. A pop shot through the room and the screen went black; smoke crept from its corners.

"Shut up, Ellen," Bekka screamed. The towel unraveled from her hair and dropped to the floor.

A giggle—just one giggle—trickled toward Bekka. She thrust the Taser toward the sound, her breath fast, heartbeat hammering.

"Who are you?" she shouted toward the giggle from the kitchen.

Another giggle. Is that a—a child? "Hey," Bekka said, attempting to even her voice, but the fear remained. "Come on out, kiddo. Are you lost? How did you get in here? I can help you."

The giggle morphed into a full-on laugh. "Help me? No, Bekka. I'm here to help you."

Bekka's grip became slack and slick with sweat as the girl stepped from the kitchen.

The Taser clacked as it hit the floor. The child, about six, wore a sheer white dress, her red hair tied in a ponytail. Her smile, pulled tight, was too wide for her face.

"Remember me?" the girl asked.

She tried to step back, but her legs betrayed her. "I—I don't know who you are. I—"

The grin split into the Joker's. "Yes you do. I was at Sisters of Mercy Nutso Hospital with you, right after you set your Gramma's house on fire. You remember, right? Your Gramma was still in it."

Memories shook through Bekka's brain with the force of a paint mixer as the smell of smoke from Todd's precious TV crept up her nose. She stood on the sidewalk, holding a teddy bear at fifteen years old, sucking her thumb as the cops and fire department came shrieking toward Gramma's house.

Gramma's inside.

I'm sorry, Gramma, I'm so sorry. Three girls were committed to Sisters of Mercy when a nurse, Nurse Carroll, escorted her to her room. One of them had—Oh my God.

"I do know you," whispered out.

The child curtsied. "I'm glad you remembered. I'm surprised; you were pretty doped up when I was there," the little girl said, her smile fading to a line across her impossibly wide face. "But it looks like you've done pretty well for yourself." She slow-clapped two, three, four times before her eyes shifted, changing into deep, black voids. "Now, let's talk business. I'm here for Todd."

What?

"Todd's not—he's not here," Bekka whispered, a hot rush of urine streaming down her clean wet leg. "He's still at work."

The girl approached Bekka in time-lapse and stood next to her in seconds.

"Oh yes, he is," she said, and pulled a kitchen knife from behind her back.

That's one of my knives, Bekka thought before the little red-haired girl slashed the blade across Bekka's belly and blood vomited across the living-room floor.

[3]

Rain erased anything important from Hiram Southwick's cattle lot. The prints, the blood, and any hope of discovering whatever slaughtered Hiram's heifer. The morning had smelled clean and fresh when Glenn stepped from the front door of his house before joining Maddy at the Southwick farm, but now, as he stood in the mud and manure, the smell as his rubber boots squished across the lot—whew. He grew up on a farm and chose another line of work when he was old enough because he got tired of smelling like manure.

Glenn pulled on a latex glove and squatted in front of the dead heifer, inserting a hand into the slit, lifting a flap of hide.

What could have done this?

"This cut looks clean," Glenn said, lifting the flap higher. The corpse had begun to stink to high heaven. He dropped the section of hide and stood. "No animal did that."

Deputy Maddy Glines stood next to him, her leather-bound notebook in hand. "That's what Dr. B said." She flipped through a few pages. "It looks like the incision was made with a CO_2 laser scalpel."

"Laser?" The glove snapped as Glenn pulled it off and stuffed it into a baggie. "Is a laser scalpel a thing?"

Maddy nodded. "Yes, sir. In major hospitals. Not in feedlots."

He handed his deputy the baggie and shoved his thumbs in his belt. The lot sat next to a gravel road softened by rain for days. Behind the lot, young fields of soybeans stretched over hills that rolled across Buchanan County. Maddy's report stated there'd been no vehicle tracks pulled to the side of the road. They'd have been obvious. So would tracks through the muddy, manure-strewn lot. There were none. Today, not even cattle tracks. After the mutilation of this beautiful brown-and-white animal, the herd had moved to the north side of the lot where some grass remained.

"What did Doc think did it?" he asked.

Maddy shrugged. "She didn't have anything definitive, although it wasn't an animal. Something intelligent did this."

"*Something* intelligent did this," he repeated, and pushed his brown felt hat farther back on his head. "I don't like where this is going."

"I'm not saying it's space aliens, Sheriff," she said. "Far from it."

He took a deep breath before speaking again. "Then what are you saying?"

"I'm saying Agent Flamank found no predator tracks anywhere near the body, I didn't find any human tracks around here, save one small set, and Dr. B said the thing used to kill this cow was probably a device too heavy to easily bring into a cattle lot, and impossible to use without a power source."

She nodded at herself, her short brown hair falling back into place when she stopped.

"And the one set of human tracks was in the picture you've already seen," she said, closing her notebook and sliding it into her shirt pocket. "It was. Dang it, Sheriff. It was the size of a little kid's, about four or five years old. From the print and sole pattern, the child wore a pair of size-ten Skechers Skech-O-Saurus." Maddy folded her arms across her chest.

"And the child didn't leave any other prints?"

Maddy shook her head. "It's the damnedest thing. No prints leading up to the animal, no prints leading away. Just the one set, like something put the child down and picked him back up again—and I'm *not* saying it was space aliens." She turned from the dead animal and met Glenn's gaze. Hers was fire. "There's an answer to this, and I'm going to find it."

A grin broke through Glenn's frustration. That intensity was the reason he hired her.

"I know you will," he said, and nodded back to his squad car. "Let's go get some coffee and eggs or waffles at Clem's. It's too early for this."

Zoe. Elizabeth finally sorted out the young nurse's name was Zoe. She nearly bumped into the girl as she stepped out of the bathroom, her tongue pressing a cinnamon disk into the roof of her mouth.

"Oh, sorry, Elizabeth," the young nurse said. She looked unusually disheveled. A strand of hair hung over one eye. "I was just looking for you."

"Looking for you" meant one of two things. Someone needed Elizabeth's help or was going to yell at her. She didn't relish either. Elizabeth held back the heavy sigh she felt like huffing, but since she'd had a couple of sips of schnapps, she thought better of it.

"Mr. and Mrs. Atkins. They're in the waiting room because Admitting told them to go home and they wouldn't listen," Zoe said in the closest thing to annoyance Elizabeth had heard from Miss Perky Just-Out-of-Nursing-School. "She's having Braxton-Hicks contractions, but she and her husband looked up her symptoms on WebPreg and they're convinced she'll have the baby any minute." Zoe attempted to blow the strand of hair out of her eye, but it lifted then fell right back.

The internet. The amount of incorrect self-diagnoses makes things harder on everyone.

"Has her water broken?"

Zoe slipped the annoying strand of hair behind her ear. "No. I told them it could be hours or days and they should go home, but they insisted on talking to someone with more experience."

Elizabeth started walking; it was jerks like this who made her consider going back to the ER. A deep fear rose in her chest; her stomach tightened. No, not just jerks like this. That devil baby. I should have gone to the ER four years ago.

She rounded the corner and entered the waiting room, *The View* on the television suspended in the corner. Mrs. Atkins lay on the couch; her husband knelt next to her telling her how to breathe.

"Well, it's about time," said the husband, who Elizabeth would eventually discover was named, for some unfortunate reason, Chaz. "Her contractions are twelve point three minutes apart."

Mrs. Atkins—Staci to her friends, so Elizabeth vowed to call her Mrs. Atkins—moaned, interrupting her perfectly timed breathing. Chaz checked his watch.

"Now it's twelve point one minutes," he said.

"Mr. Atkins," Elizabeth barked. He flinched at the sound but fell quiet. "Did your wife's water break?"

"No," he said.

Staci moaned again.

"Then she's not having contractions." He opened his mouth to speak, but snapped it shut when he caught her glare. "She's having what are called Braxton-Hicks contractions. They can happen a long time before she's ready to give birth. How many weeks is she along?"

"Twenty-eight."

Staci stopped huffing. "Twenty-seven, dear."

"Twenty-seven," Chaz repeated.

Twenty-seven weeks.

Elizabeth's arms crossed over her chest. "A full-term pregnancy is forty weeks. You two have, give or take, nine to twelve more weeks until your baby—"

"Chet," Chaz interrupted, then shrugged. "He's a baby boy. We're naming him Chet."

"Then Chet won't be here for three months," Elizabeth said. "Please go home, have a nice dinner, and relax."

"But—" Chaz started.

Elizabeth loomed over him. "Go home."

She turned and left the room, Zoe in tow, the Atkinses protesting behind them.

A tiny laugh escaped Zoe.

"What's so funny?" Elizabeth asked.

"Those two," she said. "Do you have to deal with many couples like that? They were the worst."

The worst? An invisible fist grabbed Elizabeth's guts and twisted. The eyes, those black eyes burning into her own, the smile. The damn knowing smile. The memory dredged itself from deep inside Elizabeth, a tumor she should have removed long ago.

"I've seen worse," she said.

Zoe's slim hand covered her mouth to hide her giggles. It didn't work. "How could anyone be worse? Did you smell Mr. Atkins? I think he'd been drinking."

She grabbed Zoe's shoulders and told her something she'd never told anyone before. She told her everything about the Jenkins baby.

[5]

The dark blue AA chip had begun losing some of its color around the rim in the weeks it had ridden in Thomas's left front pocket. He sat in his pickup, holding the coin signifying six months sobriety in the index fingers and thumbs of both hands, palms on the steering wheel, the wheel's plastic grip cracked beneath too many summers in the hot Missouri sun.

Thomas had walked into the local Alcoholics Anonymous meeting on a Wednesday night because he'd woken up one morning wanting a drink with breakfast. Now, as he stared at the gravel road across the rural highway, his house—Uncle Boyd's house—the gray roof, and the deep-green top of the old elm tree visible over a windbreak of tall, thin pines, all he wanted was a beer, followed by another and another. Dad's machine shed. That memory crawled from some dark hidden place in his head he didn't know existed.

And that scared the hell out of him.

He slid the blue chip back into his jeans pocket, where it would stay, at least until he earned his nine-month chip—*if* he earned his nine-month chip. As the old-timers say every meeting, "One day at a time."

He eased his foot off the brake pedal and moved it onto the accelerator. The deep, wailing honk from a tractor trailer burst through the open windows of Thomas's pickup. He mashed the brake pedal toward the floor, and the truck slid to a halt in the muddy gravel.

"Shit!" he screamed his fingers going white on the wheel, his heart pounding adrenaline through his body.

The truck, its red tractor with "Hadsell Family Farms: Easton, Missouri" painted on the door, streaked past, pulling an empty aluminum cattle trailer, manure dried beneath the vent holes in its side.

What the heck, man? Thomas's breath hammered his lungs, the blare of the air horn still rang through his head. I didn't see it. I didn't even see it. He turned and watched the Hadsell Family Farms truck disappear down the road, his heartbeat slowing like a spring on an old wind-up toy. At that moment, he'd kill someone for a beer.

[6]

Breakfast at Clem's settled on Glenn's stomach in only the way a plate of fried pork and potatoes covered in sausage gravy could. He shifted in his old office chair, the wood, after thirty years under Boyd's weight (being a Clem's fan himself), groaning with every move. Hmm. Glenn pulled at his belt; it was a little tight. Maybe I should hit the gym tomorrow, or—

Maddy stepped into the office and cleared her throat.

A flush spread across his cheeks.

"Oh, hey, Deputy." Glenn pulled his chair closer to the desk. "What can I do for you?" he asked, although the sheaf of paper in her hands told him all he needed to know.

She laid it on the desk, on a pile much tidier than Boyd's Leaning Tower of Paperwork but still a mess.

"After we left, Agent Flamank went all Aragorn from *The Lord of the Rings.*"

That meant little to Glenn. He had never read the books and only saw one of the Peter Jackson movies. "Which one's that?"

Maddy rolled her eyes. "The hot one."

Glenn shrugged.

"He was the ranger, one with nature. He could find an animal track in somebody's butt crack when their pants were on." She glared at Glenn, who attempted a smile. "Anyway. Flamank found something." She flipped the top pages to reveal photographs. One showed a print of a shoe, a child's shoe partly in mud, partly crushing grass.

Wait a minute. "Does it match?"

Maddy's face, what was it? Smug. Did she look smug?

"Well?"

"It's from a child's size-ten Skechers. The exact sole next to the mutilated heifer."

The chair creaked again as Glenn leaned back, the idea of putting on another pot of coffee crawling closer to the front of his to-do list.

"Where was it?" he asked.

"A mile away, on a spot of mud that separates a lawn from a soybean field."

Glenn flipped a few more photographs before looking back to Maddy. "Lawn? Does a child that age live in the house?"

Maddy shook her head.

"Niece or nephew visiting?"

"No."

The shoe print was only a partial, but yes, it was the same print from the mud and shit in the cattle lot. The next obvious question formed in his head, and damn, he was afraid of the answer.

"Was it the only one?"

"Yes," Maddy said, a grin hidden poorly behind her normally stoic business face.

"And?" Glenn asked.

She pulled a sealed baggie from her deep front pants pocket. It held a crushed juice box with a straw.

"Flamank found this next to the print," she said. "I know we don't have DNA databases for preschoolers, but now we have DNA matched to the only human footprint found next to the mutilated heifer. It's a start."

[7]

The call stopped the nurse cold.

"Elizabeth," Joy said from the Labor, Delivery, and Recovery nurses station, the receiver of the black desk phone cradled between her neck and shoulder. Elizabeth froze; she'd been on her way to the elevator. Too much schnapps on top of not enough food told her she needed something to calm her stomach.

"Yes?" she said, rolling a new cinnamon disc to the side of her mouth.

"Assistant Administrator Simmons wants to see you."

Her hands slipped into the pockets of her scrubs to hide their shaking. The assistant administrator?

"What is this about?" she asked, cursing herself for the quiver in her voice.

Joy cupped a hand over the receiver. "I don't know," she whispered. "But she was short."

Short? That was Joy for "angry."

The clunk of the heavy receiver slamming down signified so much.

"Donna wants to see you now," Joy said. "Do you know—"

"Yes," Elizabeth snapped, cutting her off. "I know where her office is."

She stopped at the vending machines near the elevators and grabbed a roll of little powdered doughnuts before she went to see Assistant

Administrator Donna Simmons. She'd first met Donna at the hospital Christmas party in 2019; the new assistant was a polite, introverted lady who wore clothing too large for her body. They spoke about childbirth for five minutes at most before Donna excused herself to wander off and speak with someone else. Donna was new—and important. She had places to go, people to see. Elizabeth hadn't spoken with her since.

Three floors up, she stepped off the elevator and approached the administrative offices, using her mobile phone's camera to check for powdered sugar on her face before stepping into the receptionist's office, a room full of static decorations of flower prints and a dull yellow couch.

The receptionist directed Elizabeth to sit on that couch and she did; her hands clutched her wobbly knees. The receptionist glanced at her, then back at her computer screen, and that was all.

Minutes ticked by. Elizabeth's bladder sat inside her lower abdomen like a melon.

"Dr. Simmons will see you now," the receptionist finally said. She stood and walked toward an oak door labeled "Dr. Donna Simmons."

Elizabeth followed.

The woman she'd met at the Christmas party didn't occupy this office; she'd grown. Dr. Simmons sat at her wide wooden desk, her outfit smart and professional, and it fit her.

"Elizabeth?" Dr. Simmons said. "It's been a while."

She clutched her hands behind her back. Dr. Simmons didn't ask her to sit.

"Yes?" Elizabeth swallowed the last speck of her cinnamon disc before continuing. "What do you want to see me about?"

Dr. Simmons folded her hands on her desk. The woman's eyes told Elizabeth all she needed to know. She was finished here.

"Doctors, nurses, pharmacists," the administrator said. "These are all stress-filled jobs, and the hospital understands the level of stress you're under. We understand the fact that substance abuse is common. I, myself, went through a rehabilitation program for alcohol as an intern. That's why I feel comfortable speaking with you about this topic."

Elizabeth didn't wait for another word; she sat in one of the plush chairs at the front of the desk.

"If this was just about your addiction, we would have offered you rehabilitation," Simmons said, randomly shuffling papers, her attention on her hands. "However, this meeting is about a different issue."

"I don't understand, ma'am," Elizabeth said, although she damn well did. Drinking on the job, especially this job, was worse than irresponsible, it was unconscionable. If people knew, she should have been fired already.

Dr. Simmons folded her hands, her face hard.

"You discussed patient information with someone other than the patient and the attending physician. That is a flagrant HIPAA violation, something this hospital will not tolerate." Donna stood; the sleek office chair didn't make a sound. "Please pack up any personal belongings, Elizabeth, and security will escort you from the building. You're no longer employed by Eastside Hospital."

The assistant administrator continued, but to Elizabeth it was simple ramble. Severance pay, COBRA insurance, blah, blah. But Elizabeth's mind focused on one thing. Zoe. Dr. Simmons knew about this for one reason.

Zoe, the young nurse. She told on me. That little bitch told on me.

A security guard appeared from somewhere and escorted Elizabeth to her locker, then to the employee entrance and her car, a ten-year-old Honda Civic. She never wanted to see another hospital or another stupid baby ever again.

[8]

The moment Thomas knew he wasn't going to drink that day was when he turned the key, killing his truck under the shade of the old elm tree next to the house, and stared at a squirrel on a branch staring back at him, its bushy red tail twitching like it had just done a line of coke. He didn't remember driving home. The last thing he knew, the Hadsell Family Farms truck swept by, the driver warning an accelerating Thomas to stay the hell out of his way. A left turn and four miles of asphalt were the only obstacles to him pulling into the Possum Hollow Quik-Stop in Agency and picking up an eighteen-pack of cheap beer. At that moment, the adrenaline still flowing, he didn't care what it tasted like. He just wanted to get drunk.

Then he was home. Jillian wasn't there. His old Camry she'd taken over didn't sit in its usual spot at the edge of the lawn; tire tracks marred the rain-soaked earth. He rolled up his window and stepped from the truck, the squirrel scolding him until it disappeared into the high boughs.

The door to the house was, of course, unlocked. Jillian told him long ago she'd never locked a door in her life and wasn't going to start. He paused between the screen and the old wooden front door, a long pane of window obscured by a white lace curtain. A moth of a thought fluttered through his consciousness, brief and fleeting, only to disappear into the darkness. He'd walked through an unlocked front door before, and something bad waited inside.

His hand, not as steady as he'd like, reached out and turned the knob, pushing the door open to a quiet house.

"Jill?" he said, knowing she wasn't home. He got no answer.

Inside, a note on the front sheet of a yellow legal pad sat propped against the dining-room table centerpiece.

Thomas,

I've gone to the grocery store to pick up some things for supper. Don't worry, since I'm using your money and I'm not going to cook it, this doesn't count as me presenting you with food.

Jillian

This doesn't count as me presenting you with food? The heck? Something deep down, deeper even than the memory of the cake in the machine shed, told him that fact was important, and had been important to him personally—once.

But why?

[9]

The silver Lexus SUV came to a soundless stop on the oil spot-free driveway leading to the McMansion Todd had built on a few acres of land east of St. Joseph, Missouri. The enormous lawn had been cut clean by a lawn-care service, the grass spotless and tight as a golf green. Todd Marshall shifted his vehicle—his brand-new vehicle—into park and slid from the seat. He checked his reflection in the side mirror and ran a hand through his hair before clicking the door shut and locking it with the key-ring fob. This fine-tuned machine was the reward for sales, sales, sales. Todd was the hottest real-estate agent in town and, by God, he didn't mind showing it off.

A spot of bird shit blemished the hood. He removed the monogrammed white handkerchief from the rear pocket of his slacks (new slacks to fit his ever-growing ass) and hocked a wad of spit into it before wiping off the offending stain. If it were up to Todd, all those flying rats would be exterminated, except the ducks. A group of boys at the country club went duck hunting a few times a year and, although they never came home with Daffy in tow, they sure as hell got drunk.

The white smear gone and the Lexus primo once again, he stuffed the dirty handkerchief back into his pocket. The wife would take it with his dry cleaning. And why not? It's not like she did anything but stay home and be pregnant.

Pregnant. Yeah, baby. Child numero uno. Todd knew he'd knocked up his wife that night. He felt it. She'd said she had an orgasm—no, wait, two. Yeah, two. And that meant he wasn't just doing his job, he was doing his job right. To Todd, when he was between the sheets, he was LeBron James in his prime.

He took the front steps two at a time, a little more difficult than when they moved into this house two years ago. Hell, they needed to sell it anyway. It was a four-bedroom, two-and-a-half-bath, two-car-garage split-level, but it wasn't good enough for the best real-estate agent in town, and that garage wasn't good enough to park his Lexus in.

His keys were still in his hand, but he grabbed the front doorknob first. It turned. Damn it. He'd told her and told her nobody can be trusted. Lock the door.

Todd pushed it open.

"Bekka, honey, I'm home."

Nothing.

Maybe she's in the bathroom. Pregnant women pee a lot.

Before stomping in and asking what was for lunch, he sniffed. Apart from that god-awful potpourri she insisted on littering their home with, there was nothing. No hot food, no romantic candles like she sometimes lit—but wait, there *was* something. He stood still and sucked deeply. Yes, something hung in the air. Something wet. Something metallic. Pressure pushed at his bladder.

"Bekka?"

The house felt different, heavy, like it wasn't his house, like he and Bekka and the future Todd Jr. didn't live there anymore. He felt like a stranger.

"Hon?"

A click came from up the six stairs to the main floor; the six stairs to the basement ended in darkness.

Click? What the fuck was the click? But he knew what it was. Metal on metal.

"Who's here?" Todd shouted, his face growing hot. A lub-dub, lub-dub, lub-dub, sounded in his ears. His blood pressure. Jesus. He knew he had to get that checked out. But now? "Who the fuck's here?"

A gun. Todd had a gun.

He pulled out his key chain and pushed the blades for the house, his office, and his new Lexus through his fingers. If someone was in his house, with his wife—his *pregnant* wife—that a-hole was going to pay with a ring of keys jabbed into his face.

"I'm coming," he mumbled and started to ascend the stairs to the living room.

Maybe they're in the kitchen, Todd thought. I'm going to make them wish they'd brought Rambo.

The steps, covered in tight carpet, never squeaked as Todd finished taking them to the main floor; the wet, metallic smell was stronger. He stopped and listened. Nothing. No movement, no breath, no cologne to tell him where the intruder was. He saw the pistol, a Hellcat Pro 9mm, right next to the couch.

He dashed to the couch, tripping over the coffee table, but when he came up, he gripped the Hellcat in shaky hands.

The kitchen was empty.

Todd used the end table to pull himself to his feet. What he saw was—

"Dear God." He wished he'd never come home for lunch.

Bekka lay in a pool of inky blood.

"Bekka?"

His wife was nude, a bloody towel on the floor beside her. Todd's mind couldn't quite click all the pieces in place, but he knew something was different about her, other than his wife of five years was dead. Her tummy, her eight-months-pregnant tummy, was deflated.

He took a few steps closer. The blood. Good God, the blood. The stench overwhelmed him; he dropped his hands to his knees and vomited the coffee and crullers he'd had for breakfast onto his dead wife's face.

"Jesus." He coughed.

Whoever did this. Whatever monster did this, it drew on her.

He, or she, or "it" fucking *drew* on her. Blood smeared across her belly. They painted on her stomach? With her own blood? The umbilical cord, he finally saw, lay like an enormous, bloody dead worm between his wife's legs. The baby wasn't attached. Todd Jr. was gone.

CHAPTER THREE

A WOLF SPIDER crawled across the gravel drive, thin hairy legs lifting its abdomen over chunks of rocks; the biggest was the size of a marble, but to the spider they were mountains. Jacob squatted in the drive and stared at the spider. A thick shock of black hair had fallen over one eye. He didn't brush it away, he could see well enough.

The grayish-brown spider made its way toward the thin slip of concrete that sat in front of the garage door. Linda Jenkins—he knew that was her name, although he never called Gramma that—sat in the open garage on a lawn chair, a glass of iced tea on an overturned milk crate next to her.

Condensation beaded on the surface of the glass his grandpa had stolen from a bar long before Jacob was born. "Redneck Inn" was painted in red letters across the side. A brightly colored romance book sat forgotten on her lap.

"What are you lookin' at, Jakie?" Linda asked, cigarette smoke rolling from her mouth. She brought the Pall Mall back to her lips and inhaled again.

"Issa spider, Gramma," Jacob said, picking up a stick and holding it in front of the arachnid, hoping the spider would crawl onto it.

Linda leaned forward and looked, a haze of smoke around her. She never smoked in her house, but Jacob knew when Momma had disappeared and met Daddy, his grandmother couldn't help herself. It was her house, and nobody could tell her what she could or couldn't do. Then Momma came home, alive and healthy, at least in her body (her mind, Jacob was pretty sure, had been scrambled like eggs), and carrying little Jacob in her belly, things changed around the Jenkins house. No smoking inside anymore.

No siree Bob.

"That *is* a spider, Jakie," Gramma said, then coughed, hacking up something loose she expelled into one of the many wadded tissues on the milk crate. "Just like that spider in the book Gramma read to you. Charlotte. You remember *Charlotte's Web?*"

Jacob's eyes never left the spider, but he dropped the stick. The doody-head thing walked right over it.

"Uh-huh," he said absentmindedly. Answering when Gramma spoke was what Momma called a courtesy, even though Jacob didn't care what Gramma said, or anybody else but Momma. He didn't need to listen to anybody; he was special. Momma told him so.

The spider ended its long march through the gravel and reached the concrete. Charlotte was a smarty-pants. She could talk, she could spell things. She was weak. A weaky, weaky weaker. The rat, Templeton, that's the character Jacob liked.

Templeton might not have been strong, but Templeton was clever. Jacob was clever.

He *knew* he was clever. Jacob could do things Gramma and Momma didn't know he could do.

"Say hi to Charlotte, baby." Baby. He hated it when Gramma called him baby. He wasn't a baby; he was four years old.

Jacob stood and brushed back his bangs. A smile crossed his face, the type of smile that made people in the grocery store look away and hurry down a different aisle.

"Bye-bye, Charlotte," he said, and crushed the spider under the toe of his dinosaur Skechers Momma bought at Walmart.

A gasp shot from Gramma. Ha, Gramma. You're weak too. A weaky, weaky weaker, just like Charlotte.

"No. No. Jakie," she said, her voice rough from all the cigarettes and that thing growing on her lung. "No. That was bad. Bad Jakie." She stood, her bulk tipping over the chair and sending her iced tea cascading onto the garage floor. The stolen pint glass landed in a crash. "Why did you do that? Why? That was a living creature, baby boy. You can't just kill it."

His head cocked to one side as he tried to understand what she'd just said. "Why? I'm bigger."

"Just because you can," she said, "doesn't mean you should."

The smile came back, and he spoke, his voice expressionless. "I'm gone be bigger than you someday, Gramma."

Linda froze, the color drained from her face. She never did anything to upset Jacob. There was something about the boy, something her own momma would have called "off," and Linda never wanted to flip Jacob's switch to "on."

Jacob laughed out loud, the laughter cold and emotionless. Linda cringed. She cringed at her own grandson.

"Where's Momma?" he asked.

He'd become bored with his grandmother. Linda could hear it in his voice. The switch was halfway there.

"The garden," she tried to say, but the words came in a sputter, her heart hammering; sweat streaked her round face. Linda raised a flappy arm and pointed behind the house. Jacob waved and skipped around the edge of the garage.

Linda exhaled and started to go inside, where she knew a half gallon of vodka sat under the sink, but something on the cracked, oil-stained garage floor stopped her cold. The pint glass wasn't broken; it sat on the concrete in one piece, filled with iced tea.

Jillian didn't come home for hours. Thomas made it through two episodes of *Ancient Aliens* before the creak and slam of the Camry door reached him on the couch. He got out a coaster and moved his Dr Pepper just before Jillian came through the front door, a bag of groceries in each arm. Thomas didn't move.

"Well, the honeymoon over?" she said, smiling her usual smile. Thomas couldn't remember her wearing any other expression.

That was wrong, he knew. He'd seen her angry with him before, and it had terrified him. But when? Why? The more he tried to remember, the less he could, as if a wall had been built in his brain, and the guy with the key would only let a few memories out at a time.

"What do you mean?" he asked, although he knew. He could have opened the door, he *should* have helped her inside. A boyfriend, a partner, a gentleman would have, but it didn't occur to him.

She pushed the door closed with her butt and walked into the kitchen, where her note still sat on the table. The plastic grocery-store bags landed with the clunk of cans.

Thomas finished his soda and took the remote control off his leg, changing the channel from *Ancient Aliens* to *Star Trek: The Next Generation*. Apparently the entire crew of the *Enterprise* had lost their memories.

"I picked up some microwave dinners and a couple of cans of Chef Boyardee and a frozen pizza," she said, unloading the bags. "You can take your pick. I'm not going to be home tonight."

"Oh?" Thomas asked. "Where are you going?"

She stuffed the pizza in the freezer before walking over to the couch and plopping next to Thomas, draping her legs over his. The touch brought a cringe.

"Marguerite's." The smile on her face never faded. "She finally asked me to babysit."

Babysit? After four years? This sounded wrong. Why would—

"Have you seen this one before?" she asked, pointing at Captain Picard looking confused and Lieutenant Worf overly confident. Thomas shook his head. "Too bad. It's a good one. The executive officer is really an alien."

[3]

The call on Glenn's private line blinked at him from the black surface of the office phone. The private line meant it came from someone official: a deputy, highway patrol, St. Joe Police, the FBI (like that's happened more than once). It was probably Maddy with some update on the heifer. Glenn picked up the phone to find Aaron on the other end.

"Sheriff?"

"Aaron?" The deputy's voice surprised him. He wouldn't call for an update on his case, which revolved around stolen lumber and copper wire. "What's going on?"

The deputy cleared his throat before continuing. Aaron had been with the sheriff's department almost as long as Glenn; he sounded shaken, which took Glenn off guard. Aaron was a solid officer; he'd seen a lot.

"I'm, uh, I'm at the residence of a Mr. and Mrs. Todd and Rebekka Marshall. Todd is a real-estate agent in St. Joe."

Glenn nodded along with the call. He'd seen the billboards, Todd's expensive haircut, and more expensive smile shining out over Interstate 29 claiming, "I Sell Homes FAST."

"Where's his house?" Glenn asked, expecting Aaron to answer St. Joe, so why the hell would he be there?

"Out in the country, just north of the Bessie Ellison School."

Glenn knew exactly where that was. A lot of money went into a lot of big houses out there.

"Mr. Marshall is outside with Trooper Wilmes," Aaron said. "And Mrs. Marshall. Well, she's, she's . . ." His voice trailed off.

"She's what, Aaron?" Glenn snapped. He didn't have the patience for whatever this was. "Get it together."

"She's dead, sir," he finished. "Mr. Marshall came home for lunch and found his wife deceased, murdered."

Glenn's fingers clutched the receiver hard enough it hurt.

"Sir?" Aaron asked. "Mrs. Marshall was pregnant. Can I send you a picture?"

"Yes, please." Picture of what? The body? The house? What was on the stove for lunch?

His cell phone chirped a moment later. Glenn thumbed in the pass code and clicked "Messages." The phone nearly dropped from his hand.

Mrs. Marshall lay nude on the living room floor, a bloody towel folded beside her. The umbilical cord lay detached on the floor, the baby missing. But what pulled his attention most was the blood on her stomach: drawn with the hand of a child, a bloody circle with a gaping mouth smiled at Glenn through sharp, needle-like teeth.

[4]

Jacob knew his momma was far from all right. Eleven years of her life were gone, but they weren't. Not really. The past eleven years wove themselves in and out of her conscious and unconscious life like a tapestry of insanity. She no longer woke screaming to nightmares of a demon inside her. The drugs the doctor who smelled like Mentos gave her saw to that.

Momma worried about Jacob, he knew. She struggled between loving him and being afraid of him; she especially worried when she used to scream, that her screams might wake him. She put him in a room as far away from her as Gramma's house would allow. Even as a baby—that he remembered. Oh yes, every second—he lay silently in his crib, a smile on his tiny face, as he watched the mobile above him spin one way, then the other, and back again. Occasionally lights would spark above Jacob's crib, lights of violet, green, and indigo, moving in a circle, but they wouldn't last long. And no one in the house ever saw them.

Momma's nightmares also included Daddy, the greasy boy with crazy wrapped around him like a flag. Jacob knew his father's name was Bobby, Momma met him at the mall, and Daddy died in a car accident, but that was all he knew. Jacob never asked about Daddy, and Momma was glad. As she sat in the office of one of her doctors—a talking doctor named Kermit with lots of diplomas written in Old English script that hung on the walls in gold frames—bouncing Jacob in her lap, the doctor suggested she get a hobby to take her mind off things. Like planting flowers. So she did. Momma spent lots and lots of time with her flowers. Her other doctor, the Mentos doctor, Momma went to for drugs.

Jacob's skip dropped into a silent stalk when he rounded the corner of the house, Gramma just discovering the unbroken glass. Silly old woman, he thought. Fixing the broken glass was easy. I could fix the bomb in your lungs, too, but I doan wanna.

His mother's flower garden covered half the backyard with marigolds, tulips, dandelions, roses, and things she spent hours online researching and ordering. The spot was once dead brown grass. That was before Jacob was born, but it had something to do with Daddy Bobby. Things died everywhere, but they weren't dead anymore. Momma's garden was green, and red, and orange, and gold.

Ceramic gnomes dotted this brightly colored haven, armed with ceramic rakes, hoes, and shovels. Jacob could make them be alive, but he didn't want to now. Maybe later, when Gramma came back outside.

Jacob hated the garden. It smelled funny. He liked the smell of dirt, but the flowers overpowered the solid scent of the earth. Momma bent over a plant with a funny name, hi-hi-hibiscuits. She gripped a one-hand garden rake, scraping the dirt around the roots and ridding them of the rightful owners of the gardens: the weeds that would overtake this flowering mess if she'd only let them. The weeds were strong, the flowers were weak. He walked silently toward her. Flowering bushes hid him from his mother, the person who kept things from him, information he wanted to know. She hid from him in this garden because she was the most afraid of him.

"I call you on the phone, but you're not the-re," came from her lips in off-key tones. "I sit at home alone and wonder whe-re."

Jacob's foot struck something on the ground, and he about tumbled over, but he waved his arms and caught his balance. A trowel. A trowel sat at his feet. He bent and picked it up, his stubby four-year-old fingers comically small on the handle. The blade, caked with dirt, both dried and fresh, looked dull, but he knew it was not. This blade was dangerous. He stepped behind a thick bush, purple flowers just starting to bloom, and held the trowel point first.

"Can't eat or sleep, I miss your touch," his mother sang as he came toward her. "Why do you mean so much?"

Then something moved to his right. A slight movement, and it waved at him. He turned his head fully toward the movement and saw a woman. A tiny woman with red hair in a white dress. She stood on a leaf of the weigela bush, holding onto a flower bud. Jacob stepped slowly toward her, the trowel forgotten in his hand.

"Wha—" he started, but the little woman's hand flew over her mouth, and she shook her head. Jacob knew what that meant. Be quiet. He put his own hand over his mouth and leaned close to the little woman, until his face was so near to hers she started to get blurry. The little woman leaned forward and spoke into his ear.

[5]

Dear God, no.

Glenn's eyes remained on the image until his mobile phone fell asleep, the black screen no more comforting. He knew that face. It was on the basement wall of 4244 Carlyle Street, the site of Bobby Garrett's house. It had been on Elvin Miller's living-room wall, painted in his wife's blood.

And in John and Carrie McMasters' kitchen in tiny Rushville, John sliced ear-to-ear at the dinner table, the face drawn in his blood grinned over his body.

All that was four years ago. Why the hell was it back now?

"Sheriff?" Aaron asked, a quiver in his voice. Glenn swallowed before he spoke, sure a quiver lurked in his own.

"Yeah."

"This is my first murder, sir," the deputy said. "I don't know, I—"

Don't fall apart, damn it. "Deputy," Glenn said, forcing his voice lower than was natural for him. "Detach yourself emotionally. There's no time for it now. You can have a few beers when you get home, but now isn't the time to let this get to you. You have a body." Aaron remained silent. "Deputy, stay with me. You have a body."

"Oh, yes, sir."

"And a person of interest."

"What?" Aaron asked. He sounded distant, confused. "Oh, the husband? I guess he could be, but I don't think—"

"No," Glenn interrupted. "Don't think too far down the road right now, Deputy. The spouse is always a person of interest, even if you're one hundred percent certain he didn't do it. You'll have to bring him into the station for questioning."

Probably more nodding. "Yes, sir."

"How about motive?"

"Not at this time." The quiver had disappeared; Glenn took a deep, even breath.

"Murder weapon?"

This time Aaron simply didn't respond. After a few seconds, Glenn broke in.

"Is there a murder weapon?" he asked.

"Well, sir," Aaron said. "There is. The Marshalls have one of those magnetic strips in the kitchen all their knives are stuck to, and it, well, the murder weapon, it's there. The blade's covered with blood."

What? Glenn thought. They used one of the Marshalls' own knives as the murder weapon, then put it away?

"And sir. There's a bloody handprint on the handle."

A sense of relief rushed over him.

A murder weapon covered in blood, probably the victim's, and a handprint on the handle. Find the hand that fits the print, and the case solves itself.

"Does it look like it fits Mr. Marshall?" Glenn asked.

Aaron probably shook his head before speaking, Glenn thought. "No, sir. Mr. Marshall doesn't have a drop of blood on him or under his fingernails. I checked. All I found was sugar. He told me he had crullers for breakfast. Besides, the print's not big enough."

Not what? "Big enough? What do you mean not big enough? Is it a woman's print?"

"No. That's the funny thing. It's a kid's handprint, sir. Swear to God. It's about the size of my nephew's hand, and he's in kindergarten."

"Thank you, deputy," came from Glenn's mouth, although the words sounded like something that traveled through tin cans connected by string. He missed the telephone cradle with the receiver; it bounced off the desk onto the floor. The sheriff didn't pick it up.

[6]

Jillian left before supper, planting a dry kiss on Thomas's cheek, then nearly skipped out the door and down the porch steps to the rusty Camry. Thomas leaned against a porch post and waved as she pulled out onto the gravel road and pointed the Toyota toward the rural highway that went to St. Joseph; that would be followed by a half-hour drive to Marguerite's house outside Savannah.

A thought, brief and fleeting, told him to call Marguerite to double-check on Jillian. The babysitting gig sounded wrong. He made it as far as pulling his mobile phone from his pocket, but didn't touch the screen to bring it to life. Thomas realized at that moment, this was finally it for Jillian and him. They'd grown distant over the past few months, and as he stood on the porch, the old car gone in the late afternoon, he knew he didn't care if she'd lied to him; he didn't care if she ever came home.

He went back inside for a shower. He had a meeting to go to.

[7]

Marguerite slid plates of microwaved popcorn chicken and tater tots onto the kitchen table.

"Where's Gramma?" Jacob asked, grabbing a tot and shoving it into his mouth.

"In bed, baby," Marguerite said. "Just eat your dinner, then we can watch some SpongeBob."

She squirted ketchup onto his plate, then hers, and picked up a fork. What Jacob said made her drop it.

"I saw a fairy in the garden today."

She scooped up the fork and gripped it tightly, trying to hide her shaking hand. Her hands shook a lot. Her son terrified her.

"Really?"

"Yes, Momma," he said, dipping a piece of processed chicken in ketchup, the sweet, sickly smell of the red mess wafting across the table. "She was purty. She said I was special, and she needed me to finish something she started. But she didn't tell me what that was. Somethin' about rainin' hell. What's 'rainin' hell' mean, Momma?"

Marguerite's fork clattered on the stained Formica tabletop again. Raining hell. Those words had come from her mouth once as the monster inside her commanded Jacob's father to destroy a city.

Where had he heard this? Did I scream it in my sleep?

"Did you know this woman, honey?" she asked, her voice wavering.

Jacob nodded. "Uh-huh. I think so. She said she wanted me to come visit her in her fairy world," he continued, ignoring the fact that his question went unanswered. "She's gonna come to the trees tonight and give me chocolate cake." He ate the chicken bit and looked at his mother with dead, black eyes. A second piece of chicken rolled across the plate into the ketchup, then floated up to the level of his mouth. "Can I go, Momma?"

Marguerite took a drink of white wine from a red Solo cup, the alcohol dancing on her tongue. She'd seen Jacob's trick before, but never while he knew she was watching. She upended the cup, and drained the contents.

"Fairy?" she asked, when she lowered it. "What did she do?"

"Oh, she was tiny, Momma. Little bitty. She stood on a leaf and whispered in my ear."

Marguerite stared at the boy, his hair, his eyes, his lifeless grin so much like his father's. "And she talked to you?"

Jacob nodded, the chicken bit still floating in front of his mouth, a smear of ketchup across his cheek. "Ya, she did."

Marguerite poured more wine into her cup. "Sure, baby. If a fairy comes and offers you cake, you can eat it and go to fairy world. I think you'll like it there."

[8]

The smell of warm cookies greeted Thomas when he opened the door of the Delores Hadley Community Center. A platter of sugar cookies and snickerdoodles sat between two great metal pots of coffee on a table in a corner, one pot marked "Decaf."

"Hey, Frank," Thomas said, resting his hand on a gentleman's shoulder. The man, at least seventy, reached back and patted that hand.

"Good evening, young sir." The old man's voice, rough as a diesel engine, showed drinking hadn't been his only vice.

Fourteen people dotted the metal chairs around four long folding tables; the configuration of the room was large enough for thirty. Thomas attended his first Alcoholics Anonymous meeting two years after Uncle Boyd died. Beer had become his coping mechanism for work, Jillian, and living in his late uncle's house; then drinking became his coping mechanism for drinking. He'd been nervous his first time until the meeting started. Old drunks, he discovered, are some of the nicest, most welcoming people on the planet. They confessed their problems, encouraged one another's achievements, and held hands to pray at the end.

The next week he went back, then the next, and the next. Thomas hadn't had a drink since. That was nearly eight months ago.

He grabbed a cookie and poured himself a Styrofoam cup of coffee, knowing the scalding black liquid wouldn't be cool enough to drink until the meeting was half over. Jerry smiled at the room and started the meeting. Thomas sat as Amanda read the AA creed.

That's all he ever knew members by, Jerry, Amanda, Frank, Tony. AA is anonymous for a reason; not knowing anyone's full name allows people to be truthful.

"Cell phones off, everybody," Jerry announced, like he did every week. "Tonight's for fellowship and understanding, not playing word search or whatever's popular nowadays."

Phones clicked onto the table in front of each member, face down, and Jerry went around the room for introductions, Thomas talking through his M&M cookie. Crumbs fell down his chin, and a few people laughed. About fifteen minutes into the meeting, while everyone was confessing what brought them there, a woman of about forty-five slid open the door, silent on its pneumatic hinge, and stepped in. Jerry waved her to the table and she sat.

Moments later, it was the new woman's turn.

"My name's Elizabeth," she said, "and I'm an alcoholic."

[9]

The moon rose above the dead trees at the edge of the property, remnants of Bobby's rein of destruction across northwest Missouri. With coaxing from the conservation department, and the University of Missouri Extension, new plants now grew in the once-dead soil, but the trees drained of life by the black entity that created Jacob remained dead.

Marguerite sat on a canvas lawn chair, another Solo of cheap wine in the cupholder, her mind a pleasant, numb lump. Jacob giggled as he ran across the yard, one of the only times the boy ever showed emotion, catching and squishing lightning bugs. Marguerite had long since abandoned trying to convince her son it was wrong to kill; she'd given in. Besides, they were just bugs.

But what, she wondered, did he consider bugs?

Jacob ducked behind the row of dead trees, the giggle disappearing with him. Marguerite had never wanted to be a mother. Before Bobby kidnapped her in the mall parking lot, before the demon space monster took residence inside her, before her mind became buried deep inside the blanket of darkness, she wanted to meet a nice guy, go back to school to get a degree, then a job better than the one she had waitressing at the Savannah Pizza Palace. Motherhood happened to someone else. Marguerite Jenkins wasn't going to lug what amounted to a hairless chimp on her hip, feeding it with a plastic spoon, and changing its shitty pants.

Then she had Jacob, and the boy not only kept her in a perpetual state of exhaustion—the little boy, with his dark, piercing eyes and thick black hair like his father, the boy with an otherworldly air about him, who could dip chicken nuggets into ketchup and eat them without lifting a hand—that little monster horrified her.

She took a long drink of Chablis, the wine still cold. The effects of the prior cups kept her drunk but did little to dull her fear.

The rear screen door slammed shut, and her mother stepped onto the lawn, rubbing her eyes. Her nap was short today.

"It's getting late, hon," she said, her words slurred from too much vodka.

It was beautiful. The stars burned bright in the country, and these seemed on fire. The moon had already moved from above the line of trees to over the house. Staring drunkenly at the moon, Marguerite thought about how quiet it was. No insect noises, no night birds, no faraway cattle lowing, no coyotes yipping, no—

"Jakie," she said, then said it again, louder. "Jakie?" Marguerite pulled herself awkwardly from the flimsy chair and stood, looking out toward the trees. "Where are you, baby?"

Linda stepped beside her daughter. "Where is he, honey?"

[10]

Something smelled like poop stinky.

The boy trudged through the broken branches and long-dead leaves in the small spot of woods he knew his daddy had killed before he was born. Trudged. He liked that word. It felt good in his head, although when his stupid tongue said it, the word came out "tudged." He got mad at his mouth sometimes; it wasn't as smart as his brain.

A long-fallen stick snapped under his dinosaur shoes. The sun sank low, and soon it would be dark. Jacob liked the dark, but it was hard to see. A few steps later, a light, like a huge firefly, flew in the trees. He followed it.

"Jakie," a tiny voice whispered.

A smile crossed the boy's face. It was the fairy, and she was playing a game.

"I'm coming," he whispered back, following the light.

It flittered around a dead tree, the barkless wood white in the dying light. "I'm gonna find you."

The spark in the night, that in his mind was a fairy light, ducked behind a tree and dimmed. He took slower steps toward the tree and jumped behind it when he got close enough.

I'm gonna scare you.

"Boo!" he shouted, but the fairy wasn't there, although it was. The little fairy in Momma's flowers, the one who wanted to take him to fairy world, the one who came to him when he played outside while Gramma was inside getting more vodka, stood behind the tree, but she was big now. Big like a real woman.

"Hi, lady," Jacob said, raising a hand to wave.

He stepped back. He'd never seen the fairy lady big and—and he knew her. She'd taken him out to play.

"Do you remember when we had fun with the cow?" she asked.

Jacob nodded. "Oh, yes. It was fun. The cow was so big, but it was a weaky, weaky weaker."

The lady, her hair tied behind her head in a ponytail like Momma sometimes wore, smiled the prettiest smile Jacob had ever seen. It glowed so much Jacob wondered if she had a flashlight in her mouth.

"Good," she said, stepping aside and waving her hand at a tree stump like the ladies on Gramma's game shows waved at a new washer dryer. A plate sat on the stump, and it held a piece of chocolate cake. Jacob thought chocolate cake was the best food anyone ever invented. "Then you'll really like my cake. It'll take us to fairy world, but I won't show you cows in fairy world," she said. "This time, I'll show you how fun playing with people can be."

Jacob's smile stretched wide as he stepped toward the plate. People were stupid; she was right, it would be fun. The pretty red-haired lady lifted the cake to his mouth and he took a bite. It didn't taste as good as it looked, but that didn't matter. The world started to spin, and Jacob took the lady's hand.

Marguerite stood still, and Jacob's words during what passed for supper pushed through the alcohol that clouded her brain. *"She said she wanted me to come visit her in her fairy world."*

In the trees?

She moved, staggering toward the dry, gray skeletons of trees at the edge of the lawn, and entered the miniature forest. Pines, oaks, hickories, all dead, the ground covered with brown leaves, some with withered bark, others stripped of it. In a small clearing, a china plate, white with blue flowers, sat on a stump.

"She's gonna come to the trees tonight and give me chocolate cake," Jacob had told her.

Marguerite approached the stump and fell to her knees before it. A piece of chocolate cake sat on the plate, a bite missing.

Jacob was gone.

CHAPTER FOUR

[1]

TAP.

   Tap.

   Tap.

Thomas rolled over in his sleep. Whatever caused that sound would go away, his subconscious mind told itself; it must be a bird, or the wind, or squirrels. Definitely squirrels. Sleep attempted to haul itself back over his eyes.

   Tap.

   Tap.

   Tap.

The back of his hand instinctively drew across his mouth, mopping off a glop of drool. That noise was no bird, it wasn't the wind, and it wasn't a squirrel. Someone stood at his front door, trying to get his attention—like he wanted that. He shifted his body toward Jillian's side of the bed, careful not to bump her. Waking Jillian would mean they'd talk about things Thomas didn't want to talk about, and hold a hand he didn't want to hold. But her side of the bed was empty, the sheet and comforter still tucked in. Yeah, he realized. Jillian left to babysit Jacob Jenkins, but she never came home.

"That's weird."

A memory, one of the many locked behind that wall, squeezed through. Jillian had done this once before; one night she just disappeared—for years. Thomas had been frantic. This morning, he simply rolled onto his back and stared at the white popcorn ceiling, the fan over the bed moving so slowly it wouldn't cool the room, and he smiled. At least for now, she was gone.

Bang.

Bang.

Bang.

But somebody wasn't.

"Damn it."

He sat up in bed and swung his legs over the side. Whoever it was at the door wasn't going away. For years he'd woken with a dry mouth and a nagging headache that rarely went away until that first beer of the day. Sober for more than half a year, other than a bit of lingering brain fog, he felt great. Thomas swiped a finger across his mobile phone, waking it.

It read 3:16 a.m.

"What the heck?" he hissed. Whoever this is, it's way too early.

Bang.

Bang.

Bang.

The phone slid into the pocket of the gray sweatpants that doubled for pajamas, and he walked to the door and flicked on the porch light. The figure on the other side was feminine and familiar.

"Marguerite?" he said, opening the door. She stood on shaking legs, her normally well-kept hair disheveled, a few dried leaves and a cocklebur clinging to the tight material of her yoga pants. She stank of stale wine.

"Jakie," she said, and lurched forward, falling into Thomas. Unlike the time in college when a pretty girl next to him in a hot, unmoving line started to fall, he caught Marguerite.

What happened to you? he thought, easing her onto the couch, her body odor fighting to overpower the reek of wine.

"Let me get you some water," Thomas said, holding up his hands palms out, telling her to stay put, but she didn't. Marguerite latched on to his arm, her eyes wide and bloodshot, cheeks streaked with the white crust of dried tears.

"Jakie," she said, the word thick in her mouth. "Is Jillian here?"

Jillian?

"No." What was this? "Jillian went to babysit Jake."

Marguerite's grip on his arm began to hurt.

"Babysit? I never asked her to babysit," she shouted at Thomas, her face wild, like an animal's. "I think Jillian stole him."

"What?"

Her other hand grabbed his arm, pulling him close, the stink of old wine on her breath overwhelming. "Jillian kidnapped my son."

[2]

Bruce called Elizabeth in early. Something about an emergency. Then why didn't the emergency patient go to the emergency room? she asked her boss, but Bruce mumbled something she couldn't understand before hanging up the phone. When she dragged herself out to her car, she was angry to see the sky still dark.

The man in the waiting room of the Buchanan County Health Clinic had been better. Most of his yellowed teeth were missing; his right arm had been broken at some point, and healed improperly. He sat at the edge of a chair, the faux-leather seat cracked and worn by too many butts before his. Something on his arm fascinated him, and his incessant picking drew blood, but he didn't stop.

Elizabeth had seen meth users before—not in her previous life, the life of a nurse in the birthing wing of a hospital, but now as a public health nurse, she saw them all the time. She stood in the doorway that led to the examining rooms, an aluminum clipboard in hand. In barely legible spidery script, the man listed his name as Rodney Paulson, forty-eight; address: Room 201, Starlight Motel, St. Joseph, Missouri. She doubted none of it. A lot of her patients lived in that area, if you could call it living. A thought, a memory, scratched at Elizabeth. She thought the Starlight had burned down.

"Mr. Paulson," she said. Rodney's jittery hand moved to another spot on his arm. He didn't hear her. Elizabeth cleared her throat. "Mr. Paulson."

Rodney looked up, his eyes crisscrossed with red veins.

"Yahum," he mumbled.

Great, she thought. This is going to be fun.

Elizabeth held open the swinging door and directed him inside. His height was five foot seven once she got him to stand straight, but his weight was only 112 pounds. If good old Rodney didn't get off the stuff, he wouldn't be around much longer. She directed him to a room.

"Mr. Paulson?"

Rodney shook his head as if to clear something out of the way of his thoughts, the look on his face that of a child. She directed him to a white, sterile room lined with pressboard cabinets and a sink that dripped, and asked him to sit on the examination table, wondering if the thin strip of paper pulled across the table would be enough to keep it clean.

"What are we seeing you for today?"

A hand he flung to his face in a fit of coughing kept yellow mucus from splattering the floor. Elizabeth hurried to fetch wipes and paper towels from the cabinets, thanking God medical science had long since adopted masks and latex gloves.

"Is it your cough?" she asked as he wiped his face.

"Naw. Issa demin." His tongue seemed to stumble over itself. "Issa getsus."

She didn't understand a word.

"Getsus?"

The man nodded, the movement the death throes of a mouse in a trap. He leaned back, and Elizabeth took a step away in case of another coughing fit. Instead, Rodney Paulson, methamphetamine addict, cleared his throat.

His body's uncontrollable jerking stopped, and his eyes, dear God, his eyes. A slick onyx sheen poured over the yellowed whites, filling in the iris before it sank below the bottom lid, leaving Rodney's eyes white, the iris brown, his expression blank.

Elizabeth's breath caught. She'd seen those eyes before, only once—the baby. The evil baby. Suddenly, Rodney's words were clear to her: "It's a demon."

"R-Rodney," she stuttered.

"There's a demon coming, Elizabeth Condon," he said, each syllable enunciated, his voice solid, steady, clear. "It's coming to eat us all."

[3]

Thomas sat on the couch next to Marguerite, staring out the window. The spot where Jillian always parked the Camry was empty, illuminated by the porch light, the car's tire marks still visible in the drying ground.

"I called, Thomas," she said, tears threatening to come back. "I called and called, but you never answered."

Oh, man. My phone. "I turned off the sound for the AA meeting," he mumbled.

"What?" Marguerite nearly shouted, her wild tangle of hair rendering her a villain in a Disney cartoon.

"I turned off the sound and all alerts last night and forgot to turn them back on." He pried her grip off his forearm and took her cold, shaky hands in his. "I'm sorry."

The tears started again. He wondered how many she had left.

"What time did Jake go missing?" he asked, trying to stay calm to keep Marguerite from freaking out more.

"I don't know," she said, her normally soft eyes wide and red. "Nine something?"

Okay, okay. We're going to get somewhere. "And what did you do?"

A snort erupted from Marguerite; she ran her forearm across her nose. "I–I went looking for him, of course," she said. "Mom, she stayed at the house in case Jakie came home, but he didn't."

Thomas held her hands tight.

"Why do you think it's Jillian?" he asked.

Her arm came up and wiped the tears away. Marguerite brushed some of the hair from her face, trying to compose herself.

"She's not here, and neither is Jake. And she lied to you about babysitting Jakie, didn't she?"

"Yeah, but—"

"And Jake told me a pretty lady promised him cake if he met her in the trees, and she would take him away."

Thomas's brain froze. Cake. There was cake in the machine shed once, when he was a boy and, and cake in his room. Memories began to rush in. There was a woman, a little woman in the corn; she looked nice. "*She was pretty*," he'd told his mother, "*like you.*"

"Did you see her?" he asked. His voice had lost all its strength.

"No," Marguerite said. "But I found Jillian's car abandoned on the gravel road about a mile from my house."

A knot the size of a fist hit Thomas's stomach, a feeling he hadn't had in years.

"All right. What time did you call the sheriff?"

Those red, swollen eyes grew wider, her expression wild with fear. Either from panic or booze, she hadn't called yet.

"Jesus Christ," he whispered, swiping his phone with his thumb. "I'm calling him now."

[4]

Sheriff Glenn Kirkhoff had had a bad week. After four years of minor robberies, DWIs, a car wreck here and there, and a successful election, the past few days included a cattle mutilation, a human mutilation and baby abduction, and now the kidnapping of a four-year-old boy. He sipped at the coffee Thomas Cavanaugh handed him in a John Deere mug, presumably strained through a dirty sock given the taste, and he looked at the little sister of a high-school friend. Marguerite sat on Thomas's couch as Thomas paced behind it. She'd looked better. Lots better.

"Now, Margie," Glenn said, setting the coffee cup down on the end table, not intending to pick it up again. He pulled his notebook and pen from his breast pocket. "Run this all by me again. A woman of your acquaintance, Ms. Jillian Robertson, a woman who helped rescue you during the destruction of St. Joseph Children's Hospital, came to your house and kidnapped your son?"

She'd had a shower, apparently right before Glenn arrived; Marguerite brushed a strand of still-wet hair behind her ear before beginning.

"From the day I brought Jakie home, she's asked to babysit him." Marguerite took a long drink of the water Thomas had forced on her.

"And have you?"

"Let her babysit?" She shook her head. "No. I haven't let anyone spend time alone with him except Mom. He's my first, my only. I—I guess I'm sort of . . ."

"Overprotective?" Glenn finished.

She nodded.

"What leads you to believe it was her?"

Thomas stopped pacing, rested his hands on the back of the couch, and leaned forward. "For one, she's recently been obsessing about babysitting."

"Babysitting anyone?" Glenn asked.

"No." Thomas's denial was firm. "Just Jacob. Then, last night she, surprise, tells me Marguerite called and asked her to watch him. She came home from the grocery store with food for my supper, and was gone. She didn't come back."

"Last night?" Glenn asked.

"At all. Her side of the bed hasn't been slept in."

Marguerite squirmed herself forward until she sat on the edge of the couch. "Jakie told me a woman he knew approached him when he played in the backyard and told him to meet her in the trees behind our house, and she'd take him to the fairy world."

Oh, dear Lord. "The fairy world?"

Marguerite's fist slammed into her thigh; Glenn didn't flinch at the outburst. "I know it sounds like the kind of complete BS a child Jakie's age would say, but damn it, he told me she'd bring him a piece of cake that would take him there."

The sheriff leaned back in his chair, the notebook forgotten in his hands. "Cake? That seems kind of—"

"Normal," Thomas interrupted, without looking up at Glenn. "I, um, I had something similar happen to me when I was a child. A woman approached me in the corn and told me she wanted to take me to fairy world. Then she left cake for me that would take me there. I didn't eat it."

"But Jakie did," Marguerite said.

The pen came back to life and Glenn scratched some words in the leather-bound notebook. "Okay," he said. "How do you know that?"

Marguerite pulled her mobile phone from her back pocket and swiped the screen, holding up to Glenn a photograph of a white china plate with a blue floral patten sitting on a stump. A piece of cake was on that plate; it had a bite out of it.

"Because I took a picture." She swiped the screen; another photo popped up. "And I took a picture of Jillian's car on my way over here.

It's parked just down the gravel road from my house, and it's empty. Glenn, goddamn it, that red-haired maniac stole my son."

[5]

The office door of Buchanan County Health Clinic Director Bruce Webster was open early, the ever-present smell of Tommy Hilfiger for Men telling Elizabeth she was about to time travel back to 1995. Bruce, Elizabeth knew, was unqualified for his position, but made up for it by appreciating that fact and letting those under him, those who knew more about the health profession, do all the thinking for him. He didn't pull one switch until everyone spoke their mind, and the Buchanan County Health Clinic ran as smoothly as a freshly polished Chevelle on its way to a car show.

She knocked on the open door and leaned in. Bruce pecked a few keystrokes on his laptop before looking up with a smile and waved her toward him. One step, two; her knees wobbled, and an animated vine from a bad jungle movie wrapped around her intestines, bunching them into a knot. A thirst came over her as she stopped behind a chair and used it to keep her balance; she felt like a bag of doorknobs.

"What can I help you with, Elizabeth?" the director asked.

Heat spread through her skin. Don't sweat. Please, don't sweat. If she began to sweat, Elizabeth thought she might pass out.

"I'm sorry, Bruce," she said in little more than a whisper. "All of a sudden, I don't feel well. I—" The image of meth-addled Rodney Paulson wouldn't leave her mind: the oily blackness that glossed over his eyes and disappeared beneath his eyelids, leaving clear cognizance behind. "*There's a demon coming, Elizabeth Condon,*" he'd said. "*It's coming to eat us all.*"

Her right hand slid from the chair back and she almost fell. She shouldn't have come in this morning.

No way.

Bruce shot from his chair, rounding the table to her, although he didn't touch Elizabeth. Too much state-mandated sexual harassment training for that.

"Are you okay?" he asked.

She grabbed the chair again, slowly sucking in a few breaths. Clear-headed Rodney had disappeared after those words left his mouth. Out in the hallway, he said, "Gage bow hibbidy," before he found the way to the exit. Elizabeth prayed to God, if there still was a God, that she'd never see Rodney Paulson again.

"Yeah," she said, nodding slowly to keep her head from spinning. "I just need to go home and lie down."

"Sure," Bruce said, still not standing close enough to touch her, but maybe close enough to try to catch her if she fell. "No problem. You came in a few hours early. Oh, and water. You need to drink plenty of water. There's a lot of dehydration going around these days."

Elizabeth would have laughed if she wasn't terrified.

"Of course. Thank you."

It only took her a few minutes to get into her car, although she scanned the parking lot for any sign of Rodney before she walked out. Safely locked inside the old Civic, she started it, put it in gear, and drove onto Lafayette Street before hitting South Tenth. The thought to call her AA sponsor tugged at her the farther she drove from work, but the urge to pull into the lot outside River City Liquor and Drug Store took over the steering wheel.

She'd worry about that tug tomorrow. Today burned into her mind, the kind of burn that left scars. She stepped into River City with twenty dollars in her pocket and came out with sanity-saving vodka, limes, and Tums. Home.

She had to get home to the peace and quiet she begged for; her loser husband long gone, their kids grown enough to have lives of their own. She only wanted to pass out on the couch, and to hell with anyone who tried to stop her.

[6]

A deputy stood outside Jillian's car, the doors and trunk open as the sun peeped over the horizon. She wrote in a notebook, looking up when the sheriff's cruiser pulled next to her. Thomas slowed his old truck behind it. Marguerite's hands shook; she was a mess. Thomas was surprised she'd made it to his house without wrapping her truck around a tree.

The deputy nodded at Thomas and Marguerite as the sheriff pulled away and they followed. Glines, Thomas thought. Madeline, maybe, if he remembered right. As they drove past, the deputy went back to her notebook.

Marguerite turned to Thomas as the car behind them disappeared in the dust.

"How well do you know Jillian?" Marguerite asked. She'd pulled her left leg up onto the seat, tucking the foot under her right thigh. Thomas glanced over, the fear and anger on her face painful to witness. She was a mother; he couldn't imagine what it would be like to lose a kid.

Mom and Dad would. Wait. Thomas's jaw muscles bunched as he clenched his teeth. Where did that come from? Mom and Dad would?

"What do—" He paused, a cough stuck in his throat. Thomas hadn't spoken since he'd followed the sheriff to his car and Glenn instructed him to drive "Margie's" truck back home.

"What do you mean? I've known her since—" The thought stuck in his head. How long had he known Jillian? Since he was fourteen, surely. They met at the Sisters of Mercy mental hospital, but something in the back of Thomas's head told him that was wrong. Jillian had been with him so much longer, and now she was gone and he didn't care; the spot where loneliness, fear, and longing would lie beneath the shelf of his life—a cave where the energy to get out of bed, to eat, to shower, would drain—was plugged by not giving a damn. Resentment, regret, emotional distancing had built a tower inside Thomas. Now he could look down from that tower and see the opening to the cave, and do what any guy does from a great height—spit in it.

"Shit, Marguerite," he said. "I never thought she'd do something like this. I guess I don't know her that well at all."

Marguerite sat in silence as they drove toward her mother's house, where she lived, where she'd always lived.

"She's capable of kidnapping someone as innoc—" She paused. "Someone as small as Jakie. Is she capable of hurting him?"

Innocent? The deletion of that word as it came from her mouth hit the brakes in Thomas's head. He's four. He likes *Paw Patrol*. He's not innocent?

"Hurt?" he asked, slowing as Sheriff Kirkhoff slowed, a turn signal pointing them down the gravel road toward the Jenkins house. Would she? "I don't think so."

Marguerite slapped the dash, and dust danced around the cab.

"What do you mean you don't think so?" She grabbed Thomas's arm and shook. "Would she hurt my baby?"

"She wouldn't. No," he said, shaking his head, trying to think back to just days before when he told his dad Jillian acted like she wanted a baby. "She talks about Jake all the time. What she wants is to be a mom."

Thomas knew that came out wrong as he said it; he just couldn't stop himself.

"But," Marguerite whispered as she released his arm, her voice a small girl's, "I'm his mom."

Thomas pulled the truck into the Jenkinses' driveway behind the sleek, fast sheriff's department cruiser and killed the engine. He hoped it was the only thing that died today.

[7]

Glenn stepped from the car, a six-pointed star and the words Buchanan County Sheriff's Department decorating the door. He waited for

Margie and Thomas to reach him, then followed them into the house. He'd known Linda Jenkins his whole life and although it was his job to ask questions about her missing grandson, he didn't want to be the one to knock on the door. The officer who knocks on the door becomes the villain later in the story.

"Oh, honey," Linda said, rushing to sweep Marguerite into an embrace. "Have you heard anything?"

Marguerite shook her head as she buried it in her mother's shoulder.

"No, ma'am," Glenn said, his wide felt sheriff's hat in his hands. "That's what we're here for."

A slight cough from Linda brought a rattle that sounded to Glenn like the pickup he'd owned in college, right before he sold it for scrap. She held up the arm that didn't hold her daughter and waved for Glenn to come closer.

He did, and she crushed him to her side.

"Ma'am," she scolded. "Glenny Tucker Kirkhoff, we've all known each other too long for that." Just as Marguerite's tears soaked into her shoulder, hers soaked into Glenn's. He didn't let go until she was finished.

"Margie, Linda," he said, releasing her and backing away, his back stiffening. Glenn was no longer Glenny, the little boy who had come to her house to play with her son Robbie. He was the Buchanan County sheriff. "I'm so sorry this has happened, but I promise you my department and I will do everything we can do to bring Jacob home."

Even as the words of reassurance came from his mouth, the images of the mutilated heifer with the lone pair of small footprints ("child size-ten Skechers Skech-O-Saurus") ran through his head, along with the photos of the murder weapon of Rebekka Marshall, a kitchen knife with the bloody handprint of a child—a child the same age as Jacob. These pictures didn't stab at his mind alone—there was the face. The child-like drawing of the smiling circle full of teeth loomed over all of them.

Is this why Boyd went to that house? The one in St. Joe?

Glenn grunted, the sound of his throat clearing that of a new Corvette compared to Linda's cough like a dying truck.

"I'll need to see where you last saw Jacob," he said. The words sounded stiff and impersonal to him, but he didn't know how to fix it. This whole situation was stiff and impersonal. "I need to see the plate."

The plate in the dead trees; a plate with a piece of chocolate cake. Linda shifted her weight from one foot to another with enough force Glenn noticed.

"What's the matter, Linda?" he asked.

Her eyes shot toward her daughter, who now sat on the couch, her face in her hands.

"Um, I, uh, I found something the other day," Linda said.

Something? Glenn didn't like the sound of that.

"What did you find, Mom?" Marguerite asked, her voice weak.

Thomas moved to the couch and sat next to Marguerite, holding her hand.

"I found this," she said, pulling a gallon Ziploc bag from behind a decorative couch pillow. The clear polyethylene sack held a folded square of brownish red.

"What is it?" Marguerite asked.

Linda pulled her hand across the tears welling in her eyes as she held the bag out to Glenn.

"Jakie's clothes. The shirt with the fern, and those cute little shorts with the dinosaurs."

"But the shirt's light blue, and the shorts—" Marguerite's eyes grew. "What's on Jakie's clothes, Mom?"

"Blood," Glenn said, taking the package, the clothing inside neatly folded but now stiff as a stack of matzo crackers. "Jacob's clothes are soaked in blood."

His day had just gotten a lot worse.

It felt strange to Thomas, sitting on Marguerite's couch, holding her hand instead of Jillian's. Thomas and Jillian had grown close to Marguerite the past four years, just as Thomas and Jillian began to grow apart, Jillian spending her time talking about Jacob, Thomas spending one night a week at AA meetings. Marguerite's grip seemed tighter than it should be, but Thomas didn't flinch as he held her hand; she needed all the strength he could give her.

The sheriff sat in a chair next to the couch, maybe to keep from falling, the baggie with Jacob's dried, bloody clothes in his hands. What the boy had been through, Thomas couldn't begin to guess.

"What happened, Mom?" Marguerite asked, the words soft, shaky. "Why are Jakie's clothes like that? Did he—"

"No," Linda nearly barked at her. She took a deep breath and continued. "He didn't get hurt." She leaned back into the couch, looking like she was trying to disappear. "We were outside the longest time. He was playing at the edge of the cornfield, then he was, well, he was just gone."

Marguerite nearly shot to her feet, but Thomas held her on the couch. "You let him run off?" she shouted at her mother. "What the hell were you doing?"

Linda rubbed her knees with the palms of her hands. "I went inside to refill my cup and get him another juice box."

Glenn stirred in his chair. "What day was it?" he asked.

Her forehead wrinkled for a moment, mental calculations falling into place. "Tuesday. I believe it was Tuesday."

The sheriff's face fell slack, the blood seeming to drain out. Thomas didn't like the look on Glenn.

He pulled Marguerite farther back on the couch, slipping an arm around her to keep her from falling forward, backward, or sideways if she fainted.

"Glenn," Thomas said, his emotions betrayed by a slight waver. "You know something, don't you? What do you know about these clothes?"

Glenn coughed and sat straight, attempting to put back together whatever had crashed in his mind.

"Margie," he said. "What kind of shoes does Jacob wear?"

Her head cocked. "Skech-O-Saurus. They light up. Why?"

Glenn's felt hat hit the floor. He didn't bother to pick it up. "What size?"

"I don't, I don't understand," Marguerite stuttered.

"What size shoe does Jacob wear?" he repeated.

Long seconds ticked by. "Tens," she finally said. "Jakie wears children's tens."

"Margie." Glenn unfolded his body from the chair and squatted in front of her, his eyes boring into hers. "On Wednesday morning, Deputy Glines was called to Hiram Southwick's cattle lot. One of Hiram's heifers was dead."

"I don't understand," she said, the sound weak, as if all the air had been let out of her balloon.

"Yeah, Glenn. What does that have to do with—" Thomas started before the sheriff cut him off, the man's eyes never leaving Marguerite's.

"There was lots of blood. Somebody gutted that heifer, and there was one set of footprints in the mud next to her. They were made with a pair of child size-ten Skech-O-Saurus shoes."

Linda wailed, but Marguerite sat up and returned Glenn's glare. Thomas slid his arm off her and dropped her hand. Whatever was going to happen, he figured, was going to happen.

Glenn continued, "Now, I know a four-year-old boy can't do this—"

"Then," she said through gritted teeth, "you don't know my boy."

[9]

Jacob sat on the top of a grain bin, the nice fairy lady next to him.

The world of Northwest Missouri stretched out before them, green fields of corn and soybeans black in the night, the stars shining so clearly he wondered if he could touch them. Red lights atop dozens of enormous wind turbines lined the landscape.

"When are we gonna go?" he asked.

She smiled down at him; he couldn't help but smile back. They were going to fairy world.

"Any time now," she said, her voice soft. "We're going to have so much fun."

Jacob leaned his head into her arm and snuggled in close. He was tired of his mother; this one would be better anyway. She could show him more things.

"Will there be ice cream there?"

She leaned over and kissed the top of his head.

"Of course there will be ice cream. Don't you worry." An arm looped around his shoulders and she pulled Jacob close. "Here it comes. Don't be afraid."

Afraid? Jacob thought. "I don't get scared," he told her, and she smiled. He liked that smile. It felt right.

A swirl like a dust devil began at their feet and grew tall around them, the lady's ponytail flipping behind her. Jacob giggled as the wind demon devoured them. A second later, the devil broke apart and they were gone.

Somewhere in the night a coyote howled.

CHAPTER FIVE

[1]

THOMAS DROVE HOME alone, radio off, wind from the open windows blowing empty wrappers around the interior of the truck cab. He wanted to think, but he didn't want to think. Jake had been at the slaughtered heifer and come home with his clothing soaked in blood? The thought the little boy could have killed the twelve-hundred-pound beast—an animal the size of a concert piano—was impossible. Jake was at most three and a half feet tall and maybe forty pounds with his belly full.

With blood.

Thomas tried to shake out the image of Jake standing in front of a slain heifer, its innards spilled over the muddy ground of the cattle lot, a bloody grin on the boy's face, but he might as well have been trying to dislodge a tick with the Force.

He stopped at the red sign that told him to, a few bullet holes in the sheet metal. Thomas looked both ways; no "Hadsell Family Farms: Easton, Missouri" truck bore down on him. He released the brake and eased his pickup across the rural highway onto the continued gravel beyond, his house behind a grove of trees. Thomas had called his dad on the way to Marguerite's and told him he wouldn't be in today.

Marguerite.

Her name seemed to breathe across his face with the scent of honeysuckle. He and Jillian had befriended the exhausted, drunk woman at his door the morning after Bobby Garrett blew up half of St. Joseph. She appeared in Thomas's thoughts often the past few years, as Jillian pulled away, laser-focused on Marguerite's son. When they were all together, Marguerite's gaze caught his longer than a glance, and he found himself more and more wishing they had met under different circumstances.

Then Jillian would say something Thomas never remembered and the next moment he'd be behind the wheel of his truck a quarter mile from home.

The squeal of a brake pad Thomas knew he should change pierced the cab as he stopped the truck.

"Damn it," whistled out.

He'd never questioned that before. The brain fog he'd gone through for months when he stopped drinking slowly went away, but this didn't. Whenever he and Marguerite locked eyes and he began to dwell on his empty life, he was immediately transported a quarter mile from home and never remembered getting into his truck. He was just there, the world warped outside the cab, as if he looked at it through the bottom of a drinking glass.

Eyes. Pretty. Lonely. Trust. Cold. Escape.

A horn honk from behind shot him upright on the dusty bench seat.

The blood coursing through his body surged, his heart shredding an Angus Young solo. Thomas's eyes met the rearview mirror and found—nothing. No car. No pickup. No "Hadsell Family Farms: Easton, Missouri" truck advertising it didn't want to kill him today.

A long exhale pushed out.

"The heck?"

The honk had been real. It had been. He knew it.

Jillian.

Thomas didn't know why the honk was Jillian trying to tell him something, but it was. He slipped his foot off the brake pedal and rolled toward his house, praying her car was now under the tree instead of abandoned down the road from the Jenkinses' house, and that she was sitting on the porch with Jacob. Then he could take Jacob home to his mother and be the hero, and tell Jillian they were over. They were—

Her car wasn't there. Of course it wasn't there. The sheriff's department was probably going to impound it.

Thomas parked the truck where he always did and got out, walking to the house, expecting it to be unlocked like Jillian usually left it, but the front door was locked like *he* left it. Thomas opened the door and walked inside. Nothing had changed. Not in the living room. Not in the kitchen. Not in the bathroom.

Not—

The drawers of Jillian's dresser hung open. Thomas's hands unconsciously curled into fists as he approached. Each drawer lay empty—not a stray pair of panties, not a liner sock, not a brush clogged with strands of red hair. The clothes Jillian owned were the only brand she'd ever put on this house, and she'd just erased herself from his life.

[2]

Glenn sat in his office staring at the computer screen. One day. It had been only one day since Jillian Robertson abducted Jacob Jenkins. He was certain that's what went down; he just hoped Jacob was still alive, but why had the boy killed Hiram Southwick's heifer, and how had he mutilated such a large animal?

The initial tests on Jacob's blood-soaked clothing showed it was bovine. Glenn ordered a DNA test on the blood, but his gut told him it came from Hiram's heifer. He'd find out in a couple of days. He didn't relish sharing any of the results with Margie or Linda or Hiram or the press. That information wouldn't help anyone; it would only hurt, and he didn't want to do that to the Jenkinses. Margie and Linda were good people.

Then there was Rebekka Marshall of rural St. Joe, whose belly had been sliced open with one of her own kitchen knives, her unborn baby, Todd Marshall Jr., gone. The bloody handprint on the knife handle was from a child the same size as Jacob. The department never located the baby. No anonymous tips, no unexpected baby pictures on Facebook, no baby without a birth certificate brought into any hospital within the four-state area. Nothing. The department had yet to determine who killed Rebekka Marshall, although whomever it was left a gruesome calling card drawn on her deflated torso in her own blood. A circle with a smile. Not a smile, *the* smile, filled with sharp, pointed teeth.

That image burned in Glenn's mind. He suspected the same smiling circle consumed Boyd while he was sheriff, and now it had him. What was that smiling face? What did it represent? And how did it connect everything? Elvin Miller, Carrie McMasters, Bobby Garrett, now Rebekka Marshall. Hell, probably Hiram's heifer for all he knew. How did all these things wrap together?

A tap on his office door snapped him out of the zone. He closed the laptop and looked up, a nod signaling Aaron to enter.

"Please don't bring me any bad news," Glenn said.

The lanky deputy strode into the office with more confidence than he used to possess. Glenn remembered when Boyd hired him, young and right out of the MWSCC Law Enforcement Academy in St. Joe. Aaron was so timid Boyd confided in Glenn he didn't think "the boy would last a month." Glenn was happy he did.

"No new cases," Aaron said. "But Marcus Cline called. Said he set up a trail cam on a light post on his property and he's got pictures of two guys stealing lumber from the new barn he's putting up."

The chair creaked as Glenn leaned back, his smile not revealing much joy.

"It's about time. There's a good chance they're the guys lifting all that copper wire too."

Aaron nodded. "I'm headed over there just as soon you take a look at this." He set a sheet of printer paper on Glenn's desk. Three fingerprints: one from an adult, one from what could have been a ten-year-old or a young teenager, the third from a child about Jacob's age.

"Is this—"

"We've got a match," Aaron said. "The smallest one is the print on the bloody knife at the Marshall house."

Glenn sat up straight. "Match? But these are from three different people."

"The big one is from Elvin Miller's ax," Aaron continued.

No. Numbness spread through the sheriff's fingers; his gut tingled like his body was gearing up to vomit.

"And the middle one?" he asked.

The deputy stood straight, his hands clenched behind his back; he didn't know what to do with them.

"That one was from a bloody puzzle piece at the McMasterses'."

The numbness went up his arms.

"B-but," Glenn stuttered, "these are from three different people. Could a family—"

Aaron shook his head.

"No, sir. It doesn't make any sense, but there it is. I don't know what we're dealing with, but it's one hundred percent these bloody fingerprints are from the same person."

That's not possible.

"And I've got some more good news, Sheriff," Aaron continued. "Press caught wind of the Marshall murder. A St. Joe reporter's in the lobby, and the local Fox News channel is on line two. Once this thing gets out—"

The sheriff nodded. "I know. We'll have CNN and NBC trucks parked outside the station until something explodes or the president farts on camera." Glenn's elbows thumped onto the desk, his hands reached up to rub his forehead. "Goddamn it."

[3]

The house seemed brighter somehow. As Thomas warmed a can of Chef Boyardee Beefaroni for his lunch and searched the cabinets for saltines, he also noticed the smell. No matter the season, and no matter how many Air Wicks he plopped down, Boyd's house always possessed the rich, earthy scent of ripening corn. Not today. Today it smelled like a house. A house where cheap canned pasta had begun to boil on the stove, and "ocean breeze" rose from the air freshener, although Thomas had never visited the ocean, so he couldn't tell if the odor was accurate. He didn't care, it smelled nice.

Jillian had been gone for less than a day, and darkness dissipated from everything around him. He pressed a toe over the heel of his right boot, and a push plopped the boot onto the kitchen floor. He did the same to his left boot and took a run across the polished hardwood floor, sliding on his socks like Tom Cruise in *Risky Business*.

"Damn," he said when he stopped next to the couch. "I should have taken off my pants first."

His laugh echoed throughout the house as he turned back toward the kitchen; his lunch was ready, but he froze as a crack formed in the Wall of Memories in the black recesses of his mind. The laugh died, and his face tensed as the atmosphere inside his home grew heavy, the weight of a giant settling in for a nap. Something dark waited for Thomas behind that Wall of Memories. He could feel it.

[4]

There had to be something rational, some logical explanation why three different people, three different ages, could have the same fingerprint, but damned if Glenn could come up with the answer. All the training he'd ever had told him one thing about prints—they were all different. The right index finger was different from the left, and even that one was different from the same finger at eleven years old as it was at fifty. Scars happen, burns, any kind of accident can change part of a print. Not one bit of law-enforcement education, even catching a random episode of *American Crime Story*, said two people could have the exact print, let alone three.

Glenn had always wondered why Boyd drank so much beer. Now he thought he might know.

One print at Elvin Miller's place, where Elvin's wife was hacked to death with an ax, one print at Carrie McMasters's house, where the wife gave her husband a red smile, and at Todd Marshall's, where someone sliced the couple's unborn baby from the wife's uterus, then put the knife back where they'd gotten it.

The logic was simple, but it wasn't. The obvious answer was that the murderer changed sizes from an adult to a child, to a four-year-old, but this wasn't a freaking Marvel movie, it was real life. That sort of stuff didn't happen.

It *couldn't* happen.

"Wait," he said to his empty office.

A sliver of a memory, a cockroach of a thought, crept from the darkness into the full light.

He'd read about something like this in one of Boyd's field-interview notebooks. Glenn opened the bottom drawer where he kept a few of Boyd's things, and pulled out a stack of notebooks, Boyd's squiggly script barely legible.

Traffic stop, traffic stop, an interview with that jackass from Kansas Boyd and Glenn caught stealing Donny Middleton's pigs. The guy claimed they were his and Donny took them first with some kind of a witch's spell. Then—

"Holy shit."

There it was, on a dog-eared page in the sixth notebook. July 12, 1990.

Deborah watered the garden this morning before she left for work, and someone walked out of the garden, into the house, turned into a little girl as she made her way up the stairs. Then she smiled at me while she vanished.

Deborah Cavanaugh, Boyd's sister, Thomas Cavanaugh's mother, had left the garden ground soft, and a person Glenn could only assume was an adult walked through it into the house, turning "into a little girl."

"Then she vanished?"

Aaron appeared at his door, Chad Clayton from the *St. Joseph News-Press* behind him. Great. Glenn knew reporters were just doing their job, but it didn't mean he had to like it.

"Sir?" Aaron began, but Glenn waved him off and the deputy stepped back from the doorway.

Clayton walked in, notebook in hand, and sat without invitation.

"You know I'm sorry to be here, Sheriff."

He knew. Clayton was a decent guy who did good work four years ago on what every news organization in the country called "The Day St. Joseph Died."

"I gotcha," Glenn said, leaning back in his chair, knowing he really needed to oil the springs.

The reporter produced a pen and flipped through his notebook.

"What we have so far is: Rebekka Marshall, the pregnant wife of real-estate mogul Todd Marshall, was found by Todd murdered in their home, their unborn baby removed from her womb." Clayton paused, looking at Glenn for a change of expression that never came. "I have day, time, and address, Sheriff. What I don't have are suspect, motive, and the condition/location of the baby."

Glenn crossed his arms on his chest, his jaw muscles clenched.

"Oh, come on, Sheriff," the reporter said. "I'd hate to drop a 'no comment' on our readers."

The chair creaked and Glenn scooted closer to the desk, personalizing the distance between them.

"I know, Chad." His voice soft, gentle, understanding. "You have a job to do, and I respect that. However—" He hesitated, giving time for his words to form. "It's way too early in our investigation to reveal facts that may hinder that investigation. I'd hate to lie to you," he said, lying to him, "but we don't even have the murder weapon. Hell, our forensics team is still at the house. So . . ."

He theatrically laid his right palm on the desk as the reporter wrote down every word. Clayton stopped writing, but the tip of his pen still rested on the reporter pad.

"Even though I know there's really no such thing as 'off the record,'" Glenn continued, "if you could hold off on things like no murder weapon and no suspects, I'll give you what I can now, and—"

Clayton squirmed in his seat, ready to drop something about the First Amendment, Glenn figured.

"*And* as soon as we have information I can release to the press, I'll call you first. That okay with you?"

The reporter stared at the sheriff, although Glenn didn't think the man really saw anything. He was thinking.

"Okay," Clayton eventually said. "But will you answer some of my questions?"

Got him. "Of course," Glenn said when the phone rang. "In a minute." He reached and grabbed the receiver off the black office phone. "Sheriff Kirkhoff."

"Sheriff?" It was Deputy Glines. "I'm out in a cornfield off County Road 53, just east of Blakely Cemetery."

Glenn knew exactly where that was; his grandmother was buried in that cemetery. He looked at the ceiling, anywhere but at the reporter.

"Go ahead, Maddy."

She took in a deep breath before speaking. "I think you need to get out here."

What now?

"Why, Deputy?" he asked. Glines wouldn't ask him to come out without a good reason.

"Because," she said. "I don't want anybody to overhear this."

Now his eyes shot to Clayton's; the reporter's were wide. "I have someone in my office, Deputy. I'll be done in five."

"Something wrong, Sheriff?" Clayton asked when Glenn disconnected.

"Nope. Surprise party, but you heard the time. You have five minutes. Ask away."

As Clayton scratched something in his notebook, Glenn wondered what fresh hell awaited him in that cornfield.

[5]

A new face walking into the Delores Hadley Community Center was nothing odd; new faces came in all the time. Most Thomas never saw again, but some, like the nurse, stayed awhile. He enjoyed the new people, because new people meant hope, and some days, hope was all a person had.

The man, probably in his thirties, his face gaunt and saggy like he was in the process of losing a lot of weight in a short time, came in late and sat in the first available chair, right next to Frank, who nodded at him and smiled. Frank missed most of the teeth on the left side of his mouth, a souvenir of the last bar fight he'd ever started and not finished. The wrinkled, smiling man, probably pushing seventy-five, had been angry when he came home from Vietnam and took it out on everyone who looked at him funny. Frank told the story often during confession time, a way to cleanse and re-cleanse his soul. By the time he was forty-four, he'd lost a step, and beating up twenty-one-year-olds who may (or may not) have disrespected him turned into twenty-one-year-olds beating the snot out of a guy who would have known better if he hadn't been so drunk.

Frank pushed an M&M cookie on a paper napkin toward the new guy. The man looked at the cookie for a moment as if Frank's gnarled, scarred fingers would latch on to him if he got too close. He finally nodded and took it. The new ones who sat next to Frank always took the cookie.

Thomas stood and walked to the snack table a few seconds before the meeting started, putting his Styrofoam cup beneath the spigot of the big aluminum coffeemaker and flipping the lever. Someone slid in front of the decaf coffeemaker next to him.

"I don't know how you can do it," a woman said. Thomas froze at the strange voice. A deep, haunting feeling, like a crack had formed in his Wall of Memories, washed over him. What is it I can do? He had no idea. Thomas looked over and found the nurse in blue scrubs, Elizabeth No Last Name.

He watched his cup fill slowly because the early drunks got the freshest coffee, and he usually got the bitter dregs. "What do you mean?" he asked.

She nodded toward the coffee dispenser before him. "Drinking the hard stuff this late in the day. I'd be up all night."

The hard stuff. Alcoholics 101 for caffeinated. "Right?" he said. "I have enough baggage to keep me up late anyway."

A sigh escaped the nurse as she flipped off the heavier flow of decaf. "Don't we all, honey," she said and went back to her seat.

The gavel tapped, and Thomas made his way back to the table after grabbing a cookie. Sweets were one of the perks of AA meetings. Cookies and, sometimes, if they were lucky, cupcakes came in from the local grocery store by whomever felt like buying that week. Alcohol is created by the fermentation of sugars, so removing that ingredient from daily life leaves a void as deep as a well. Thomas had gained ten pounds in the past eight months by giving up beer.

"Who'd like to share?" Jerry asked after reading the AA mantra, his big walrus mustache covering his mouth.

Conrad raised a hand, tears in his eyes. A small man with a St. Louis Cardinals baseball cap pulled low over his eyes, he leaned back in his metal folding chair and stared at the ceiling before he spoke.

"I was offered a job in Alaska for three months," Conrad said, never looking down from the expanded polystyrene tiles, his hands in his jeans pockets. "I help install those big, white wind turbines." He paused to lick his upper lip. "I haven't accepted the job yet. It'll—" He stopped and sat forward, his elbows on the table, his face in his hands. "It'll be financially important to my family, but I know if I leave them for three weeks, if I leave you all, I'll drink. I fucking know it."

He looked up, eyes slowly landing on everyone in the room. "Sorry for my language."

"It's okay, Conrad." Jerry folded his hands on the table, adopting his Everyone's Grandpa pose. He was good at this. "One day at a time, my friend. You know they have meetings everywhere, even in Alaska. I went to one in Fairbanks once. Good people up there."

Conrad nodded and slumped in his chair, a few other members offering to pick up their phone at any time of day or night to talk him off the ledge. This was one of Thomas's most and least favorite parts of meetings; seeing people's despair, but also hearing others talk them up.

Frank elbowed the new guy, and the man shook before realizing what had happened.

"Go ahead," Frank said; a life filled with too many cigarettes left his voice low and gravelly. "Introduce yourself."

The cookie snapped in the man's hands.

"Uh, uh, hi," stumbled out. "I'm Todd. My, uh, my name's Todd, and I'm, I'm an alcoholic." He paused, glancing at Frank. "Do I have to say anything like that guy?"

Frank shook his head. "No, sir. Just say you pass."

The man took a bite of cookie before he had enough will to say anything else. "Then, I pass. Thank you all for having me here."

Jerry nodded at Todd, then looked around the table. "Who'd like to go next?"

Elizabeth fumbled with her coffee cup and then raised her hand. "I'll go," she said, her voice wavering. "My name's Elizabeth, and I'm an alcoholic."

Thomas sat up. The nurse had been coming to meetings off and on for months, sitting quietly and drinking decaf. Her "I don't know how you can do it" was the first time he'd heard her say anything but the AA mantra.

"I'm a nurse," she said, moving her hands across her scrubs top like a spokesmodel presenting a game-show prize. "I worked in labor and delivery for years. I'd only drunk socially before—" The next word caught in her throat. "Before that lady came in, the one that awful Garrett man kidnapped."

The room fell deathly quiet, most members' eyes on their hands, but Thomas's locked on Elizabeth. A thump like a fist landed on his chest.

Marguerite?

"She—" Elizabeth's voice had gone from firm and steady to a whisper. "She was fine. She was too fine for a woman in labor. She didn't sweat, she didn't scream. All those normal things a woman giving birth goes through."

Thomas's hands balled into one big fist in his lap; the nurse dug at her Styrofoam cup with a thumbnail.

"And when the baby was born, it just came out. There was no crying, no sound at all from the baby, and the mother laughed. I have two children, and I've helped countless women give birth over the decades, and no one—no one—laughs when they have to force a body the size of a small pumpkin through a hole the size of a kiwi."

From across the room, Frank coughed.

"But it wasn't her, it was the baby. I remember everything about it. Its look, its name, the way it came out of the womb. Everything." Elizabeth took a deep breath and continued. "It was born without an umbilical cord; that never happens. *Never*. Its eyes were black, and it smiled at me." She wiped the back of her hand under her suddenly running nose. "It smiled at me like it knew something. Like that demon baby *knew* something."

The coffee cup snapped in her hand; the remaining decaf gushed across the table and dribbled off the edge.

[6]

It was 6 p.m. by the time Glenn pulled up to Maddy's patrol car and got out of his own, the early evening hot enough he could feel the beginnings of sweaty moons forming under his arms. The coroner's van sat idling at the edge of the field, and a man in a white T-shirt and blue jeans stood next to coroner Phil Rolfson with his hands in his pockets. Glenn guessed it was the landowner. Maddy stood in the field taking photos of something in the corn with her iPhone. Apart from a traffic stop on US 36, the radio stayed silent.

He nodded at Phil as he strode into the field toward Maddy. Phil was a nice enough guy; Glenn always sure as hell hated to see him, though.

"What do we have, Deputy?" Glenn asked, stepping into a curved line of flattened corn. He hoped that wasn't what he got called out here for. A crop circle alongside headlines of Hiram's heifer, and those UFO nuts would be out here like it was a *Star Trek* convention or something.

Maddy held up a hand for him to stop, and he did. Something about her face, the set of her jaw, maybe, told him to keep his distance.

"How's your nerves?" she asked.

"Fine, I gu—"

"And your stomach?" she interrupted.

My stomach? "It's fine too. What's this about?"

The inhale she sucked in seemed to Glenn to take longer than lungs should take. Finally, his deputy answered, nodding toward the man standing next to the coroner.

"The landowner, Palmer Abbott, stopped here because some turkey buzzards were circling overhead and—" She stopped to swallow. Maddy seemed nervous, shaken. Glenn had never seen her like this before. Maddy's as tough as an MMA fighter. "He found a body," she said. "I think it's the missing Marshall baby."

Glenn's stomach dropped off a cliff. "Body?"

Body could mean only one thing: Todd's baby was as dead as its mother.

Maddy nodded. "Most of it."

CHAPTER SIX

MOST OF IT?

Glenn removed his hat for no other reason than respect of the dead, his feet unsure on the dirt clods between the rows of deep-green knee-high cornstalks. More lines of crushed stalks wove in and out of the otherwise healthy field. He swallowed hard and stepped next to his deputy.

The tiny body, maybe six pounds, lay on a path of the flattened corn, wrapped in nothing, his skin still spotted with cheese from the womb—and blood, lots of blood.

"It doesn't have any fingers or toes," Glenn said, telling Maddy something she already knew.

"There are bite marks at the base of them all," she said. Her throat sounded dry. Glenn imagined it was. "I've already asked Phil to determine what type of teeth removed the digits."

Removed the digits. The words distant, cold.

"Animal predation?" Glenn asked.

She shook her head.

"I already called Agent Flamank with the Department of Conservation. He's on his way, but I don't think it is." Maddy pulled a pen from her pocket and squatted close to the body, pointing at the ground around it. "There are no footprints, no traces of fur, no scat, nothing to indicate an animal had come close. Even then, it wouldn't have gone for the fingers and toes first. It would have gone for—"

Jesus Christ.

"That's enough, Deputy," Glenn said. "I think I got it."

She was right, he knew. No animal did this, but there were no footprints other than Maddy's and his. Just like Hiram's heifer—almost. The heifer crime scene had one set of footprints, impossible footprints.

"What are these mashed lines of corn?" he asked. "And don't say 'crop circle.'"

Maddy shrugged. "I was going to say 'crop circle.'"

"Get Zach out here with that drone of his and show me what this looks like from the air," Glenn said. "It may give us an idea of what kind of psycho did this."

The sheriff stopped at the coroner's van to talk with Phil and the farmer, Palmer something, but his mind was miles away.

[2]

Elizabeth's words about Jacob's birth stung as Thomas drove home, the imagery unfolding in his mind. "*It wasn't her, it was the baby . . . It smiled at me like it knew something. Like that demon baby knew something.*"

He wondered if that nurse was on something. Jake was a little standoffish for a four-year-old and rarely laughed, but he wasn't a "demon baby."

A sheriff's department cruiser closed on Thomas's pickup fast, its roof light bar pulsating. A year ago, when Thomas still threw down beer at the same rate as his dad, he'd have tossed the can through the window that opened to the truck bed and grabbed the bottle of Scope he kept on the dash. The plastic bottle still lay there, the label bleached white by the sun, the blue liquid now mostly clear, but he was sober as a Southern Baptist and had the cruise control set at 65 mph, which was the speed limit on this stretch of East US 36.

His pulse raced anyway, and he reached for the Scope but pulled his hand back. Old habits, he thought, deciding to throw the Scope in the garbage when he got home. Tonight he had nothing to worry about from Johnny Law. But he wondered what the heck was going on. A truck from KMBC-TV9 out of Kansas City had pulled up to the law-enforcement center about the time he left the AA meeting. Long-time reporter Kris Ketz sat in the passenger seat. Something big must be going on.

A quick flip of his hand and the truck's signal light came on; Thomas slowed the vehicle, directing it toward the shoulder. The rumble strips to keep drivers from falling asleep rattled beneath his front wheel. The patrol car's blaring siren grew as it approached and fell as the vehicle blasted past him. The car had to be doing at least ninety.

Thomas whistled in the now-silent cab and pulled back fully onto the highway. "Not going to bust up a high-school party there, are you, chief?" he said to nobody but himself.

The patrol car disappeared over the hill and reappeared speeding up the next one before Thomas reached the top. He whistled again and punched the speed up to seventy. As the truck reached the peak of the next hill, the patrol car's brake lights flashed and it turned onto a gravel road.

"Whoa," Thomas whispered.

Whatever emergency needed warp speed, Thomas was headed right for it.

[3]

Elizabeth sat in her car, the light of the sun dropping behind the brick-and-glass facade of the Delores Hadley Community Center painting the sky in pastel yellow, orange, and a pink stripe like God had wiped His face after finishing a rare steak. Her eyes ached, but the tears were gone. She couldn't cry anymore.

Marguerite, the mother who didn't scream during childbirth, lived in the back of her mind; she and the demon baby. That monster's eyes, black and inky, still woke her screaming in the stillness of night, its wicked, toothless smile branded into her memory. Elizabeth had hidden the memory after that day in the birthing room. She'd buried it deep behind her divorce, her daughter going to rehab for a heroin addiction, and the six months of hell living with Bernie, who drank Milwaukee's Best by the case, chewed Red Man leaf tobacco, and thought having a steady job was for people like Elizabeth, not for a free thinker like himself.

She never talked about Bernie, who knew he was on borrowed time when she kicked him out. There was no reason to bring up that embarrassment. But the baby?

After months of attending AA meetings and hearing the deep wounds that still haunted old-timers like Jerry, Frank, and Conrad, it was Elizabeth who brought up the woman and her devil baby. The story of that day in the birthing room flowed out because her mind wanted to purge itself of the memory, the injection of adrenaline, the fight-or-flight panic that racked her body.

All she did was make the memory real again.

Elizabeth started her old Civic and pulled onto the street in the middle of a cluster of cheap faux-brick facade low-income housing, and stopped at the first convenience store she found.

The beer was too expensive, but she bought it anyway.

[4]

"What's happening?" hissed from Thomas as he turned a long corner on County Road 53. Four patrol cars, three brown Nodaway County cruisers, and one blue Missouri State Highway Patrol vehicle, rested at the edge of a cornfield next to a white van with the words "Buchanan County Coroner" on the side. A pickup pulled onto the gravel from the field and disappeared over a hill. His foot instinctively fell onto the brake pedal and slowed his own pickup to a crawl. Rubbernecking in the country wasn't a hobby, it was a way of life.

"What's going on?" he whispered. No car crashes with mangled bodies, no redneck swinging a shotgun—nothing.

A figure broke from the cluster of officers next to the van. The man, tall and lanky with the beginnings of an awkward paunch, approached the road and Thomas pulled the pickup to a stop. The Buchanan County sheriff appeared in the open passenger window, red stubble on his face more telling than the shade under his eyes.

"Hey, Glenn," Thomas said. "Everything okay?"

The sheriff shook his head.

"No."

Glenn's eyes dropped to his boots, the scratch against gravel enough to tell Thomas he kicked the road. This is something bad.

Thomas coughed into his hand before trying another question. "You need something?"

The sheriff shook his head. "Not really." He pushed his hat back on his head and wiped greasy, sweaty hair off to the side before dropping the felt Stetson back down. "You seen Margie?" he asked.

The name *Margie* always caught Thomas off guard. Glenn meant Marguerite. The question hit him like a punch to the face.

"Is that Jacob?" Thomas asked, his voice sounding to him like it came from somebody else. "Did you find Jacob?"

No words. No body language. Nothing.

"Glenn?" Thomas pushed himself across the bench seat in the cab of his truck and looked the sheriff in the eyes. The man was shaken. "Did you find Jacob?"

"No." Glenn shook his head before he said any more. "It's, it's not Jacob. It's the Marshall baby. I was just worried about Margie. I've known her since she was a kid. She's been through so damn much. If this gets to her she's going to think all kinds of things about her boy."

Thomas patted the sheriff's arm that leaned on the window frame, Glenn looking less a man of the law and more like a lost little boy. The urge to ask about Jacob opened his mouth, but the urge to not hear about Jillian shut it. If there was any news, Thomas figured Glenn would tell him.

"I'll go see her," Thomas said, and slid back under the steering wheel. His last words caught Glenn before he walked away. "If you find anything about Jacob, you'll let us know, right?"

[5]

The stupid road kept moving on Elizabeth, or the car did. No, it couldn't be the car. She cruised a country highway like she and her best friend Kathy did on Friday nights in high school when all those sports dorks and cheerleaders were at the football game. When she and Kathy had drunk just enough beer and the road got naughty, they played Pac-Man, the car gobbling up those lines in the center that looked like dots when they drove fast enough. But that was a long time ago.

Damn it, she thought. I haven't talked to Kathy since her funeral.

A laugh burst from Elizabeth as she tossed another empty beer can out the passenger-side window of her Honda, the can going into the ditch of the rural highway. Drunk driver's trick: tossing the can out the driver's window leaves a bread-crumb trail for the cops; tossing the can out the passenger side puts it in the ditch. That way, you're not littering, you're recycling.

The rest of the cans in the twelve-pack rattled as she reached for another and pulled it out. The dumb things were starting to get warm. It cracked as she pulled back on the tab, spraying foam onto the dash.

"Ju-das," she slurred toward the can, then put it to her lips, the beer still cool but not cold.

She hadn't had a drink, not even a breath of alcohol, since the day Rodney came to the health center. Alcoholics Anonymous kept her sane, it kept her dry, but too much pain stayed with her, lurking in the dark corners, waiting to come out and claim her, like it failed to do when that stupid Mentos doctor handed the monster baby to its clueless mother. The claws of that black-eyed hell beast latched on to her again and dragged her to the convenience store. Silent whispers from the little bastard told her to get a drink. Get good and drunk. To—

A thought shot through her alcohol-fueled brain.

No. No, no, no. The thing was here to kill everyone. To drink from us, to suck the souls from our bodies while his minion—the image of a beautiful red-haired fairy flashed in her mind.

"No," she hissed, and yanked the wheel to the right, putting the car back into the driving lane. Another vehicle, long and brown, snuck up on her. It snuck up on her and drove by. The driver wore a brown cowboy hat.

Red and blue lights fired up on that long, brown car's roof. She hit the turn signal and pulled the car to the shoulder, the passenger-side wheels ending in the weeds at the top of the ditch.

Gum, she thought. I need gum.

Elizabeth dropped a hand into her purse, but the cop stood in her window before she could find her packet of Dentyne.

"Damn it."

"Good evening," the man in uniform said. He motioned to the mostly empty twelve-pack box on the seat beside her. "Been drinking tonight?"

Tonight? Yes, it was night. What happened to the day? The sky had darkened, the horizon beyond St. Joe a streak of pastels. The headlights were on. When did that happen?

"Yes," she said flatly.

The officer nodded, raising a hand to tip his hat farther back on his head.

"Would you please step out of the vehicle, ma'am?" he asked, his words calm, like he was just doing his job.

Her shoulders slumped. "Sure," she said, and unlatched the door, stepping out into the early evening. A DWI was always a possibility for somebody who drank; she was surprised it had taken this long.

"May I see your license?" he asked, holding out a hand.

The man seemed nice. Not like a lecture waited somewhere behind his straight white teeth. He'd get down to business and, well, damn. Elizabeth hoped he'd drop her off home instead of arresting her.

She retrieved her purse and found her wallet, and that stupid pack of gum that didn't do her any good now.

"So, Elizabeth," the officer said. "I'm Sheriff Glenn Kirkhoff—"

Kirkhoff? "I . . . I voted for you," she said, interrupting him.

He nodded, a Mayberry, North Carolina, "aw shucks" on his tired, lined face.

"Thanks, Elizabeth. I really appreciate it, and I hope tonight won't change your opinion of me if I decide to take you in." His eyes narrowed.

"No," she said before he could say more. "You did a great—um, a great job with the whole cleanup thing after your pred-pred-predecessor died in that explosion." A slight hiccup cut her off. "You showed strong lea . . . leadership when St. Joe went, you know." Her hands flared in front of her as she mouthed "boom."

The man's thumbs tucked into his black leather police belt.

"Thank you, Elizabeth, but that doesn't have anything to do with the fact that you were swerving like you were avoiding machine-gun fire."

Oh, man. This guy knew. A picture of the demon baby crawled through Elizabeth's brain, the boy aged until it wore a T-shirt, shorts, and dinosaur tennis shoes; the little monster stood before a cow, stuffing ripped, bloody flesh into its fetid maw. Raw fear ran through her.

"Jacob Jenkins," she said, her voice straight and hard, not a trace of the terror that coursed through her. At that moment, she understood the sheriff knew about that, that thing. Then she repeated the words Rodney Paulson said to her in the clinic. "There's a demon coming, Glenn Kirkhoff. It's coming to eat us all."

[6]

A knock on the door—an odd thing at 7 p.m., Todd Marshall thought as he sat on the floor between the living room and kitchen, on the spot where his wife was murdered.

Todd's days began at 3 a.m. when he woke, took a dump, and then poured a glass of water from the dispenser in the refrigerator door and sat down to join Bekka on the floor.

He lay with her for hours, talking to her about the work he didn't go to anymore and what he watched on TV. About the baseball glove he'd planned to buy Todd Jr. on his first birthday. About the name for the girl they'd have when Todd Jr. was two. Then, by noon, he'd open a bottle of vodka and drink until he fell over the place where some shit stain had sliced open his beautiful Bekka with their own kitchen knife and stolen their unborn child.

The crime-scene cleanup crew made the life his Bekka—the love of his stupid life—had bled out across their zebra-wood floors disappear, leaving a lemon scent just like a household cleaner commercial.

Todd tried not drinking vodka all day. He went to his first AA meeting ever and listened as a nurse talked about a woman who had a baby. Sure, the baby was evil, but at least the mother got to keep him, to take him home and watch him grow. Todd bit his knuckle, then screamed all the way to the liquor store, biting the inside of his mouth when he went inside because businesses frown on screaming. He'd never expected the nurse lady's story, but Todd tried not to expect much out of life anymore.

He sure as hell didn't expect a knock on the door at 7 p.m., unless it was another TV reporter. The vultures wanted to know every detail.

The pretty thing from Fox News had the balls to ask him to describe what his wife looked like, on the floor, sliced open like a fish.

Todd pushed himself to his feet; the living room spun until his brain's vodka bath stopped sloshing.

"Hey," he called to the door. More words had been attached to his shout, but they'd evaporated by the time they got to his mouth.

The doorknob turned freely in his hand because he'd stopped locking the door. There wasn't anything inside his house he cared about anymore, even himself.

When the door swung wide, a sheriff's deputy, about thirty, stood on his concrete stoop.

"Whadayawant?" Todd slurred, angry a cop showed up at his house. Dinn I have nuff problems?

"Mr. Marshall?" the deputy asked, her hands grasping each other behind her back. "Mr. Todd Marshall?"

"Yeah." He propped his right hand against the door frame to keep himself vertical and noticed he still held the vodka bottle.

"I'm Deputy Maddison Glines with the Buchanan County Sheriff's Department and—" She paused for a moment, tears beginning to well in her eyes.

Are cops s'posed to cry?

"I regret to inform you this afternoon we discovered the body of your son in a cornfield in the eastern part of the county." Deputy Glines stood still as she stared at Todd with those weepy eyes. "Are you in need of assistance, Mr. Marshall? Do you need me to contact someone close to you for support, and do you need someone to stay with you until they arrive?"

Fuckyatalkinbout? Then his red, swollen eyes stopped swimming.

"My son," he whispered. "My son's dead."

"I'm so sorry, Mr. Marshall, I—"

"Get da fuck offa my property," Todd said before slamming the door in the deputy's face.

He wanted the bottle to smash when he threw it against the living-room wall, but the plastic container simply bounced off and rolled onto the floor.

My son. My wife. Gone. Sobs shook his torso. "They're gone. All gone."

Frank.

He didn't know where the word come from, but it ran through his head clearly, like the ting of toasting glasses. Frank from AA gave Todd his number at the meeting. "Call anytime you're feeling down. Before you drink. Before you do anything foolish, you just give me a call," the old man with half his teeth had told him.

Frank.

Todd stumbled to the center of the room and plopped onto the couch. The note and the phone were in the end-table drawer. Frank. Gotta call Frank.

Fingers, fat and stupid from booze, fumbled with the drawer before it shot from its slot in the table and overturned on the floor. His iPhone dumped out, right alongside the Springfield Hellcat 9mm. "*It's for home protection, baby,*" he'd told Bekka the day he showed it to her. "*Nothin's going to come into our house and threaten my family.*"

But it did. It absolutely did.

Tears flowed in steady streams as he bent over and wrapped his hand around the pistol's handle. The cold metal grip felt good in his fist.

I can see Bekka again. I can play with Toddy. "God, Jesus Christ. I miss you so much, honey."

Todd Marshall pulled back the slide with a click, and wedged the barrel firmly under his chin. Just a click, one little click, and he'd be with his family.

The name Frank appeared in his head again, but it was dim, almost silent.

"I'm coming," he whispered as he started to squeeze the trigger.

A giggle, the giggle of a child, laughed in the kitchen.

"Wha—" he managed, turning his head toward the sound, a sound he should never have heard. Then the pistol fired.

[7]

The sheriff turned his patrol cruiser onto Tamara Drive, Elizabeth Condon asleep next to him. Glenn knew he should have slapped the cuffs on her and shoved her in the backseat, driven straight to headquarters and locked her in a cell until she came to in the morning wondering what the hell she'd done. But Boyd told him a story when he picked up Elvin Miller, drunk, the night he found Elvin's wife chopped up with an ax. Boyd knew something was wrong with Elvin's story, something dark, something wicked, something that had nothing to do with Elvin. Driving drunk that night wasn't Elvin's fault.

When Elizabeth looked into his eyes, hers suddenly as sober as a Mormon's, and she said, "Jacob Jenkins. There's a demon coming, Glenn Kirkhoff. It's coming to eat us all," Glenn knew that was his Elvin moment. The woman who said those words from the front seat of her car wasn't Elizabeth.

Thoughts crashed into one another. Then who was it? Glenn had grown up in the Methodist church, stood there while the preacher sprinkled him with glorified tap water. He'd read all that stuff by Zecharia Sitchin in high school, the books about giants coming to Earth from the Twelfth Planet and turning protohumans into Homo sapiens. Then he'd stopped believing in anything but the law of the state. What was this madness that crept into his life?

For about four seconds, Elizabeth Condon wasn't Elizabeth Condon. Of that much he was certain.

So, he took her home. She fell back into a drunken slouch and slobbered out her address when he asked. He'd get her to bed; she'd have to figure out how to get her car tomorrow, but she was damn lucky. He hoped she woke up knowing that. Soft snoring was coming from the passenger seat by the time he pulled into her driveway. She woke to open the door, and Glenn dropped her on the couch and made sure she lay on her side before leaving.

Boyd didn't warn him enough about this job, or did he? The late sheriff's field-interview notebook kept replaying in his mind.

. . . Someone walked out of the garden, into the house, turned into a little girl as she made her way up the stairs. Then she smiled at me while she vanished . . .

Turned into a little girl? Vanished?

"What did you mean, Sheriff?" he asked the interior of his patrol car. The air inside still smelled like the nurse's beer breath.

But Glenn was sure he knew damn well what Boyd meant. The sheriff didn't mess around, and he wouldn't write something arbitrary or flat-out false in his interview notebook. Whatever walked into the Cavanaugh's house more than thirty years ago wasn't a little girl, but it somehow became one, then when she did, she disappeared in front of Sheriff Boyd Donally like Harry Potter.

Maybe it was Elizabeth Condon's demon.

[8]

A night bird's call pierced the air; a little too early at dusk, but hunger is a heck of an alarm clock. Thomas sat, leaning over the steering wheel of his pickup at the spot where Deputy Glines investigated the Camry, the car now back at his house. The tow truck should have brought the car to the Buchanan County impound lot, but being the nephew of the county sheriff's mentor apparently bought some kind of privilege.

Jillian. It had only been a couple of days since she disappeared, and Thomas had trouble remembering details about her. She had red hair and stood a bit shorter than he did, but her voice? What did it sound like? What did she like for dinner? Where did she work (*if* she worked)? How long had he known her? She'd lived with him for, he couldn't remember how long, but long enough. All he knew for certain was a conversation about babies she'd had with his mother at the kitchen table of his parents' farmhouse.

"*Don't you just want to eat their toes?*" Jillian asked, and his mom said, "*Oh, yes, yes, yes. They're like little bits of popcorn chicken.*" Now Jillian was gone, Marguerite's son Jacob was gone too, and the sheriff's department discovered a dead baby in a cornfield. He wondered if it still had its toes.

"This is a nightmare," he said under his breath as he put the truck in gear and drove the rest of the short distance to the Jenkinses' place in silence, pulling his pickup to a stop in the gravel driveway next to a car he didn't recognize.

He took out his smartphone and thumbed, *Mind if I come over?* to Marguerite in a text.

She texted back seconds later. *Of course!* ♥

Good, because I'm outside.

The curtain in the front window peeled back to reveal Marguerite's face; the flutter in Thomas's stomach was strong enough he wondered if he had a tapeworm.

You're such a goober! ☺

Thomas never quite got the hang of emojis, but her second one made more sense than the first. A few moments later, the door opened and Marguerite stood in the light that poured from inside into the darkening evening. She waved before bounding into the yard as Thomas got out of the truck.

"Hey," he said as she took his hand.

"I'm glad you're here," she said, drawing him in for a tight one-armed hug, the strength and warmth of her body as comforting as home when he'd been away too long. He returned the hug, not too hard, not too loose.

When she pulled back, his hand still in hers, he missed the hug already.

"Any news on Jakie?" she asked, her eyes wide like she anticipated him to have something, but her voice carried no conviction. Jillian had stolen Marguerite's son—both she and Thomas knew that. Marguerite also knew Jillian, probably better than Thomas did at the moment, and had to realize by now that she wouldn't hurt the boy.

"*Don't you just want to eat their toes?*" whispered inside his head.

Or would she?

"No," he said, understanding at that moment what Glenn had meant. Marguerite didn't need to know about the Marshall baby. Not a thing.

Her smile fell, but a half smile returned.

"Aunt Kathy's here to look after Mom tonight," she said, squeezing his hand. "You want to come in and watch a movie? *Invasion of the Body Snatchers* is coming on TNT, the one from 1978 with Donald Sutherland, Jeff Goldblum, and Spock."

Her touch stirred the nonexistent tapeworms into a frenzy. He let Marguerite lead him toward the house, although *Invasion of the Body Snatchers* didn't sound like the movie either of them needed to see tonight.

"Hey," he said, pulling her to a stop. "It's a nice night. How about we go for a walk?"

She nodded, her eyes shaded by the dying light of the day.

"Sure," she said, leaning toward the gravel road. "This way."

The crunch of shoes on gravel, loud to Thomas's ears, seemed to consume the night. Marguerite walked close to him, but their hands parted, Thomas's shoved into the front pockets of his jeans. Unless he was at work, he never knew what to do with them.

The flash of lightning bugs, the yip of a red fox; the lowing of a cow in a nearby pasture. Marguerite stepped from the gravel road and into a grove of dead trees by their house, trees he was sure died when, when . . . damn. Like forgetting any detail about Jillian, Thomas couldn't remember the event that killed the trees, but he knew he was there, somehow in the middle of it all. After about twenty or so yards, Thomas and Marguerite stepped from the straight, stripped trunks and bare limbs into a crime scene.

Yellow tape bearing a continuous scroll of the warning POLICE LINE DO NOT CROSS stretched through the limbs of dead saplings and naked bushes.

"This is where it happened," Marguerite said, her words flat, emotionless. "This is where Jillian kidnapped Jakie."

The night sounds disappeared when they stepped into the clearing, Thomas's heart beat against his shirt and he realized he'd stopped breathing.

"He could do things," she continued, then laughed; there was no joy in it. "Scary things people aren't supposed to be able to do." She stopped and kicked at something on the ground. "This is going to sound terrible, and I won't blame you if you leave, but sometimes when I think of some of the things Jakie did, I don't miss him."

No. That doesn't sound terrible, he wanted to say, although the words were callous, even wicked, but she kept talking, her thoughts flowing out in a steady stream.

"He could feed himself. Not with his hands. The food *floated* to his mouth. My mother—" Her voice squeaked and she stopped to swallow. "My mother died." Marguerite let out a long breath, grabbing the front of Thomas's shirt. "Jakie told me, 'Gramma's sick. She has the cancer. She'll feel better when she's dead.' Then my mother grabbed her chest and collapsed on the kitchen floor. He killed her. I know he did. Jakie made Mom's heart stop."

Marguerite's arms wrapped around Thomas's neck and her face pressed into his chest, tears soaking his shirt. He had no idea what to do.

"I—I screamed at him, 'Jakie, what did you do?'" she sobbed. "And he said, 'Gramma don't hurt no more.'" Marguerite stood back, brushing the pinch marks of her fists from his shirt. "I told him Gramma needed to be alive again, and he shrugged. Then she coughed, and you know what?"

She ran a hand under her leaky nose, then wiped it off in her armpit.

"She stood up. Mom was alive. Jacob stopped and started her *heart*."

Jesus H. Christ. That's not possible.

Thomas reached out and took Marguerite's sweaty, snotty hands in his. "I'm sure there's a better explanation."

She threw off his grip and grabbed his shirt again.

"He told me a fairy talked to him in the garden. He said she wanted him to come to fairyland. She'd feed him cake and they'd go." She spread her arms. "This is it. There was a plate on that stump in the middle of this clearing with specks of chocolate cake on it, and specks of poop." Marguerite pointed at the stump. "Glenn took it for evidence, but it was there."

No.

Thomas's knees buckled, and he reached out; his hand found the trunk of a dead tree. The fairy, the plate, the cake, the shit. The memories that had escaped him, the image of Jillian's face, her destroyed desert world, meth-head Rodney with a pistol, the needle-toothed devil that looked like his father, the explosions that destroyed downtown St. Joseph. Whoa. The memories . . . were suddenly all there. His stomach twisted into a bunch and he dropped to his knees; vomit spewed onto the leaf-strewn ground. A moment later, Thomas looked up, specks of puke on his lips, his chin.

He remembered it all.

PART 2

CHAPTER SEVEN
Ālfheimr

JACOB SAT ON a flat gray rock and glared at the fairy lady, her long red hair slow-dancing in the hot desert breeze. To him, her hair looked like seaweed in nature shows.

The whirlwind that took them from the top of the silo dropped them here—in this stupid hot place, with its stupid hot air, and its stupid hot everything everywhere—and then spun into the sky and disappeared, leaving him with the fairy lady. Too late, but Jacob realized she was stupid too.

"There's no ice cream here," he said, his voice flat. "This place is dumb."

She took a step toward Jacob and sat next to him on the rock.

"The rock's hot," he said. "Rocks are stupid."

The fairy lady's smile seemed to cover more of her face than her mouth did. "This used to be a nice place, Jacob," she said.

"Was it hot?"

A slight laugh escaped her.

"Sometimes, but mostly it was warm and comfortable. It rained, and the rain nourished the trees, and the grass, and the flowers, and the fish in the sea." Her smile shrank until her mouth formed a line like in a cartoon. "The air was full of scents, and the birds sang. This place was once beautiful."

Jacob shook his head. "Yuck. It's ugly. What happened?" he asked. Talking to grown-ups never scared Jacob. With the things he could do—that they couldn't—he thought adults should be scared talking to him. Momma was, Gramma was. Why wasn't this lady?

Her slim fingers wrapped around his small hands, the fairy lady's touch cool in the heat. She took a long time before answering. Jacob thought this was boring.

"Dauðr," she finally said. "A monster came."

Jacob snorted. "I know what monsters are. There's vampires, and werewolves, and bigfoots and Frankensteins all over the place, but I never heard of that one."

The fairy lady squeezed his hands until it hurt.

"Ow," he said, and thought her away. The fairy lady vanished.

Less than a second later, she stood next to the rock.

"Dauðr was real," she said as if she'd never disappeared and reappeared. "Then a man named Thomas killed it." The fairy lady knelt in the sand before the boy. "Dauðr was my mother. Thomas killed my mother."

Thomas?

"I know Thomas," Jacob said. "Momma thinks he's hamsome. He's nice."

A strawberry stain swelled on the fairy lady's face and her hands clenched into fists.

"Dauðr is gone, and this place can be happy again." The words came through clenched teeth.

Jacob looked at her through tight eyes. "You said I'd get ice cream."

She smiled again. This time her teeth looked more like a crocodile's. "And you will," she said. "Just as soon as you bring back the plants. You can do it, Jacob. You're smart. You're strong. You can do anything."

She nodded, and he suddenly knew he could do anything she asked him to. He stretched his hand over the dusty earth, and the ground began to vibrate.

[2]

The second anniversary of the disappearance of Jacob Jenkins and Jillian Robertson came and went the way it had the year before: Thomas invited Marguerite to dinner at the San Miguel Steakhouse right off the interstate in St. Joe. They went, ate, talked about their lives and if they'd ever find Jakie; Marguerite had too much wine; and Thomas drove her home. This year, Marguerite still had too much wine, but she didn't want to go home. Linda had packed up Jacob's clothes and toys and put them in the garage. Marguerite said it didn't feel like home anymore. They went to Thomas's house, the former home of Buchanan County Sheriff Boyd Donally, who was murdered by the father of Marguerite's child. Life, Thomas realized, is just a soap opera.

Thomas hadn't brought any women to the house, although a little over a year after Jillian vanished, he'd briefly gone out with Claire, a loan officer he'd met on Hinge. They'd hit it off enough to make out, but not enough to invite each other home. He'd always been attracted to Marguerite—the way she smiled, the way she laughed, her inappropriate jokes—but Thomas had never stepped off the friend path into oncoming traffic. Respect your boundaries, sir. So Thomas's dating life was much like it had been in high school—nonexistent.

"Whoa," he said, catching Marguerite around the waist as he escorted her from his truck and she slipped negotiating the steps that led to his front door. "Maybe you'd better let me drive up the porch."

When they reached the top, Marguerite stopped and faced Thomas, throwing her arms around his neck.

"Why?" she said, her eyes glassy. "Why, oh why, have I never met a nice guy like you, Thomas Cavanaugh?"

Her warm breath caressed his face, the scent of wine fruity, but it didn't trigger him. Instead of itching for a drink, it was warm and comfortable as snuggling under a blanket.

"Well, technically, you have."

It took a few moments for her eyes to widen. A smile took hold and grew playfully.

"Oh, I have," she said, her voice going all Marilyn Monroe. He'd never heard her talk like this. The flirtatious tone sent some kind of insect fluttering in Thomas's chest. Butterflies? No. More like methed-up dragonflies bouncing around his rib cage.

Marguerite leaned into him; her lips brushed his for a moment before she pressed into a deep, warm kiss. She didn't kiss like Jillian. The kisses from Jillian now felt like frauds. Everything about Jillian felt like a fraud. Marguerite's lips were soft, but her kiss firm, her tongue flicking his own. When Marguerite kissed him, she meant it. The guilt of thinking about Jillian while he kissed Marguerite poked him in the chest.

"Hey," he said, trying to pull away. Her arms tightened and brought him back in. He let her.

Moments later, Marguerite broke off the kiss and looked at Thomas through tired eyes. She unfolded her arms from around his neck and wiped her bottom lip with the back of a hand.

"I've wanted to do that for a long time. A *really* long time," she said, never breaking eye contact. "I hope it was okay."

Okay? Thomas reached out and grabbed the porch railing to support his wobbling knees.

"Yeah. It was more than okay."

"I'm glad." Her smile came back as she turned toward the door. "But I'm really tired, and need to go to sleep. Can I sleep on your couch?"

It was his turn to smile.

"Not on your life." He unlocked the front door and escorted her inside. "You get the bed. The couch is mine."

She lay her head on his shoulder and they walked.

"See. I told you you were nice."

[3]

Ālfheimr

Storm clouds rolled above, blacks and grays painting the sky to the bare horizons. The elf lady and Jacob stood on a dusty rise, looking out over a plain that used to be a sea. The change in air pressure sent a cold wave through the hills, and her hair moved with the breeze. Rain fell in the distance in a great moving curtain. A cold, fat droplet struck Jacob on the forehead as the front neared. He wiped it off.

"I don't like the rain," he said. "Being wet is yuck."

"Then why are you making it rain?" the fairy lady asked, looking out over the dead sea, her teeth still like a crocodile's. He liked her better that way. Every time she and the Thomas guy came to visit Momma, Jacob had always thought the fairy looked like she was wearing a mask. Now he could see what she was hiding, and it fit her. It fit her just right.

"Because Momma grows a garden with flowers, and she said the plants need water to grow." Jacob looked up at the fairy lady through a suspicious squint. "There aren't any kitchen sinks around here to get water. There aren't any kitchens anywhere. How am I going to get ice cream?"

The crocodile smile broke larger, splitting her head in half. "Just as soon as you're finished," the fairy lady monster woman said.

Jacob didn't like grown-ups sometimes.

Gray and yellow dirt stretched everywhere. The place looked and smelled like a sandbox, and Jacob Jenkins didn't like sandboxes. Cats pooped in them, and the sand always got in his shoes. He raised his arms toward the sky, a coldness seeping into his hands, not like when he played outside in the snow, but like he'd held a can of soda too long. More clouds appeared, black and churning, to join the spotty gray clouds that dropped a raindrop here and there. Jacob thought about water shooting from the shower head, and rain began to pound the ancient seabed in the distance.

The fairy lady squealed like a dog toy or a dolphin. "You're doing it, Jacob," she said, her voice weird, he thought.

"Is something wrong?" he asked.

A slim hand rested on his head and mussed his black hair. "I'm just happy, Jakie boy."

A frown spread over him. "Don't call me that," he said. "Only my momma calls me Jakie, and you're not Momma."

The fairy lady lowered herself until she knelt close to eye level with Jacob; her eyes were different. They were black, with no whites, no—what did Momma call them? Irishes?—yeah, no Irishes.

"I'll never be your momma, honey." Her words came out sweet, like they wanted Jacob to trust her.

He nodded because he wanted her to think he did, but he didn't. Nope. He didn't ever want to trust the fairy crocodile woman.

"Why did you bring me here?"

His defiant tone pulled a laugh from her.

"Because you're the only one who can help me. You're the only one strong enough." Her smile had shrunk to a normal mouth with normal teeth. "You do want to help me, don't you?"

"You promised me ice cream," he said to the fairy lady in close to a pout, his arms crossed.

She squealed, her hands bunched in fists in front of her mouth. She looked out over the old seabed at the cascading rain and laughed.

"Ice cream," he said again.

"Yes, yes, yes. All the ice cream you can eat."

More raindrops fell, splattering the dusty ground at Jacob's feet, absorbing into the dust and sand. The fairy lady began to dance. She's weird, ran through his young but impossibly old mind. A layer of mud formed at his feet, its surface undulating as if alive. Green leaves sprouted from the mud in jerky time-lapse motions. Water collected in the dry seabed, the heaviest rains settling over it. Trees erupted from the earth behind Jacob, and the fairy lady cackled like Momma watching *The Bachelor* after too many cups of Mommy Juice from the big box in the refrigerator.

"You're doing it," she said, thunder in the distance punctuating her words. "You're powerful, Jake. You're more powerful than God."

He didn't know what she was talking about. All he wanted was ice cream, and he figured he wouldn't get any until he fixed this place, like the fairy lady wanted. He'd tried making his own ice cream before, but whatever appeared in a bowl before him tasted yuck.

The sky cleared overhead, although heavy black clouds still dumped rain into the old ocean. The growing plants slowed. A bird chirped from somewhere behind them, followed by another and another, until their song filled the day. Jacob reached to the new full, green bush that grew beside him and plucked a fat blackberry. It squirted juice inside his mouth when he chomped down. Sweet and slightly sour. Jacob loved blackberries. The fairy lady screamed a laughing scream as a stream sprang up beside her, its bed crawling with fish. She knelt beside the water, the knees of her blue jeans soaking up mud. She cupped her hand and drank a scoop of water.

"So pure," she shouted. "Jacob, this is perfect!"

He willed a breeze and stood still in it. The wind was light and warm and smelled like Twizzlers. Jacob liked Twizzlers, but he liked ice cream more.

"Now?" he asked.

The fairy lady scooped him off the ground and held him tight. "You can have anything you want, Jake," she said. "Oh, the things we will do."

He didn't know what she meant, but as she began walking toward a place she called the City, he decided he should leave the rain on for a while. That ocean wasn't going to fill itself.

"You can change worlds, Jacob."

Jacob wasn't sure he wanted to do that.

[4]

Glenn sat in his office staring at his computer screen. Two years. It had been two years since Jillian Robertson abducted Jacob Jenkins. He was still certain that's what went down. The poor kid would be six now.

What has that boy been through? he wondered, hoping that somehow, by some gift of God, Jacob was still alive. Most missing children weren't, after two years.

Glenn suspected Jacob might be special, because it had also been two years since someone gutted one of Hiram Southwick's heifers, and by someone, Glenn knew—however impossible it seemed—it had been Jacob Jenkins. Initial tests on Jacob's blood-soaked clothing was bovine; a later DNA test showed the blood came from Hiram's heifer. Glenn didn't share either result with anyone.

It had also been two years since Todd Marshall's gruesome and heartbreaking discovery, two years since he'd shot himself in the head the day Deputy Glines went to his house to break the news she'd found his baby, and something—someone—had eaten its fingers and toes. The teeth marks were from an adult human. Todd might have been of some help during the investigation, but Glenn would never know; he died in the ER a couple hours later.

The bloody handprint on the knife handle was from a child, although the prints didn't match Jacob's. The department had also never determined who killed Rebekka Marshall, although whoever it was left the gruesome sharp-tooth smile calling card drawn on her deflated torso with her own blood.

That image burned in Glenn's mind for years. He suspected the same smiling circle consumed Boyd while he was sheriff, and now it had him. What was that smiling face? What did it represent? And how did it connect everything? Elvin Miller, Carrie McMasters, Bobby Garrett, now Bekka Marshall. Hell, it was probably carved somewhere inside Hiram's heifer for all he knew.

"How do you fit, Jake?" he whispered to himself, and how did any of this fit with Marguerite's disappearance eleven years before?

[5]

The smell of coffee welcomed Thomas to the morning before his alarm clock got the chance. He sat up on the couch and looked into the kitchen. The fear that Jillian had come back vanished when Marguerite turned around; her shirt was untucked but she was still dressed in what she wore to the restaurant last night, her hair a wonderful mess. She saw him and smiled over her coffee cup.

"Good morning," she said, eyes locked on him.

Did any of that happen last night? Thomas wondered, then knew it did. He was still an alcoholic, he always was, always would be, but he hadn't had a drop to drink over dinner. However, Marguerite did, and Marguerite kissed him, long and deep. The question was, after all that wine, did *she* remember?

Marguerite poured coffee in a second cup and walked to the couch, handing the cup to Thomas before sliding next to him, her leg pressed against his.

"It's black," she said. "You look like you drink your coffee black."

He took a sip before answering. "What's that supposed to mean?"

Her mug clinked as she set it on the coffee table. No coaster for her.

"My Gramma always told me a man who put sugar and milk in his coffee was a dandy or British and you wouldn't want either to take you to the Fourth of July parade."

His laugh came out in specks of coffee that tasted a hell of a lot better than he'd ever brewed. He wiped his mouth. "I'm going to take that as a compliment, although I'm not sure what any of that means."

Marguerite's hand, soft but strong, rested on his forearm. A shock, like brushing against an electric fence, ran through him.

He sat straight.

"Gramma was full of sayings that didn't make much sense." She eased Thomas's cup from his hands and set it on the coffee table next to hers. "What happened last night wasn't because I was drunk," she said. "I kissed you because I've wanted to for a long time. I sure hope you're cool with it, because I'm going to do it again."

Thomas's mouth became dry; he tasted last night's garlic mashed potatoes over this morning's coffee. He opened his mouth to protest, but she was already there, her lips meeting his.

How is this happening? Why is this happening? I don't deserve—

His brain dumped a sweet cocktail of dopamine, serotonin, and oxytocin into the pleasure centers, and Thomas's eyes rolled backward; he drank in more happiness than booze had ever brought him.

Then she pulled away and kissed the tip of his nose.

"I used your toothbrush this morning," she said. "After we'd had our tongues in each other's mouths last night, I figured you wouldn't mind."

Thomas, what have you been doing with your life?

This time, he kissed her. When he broke it off, her eyes were still closed.

Her smile slowly spread, her eyes opened a crack. "Those garlic potatoes were awesome, weren't they?"

His face became hot. A playful slap hit Thomas's shoulder, and her hand slid into his before he could consider what to do next.

"You need to take me home," Marguerite said, resting her head on his shoulder, the meth dragonflies back in Thomas's chest. "This round of chemo has been rough on Mom. Aunt Kathy looked after her last night, but I know my mom. I'm sure my aunt needs a break."

She sniffled, and Thomas raised her face toward his. A tear trickled down her cheek. He wiped it off.

"I'm glad your mom has you," he said. "You're the strongest person I know."

She punched his arm. "Damn straight, and don't you forget it."

Marguerite snuggled in for another kiss. When she sat back, she said, "I was serious when I said last night wasn't because I was drunk—it wasn't."

Every speck of self-confidence he could scrounge up during the night had still told him that was exactly the reason.

"Of course not."

A grin crept over her lips. "You're a terrible liar," she said. "That's one of the things I look for in a man."

[6]
Ālfheimr

Jacob stood in the entrance of one of the homes that honeycombed the cliff the fairy lady called the City. It didn't look like a city to Jacob. He'd been to St. Joe, he'd been to Kansas City, Momma and Gramma even took him to the zoo in Omaha. These places weren't holes cut into mountains; cities were made of buildings. This dirty place looked like something from that old Flintstones cartoon.

In the distance, rain continued to fall over the sea, the water starting to collect in its basin. Inside, the rock room was carved into what looked to Jacob like a living room and kitchen for those cartoon cavemen.

"I wanna go home," he said.

The fairy lady stepped beside him, holding a black wooden bowl filled with mushy white lumps.

"Sorry. Not yet. We still have work to do."

She handed him the bowl, the surface polished smooth as glass. "See? I told you you'd get ice cream."

He took it and wrinkled his nose. "It doesn't look like ice cream."

"You take what you get," she said, her smile back to the crocodile teeth. Jacob guessed she didn't have to pretend to be pretty for him anymore.

The lumps of white had already begun to melt; a waft of microwave fish sticks pushed its way into his nose.

"I need a spoon."

The fairy lady's laugh ground like gravel. "No, you don't. You can eat it with your thoughts."

The fairy lady wasn't as nice as she'd seemed in Momma's garden, and Jacob didn't want ice cream anymore. He walked to the open door-way and threw the bowl onto the rocks below.

"You want to hear something silly?" the fairy lady said.

He nodded, and a shock of deep black hair dropped over his fore-head. Something silly was better than anything he'd seen so far.

"When you go home, you'll be the same, but everyone you know will be old. Your Gramma will be dead." She laughed again. "Isn't that funny?"

No. He didn't think that sounded funny at all. It would have before he came here, before the fairy lady showed him who she really was. But not anymore. Jacob saw he'd been mean to his family, mean like her, and he didn't want to be like her.

Not at all.

"What else do you want me to do in this place?" He folded his arms across his chest as he looked out into the day, the once gray-and-brown world now blue and green and happy with colors.

A hand slid onto his shoulder and squeezed too hard. Jacob almost said ow, but he didn't want the fairy lady to know it hurt.

"Oh, honey." The fairy lady's words were hard. "You're rebuilding it into something worthy to be my kingdom."

Jacob squinted. "Kingdom? That needs a castle, and a king."

Her laughter was sharp. "Ha, a king, yes. I once thought that would be Thomas Cavanaugh, but he's too weak, too pliable. Even our former consorts, the Norsemen of your world, are but shadows of what they once were."

She looked down at Jacob and pinched his cheek. He didn't like this lady anymore.

"Maybe one day when you grow up, you'll be my king, little man." She released him and looked out upon her healing lands. "But first, I need to devour the strength of your world."

"I don't even know what that means," Jacob said.

"A queen must be strong, and your world, I'm afraid, will have to make sacrifices."

His eyes met hers, only for a second. "What's a sack-fice?"

"Oh, you're full of questions. Your world is full of souls. They're in the water, they're in the plants, they're in the people. Souls fulfill me. They make me strong. When I take you home, I'm going to swallow them all."

A bad feeling crept through Jacob. He wanted to go home—now, but he didn't want her to come with him.

"When Dauðr sucked the life from this world, many of my people escaped death in yours." The strawberry patch on her face flared to life; Jacob only saw it when she got angry. "But a kingdom needs servants, so I need you to call my people home," she said, kneading his shoulder.

"Now?" he asked.

The hands on his shoulders turned him from the den opening to face the scary-tooth fairy lady who squatted beside him.

"Your world needs to suffer as much as mine needs to live," she said as flatly as if she'd said "have a nice day."

She released him and stood, her smell going from Twizzlers to the inside of that dead cow. "You ask too many questions, you know that?"

He squinted at her. "I shouldn't talk to you anymore. Momma said I shouldn't talk to someone if I don't know their name."

The fairy lady pulled a black circle from the back pocket of her jeans and used it to tie her hair into a ponytail.

"I cannot give you my real name," she said. "In my world, names are sacred and must be protected. However, in another language, it would be Alvilda."

"You can't tell me your real name?" he said. "Everything here is dumb. I wanna go home now."

"Names mean things. Thomas knows my real name, but he doesn't know what he can do with it," she said, ignoring his words. "Do you know what *Jacob* means? It means 'supplanter.'"

Jacob's frown fell into confusion. "Sup-what?"

"Supplanter," she continued. "It's someone who takes over a kingdom, or a world. Your name is noble. It means you're going to control your home, Jacob. You're going to be a king. Remember?"

A king? Jacob didn't much want to be a king. He wanted to be a firefighter, or one of those guys who drove the garbage truck. Being a king looked like too much work.

"What does *Alvilda* mean anyway?" he asked.

Those crocodile teeth split until he could see her tongue. It wasn't a people tongue anymore either. It was pointed and split at the end.

"It means 'Battle of Elves,'" she told him. "Now get to work calling my friends. Trust me, I'm ready to get you home too."

A frown formed on Jacob's little face. "You're mean."

"Not as mean as the child who killed his own grandmother." The pointed teeth seemed to fill her whole face. "Now, call them home."

[7]

The smell hit Elizabeth as she opened the door to the Buchanan County Health Department's Examination Room 2. Not the sour, rotten body odor of a great number of their clients—the poor, the uninsured, the homeless. This was, what? Aramis? She didn't realize Estée Lauder still made that cologne. The file the receptionist handed her was light, but it contained a chart; this patient had been in before. She stepped inside the white room and found a man sitting on the examination table in clean jogging pants and a gray "Property of Bishop LeBlond High School" T-shirt. Thick brown hair, cut and combed; a beard, short, neat, and speckled with white. The man looked healthy, but the sudden involuntary muscle twitches and the still-healing sores on his mottled skin told enough of his story.

The manila folder flipped open with the flick of her thumb, and— Dear God.

Elizabeth's attention shot back to the man on the table. The sober meth addict in clean clothes and a shower was—no, no, no. Rodney Paulson.

"Hello, Elizabeth," Rodney said, his voice steady, deep, and clear, unlike the rattly gibberish he'd spouted the last time they met.

In that same room, Rodney had once warned Elizabeth a demon was coming to "eat them all." His eyes, which had gone from bloodshot to black, were now clear, brown, lucid. She'd left work early that day two years ago and got drunk as hell. She woke at home with a foggy memory of the sheriff bringing her there. It was the last time she'd had a sip of alcohol. Elizabeth shut the door, pressing her back into it, staying as far away from her patient as she could.

"Hello, Rodney," she said, trying to keep panic from winding her tight and letting her go.

He smiled awkwardly, meth mouth rendering his remaining teeth riddled with deep, black holes and scorch marks from anhydrous ammonia, hydrochloric acid, and lye.

"I frightened you once," he said. The hands resting on his knees couldn't lie still. "I wasn't in control of my life then. I am so, so sorry."

HR procedures from the hospital and the county health center about potentially dangerous patients ran through her head. Not one thing applied.

"Well," she said, pressing harder against the door. "That's fine. Thank you. What can we do for you today?"

Rodney's right hand smacked his head and dug into a spot.

Elizabeth jumped, the folder dropping from her hands; its spine thwacked against the tile floor.

She bent and scooped it up.

"Uh, Rodney. How, how, ho—" She wiped the back of her hand across the sweat on her lip. "How do you feel?"

He stopped the furious scratching and slapped his hand back into his lap.

"I need something to help with the voice," he said.

The voice?

A shimmy worked through his shoulders.

"A boy," Rodney said. "A little boy talks to me in my head. He's telling me to come home."

Alarm klaxons sounded deep inside Elizabeth.

Schizophrenia?

Abduction?

"Well, hearing voices could mean a lot of things—" she said before Rodney sat up straight, the sudden movement sending tremors through her body.

"No," he snapped. "It means one thing. *One.*" His gaze hit the floor, and he shook his head. When he looked back up at Elizabeth, the eyes were green. "Elizabeth. I'm not from here. This city. This state. This world." The green glowed, an electric fire behind his stare. "I escaped a monster in my world once, and it's calling me back. Methamphetamines kept my mind stupid, they kept me safe, but the drug was killing me. I need something to dull my head, another drug to deaden the voice of the boy, that damned boy."

Elizabeth stepped forward, captured in the emerald glow. "Do you know who the boy is, Rodney?"

The clean meth addict nodded.

"Yes. It's Jacob Jenkins."

Elizabeth shot toward Rodney and slapped him across the face.

The inside of the Buchanan County Sheriff's Department reeked of coffee and anxiety. Aaron sat at his desk, a hand shoved into his thinning brown hair, the other holding a telephone receiver to his ear.

"Yes, ma'am, I do take your concern seriously," he said. "But President Kennedy's been dead for more than sixty years. I don't think we can do anything to help him."

Glenn patted the deputy's shoulder as he walked by. Maddy stood from her desk, spraying her peace lily before joining him.

"Sounds like Mrs. Teal's off the rails again," she said, following Glenn into his office.

The sheriff slid his Styrofoam cup of convenience-store coffee next to his laptop and sat, the well-worn chair moaning. "We need more like Mrs. Teal, Maddy. She works parts of our brain that don't get enough exercise."

Maddy laughed, more from courtesy than humor, and pulled a thumb drive from her uniform pocket. She handed it to Glenn.

"What's on this?" he asked, taking the memory drive.

The deputy bit her lower lip before answering. "You remember you asked me to get Zach out to photograph the field where the Marshall baby was found?"

Remember? Yeah. "Sure I do, but that was—" Glenn trailed off. He leaned back in the chair, folding his hands across his belly. "You know, I never saw it."

"Yeah," she said. "Zach said the file was corrupted and by the time he got back out to the field to shoot it again, Palmer had plowed that spot under."

"So? What about it now?"

Pink spread over her cheeks; it always did when she got nervous. "Well, Zach came in early this morning and gave me that drive." She paused, sucking in a deep breath before continuing. "He got some kind of new software and ran some old files through it. He was able to recover the video."

The chair creaked again as Glenn leaned forward and opened his laptop. "Have you seen it?"

She nodded.

"And?"

She shook her head; the deputy's short hair barely moved.

"I think you'd better see it yourself," she said.

Glenn's fingers clicked over the keys, then Enter, telling the computer the password. He pushed the stick into the USB port. "Then, let's see what we missed."

Glenn double-clicked on the drive icon, then on the MP4 file labeled PALMERABBOTT_FIELD_6_10_2021. Zach Davees's stubbly face appeared on the screen.

"It's June 10, 2021, and I'm at the property of Palmer Abbott, County Road 54 just south of Blakely Cemetery. The crime scene involves the body of a newborn, one Todd Darren Marshall Junior removed by the county coroner, so the aerial footage will not be of the body, it will be of the odd flattened lines of corn that surrounded the body. Here we go."

Zach's face gave way to the deep green of the young corn, the mashed pattern only a curved line from the low altitude.

"Here we're going up from ten feet to twenty," Zach said, the image no clearer. "Now thirty, forty."

Bits of the lines began to form a picture, a long curve that started to grow into what Glenn suspected would become a circle; diagonal lines cut through its center.

"We're now at one hundred feet," Zach said, his voice softer, unsure. "What the hell *is* that?"

"You see it?" Maddy whispered.

The curved line did form a circle, split by a huge triangular mouth and pointy, shark-like teeth. Glenn had seen that same image in photos of Elvin Miller's house, of Carrie McMasters's house, Bobby Garrett's basement, and on Rebekka Marshall's butchered belly. The smiling face that had tortured Boyd.

"Motherfucker."

CHAPTER EIGHT

FRANK STOOD WITH his right hand in the pocket of his faded blue jeans, a Marlboro smoldering in the other. The old man took a deep drag and held it in awhile before exhaling. He coughed as he grinned at Thomas standing next to him, nodding and saying good night to members of AA and Al-Anon as they filed from the Delores Hadley Community Center.

"You know smoking's bad for you, right?" Thomas asked.

The old man coughed out a laugh before answering.

"We all got problems, Tommy," he said. "Wouldn't be here if we didn't." Frank sucked in another lungful of cancer smoke and pushed it out through tight lips as he leaned his back against the brick building. "Smokin's the worst thing I do now. Booze and fighting would have killed me long before now if I hadn't found the program."

He dropped the spent filter into the sand bucket by the door. Frank wasn't the only alcoholic who smoked. Not by a long shot. The kindly, genial man grinned, the mouth half-filled with teeth. Time and sobriety changed a guy.

"It'll kill me one of these days," Frank said. "But fuck it. At least my liver will be okay."

From the sound of Frank's cough, Thomas wondered if it wasn't killing him already.

A trio of Al-Anon wives stepped from the front door laughing at something Thomas missed. One of the aspects of both sides of AA that still surprised him was the humor. Some people were angry, sad, bitter, but most people who lived inside the cult of the Big Book were happy as hell.

He walked with the ladies a few steps before turning toward his truck, patting a new recruit named Pope on the shoulder as he passed. Pope, a husband and father of two, was trying to kick oxycodone dependence. Apparently, opioids were a bitch. It was a good meeting with a lot of new faces. Thomas hoped he saw some of them again.

His keys were near the door when Thomas realized someone was walking behind him. He slowed.

"Thomas?" The voice was a woman's. He turned. The nurse stood about ten feet away, her hands held in a bunch before her.

"Yeah," he said. "Elizabeth, right?"

She nodded, and her gaze shifted from Thomas to her hands to the asphalt.

"Are you—" She coughed into her hand before continuing. "Are you Thomas Cavanaugh?"

He unlocked the pickup door and opened it, his senses on alert. The second word in AA was *Anonymous* because no one ever gave their last name. What the heck does she want?

"Yeah," he said. "Why?"

She took a step forward, and Thomas took one back, resting his butt against the pickup's bench seat. He didn't keep a rifle in his truck like Dad, but an aluminum softball bat lay hidden behind the seat, its handle about six inches from his left hand.

"I'm so sorry," she said, shaking her head, her hands in front of her. "I didn't mean for it to be like this."

The hair on his arms tingled like he was Spider-Man or something.

"Be like what?" he asked, his tone harsh, suspicious.

She took a step back. "I'm sorry," she said. "This is just as uncomfortable for me." A light cough came out into her hand as she cleared her throat. "One of my patients. He, uh, he told me I had to find Thomas Cavanaugh."

Thomas opened his mouth to speak, but Elizabeth continued.

"His name is Rodney."

"Rodney?" he started, then stopped. Rodney? The name seemed familiar maybe, a remnant of a former life, but he couldn't place it. "I'm not sure I know a Rodney."

"He—" She shifted weight from foot to foot before finally looking him in the eye. "He told me you once fell through a portal into his apartment, then broke his arm with a table leg."

"His arm?"

Oh no. The memory flooded his brain. Jillian, a desert land, Twinkies, falling through nothingness and crashing into a trashed room of a trashed motel to find a man decimated by methamphetamines. The man pointed a pistol at them. "I could have handled Rodney," Jillian had said as they walked out of the motel room into a snowy night after Thomas broke Rodney's arm.

"I did," Thomas said, the words falling out in a mumble, the softball bat forgotten.

She stepped toward him; this time he didn't shrink back.

"He said there's a devil coming here, and . . . and the voice of a little boy is trying to call him home. Someplace far away."

Her words dragged sharp, jagged images from the depths of his memory, like a barbed-wire fence pulled through his brain. Far away? A name . . . Jillian took him to this faraway place, an awful place, and it had a name.

Alfmeyer? Ālrfhimer? No. No, it's Ālfheimr.

The Land of the Elves.

No. Not this.

"A little boy?" he said, his skin crawling as the gooseflesh rose. "A little boy is talking to him?"

"Yes." Tears began to run down Elizabeth's cheeks. "And I helped deliver him. It's the devil boy, Jacob Jenkins."

[2]

The video of the crop circle, frozen on the screen of the laptop, smiled at Glenn, the slicing needles for teeth, the grin of death. The grin that devoured the fingers and toes of the infant this monster sliced from the womb of a pregnant woman. He reached up and shut the lid.

"You okay, Glenn?"

The voice shook him from a trance. He'd forgotten Maddy was still in his office, still in the hard wooden chair across from his desk, her forehead pinched.

"That face. That goddammed smiley face with the teeth." He rubbed a calloused hand across his chin. "It's been at the scene of six murders in Buchanan County. Six murders we haven't come close to solving."

Maddy squinted, her head cocked to one side. "But Sheriff. Elvin Miller's in prison down in Cameron for murdering his wife, and Sheriff Donally and his girlfriend, uh—"

"Emily."

She nodded. "Yeah, Emily. That was Robert Garrett, and Carrie McMasters is still in the Fulton State Hospital. That only leaves—"

Glenn held up a hand and his deputy stopped.

"From our investigation, nobody who knew Carrie McMasters believes she could kill her husband. They held hands when they went to Walmart, for Christ's sake. She still claims she doesn't remember what happened before she woke sitting straight up in her kitchen chair covered in blood."

"That doesn't—" Maddy began. Glenn talked over her.

"And Boyd was convinced Elvin had nothing to do with his wife's murder. If Boyd believed it, that's good enough for me." He started counting off the rest on his fingers. "Now, Boyd and Emily died in Robert Garrett's house, but we don't know it was Garrett who pushed the button. When the house exploded, Garrett was at the children's hospital he'd rigged to explode facing off with Tommy Cavanaugh and . . ." Glenn's voice trailed away.

"He was with Jillian Robertson," Maddy finished for him.

"Jillian," he blew out in a whisper. He grabbed his sheriff's hat and rolled it in his hands. His eyes met Maddy's.

"The same names keep coming up. Bobby Garrett, Thomas Cavanaugh, Jillian Robertson, Boyd Donally. Those names are connected with a few of those deaths," he said. "Because of that, that damned smiley face, I'll bet dollars to dog nuts some of those names are connected to the rest."

"There's another one, Sheriff," Maddy said. "Rebekka Marshall."

He exhaled slowly. "Yeah. She's not connected to any of these."

"But she is," Maddy said, and Glenn's chin dropped. "I did some digging. Rebekka was at Sisters of Mercy the same time as Thomas Cavanaugh and—"

"Jillian Robertson," he finished for her. Glenn rose from his chair, the old wood protesting.

She slipped her hat over her close-cropped hair. "Where are we going, Sheriff?"

"We? Going?" he asked.

She stood at military attention, her army service not lost on Glenn. This kid was starting to impress the heck out of him.

"I'm part of this, sir. The Marshall boy is my case." She paused and swallowed, the subconscious reaction so tight Glenn worried she might choke on her emotions. "I also suspect Hiram's heifer might fit into all this somehow."

It was Glenn's turn to choke.

"My car, Deputy," he said, crushing his hat on his head. "I'll fill you in."

She took a step toward the office door before turning toward Glenn.

"We're going to find Thomas Cavanaugh," he said. "I don't think Tommy did anything, but he lived with the Robertson woman. I think he knows more than he's told us."

Silence paced the officers as they left the office.

[3]

Ālfheimr

Another vortex swirled into existence above the grassy plain, Jacob sitting on the long, flat rock, Jillian standing beside him, her thin, strong fingers on his shoulders. She made Jacob feel yuck.

"I'm hungry," he said. "I want chicken nuggets and ketchup."

"You talk too much." Her fingers gripped him tighter as a pair of legs slipped through the spinning hole in the universe. "Besides, ketchup is disgusting."

Ketchup's not 'skusting, he thought.

The legs hung in the sky for a moment, like the person falling into this world got stuck. They kicked, and a woman dropped into the thick grass, falling on her bottom. Jacob would have laughed, but the stupid fairy lady made him mad.

A deer, followed by a white-speckled fawn, strode onto the bluff. The doe ignored them and dipped its face to the young grass, tearing out a mouthful. It chewed like Jacob didn't just create it out of nothing.

Another human-looking person fell from another hole in the air. When the man stood, he looked up the hill and saw them—then screamed.

"There are still more," she said, glaring at the man. His body convulsed, the flesh from his arms and legs sucked into jerky, the skin on his face pulled tight into a Halloween costume. A second—just a second—later, a breeze kicked up and swept the man away in a cloud of dust. The fairy lady licked a couple of fingers like she'd just eaten barbecued ribs. "Find them. And after you do, you can go home and eat your nasty chicken nuggets and ketchup."

Jacob closed his eyes and concentrated on people who felt like the awful fairy lady until he found one. His arms rose over his head, little pudgy fingers reaching into nothingness until he grabbed the fairy person, and he pulled.

[4]

The Starlight Motel stretched its sagging roof across half a crumbling city block about four miles from the Delores Hadley Community Center. Thomas had never wanted to see this part of St. Joe again. Jillian had once lived in this meth-infested hole, using it as some kind of base of operations as she hunted for him. The thought tied his stomach in knots. Rodney had lived in this place when Jillian dropped them back into his world from the hellscape of her own.

Did that really happen? he wondered, but knew it had. If it hadn't, how was he here?

The truck idled in park across the street as he stared at the motel. The crappy motel, once with gang graffiti, rusted cars without tires, and a dead dog rotting in green muck at the bottom of the small concrete swimming pool, now glowed with light, the graffiti painted over, the abandoned cars replaced with clean, polished vehicles with inflated tires, and people; people laughed and splashed in the pool.

Thomas didn't believe what he saw. The motel appeared new. The lighted sign near the manager's office—all the bulbs working—read, "No Vacancy."

He shifted into drive and pulled onto the asphalt of the freshly paved lot, parking next to a silver Kia Soul with a Northwest Missouri State University sticker in the rear window. Children's laughter rose amid splashes from the pool. Thomas stepped from the truck, and a beach ball rolled toward him.

"Hey," a high, light voice called from the pool.

Thomas bent and picked up the ball, and punched it back underhand volleyball-style toward the pool before turning to approach the motel, followed by a few scattered thank-yous.

The lights of the rooms were off, except one. Thomas couldn't see the number from his spot in the parking lot, but the chill that ran through him guaranteed it was Room 201. That was Rodney's room, Jillian's room. Thomas and Jillian had fallen through the ceiling, crashing among moldy carpet and splintered furniture. He'd snapped the room's only resident's arm with a table leg. The scent of death crawled into his nostrils, and Thomas shook his head. The smell had gone, but had he really smelled it, or was it a memory?

The air he sucked into his lungs was somehow hotter than the evening as he mounted the freshly painted metal stairs, until he exhaled. His breath blew out cold; it came in a fog.

The cheap 201 numbers on the door shone as if recently polished. Thomas's hand shook as he made a fist and rapped once, twice, three times. This was wrong. No one would spend the kind of money it would take to revive this crumbled memory. They'd tear it down.

He flinched at a child's laugh from the pool.

The door cracked open, snapping at the end of the chain. One eye from a bearded face glared at him, the man's identity clouded in silhouette from the lit desk lamp behind him.

"Thomas Cavanaugh," the man said. "You once broke my arm."

Thomas exhaled; the hiss came out slowly. "Yeah," he said. More laughter and splashing from the families below him came from the forecourt. "I'm really sorry about that, Rodney, but we need to talk about Jacob Jenkins. May I come in?"

Rodney shut the door, the chain rattling as it was pulled back through the rail of cheap metal that gave people a false sense of safety.

Then the door swung wide. Thomas stuffed his hands in his jeans pockets and stepped inside, his right hand wrapped around his pocket knife.

The bullet holes that once decorated the thin walls and the water stains dotting the ceiling were gone, the holes patched and everything painted. Freshly vacuumed carpet stretched from wall to wall, the bed made with a clean comforter. The 1970s paintings of sailing ships were replaced by reproductions of Munch paintings. *The Scream* on the far wall was ominous.

"What happened?" Thomas asked, taking in Rodney. The emaciated, greasy-haired, wild-eyed meth head stood straight, his hair washed, cut, and combed, his beard trimmed, his clothes clean, and his eyes clear and bright.

"I stopped ingesting methamphetamines," he said simply. Slight tremors still shook him; meth had left its mark.

He motioned Thomas away from the door, and Thomas moved. The motel door cutting off the outside world didn't bother him as much as he'd thought it would when he approached the motel.

"You told Elizabeth the nurse about Jacob Jenkins," Thomas said, then sniffed. The time Thomas ran from this room, it reeked of the chemicals Rodney used to cook his drugs. Now it smelled of cinnamon, which Thomas suspected came from a lit candle on the kitchenette table. "I know Jacob. I—I'm friends with his mother."

A twitch jerked Rodney's head to one side. "More than friends," he said.

More? This flat statement caught Thomas like a cross-check, and no referee to blow a whistle. Yeah, maybe.

Thomas cleared his throat. "So, you're, uh. You're a fairy like Jillian?"

Rodney's air of indifference shifted as he gritted what was left of his teeth. "I am *álfr*, yes, but not like her. I came here to escape Jillian." His gaze shifted from Thomas's. "But she found me."

"I'm here because—" Thomas's hand involuntarily squeezed the knife handle tighter. "Because Jillian kidnapped Jacob." A plea not absent from his voice. "Elizabeth said he talks to you. How? Where? I need to find him."

Rodney's unblinking eyes stared into Thomas's. "He is in Ālfheimr with the beast you call Jillian. He is safe, but I am not. You are not." He spread his arms wide, and the sudden movement sent Thomas back a step. "This place, the place the beast's *móðir* failed to destroy, is her next conquest."

"*Móðir?*"

"Her mother."

Mother? His stomach crawled.

"The dark creature at the hospital you destroyed with your talisman. You remember her." It wasn't a question. The monster that looked like his father with a too-wide mouth and teeth of a T. rex. It tried to kill him. A sudden weakness in Thomas's knees sent him back three steps until he stopped against a table, newer and sturdier than the one that once collapsed beneath him.

"That thing? Dauðr? The death monster with the teeth was Jillian's *mother?*"

Rodney's forehead pinched as he considered Thomas's words. "Yes, of course. You didn't know?" Thomas didn't move, couldn't move. "No, of course you didn't. Did your Jillian tell you Dauðr was the destroyer of worlds?"

Thomas's head involuntarily nodded.

"You may not realize it, but that's why you're really here," he said. "You want Jacob Jenkins back, but you want to stop Jillian." Rodney walked to Thomas, standing inches from him. The man who once pointed a gun at him took Thomas's hands in his own. "Jacob Jenkins is dangerous. Dauðr's soul is inside him; he is a demon capable of much darkness. But the beast is what will ignite it. Save him, Thomas Cavanaugh. Take the boy from Jillian, and you save him, save this place."

A memory, scant and dark, dredged itself from the depths of that night, the night he'd killed Dauðr. The thing crumbled to ash and dropped him to the frozen pavement, snow and flakes of Dauðr fell to the ground around him, and a tornado of souls of people slaughtered in the hospital explosion dissipated into the night. Flashing lights and sirens approached, but Jillian ignored them, ignoring Marguerite as she searched the ashes of the monster for something, screaming, "Where is it?"

Fear shivered through his frame; he'd forgotten that moment. Dear God, what is she?

[5]

The small farmhouse sat dark when Glenn pulled into the yard. He couldn't count the number of times he'd parked there for work, to listen to Royals games on the radio with Boyd, or for a Sunday-afternoon barbecue. An alien shadow seemed to hang over the home in the waning evening light, the windows dark and lifeless.

"Nobody's home," Maddy said, holding a cup of convenience-store coffee in both hands. She took off the lid and blew over the top.

Jillian's car sat exactly where the Sherman's Towing truck left it. Glenn gave Thomas instructions not to drive it or even open the door. That car was still connected to a kidnapping.

"Don't ever assume, Deputy," Glenn said. "We deal in facts, not conjecture."

She took a sip before answering. "Do you want me to go up and knock on the door?"

"Why?" he asked, a grin drifting across his lips, then disappearing "Nobody's home."

"Then why did you—" Maddy shook her head and took a sip from the cup. "What do we do? Wait here until someone shows up?"

The sheriff nodded and leaned the driver's seat back, tipping his hat over his eyes.

"Yep. Wake me when they do."

[6]

A chill wind swept through the motel room; it smelled of red licorice. Thomas braced himself against the table.

"What's happening?" Terror trembled in his voice.

"Something's coming," Rodney said, his voice placid.

Thomas stepped forward and pulled his hands from his pockets, grabbing Rodney's slim shoulders. "What's coming?"

"Ālfheimr. It is coming to take me home." Rodney pulled himself from Thomas's grip with a slight shove, as if Thomas's strong hands were as weak as a child's.

The increasing cold wind pulled a note from beneath a magnet on Rodney's mini-fridge door and twirled it around the room. Thomas fell against the tightly made bed; the wind grew stronger, erupting into a frigid gale, shooting through the motel room, knocking paintings from the walls.

The Scream crashed into a lamp, sending both to the floor. Rodney opened his mouth to speak when a perfectly circular hole appeared in the carpeted floor beneath him and two small hands reached through it. Thomas stood, holding on to the bed's headboard as Rodney reached for the door to run, to escape this horror, when the child's hands grabbed Rodney's pants legs and dragged him into a whirlpool of darkness.

Thomas's scream ripped through the night.

[7]
Ālfheimr

The stupid man fell from the stupid purple whirlpool in the sky and landed in the stupid grass. A giggle burst from the stupid fairy lady as she sat on the stupid rock next to Jacob and watched the stupid man roll down the stupid hill.

"Can you feel anyone else, Jakie?" she asked.

A burst of wind shot out of Jacob as he forced a cartoon sigh. He'd asked her not to call him that.

"No," he said, then stuck out his tongue at her; her eyes were still on the man, who'd by now reached the bottom of the slope and stood, brushing himself off. "I brought 'em all here to this dumb place."

"Good." She rose and took his hand in hers, pulling Jacob to his feet. The fairy lady then knelt before him, her hands softly gripping his arms. "I have to talk to this one," she said, "to teach him a lesson. But when I'm done, I promise I'll take you home. You'll be knees-deep in tater tots and fried chicken things before you know it."

The red-haired elf-person grinned at him, the faint smile mean, like a bully's. Her hand shimmered as it grew into a sword, the skin now shiny and sharp as metal. The point touched the center of Jacob's chest; pressure pushed him a step backward.

"Ow," he said. Jacob's eyebrows pinched as she poked him. He wished he hadn't come with the fairy lady at all.

Her sword shrank back into a hand, and she rested her fists on her hips. The spot on his chest was unharmed; the hole her blade made in his shirt knitted itself back together.

"You're stronger than I thought," she said. "No matter. You've served me. I'll come for you when *I'm* strong enough."

Jacob squinted. "How do you get strong?"

An easy grin crossed her face, the kind of grin he felt he shouldn't like to see on a grown-up.

"Just like you, baby. I feed," she said. "Watch."

The fairy lady took a step onto the slope but didn't fall like the man she'd made Jacob grab. She glided down the hill until she reached the bearded man. He flinched as he saw her approach, his head darting around to find a place to run, but there was nowhere. The man screamed when the fairy lady spoke to him, then his body withered and blew away; his empty clothes fell to the ground.

Jacob looked away. He was getting away from the mean fairy lady. He was going home.

[8]

Rodney disappeared and the freezing wind died; the few things blown loose in his clean room dropped silently onto the carpet. Thomas didn't release his grip on the headboard, not yet. His heart pounded; his eyes were wide.

"What just happened?" he whispered.

Seconds passed, then minutes, before Thomas dropped back onto the bed.

The hole in the floor was gone, closed, shutting off this world from the next. Heaven? Hell? What Thomas remembered of it, it was hell. The footboard tipped backward and fell as the bed legs collapsed, spilling Thomas onto the floor; the tight, clean carpet gone. The maroon shag now beneath him was encrusted with dried human waste and blood.

What?

A chunk of plaster ceiling crashed down beside him. Thomas rolled to one side and pushed himself to his feet. The door fell in, and the smell of old smoke permeated the room.

Run, Thomas, he told himself. *Run.*

He crossed the room in seconds and shot onto the crumbling mezzanine, the parking lot below dotted with garbage; the shiny, new cars were gone, two rusty burned-out wrecks in their place. No one played in the pool, the filthy concrete basin now just an empty cistern.

The mezzanine guardrail in front of Room 201 tipped over and fell into the parking lot; the rest of the rail followed, peeling off like a length of old tape.

"Shit."

Thomas ran for the stairs. Chunks of crumbling concrete dropped as he made the landing and pounded down the steps to the asphalt parking lot; dead weeds jutted from the cracks. He skidded to a stop at his pickup and turned back toward the motel as his lungs fought to catch a breath.

Fire had raged inside that structure, but not recently. Black, jagged support columns pointed toward the sky; most of the mezzanine collapsed along with the second floor. Then it was gone. All of it. The site of the Starlight Motel was empty—the ruins, the pool, the cars were now a plain of cracked concrete, the building long gone.

Thomas fell back into the door of his pickup, the world around him suddenly soft, suspect, like reality might crumble beneath his feet.

"What the hell just happened?" he wheezed, his legs shaking.

But he knew. Somewhere deep in the pit of memories, he knew. The motel had been an illusion—Rodney's illusion. Thomas wondered if he was the only person who could see it. As he leaned on his truck facing the empty lot, the lack of emergency-vehicle sirens approaching told him he was.

His hand, weak and unsure, opened the pickup door. He slid onto the bench seat and leaned forward over the steering wheel, staring at the blank spot where a ruined motel had disintegrated beneath him.

He didn't know how long he sat there until his mobile phone rang. The caller ID read "Marguerite." He picked it up and slid his finger across the screen.

"Hello?" he said.

"It's Jakie!" Marguerite screamed into his ear. "He's home."

CHAPTER NINE

WARM SUMMER AIR flowed through the open windows of the pick-up's cabin; a Burger King hamburger wrapper was caught in the cross breeze and lifted from the floor, landing on the bench seat before the wind whipped it out the window. The center dashes on the rural high-way disappeared behind Thomas's truck, the ten-foot-long stripes noth-ing more than dots. With the destruction of the Starlight Motel still ripping at his brain, Marguerite had called him, ecstatic.

She hadn't called Glenn. A lump formed in Thomas's throat. No. She didn't call the law. He was the first one she'd told.

Thomas flipped on the indicator and slowed, pulling onto a gravel road that led to Marguerite's house. The truck ground to a halt, the tires throwing gravel as the brakes locked. He slowly sucked in air, try-ing to calm his hammering heart, then scrolled through his phone to find Glenn's number. He put the call on speaker.

One ring. Two.

"Heh—hello." It was Glenn's voice, but thick, slow.

"Glenn?" Thomas asked, pulling his foot off the brake and easing down on the accelerator, trying to keep his urgency from the sheriff's ears. "That you?"

Glenn coughed and, what was that? A slurp?

"Did I wake you up?"

"No, no," the sheriff said, coughing before continuing. "I was looking for you, Thomas. I'm at your house. Where are you?"

My house?

"I'm heading toward Marguerite's," he said, holding the phone close to his mouth. Why are you at my house? "Jacob's back."

The line went silent. Thomas's eyes shot to his phone for only a second. He had four bars.

"Glenn?"

Someone spoke in the background, a woman's voice asking what was happening.

"Jacob Jenkins is *home?*" Glenn asked, each syllable slow and exact. "Did Margie tell you this?"

Thomas's teeth clenched.

"No, Glenn. I'm punking the fucking *sheriff*." His hand squeezed the phone tight. "Of course Marguerite told me. Why else would I say this?"

The line fell quiet again.

"Come on, Glenn."

"Yeah." The tight roar of the sheriff's cruiser came to life as background noise. "Right. Of course. Sorry. We're on our way."

He disconnected. Thomas dropped his mobile onto the dusty seat and punched the accelerator, sending the truck tearing down the gravel road toward the Jenkinses' house. The back end of the pickup fishtailed from ditch-to-ditch until he got it under control. Something was wrong—a Rodney-level of wrong. He never thought he'd see Jacob again, but here he was.

[2]

Gramma's house was dark. Jacob sat at the kitchen table, shadows hanging in the corners of the room. The light fixture above the table had three bulbs, but only one of them worked. Momma sat opposite him, drinking her third glass of Momma Juice. Her hand shook and the pale-yellow liquid tried to splash over the side, but she'd drunk too much of it for that. He picked up a chicken finger and dipped it in the pool of ketchup Momma squirted on his plate over Elmo's face. She said she didn't buy chicken nuggets anymore because Jacob had been gone so long.

"Silly," he'd said. "The mean fairy lady took me just yesterday."

Momma didn't say much after that.

"I wanna see Gramma," he said through a mouthful of chicken.

Momma set her glass on the table, and her hands fell to her lap.

"Gramma's really sick," she said, her voice sad and scared at the same time. "She sleeps a lot. It's probably best you see her in the morning."

No. No, no, no.

Gramma was dumb, but not like that fairy lady with the weird name. The fairy lady. She was mean, the kind of mean that wanted to do bad things for no reason. For no reason to people who didn't do anything to her. He knew Thomas, the man Momma liked, and the bad fairy lady wanted to hurt Thomas. Jacob could feel it deep in his tummy.

"I can fix her." Jacob's eyes pinched shut while he grabbed another chicken strip and dipped it in the center of the ketchup mess. Gramma's okay, but the fairy doesn't want Gramma. "She's all better now, and she wants a sandwich."

Momma lifted her glass and drained it.

"How do you know that, honey?" she asked, standing and moving backward toward the refrigerator, her eyes never leaving him.

Jacob took a bite, then shrugged. "Just do. You can go check if you want."

The base of the glass clicked against the counter after Momma filled it from the box in the fridge and set it down.

"She has cancer, Jakie." Momma lifted the glass and drank it all before opening the door and filling it again. "Cancer's bad, baby. She's not going to stop being sick."

No, Momma.

"The ball growing in her lungs made her sick. It sent little fingers all over the place," he said. "But if the ball and all the fingers go away, she won't be sick no more."

"But—" Momma started.

Too late.

A thunk landed somewhere past the living room, followed by a muffled word Jacob knew he wasn't supposed to say, but Gramma could. Momma took a step toward the door to the living room, then moved back to the counter to grab her drink.

"Margie?" came from deep in the house.

The glass slid from Momma's hand and crashed onto the floor; slivers scattered everywhere. Jacob knew his mother would worry about that later, but she didn't need to. As with Gramma's iced-tea glass, the shards skittered across the floor back toward each other, the splinters and chips melding into larger fragments until the glass stood on the floor next to the cabinet, filled with the pale Momma Juice.

His mother looked at him, eyes as wide as a funny drawing.

"Jakie," she said, the sound soft, like the word didn't want him to hear it. But Jacob did. He heard everything. "Honey, did you do that?"

He smiled, but it faded when Momma didn't seem happy. She should be. She didn't have to clean up the mess she made.

Before he answered, a shadowed figure stood in the doorway to the kitchen.

"I'm so damn hungry."

Jacob's mom turned toward those words and screamed. Gramma stepped backward before shuffling into the room, the light casting deep shadows on her hollow eyes. She reached the table and sat in a wooden chair that had seen too many meals.

"Mom?" Jacob's mother whispered.

"She's all better," Jacob said. "But she really wants a sandwich. I told you. Ham and cheese with mustard."

"Ham and cheese?"

Jacob cleared his throat. "With mustard."

Old, wrinkly hands with blue spiderweb veins grabbed Jacob's small ones. Gramma's hands were dry and cold.

"Jakie?" Gramma said; tears ran down her cheeks. "Jakie, you came home."

Why did she say that too? he wondered. These people are dumbest dummies. "I was only gone one day."

The doorbell rang.

A whoosh came from between Jacob's lips. He just got home and was already tired.

"It's Thomas. The fairy lady hates him," Jacob said flatly. "She wants to kill him, but she can't because Thomas is a good guy, like Freddie, and she's just the bad guy in a mask."

Momma's eyes grew narrow. "Freddie? From *Scooby-Doo?*"

Jacob nodded, then stopped.

"The sheriff man is coming," he said. "Would you fix Gramma a sandwich? She's super hungry."

[3]

Thomas launched himself from the pickup the moment he killed the engine.

The door to the kitchen opened at the first knock, the smell of wine hitting Thomas before the chill of the air-conditioning. Fear drew Marguerite's soft, pretty features gaunt. My God. He pulled open the screen door and stepped in. She wrapped her arms around his neck and buried her face in his shoulder.

"Jacob?" he asked.

"Hello, Thomas," the four-year-old boy said from the kitchen table in a voice too old for him, ketchup smeared at the corners of his mouth. Marguerite's mom sat at the table with him, eating a sandwich, her normally pallid skin full of color.

Yesterday all she could stomach was Ensure. Her doctor said she'd be dead in a week, but now? She looked like she'd just gotten over the flu.

Cold gripped Thomas in its fist and squeezed.

"That's not possible," he whispered, stroking Marguerite's hair. "He hasn't aged."

She pulled back and looked up at him, her eyes swollen with tears. "Jakie said 'the fairy lady' took him away yesterday."

Yesterday? "Time," Jillian once told him in a voice he didn't quite remember. "Time moves much faster here than it does in Álfheimr."

"She did," Thomas said, pulling Marguerite's arms from around his neck and sliding his hand into hers. "Jake?"

The little boy ignored Thomas. "Momma," he said. "Can I have a soda? And Gramma wants a milkshake." His gaze latched on to Thomas's like it was armed with hooks.

"Jake," Thomas said again. The little boy smiled, his eyes wide and dark. "The fairy lady. Did she have red hair?"

Jacob thought a moment before responding. "No, not really red. It was kinda orange-y."

Thomas attempted to smile but didn't think it was convincing at all. "Of course. Right. That's what I meant. Orange-y." He stepped closer to the table, releasing Marguerite's hand, and squatted, eye level to Jacob. "Did this fairy lady take you someplace you'd never been before?"

The boy nodded. "Yes. It was hot and dirty. There was dust and rocks and junk everywhere. But I fixed it."

Fixed it?

"Did she call this place by a funny name?" Thomas asked.

Jacob nodded again, his black, straight bangs falling over his right eye. At that moment, Thomas thought he looked just like his father—the St. Joe Angel of Death.

"Alf something."

It was Thomas's turn to nod. "Ālfheimr," he said, and turned to Marguerite. "Time moves differently there. He's right. He was only gone a day. One day."

Thomas's mobile phone vibrated in his pocket. He pulled it out. The caller ID read "Glenn."

[4]

Headlights cut through the country night; the stars gleamed bright, a lack of city lights allowing them to sparkle like crystals. A coyote dashed in front of the sheriff's car from the cornfield on one side of the gravel road and disappeared into the cornfield on the other. Glenn never slowed the vehicle.

"Are we close?" Maddy asked. She'd finished the coffee a few miles back, now content to dig furrows into the foam cup with her thumbnail.

Glenn nodded. "About fifteen minutes. It's just up—" Dear God. He threw his shoulders back into the seat as he slammed both feet onto the brake pedal, the car scattering gravel as it skidded to a halt.

"Whoa," Maddy hissed, the empty cup crushed in her hands. "What was that?"

The sheriff raised his right hand and pointed out the window at a figure standing in the roadway, the dust churned up by the car's tires floating around the figure in a fog. As the dust dissipated, the headlights shone their white light onto a girl, maybe ten years old. She stood in the middle of the road in a white dress, chewing on her index finger.

I almost killed the kid.

"Go see about her," Glenn finally said, the sentence shaky, his breath out of reach.

Maddy's door flew open and she jumped out. Glenn's door clicked and he unfolded himself from the seat, trying to find his wind. Maddy had already knelt by the little girl by the time he made it around the big car.

"Are you all right, sweetheart?" Maddy asked.

The girl pulled her finger from her mouth and nodded, her red hair bobbing in a ponytail. Glenn squatted next to Maddy and tried his best to smile. He hoped he succeeded.

"Hey, kiddo," he said in the same voice he used on his niece when she was upset. His head swam. Dakota. I could have run over Dakota. "Whatcha doing out here all alone in the dark? Are your parents around?"

The ponytail danced as she shook her head.

"Is anyone out here with you?" he asked.

"No, sir."

"Hey, honey," Maddy said, slowly reaching out a hand. The little girl took it without hesitation. "We're here to help you. Can you tell us your name?"

The girl put her dirty index finger back into her mouth.

"No," she mumbled through the digit.

"Your parents' names?" Maddy continued. "Where you live?"

Glenn stood and rested against the grill, trying to will strength back into his knees. There was something wrong here. A girl this young out in the boonies in the dark. There weren't many houses close enough for her to have wandered from.

"What can you tell us, honey?" he asked.

The child stepped toward Glenn and held her hands toward him. He knew that body language from Dakota, so he lifted her; she leaned into his shoulder. A warmth spread through his chest. He had to protect this child.

"I don't remember anything," she said. "I just wanna go someplace safe."

"Okay, kiddo," he said, nodding to Maddy, who now stood beside him. "Deputy Maddy and I will take you somewhere safe where people will feed you and let you take a bath, and a doctor will see you're just fine, then they'll put you to bed. That sound good?"

He knew the events wouldn't be in that order; the doctor would have to check her out first just in case sh—he choked back the thought. Human beings could be the worst kind of people.

She wrapped her arms around his neck and squeezed. "Yes, sir," she said.

The girl and Maddy took the backseat. After Glenn shut his door he turned toward them and handed his mobile phone to Maddy. "You'd better call Tommy and tell him we're going to be late."

She punched a few buttons and held the phone to her ear as the air began to crackle; frost spread across the windows, and the little girl laughed.

[5]

Marguerite poured herself another glass of wine and stumbled slightly as she walked back to her chair. She sat next to Thomas and grabbed his hand under the kitchen table; the hand holding the glass never let go, the fear radiating from her as solid as the floor. Linda sat across the table holding Jacob on her lap. Although color had returned to her face, the dark half-moons beneath her eyes looked like she'd gotten into a fistfight.

Linda squeezed Jacob and kissed the top of his head.

"I have to lie back down. I'm tired, honey," she said, slipping him onto his feet. "I'm so happy you're home." She reached up to her eye to wipe away a tear. "Come to my room later, and if I'm still awake, I'll read you a book before bed."

"Okay, Gramma," he said before looking over the table at Marguerite. "Can I watch TV now, Momma?"

Her hand tightened on Thomas's until his knuckles nearly rubbed together.

"Sure, baby." She forced a smile. "Love you."

The boy picked the last bit of chicken from his plate and popped it into his mouth before following his grandmother's path into the living room. Seconds later, SpongeBob giggled from the television, and Marguerite collapsed into Thomas's arms, her sobs buried in his shoulder.

"I'm tired," she said, snorting. She wiped her face across his shirt before looking up at him. "And I'm scared. He's my baby, and I'm happy he's home, but he scares the shit out of me. The last two years have been, have been. Well, they've been peaceful."

He kissed her forehead, his lips meeting a sheen of oil. Today had exhausted her. Thomas's phone on the table vibrated. It was Glenn.

"Hey—"

"Did you talk to the cops?" Marguerite asked. Thomas nodded and she reached for the phone, engaging the call. "Hello," she said, holding it to her ear. "Yeah. Okay. I understand. We'll be here. Uh-huh. We—" She pulled the phone out to look at the screen. The call was still engaged. Her thumb hit Speaker. "Hello? Deputy? Hello?"

"Yeah, I-m . . . ere," Deputy Glines's voice said, the words choppy as the signal threatened to drop off.

"Are you almost here?" Thomas asked.

"Neg-tive," the deputy said, the sound popping in and out. "We found a little girl wandering in the dark. We'll be there after we get her to the shelter."

Little girl? The knot hit him like a fist in his stomach. He winced. That knot plagued him as a child whenever fear, the unknown, the dark, jumped into his life.

"What does she look like?" he asked.

"Red hair and a white dress," the deputy said.

No, no, no. Red hair and white dress. Red hair and white dress. He knew that little girl.

"What's her name?"

"Name? Let me check again," she said, presumably turning toward her. "Honey, will you tell me your name now?"

"Jillian."

The knot formed into a boulder.

"I know that voice," stumbled from Thomas. "I know that *voice*."

Marguerite squeezed him, hard. "What's wrong?"

"Get out of the car," he said, pulling Marguerite's hand with the phone toward his mouth. "Get out of the car!"

Marguerite pulled Thomas's face to hers. "Thomas?"

A woman screamed through the static.

"Maddy!" Glenn's voice screamed before the call died.

The hair follicles across Thomas's head squeezed tight; gooseflesh rose on his arms.

"What happened?" Marguerite asked.

"Call 9-1-1," Thomas said, pulling himself away from Marguerite and shooting to his feet; the chair clacked to the floor behind him. "Tell them to head this way and look for a red-haired girl in a white dress, but do not approach her."

Her slightly drunken eyes widened. "Is it her? The monster who took my baby?"

"I think so," Thomas said. "Glenn and his deputy are probably dead." He bolted for the door to the sound of SpongeBob's cackle on the living-room TV.

[6]

The engine died; Glenn slammed his fist into the patrol car steering wheel. In the backseat, Maddy turned toward the little girl.

"Honey, will you tell me your name now?" she asked.

"Jillian," the girl said.

Glenn tilted the rearview mirror toward the girl.

Solid black eyes framed by a pale face stabbed at him.

"What?" Maddy asked into the phone, then toward Glenn. "I've got three bars, Sheriff, but the call keeps cutting out. I can't understand what he's saying."

"Is that Thomas? I know Thomas." Jillian giggled. "I used to be his girlfriend."

Glenn turned to face the child; the words she said were wrong.

"You were what?" he asked, but other words never made it out.

What sat next to his deputy looked like a ten-year-old girl, except for her mouth; it stretched across her face in a smile too wide for her lips. The teeth showing were a monster's. Glenn's crotch grew warm as urine soaked his pants. This was the face. The face in the pictures. The face painted in blood at the scene of murders all around Buchanan County. The face that had haunted Boyd. The face that now haunted *him*.

"Dear God," he whimpered.

Maddy screamed, and the girl lunged for her; the impossible maw gaped open, saliva strings dripping from those teeth as they plunged into the deputy's neck. Blood from her severed jugular splattered across Glenn's face, the hot, sticky liquid a stain that would never leave.

"Maddy!"

The monster jerked its face away from Maddy's neck, and a great chunk of dripping flesh ripped with it, flinging blood across the back of the seat. Glenn screamed as the thing chewed once, twice, then swallowed. A lump too wide for the neck slid down, just like a snake. The smile never faltered. Maddy's lifeless body slumped in the seat when the beast in a girl's body released her, the white dress smeared in blood.

"I'm the one who took Jacob Jenkins," it said, blood dripping from its delicate, pointed chin. "He's fine, you know? As fine as a demon can be." It wiped a finger across its face, red glistening on the tip. The monster sucked the blood from its finger. "Now, what does sheriff taste like?"

It launched its small blood-streaked body into the front seat.

Glenn's vehicle sat sideways in the road as Thomas's pickup skidded across the gravel and stopped about twenty feet away. The driver's-side door of the patrol car hung open; the dome light lit the interior, the windows painted red. Thomas opened his truck door and slid out, gravel dust floating around him. Nothing moved in the patrol car, but he knew that didn't mean a thing.

"Glenn?" he said, not loud enough to be heard over the car's engine. He tried again, "Glenn?"

Still no answer.

Gravel crunched under his boots as his steps took him slowly toward the car. The only weapon he had on him was his pocket knife. He left it in his pocket; it wouldn't do any good.

"Glenn? You there?"

Thomas approached the driver's door, the radio shouting.

"Sheriff. Sheriff? Glenn? Damn it, answer me."

Stepping around the door, Thomas walked into a horror movie. Blood dripped from the rearview mirror, the seat covered in a red sheet of it. A bloody handprint on the dash told him what he already knew; the child who wasn't a child was here. She was back. *It* was back.

"Glenn," the dispatcher shouted.

Thomas leaned into the car, and the blood's sharp, warm tang nearly pulled up his lunch. Careful not to touch the interior, he took the mic from its place on the dash and lifted it to his mouth.

"This isn't Glenn," he said. "This is Thomas Cavanaugh, the late Sheriff Boyd Donally's nephew."

The speaker hissed before the voice came back.

"Yeah, hey, Thomas. This is Aaron at the station," he said, his voice on a knife's edge. "Where's Glenn?"

Thomas pulled his head from inside the car, the summer heat making the stench uncomfortable. When he did, Maddy's lifeless eyes caught his, her head hanging at an odd angle, her throat chewed through. His vision dimmed and he dropped, rocks stabbing his knees. Thomas vomited onto the gravel.

"Thomas?" Aaron asked.

More puke spewed out, bouncing off the uneven road surface and splattering his hands.

"Hey, Thomas. Come back."

He wiped the back of his hand over his mouth and pressed the side of the mic.

"Shit, Aaron." He stopped to cough. "Aaron, goddamn. Get somebody out here."

"Slow down," the deputy said in his 9-1-1 dispatcher voice. "What's the emergency?"

"The deputy with Glenn." He swallowed, forcing more puke to stay down. "She's dead."

The radio went silent.

"Aaron?" Thomas asked.

"Maddy's dead?" His words like a little lost boy's. "I had lunch with her today at Clem's."

"Aaron, stay with me." Thomas hocked and spat onto the vomit-soaked gravel. "The car's out on County Road 227, about two miles from Marguerite Jenkins's place."

"Jenkins?" Aaron wasn't making connections.

"Yes, Jenkins. The woman whose little boy was kidnapped by Jillian Robertson."

Seconds ticked past before Aaron came back. This time more urgency filled his voice.

"I know where that is. Have you seen Glenn?"

"No," Thomas said, lifting his gaze from the rocks. The different angle revealed a set of small, bloody footprints. "But I know where he went, and the person who killed the deputy followed him."

Aaron's response was swift, loud.

"Thomas Cavanaugh. Remain at the car. Do not—I repeat—*do not* follow them."

Thomas pulled the mobile phone from his pocket and engaged the flashlight. The white beam cut through the darkness, lighting the bloody prints that went directly into the corn. Thomas stood straight and clicked the mic button.

"Sorry, Aaron. Glenn needs help."

He dropped the mic, the coiled chord snapping it back into the bloody cab. Thomas leaned inside and yanked the blood-splattered shotgun from the gun mount between the bucket seats, Aaron shouting at him to stop.

Clouds masked the crescent moon that hung low in the night sky as Thomas stopped at the ditch, his phone lighting the path made in the dirt by a man's boots, followed by a child's bare feet. Those feet grew to adult size, like they did that day in his house.

That terrible, terrible day.

Thomas clicked the safety off on the shotgun and followed the footprints into the field.

[8]

The slamming door told Jacob Thomas had gone; Momma sat at the kitchen table, her sobs carrying into the living room. SpongeBob interrupted Squidward's clarinet practice and Squidward got mad. SpongeBob did this all the time, Jacob knew. If it made Squidward so mad, why didn't Squidward just move?

He pushed himself off the couch and tiptoed, like a sneaky sneaker, and peeked into the kitchen. Momma's tears pulled at a place inside he'd never felt before, a place where seeing his mother cry made him want to cry too.

She looked up at him and tried to smile.

"Momma?" he asked, a tear running down his cheek.

Jacob scurried to his mother and held his arms to her. "Up," he said, like he had when he was tiny.

She wiped her nose on her shirtsleeve and lifted him onto her lap. Jacob threw his arms around her neck, nuzzling close to her ear.

"What's wrong, Momma?"

Then she did something she hadn't done in so long Jacob couldn't remember. She wrapped her arms around him and squeezed. Warmth grew inside.

"Something bad's happening, baby," she said, wiping her nose again, this time on his shoulder. "My friend Glenn might be hurt, and Thomas, oh, Thomas." She paused and took a deep breath. "You know Mommy likes Thomas, don't you baby?"

He nodded.

"I think Thomas might get hurt too."

"By the bad fairy lady who took me?" he asked. He knew her answer would be yes, but sometimes grown-up people were kinda dumb.

She nodded. "Yes, baby."

He thought for a moment, reaching out his mind like he did sometimes when he was lonely. He could see Thomas and the sheriff-man and the fairy lady; she was pretending to be somebody else because she was scared. Jacob could feel it.

"Thomas won't let her hurt him," he said, holding her tighter. Thoughts from the bad fairy lady snuck into his mind; she didn't think she could hurt Thomas all by herself. She needed somebody else to do it for her. But she could eat the sheriff man. "She *can't* hurt him."

Momma pulled Jacob away from her; he could stop her, but he knew she just wanted to look at him.

"What do you mean, 'she can't hurt him'?"

Jacob's shoulders went up and down, too theatrical for a real shrug.

"I dunno. Sometimes I hear things people think, that's all. Sometimes things that scare people, like that the fairy lady can't hurt Thomas. He can't do things like me and the fairy, but his insides are strong, like a wall. She could try to hurt him, but—" His voice trailed off, Jacob's still-four-year-old mind trying to find the words. "But I think it might bounce off. He's stronger than her magic. He just doesn't know it."

Momma's eyes widened. "Do you know where they are right now?"

He buried his face in her neck again. The hug she returned brought out emotions he'd never felt, and a smile spread over him. Momma loved him, she did. She really, really did. Then her question came back to Jacob.

"They're in a cornfield," he said, his young voice stern. "And the fairy lady wants to do something bad to Glenn."

[9]

The phone buzzed in Thomas's hand. He ignored it, keeping the flashlight on the path ahead of him, the bladed corn leaves scraping his pants and shirt, the season too early for them to grow over his head. Still, the quiet field—lit by only his phone and a sliver of moon—scared the hell out of him. The corn always did.

A gunshot echoed through the night. Thomas ran toward it.

About forty yards—or fifty, or a hundred, Thomas couldn't tell—he pulled up to a black circle seared into the cornfield; Glenn sat on the scorched earth, sidearm in his hands. The light from Thomas's mobile phone showed a ragged shoulder injury. A figure stood over Glenn.

Thomas knew that shape. It was Glenn's deputy, Maddy. But it wasn't.

"Welcome to the party, pal," the deputy said.

No. He tried to sound calm as he sucked air into his heaving chest.

"You're quoting *Die Hard*, Jillian," he said. "Maddy didn't know that was my favorite movie. Actually, even if she did, she couldn't quote it, because she's dead."

The Maddy figure slipped thumbs into its belt and smiled at Thomas. White moonlight shone off that big smile of needle teeth.

"Oh, how I've missed you, baby," it said in Jillian's voice, taking a step away from Glenn and toward Thomas. "Do you think we can reconcile?"

The phone slipped into Thomas's shirt pocket and he gripped the shotgun with both hands.

"Not another step," he said, cocking the weapon, the click loud in the night. "Now stop the charade. If you're Jillian, show me Jillian."

The form shimmered like heat on a summer blacktop, and the figure of the former Buchanan County Sheriff's Deputy Maddy Glines melted into the trim body of Jillian Robertson, the red-haired beauty who'd tortured Thomas most of his life. Her smile normal, kind, a sharp contrast to the blood that soaked her white dress. She waved at him before vanishing.

"Jesus Christ," Glenn said, his voice weak, shaky.

Thomas hissed at him to shush, the stock of the shotgun still pressed hard into his shoulder.

Jillian popped back into the burned circle of corn, her chest level with the barrel of the shotgun, her smile again like a shark's.

"Didn't you miss me too?"

"No," Thomas said, and squeezed the trigger.

PART 3

CHAPTER TEN
January

[1]

A CHILL CRAWLED across the bedroom. The cold had somehow worked its way beneath the duvet and sheet, sending a shiver across the parts of Thomas not warmed by spooning with Marguerite, her soft snores the only sound in the shadow-draped bedroom. He snuggled his nose into her hair, sniffing in coconut before he pulled away and slid from beneath the covers.

Uncle Boyd's cardigan hung off the back of a desk chair; he slipped it on, the old heavy cotton sweater comforting in the night. Mom had cleaned out her brother's house after he was murdered in Bobby Garrett's bloody rampage and donated most of Uncle Boyd's clothing to Goodwill, but Thomas kept the cardigan. Uncle Boyd had worn the sweater whenever the family came over on a Sunday in the fall to watch football. The sweater hung loose on Thomas; Boyd was a much larger man. He grabbed his mobile phone and tiptoed into the hallway.

A sharp pain stabbed the ball of his foot. Thomas's hand found the wall and he skipped away from whatever the hell lurked on the floor. Pointing the phone's flashlight at the hardwood, he saw a yellow two-stud Lego in the clean path through the dust. A grin pulled at the corner of his mouth; this had happened so many times. This was what it was like being Dad, a job he never knew he'd enjoy so much. Jacob wasn't the same kid anymore. He was, well, normal. At least as normal as he could be. Normal enough his mother wasn't afraid of him anymore.

Thomas limped down the hall to the thermostat. Sixty-one degrees? He paused and listened; the furnace was running. It should be sixty-eight in the house.

The chill grew worse as a slight burst of frigid air slid over his face, sending a shiver down his frame. The breeze came from the end of the hall—Jacob's room.

Marguerite and Jacob had moved in with Thomas after Linda went on vacation in Florida to see her sister and decided to stay there. Palm trees and water were apparently hard to pass up. The boy had taken to Thomas, and it was like Jacob's history, his father, the things the boy could do, were gone. Jacob was suddenly just a boy—a boy who played with Legos. Thomas knew Jacob could cause the breeze but doubted he did. That didn't erase the fact that, as Thomas stood sock-feet in the hall, the chilling wind that brushed over him came from the boy's room.

Thomas rapped on Jacob's door frame, the old wooden farmhouse door half open. He didn't wait for the boy to reply before he pushed the door fully open to walk in.

Jacob lay on his stomach sideways across his bed, staring out the window, the old wooden frame level with the mattress. The window was open.

What the heck are you doing, kiddo?

"Hey, bud," Thomas said, stepping into the room and kneeling next to the bed, leaning his upper body across the mattress next to Jacob. "The window's open."

Jacob didn't move. "Yes," he said.

"You cold?" Thomas asked.

"Yes."

Thomas scratched his chin. "Well, you can put a stop to that, you know. You can just reach out and pull that window shut."

"I know," Jacob said, not moving.

Thomas shook his head. Times like this, he was sure he wasn't cut out to be a parent.

"You remember it's winter, right?" Clouds covered the world outside to the horizon, the half-moon somewhere in the sky, and the bulb on the outdoor pole lighting the backyard with enough of a glow to show the shadow of the small tool shed at the corner of the yard. The huge black silhouette of a far-off barn slumped in the distance, lying in ruins. "The weather man on KQ2 said the snow's supposed to get heavy."

"Mmm-hmm." Jacob's chin rested in his hands, and his eyes never left wherever he was staring.

In the past few years the kid had turned from a creepy messed-up little weirdo into a normal seven-year-old. Thomas did something he would have been too scared to do two years ago. He reached out and patted Jacob's back.

"Then what's going on, pal?"

Jacob didn't move; his tone of voice didn't change. He simply looked ahead.

"She's out there," he said.

She? The freezing wind kicked up, pushing into the room. A bite peppered with snow stung Thomas's face. Jacob didn't flinch. Thomas's stomach sank in an elevator drop; he knew the answer to his question before asking it.

"Who's out there?"

Jacob lay quiet, glaring into the yard.

"Jillian," he said, the word so soft Thomas barely heard it.

Thomas had shot her point-blank with a shotgun, and she shook it off, the gore-splattered rip across her chest stitching itself together as he watched; then she simply vanished. Adrenaline sent Thomas's heart racing. Sweat beaded across his forehead. The past two years had been quiet, so, so blissfully quiet. And now—

"Jillian?"

Jake nodded but didn't turn his head. "The fairy who took me to Álfheimr."

"Frickin' great," Thomas whispered as he scooted closer to the window. The yard stretched to a field where Thomas's neighbor Trent Parman usually rotated corn and soybeans, although he'd left it fallow the past couple of years. Droughts dried up most field crops in the area. The yard and field were white with snow, the shed dark in the shadows.

"Where is she?" Thomas asked.

Jacob nudged himself toward the window. "Out there. In the field. Don't you see her? She's dancing."

"Dancing?" Thomas squinted as he scooted to the window sill, pulling his whole focus toward the field. "I—hey, wait."

A shadow flickered in the snow, like a weak signal on an old cathode-ray-tube TV, the kind of signal you had to adjust the rabbit-ear antenna to bring in clearly. Thomas rose onto his elbows, and the slim black figure disappeared.

"Hey," he hissed. "Where'd she go?"

Jacob patted the bed, dropping his chin back to the mattress.

"Down here," he whispered. "If you want to see her, you have to know where she's hiding."

The words cut through Thomas as he sank into the bed, the sheet wet from snow that now fell with anger. The field lay empty, a white-blanketed expanse that stretched to County Road 478, but Thomas couldn't see that far, the darkness and the driving snow creating a thick, surreal scene that hid every shape, every old furrow in the field, every—

The cold, suddenly forgotten, painted Thomas's hair white with snow, his cheeks pink. His once girlfriend, his once lover, a fairy, an otherworldly monster that had nearly killed him, stood as a thin human shadow trembling at the line that separated Thomas's property from

Trent's before finally coming into focus. The Jillian shadow spun in a silent ballet, circling a spot in the backyard over and over.

Thomas scrambled off the bed, his breath coming fast and shallow. He couldn't catch it.

"The bad fairy lady. She's out there, Daddy Tom," he said. "She's come back."

Thomas leaned forward and slammed the window into place, locking it in two quick flicks of his thumbs. Jacob looked up at him, his eyes calm. Thomas reached out and wrapped his arms around the boy.

"You've got school tomorrow, bud," he said. "So you're sleeping with us tonight. Mom needs snuggles."

"Cool," Jacob said as Thomas lifted him from the bed, pausing for one last look out the bedroom window.

The shadow figure, tall and straight in the dead field, flickered again, then vanished into the increasing snow. Thomas wasn't sure, but it looked like the shadow waved.

[2]

Tiddlyink.

Tiddlyink.

Tiddlyink.

Elizabeth's mobile phone lit the bedside table, glowing over a few used Kleenex and a bottle of Tylenol, the light perfectly clear through the half-empty fifth of cheap vodka.

Tiddlyink.

She reached toward the phone with geriatric speed for fear of moving too soon, too fast, although her head wasn't as sore as she'd feared. A thumb swept across the screen, disabling the "fairy wings" alarm sound, as different from the "rotary dial" ringtone as she could find. She didn't want to ever confuse the two; Elizabeth could ignore a phone call, she couldn't afford to ignore any more alarms. She lifted the phone: 6:45 a.m. Elizabeth already knew it was 6:45 a.m. because that was the time she'd set her alarm for, but in the early morning before any sense had found its way into her head, she sometimes didn't believe it.

Swinging her feet to the floor as she sat up felt like sticking an egg beater into her stomach and giving it a whirl.

"Oh no," she whispered, freezing for a moment, or ten. Right now, time wasn't that important.

Brrring.

Brrring.

Goddamn it. The rotary dial rattled from her phone. Who the hell's calling me when—a stab of pain lanced her forehead and she winced —I'm hungover?

Brrring.

Brrring.

Brrring.

Her hand fumbled with the device until the name on caller ID was right side up and in focus. It read "Bruce." Great. Her boss, Bruce Webster, Buchanan County Health Clinic director, never called unless it was an emergency. And "emergency" always meant she had to drive her happy ass into work early.

The thumb she used to turn off the alarm turned on the call.

She took a steadying breath, the egg beater in her stomach spinning like it wanted to whip up meringue.

"Hello," she said, her mouth as dry as a box of saltines.

Bruce exhaled on the other side of the call.

"Elizabeth." He sounded relieved. "Oh, dear Lord, Elizabeth. I can always count on you."

Running a hand through her knotted hair, she knew he really couldn't.

"What's the matter, Bruce?" Her face rested in her right hand. The coolness of her palm should have helped with the pain, but didn't.

"I need you to come in early," he said, a tinge of panic in his voice. "It snowed overnight."

Seriously?

"It snowed? Bruce, it's winter. It snows all the time."

He cleared his throat.

Elizabeth pictured the antsy little man, smelling of Tommy Hilfiger for Men, clenching his butt on the wide leather office chair, chewing his nails.

"But people are panicking," he said. "They'll flood the hospitals, and the rest will come here."

She tried to massage her scalp, but the room started to spin.

"Because of some snow?" she asked. A thought burrowed through the poison residue in her brain, a thought that might drop her back into bed. "Is it dangerous to drive, Bruce? Because I'm not a good driver in the win—"

"Haven't you looked outside?" he snapped, his voice high.

Looked outside? Elizabeth thought. I haven't even looked outside my eyelids.

"What's outside?" The words hit hard, like the tiny fairy in her head wielded a hammer. She figured the positive assessment of her hangover was premature. "Why are people panicking?"

"What's outside?" Bruce shouted. "Elizabeth! The snow's black."

Her feet fumbled with the floor, but Elizabeth made it to the window; she shoved open the heavy curtains she'd purchased to keep out the morning sun, Bruce's call still in her left hand. The world outside her bedroom window—the neighbor's split-level, their privacy fence, Elizabeth's birdbath and shed, the backyard neighbor's lumpy, hole-riddled yard covered in dog turds—was black, night black, from the flat charcoal shelf of clouds to the pitch that covered every surface from the window sill to the end of the neighborhood.

"What's happened, Bruce?" she asked, her tongue like sandpaper.

He didn't immediately respond.

The rustle of paper and foil came across the call, telling Elizabeth he'd unwrapped a stick of wintergreen gum. Bruce chewed gum when he was nervous.

"I don't know," he said. "The CDC hasn't responded, but I do know we're public servants, and we have to be here when the people need us, and they do need us. They're going to think it's radiation, or a biological attack, or a meteor, or an alien invasion or something."

"Well, is it?"

The seconds ticked off. Elizabeth worried her boss may have had a stroke.

"I don't know, Elizabeth!" he screamed. "I need you here in case it's any of that shit."

She wiped the greasy film from her forehead with the sleeve of the scrubs she hadn't taken off the night before. Whatever Bruce's situation was, it was serious. The man was a real-life Ned Flanders. He never cursed.

"I'll be in ASAP," she said, and ended the call.

Staring out the window, obsidian flakes falling onto the black-coated landscape, she wondered if this is what hell looked like.

[3]

The scroll on the bottom of the morning newscast listed the area schools closed for the day; Thomas suspected it was all of them. He sipped his coffee and stared at the screen, the bass-voiced talking head turning the show over to one of those perky right-out-of-college reporters with a name like Alexa or Jennifer. She stood outside a redbrick building, a giant white ball atop the radar tower behind it like God was playing golf. The woman, maybe twenty-two and bundled in a KQ2 parka and a furry aviator cap, held the mic close, the wind blowing black snowflakes into her face. A thick layer of dark snow rested on the flat building and the ground behind her; the walkway to the front door, shoveled at one point, had started to fill in again, the jet snow covered in footprints.

The camera operator pulled back to reveal a woman in fogged glasses standing next to the reporter.

"Thanks, Cal," the reporter said. The text under her name read Makayla Creston. "I'm here with Laura Corrales, senior meteorologist at the NWS Forecast Office in Pleasant Hill, Missouri."

Laura pulled off her glasses and cleaned them with a mitten before sliding them back on.

"This bizarre phenomenon that has struck the four-state region from Butler, to Topeka, to Omaha and Des Moines, has canceled school, concerts—factories have shut down, and churches are filled with parishioners wondering if this is the end times," Makayla continued.

Cal chuckled, and the broadcast cut to him. He looked at the camera, his unnaturally white smile assuring viewers everything was fine.

"It surely can't be that bad," he said. "*We* came to work."

Makayla laughed at Cal's joke because that's what she was paid to do.

"Right, Cal," she said, the video switching back to her. "Laura. The National Weather Service has been on the black snow since it began falling in our area last night. What can you tell us about it?"

Laura cleared her throat. "It's actually called dark snow, and the scientific community has known about it for a long time," the meteorologist said, her voice calm, firm—the kind of voice people believe. "Through deforestation, the increasing number of wildfires, pollution from industry and automobiles, dust, and soot, ultra-fine black carbon particles spread through the atmosphere and return to earth in the form of gray or black snow."

Makayla nodded, her serious face on.

"But is it dangerous?" the reporter asked.

A smile graced the scientist's face. "Only as dangerous as dust, soot, and pollution can be. I'm out here breathing the air, but if you're worried, a mask would keep out most unwanted particles."

A yawn from the hallway told him Marguerite was awake; he picked up the remote control and muted Makayla.

Marguerite stumbled and bumped against a wall, then emerged and went right to the kitchen, her hair like she'd run a hand mixer through it. The coffeemaker carafe tinked against the cup she pulled from the cabinet; she grumbled as she poured it. The coffee Thomas made was always too weak for her; Marguerite's coffee tasted like it was brewed by J. A. Folger himself. Sucks to wake up second.

She slid next to Thomas and rested her head on his shoulder, the hot, steaming cup cradled in her hands.

"Your coffee tastes like ditch water," she said.

He leaned into her. "Mmmm, smooth, delectable ditch water."

She breathed across the top and took a sip. "How come all the curtains are drawn?" she asked.

Thomas didn't know why country homes had curtains or blinds; they lived far enough away from people, what went on inside their home didn't matter. But Boyd had them, or more likely his late wife had them, so when Jillian showed up in the field next to his backyard, Thomas closed them all.

"Because Jacob saw Jillian last night," he said, lifting his feet and setting them on the coffee table. Thomas took a long drink of his now-tepid coffee before he spoke. "And I, uh, I saw her too."

Marguerite's coffee mug thunked as she set it heavily on the table. She turned and sat cross-legged facing Thomas.

"You *both* saw Jillian?" she asked. "And you didn't wake me, why?"

"What would you have done, honey?" he asked, reaching out to take her hand. She hesitated, but only for a moment.

"Panicked," she said. "I—"

Jacob leaned over the back of the couch between them. His mother swallowed a shout of surprise.

"Jillian isn't going to hurt us," he said.

"Hey!" Marguerite shouted at Thomas.

"Jillian isn't going to hurt any of us," Jacob said. Thomas and Marguerite turned toward him; he nodded at Thomas. "He won't let her."

"What?" Marguerite started.

Thomas opened his mouth to respond, but Jacob cut him off.

"You don't understand," he said, his fists clenched in tight balls. "The big black monster that was inside you—I'm what's left after Daddy Tom killed her." His dark eyes looked up at Thomas, and Thomas thought he might cry. "But she's gone, mostly." Jacob wiped his wrist across his running nose. "She made me want to hurt—she made me want to hurt everybody. I don't want to anymore. I just want to be me."

Marguerite pulled Jacob close. "I love you, baby," she whispered.

Thomas's eyes focused on the television.

"Hey," she barked at him. "That's not the way to comfort us."

Thomas pointed the remote at the TV and unmuted it. "Sorry. Something's happening."

"Thanks, Laura," Makayla said, turning from the guest toward the camera, but the camera operator didn't move to frame only the reporter. The meteorologist had grabbed her stomach, her complexion pale. The reporter saw none of this. "If this were December, it wouldn't be a white Christmas, but it also wouldn't be the end times. I'm Mak—"

Laura doubled over; crimson vomit spewed onto the black snow, coating the reporter's beige slacks. Makayla's face drained, as white as the snow wasn't. Her eyes rolled back in her head and she dropped to her knees in the charcoal snow, her bloody vomit spraying across the screen. The camera dropped to the snow-covered sidewalk and spun. The world went sideways and the camera operator fell beside it. The expensive piece of video equipment stopped moving and auto-focused on the man's whisker-stubbled face when bloody vomit erupted over the lens.

"What's going on?" Marguerite asked, squeezing Thomas's hand.

"It's Jillian, Momma," Jacob said, buried in his mother's arms. Thomas clicked off the TV just as someone in the studio switched from the live feed back to Cal, his perfect smile replaced by a look of horror. "Jillian's going on."

[4]

The black snow continued to fall; Elizabeth's too-old car struggled through the slippery mess to the health department. She hadn't had to step outside into the snow. Her car sat all warm and cozy in the garage, and her remote opener kept her from stepping outside to pull the heavy door closed.

The dark, alien landscape her car crawled through was more a dystopian nightmare on Netflix than a drive to work. No one walked the sidewalks, not dog walkers, not insane early-morning runners, not commuters. A St. Joseph Public Works plow drove past her, throwing a sheet of iron-flavored slush across her windshield. She slapped a middle finger against the inside of her window as the truck drove away.

A sleet of slate hung low, the gray like smoke; the rest of the planet seemed to be on fire.

Two rows of parking spots lay to the rear of the health department; the ones close to the door were reserved for Bruce and the board of directors. Since none of those better-than-thous besides Bruce would be in today, Elizabeth drove through the back part of the lot and parked next to the door, wrapping her nose and mouth in a scarf before grabbing her duffel bag and bolting for the entrance, coughing once she got inside.

The locker room and showers were her first stop. The snow was black. The *snow* was black, and the CDC hadn't made a peep. She was going to shower, change, and wash every stitch of clothing that came in contact with the hell-snow before she talked with Bruce.

Safety first.

She hadn't been there five minutes before he began beating on the door.

"Elizabeth? Elizabeth? Is that you?" he shouted. She'd never heard him so urgent. The man was usually as laid back as a recliner.

"I'm just getting dressed," she shouted back, hoping he didn't throw open the door to the locker room. "I'll be out in a minute."

"There's a kid in Roo—Room 2," he stuttered. "A kid, like seven, eight years old. Alone. Parents didn't even bring him in. He's wearing pajamas, for God's sake, and he's been out in that black stuff. Hurry, Elizabeth. Please hurry."

Numbness spread down her arms and through her fingers. The brush she held dropped from her fingers, clacking to the floor. A kid? She bent and grabbed the brush, her hands swollen and useless.

"I'm coming."

Bruce was gone when she opened the door, probably hiding in his office.

She tapped on the closed door of Room 2 and waited for a reply. There was none. The handle turned quietly and she pushed open the cheap pressboard door.

The examination room seemed empty.

"Hello?"

Nothing. The paper pulled across the examination table as straight and undimpled as when she'd left the night before, the pillow fresh. Nothing was out of place.

"Is somebody in here?" A quiver ran across her.

Elizabeth stepped fully into the examination room and jerked the door toward her, expecting a small child, its ink-black eyes staring into hers, its heartless smile threatening to eat her alive like the monster Jenkins baby.

No one. The room was empty.

Her exhale seemed to take forever.

"Well," she said to herself. "Where'd he go?"

Elizabeth turned toward the door, her eyes locking on the white-board where nurses wrote their schedules. Written in blue dry-erase marker was, "Treat people sick with the black snow with vitamin E and selenium."

She took a few steps forward and put her palm on the wall, resting her weight there.

"I'm all better now!" it continued. "J. J."

"J. J.?" she whispered.

But vitamin E and selenium. Vitamin E and selenium? It meant something. Where have I heard this? Then it hit her. Arsenic. Vitamin E and selenium, coupled with hydration, was an effective treatment for arsenic poisoning.

Poison?

"The black snow is poison."

[5]

Marguerite swung her head toward her son's voice. The boy, resembling his father less and less as he grew, stood behind the couch, his disheveled hair something people in California pay big money for.

"How much did you see, baby?"

He shrugged. "I dunno. I saw some people get sick. It looked like that time I drank too much Hi-C." He leaned against the back of the couch, resting his chin on his arms folded across the couch back. "Do I have to go to school?"

"No school today, buddy," Thomas said, motioning Jacob to come over the couch and sit between them. The boy smiled, threw himself over the back of the couch, and fell onto the cushion, grinning as he sat up. Thomas rubbed the boy's tousled hair. A couple of years ago, Jacob was a kid from a horror movie, now he was just a kid from a Marvel movie. "Do you know where Jillian's been?"

Jacob shook his head. "No, but I know what she did."

Marguerite wrapped her arms around her son and held him tight. "What'd she do?"

"She poisoned the snow," he said matter-of-factly. "That's why it's black."

"Poisoned?" Thomas gently grabbed Jacob's shoulder. "Why?"

The boy tried to push his mother away when she kissed his forehead, but finally gave up. Marguerite snuggled in closer, and a small sniffle came from her face, hidden in his hair.

"Because she gets stronger when people die," Jacob said, wrapping his hand around the remote control. "It's like her food or something."

"Dear God," Thomas whispered. The memory of downtown St. Joe in flames rushed over him; the ground rumbled as the children's hospital crumbled and crashed into the ground, the black monster sucking on the souls of children. That's what Dauðr was making Bobby do. Feed it.

"We have to stop her," Thomas said.

Jacob's arms wrapped around Marguerite's neck and she hugged him back. "It's okay, Mom," he said. "There's a cure."

"Cure?" Thomas's palm slipped off Jacob's shoulder and held up the boy's pointed chin, gently turning his face toward him with his fingertips. "A cure for the poison in the black snow? Do you know what it is?"

The boy nodded and Thomas dropped his hand to Marguerite's.

"Well, what is it?" Thomas asked, trying to keep his excitement under control and failing. "We can fix this thing before it gets bad."

The television clicked on, and the news flickered as Jacob changed the channel to an old episode of *Dexter's Laboratory*.

"I already did. I told Elizabeth what it was."

Thomas grabbed the remote from Jacob and clicked it off. "Who's Elizabeth?"

"She's the nurse in the delivery room when I was born." Jacob turned toward Marguerite, who'd pulled back to stare slack-jawed at her son. "You remember her, Mom? She started drinking a lot after I was born and went to those meetings with Daddy Tom for a while."

What? How?

"I know her," Thomas said, his voice distant, dream-like.

"I told Elizabeth to treat people sick with the black snow with vitamin E and selenium." He wormed the remote from Thomas's hand and turned Dexter back on. Dexter's sister DeeDee pushed a button she wasn't supposed to—again. "What's for breakfast?"

"Wait, baby." Marguerite gripped his shoulders with soft hands. "I'll fix you whatever you want, pancakes or eggs or whatever, but why vitamin E? And what even is selenium?"

"No, Mom," Jacob whined. "Your eggs are always too dry and your pancakes taste like cardboard. Daddy Tom cooks better."

A monkey bounded across the screen and Jacob laughed, its innocence lost in his words. Thomas sat still, his brain slow to push his muscles into movement. Marguerite stood and walked toward the windows, heavy drapes pulled shut.

"Honey," she said. "Focus. Selenium."

"I don't know what it is," he said. "I just know it will work, okay?" Two pokes of the thumb brought up the sound. "But we don't have to worry about the selenium stuff or the vitamin E."

"Why?" Thomas finally asked.

The room sprang to life as Marguerite pulled open the curtains and sunlight poured in.

"Uh, guys," she said. "Why is our snow white?"

[6]

The Buchanan County Sheriff's Department front office was cold, the kind of cold that didn't only come from the weather. Glenn sat in his chair and looked over his open laptop into the pit of deputy desks. Aaron was out assisting the Highway Patrol with a wreck on US 36. A tractor trailer had slid on the black snow and overturned.

"Masks on," Glenn had said to Aaron before he left, turning to catch the attention of Deputies Murphy and Clyde. He pointed his finger at each one. "And when you go out, I want everyone to take extra filters. Nobody, not the CDC, the World Health Organization, the American Public Health Association, has been able to tell us what this black snow is, but apparently it causes internal bleeding. If I find out anyone didn't wear a respirator after they step outside this building, it's their ass. Got it?"

A chorus of "Yes, Sheriff" died quickly in the room.

Deputy Brittany Curtright came to his department from Sheriff Bob Gonnor up in Andrew County. "She wants to trade the lights and action of farm crimes for the romance of meth labs and shootings down in Buchanan County," Bob had told him, two months after Glenn had picked up the little girl with the teeth. "She's ready for it, Glenn. Brittany's a good deputy." Brittany sat at Maddy's old desk, pounding on her computer keyboard, hopefully finishing her report on the break-in at a summer cabin down near Bee Creek.

Maddy. He tried not to think of Maddy, but he couldn't stop. Every damn day. Her appetite for a good Clem's breakfast, the way she could cheer up Aaron when another girl dumped him, her head nearly shorn off by a ten-year-old with a mouth full of razor teeth, the blood spraying across his face as he watched the monster they thought was a lost girl rip out most of her neck and swallow it.

Glenn almost resigned that day. And he would have if it weren't for what he'd seen after the little girl murdered his deputy.

"*I'm the one who took Jacob Jenkins,*" the monster said. What else could it be but a monster? The monster that tormented Boyd, the monster that had returned. "*Now, what does sheriff taste like?*"

And Glenn ran. He just fucking ran. Like a coward.

[7]

A tickle brushed Elizabeth's nose, like wind catching a strand of hair if hers were long enough. It wasn't. Today had been so long, and she was so tired. The black snow brought in many patients that she treated with vitamin E and selenium, like the stranger had written on the whiteboard. The tickle returned. She tried to reach up to brush it off, but her arms seemed caught, twisted in the sheets.

"No," Elizabeth moaned, the taste of vodka still heavy on her tongue. Her mind told her shoulders to roll to the side; maybe a new sleeping position would keep whatever bothered her nose at bay. Her shoulders were bolted to the bed. "Huh?"

Her eyes batted open, the drapes pulled tight, the room black except the digital clock. Its red display read 3 a.m.

"What the—what the heck?"

Her abdominal muscles contracted, trying to lift her bit by bit from the mattress, but nothing moved. Cold seeped into her bones.

"You're awake," a small voice said. "*Finally.*"

"Wha—" Elizabeth mumbled. "Who—who's here?"

A figure moved into her vision, a small figure, the size of the Skipper doll she'd had as a girl. Not as tall as Barbie, but close. She was thin, wearing a form-fitting white dress, her hair red like a cartoon's. The woman, the tiny woman, walked across Elizabeth's face and rested a hand on her nose, cocking a hip. She shouldn't be in focus, Elizabeth knew, but she was. That little woman was as clear as HDTV.

"I'm drunk," Elizabeth whispered.

"You sure are," the little woman said, "but that doesn't have anything to do with seeing me, Elizabeth Condon, RN. I'm one hundred percent real. Crazy, huh?"

A scream stretched the back of Elizabeth's throat, but her mouth wouldn't release it.

The little woman stood straight and cracked her knuckles, although Elizabeth couldn't hear it.

"I'm here for a very important reason, Elizabeth, honey." She folded her little arms under her little breasts and grinned. "It's because you know Thomas Cavanaugh. It took me ever so long to find you."

CHAPTER ELEVEN
May

[1]

THE SILVER SUBARU Outback turned off SE 50 Road and pulled to a stop in a rough gravel quarter-moon of a parking spot in the Pigeon Hill Conservation Area, just south of St. Joe. Pope Daugherty smiled and patted his wife's leg.

"We're here, folks," he said, grabbing the soft flesh of her thigh and shaking it as he looked in the rearview mirror at twelve-year-old Jaden and eight-year-old Olivia. Olivia smiled back at him. Jaden groaned and held up his Nintendo Switch.

"Can I stay here?" he said. "I'm almost done with this level."

Pope glanced at his wife of fifteen years, his grin beaten back by her glare. Amanda's arms were folded across her chest.

"No way, bud," Pope said, reaching across Amanda's lap for the glove compartment. He pulled the handle and the door dropped open to reveal a lumpy Crown Royal bag. Pope pulled it out and shut the door. Amanda huffed when he pulled away; tension vibrated throughout the cab.

"What's in the bag, Dad?" Olivia asked.

He inhaled deeply; the smell, like a pine forest if the forest were cardboard, seeped from the Christmas tree freshener that hung from the rearview mirror. The innocent cheerfulness in Olivia's voice gave him strength, at least enough strength to continue.

Pope turned the whisky bag in his hands.

"It's—" He stopped and looked up at Amanda; her face was hard, unchanged. "It's . . . it's. This . . . this bag contains everything wrong with our family. We're in a dark place, and we need to get to the light, so we're going to walk into the wilderness and bury all the dark things. We're starting over. We're going to be happy again."

Amanda coughed a laugh from the passenger seat, dragging a grimace across her husband.

"But what's *in* it, Daddy?" Olivia asked.

Amanda grabbed his arm, her well-manicured stiletto-shaped nails digging into his skin. "Don't, Pope."

Her sharp nails raked shallow furrows across his arm as Pope yanked it from her grasp. Blood welled in the scratches.

"Well, honey," he said, pulling a tissue from the Kleenex travel bag stuffed in the drink holder and dabbing his arm. "From you, last quarter's report card. From Jaden, the disposable lighter he and Calvin used to try to set the Methodist church's tool shed on fire."

A groan came from the backseat. "Come on, Dad."

"From me—" He pulled at the cord holding the neck of the bag tight, reached in, and pulled out an orange translucent bottle with a white cap. He shook it, and it rattled with pills. "The last of the oxycodone I got hooked on." He dropped it back in the sack and pulled out a folded paper. "And this is Mom's. A credit-card statement showing she rented a hotel room in Kansas City the same weekend she said she was at a conference in St. Louis."

"Screw you, Pope."

"Mom!" Jaden shouted. Olivia slapped a hand over her mouth.

Pope slid the statement back into the bag and pulled it tight. "Now, Amanda, that's not constructive. This trip is about healing." He opened his door. "Now, let's go heal. I'm missing a meeting tonight for this."

The ball flew over Jacob's head, then stopped in midair and came back to the boy's baseball glove. He pulled it out and threw it back to Thomas.

"You know you can't do that in a game, right?"

Jacob shrugged, his red St. Joe Mustangs cap akilter. "What fun is that?"

The boy, at seven, had grown, matured, and it was clear he'd be incapable of becoming his father, Bobby.

Thomas tossed the ball back to him. Jacob stood unmoving as it flew over his head again; this time he allowed it. The ball hit the grass behind him and rolled to the edge of the lawn to Trent Parman's fallow field.

Thomas's glove and right fist rested on his hips. "You didn't even try to catch it."

"Catch it?" The boy grinned. "Is that a thing?"

And he's a smart-ass to boot.

"Yeah, it's a thing." Thomas could do nothing but smile at the tall, lanky kid. "I don't see you do that much anymore."

"Do what?"

Thomas shrugged. "I don't know what you call it. Your powers? Magic? You know, like catching the ball without any hands."

"I dunno," the boy said, kicking at the grass before looking up at Thomas. "When I was little I used it for stupid stuff, like eating chicken nuggets, then I almost used it to kill Gramma, and I helped Jillian do things to hurt people and, and—"

"The cow?" Thomas asked. He'd never broached this subject with Jacob before, and didn't know how the boy would take it.

Jacob simply nodded. "Yeah. Then me and Mom moved here, and everything was nice, and happy, and I just stopped. There's no reason to do those things. I don't even know if I can do anything big anymore. You know, the bad stuff."

The warmth in Thomas's chest hit him suddenly. He wanted nothing more at that moment than to walk over to Jacob and wrap him in a bear hug, but he held his ground. Jacob was accepting being normal, just a boy, and he wanted to keep him that way.

"Unless you're cheating at baseball," Thomas said.

A half grin lifted a corner of Jacob's mouth. "Yeah. That."

"Then how about you go get that ball you let sail over your head?" Thomas said.

Jacob snapped a mock salute before turning and running toward the baseball. The boy, all knees and elbows, trucked to the edge of the lawn and stopped. His face turned toward the ground.

"Jake?" Thomas called.

He didn't move.

Thomas took a step forward. "What's going on, bud?"

Jacob's throwing hand lifted in the air and he beckoned Thomas to come.

It's a dead animal, Thomas thought. Or a pile of shit. Guaranteed.

He walked to Jacob and lay a hand on the boy's shoulder. "What's u—" His voice caught in his throat. Jacob stood outside a ring of mushrooms in the grass at the edge of the field, the wide, flat caps like brown fried eggs atop a stem. The fungus formed a perfect circle.

"Huh," he said. "That's weird."

Jacob shook his head, and the ball cap shifted, dangerously close to flopping off. "No. It's not."

"Okay, yeah, I know," Thomas said. "These circles are caused by a big fungus under the ground that sprouts mushrooms along its edges. It's just nature."

The boy looked up at him, his eyes wide. "No. That's not it at all. You should know this. It's a fairy circle."

Fairy circle? The words, hard and emotionless, raked cold chills across Thomas's back. Fairies. Jillian. The cornfield. Explosions in the snow. No.

"It's a natural phenomenon, bud. Nothing magical here." Although Thomas knew that when they'd lain on Jacob's bed, looking through the open window into the cold wind, this was the spot where Jillian danced in the snow. Nothing magical here?

Jacob didn't move, his glare unchanged.

"She made this," the boy said. "It's a door to the fairy world, the world Jillian took me to. If we stand in this circle, we can go there, you just need to know how to knock."

Thomas raked his own ball cap toward the back of his head. Knock, knock, knocking on fairy doors. When is this nightmare going to be over?

"Yeah," Thomas said. "I even think I know how." He patted Jacob's back. "Let's go. It's probably dinnertime and I gotta get going. It's my meeting night."

Jacob lingered at the fairy circle a moment before he turned and followed Thomas to the house.

"Hey, Thomas."

He slowed as the boy ran up next to him. "What?" he asked, looking at Jacob, who'd stuck his hands in his pockets, his ball glove pinched in his armpit.

"I heard at school that festival in St. Joe, Jesse James Days, is in a day or two." Jacob kicked at a dandelion before continuing. "And, you know, they have a roller coaster and a Tilt-A-Whirl."

Thomas tried not to laugh out loud. Instead, he coughed, and swallowed the laugh.

"Really?" he said. "Sounds like fun."

"Uh-huh."

The kid couldn't hold back his excitement. Thomas hoped he didn't pee himself.

"And, you know, ever since I was kidnapped, Mom's been, uh—"

"Protective of her only child?" Thomas finished for him.

Jacob shrugged. "I was going to say weird. She won't let me do anything."

Thomas stopped and squatted to Jacob's eye level, the little boy's hopeful face like something from a Dickens novel.

"And you want me to talk to her about it, right?"

He nodded; the Mustangs hat fell to the yard. Thomas picked it up and propped it back on Jacob's head.

"You bet, kiddo. I don't do roller coasters, but I might ride the Tilt-A-Whirl with you."

Thin, gangly arms of a boy growing faster than his body knew how to handle wrapped around Thomas and squeezed as hard as they could. The warmth in Thomas's chest grew from somewhere deep. He never wanted this to end.

[3]

The Daugherty family trudged down the cedar-chip surface of the Pigeon Hill walking trail, Pope leading, a shovel over his shoulder, the Crown Royal bag in the side pocket of his cargo shorts. Olivia bounced beside him; Jaden, hands stuffed into his pockets, leaned into his mother, who didn't want to be there either.

"How much farther, Pope?" Amanda asked, her voice flat. Jaden slapped at a buzzing fly.

Tree limbs thick with leaves draped a canopy over their heads; the pin oaks, maples, and ash held the forest hushed, silent. The stifling late-spring heat and the semen-like odor of the Bradford pear radiated the feel of a porn-loop booth at a strip joint.

Pope knew that smell, and given the events of the past year, he thought Amanda might too.

He breathed in deeply through his nose and exhaled through a tight grin. "Soon, honey. I'm waiting for a spot to feel right."

"Feel right?" Jaden said. "What kind of hippy stuff is that?"

Pope stopped, Olivia taking three steps before she realized her father wasn't walking anymore. Jaden thudded into his back.

"You're not embracing the family, son." He turned, and Jaden took a step backward into his mother.

"Pope," Amanda said, her hands on Jaden's shoulders. "You're scaring us."

"No, he's not, Mommy," Olivia said, slipping her arms as far around Pope's back and his beer-belly tummy as she could. "Daddy's trying to help us."

A huff blew from Jaden. "Come on, Dad. Can't we just bury our shame and go home?"

No. No way, Pope thought. I could slam this shovel on top of his smart-assed head and be done with it. Olivia squeezed and he looked down, her wide hazel eyes melting his anger. A smile teased Pope's lips. Amanda rolled her eyes.

"Okay, guys. Let's find a willow tree. We'll bury this at the foot, then go to that frozen-yogurt place on Fredrick Avenue." The knuckles on the hand that gripped the shovel handle grew white. "How does that sound?"

Olivia jumped beside him. "Oh, Daddy. Can I please have gummy worms on mine?"

He squeezed her with his free arm. "Anything, baby."

"Come on, Pope," Amanda hissed. "Just get on with it."

Pope Daugherty had never hit a woman in his life. Nope. Not once. His family preached the sanctity of marriage, the responsibility of the husband to take care of his wife and children, and the sense to know that striking a woman was nothing a strong moral man did. That was for trailer fodder and alcoholics. But his wife—the woman who pledged herself to him before God and his mother, then fucked their insurance agent, Chip Sanders, in the airport Hilton—tried to burn holes into him with her eyes. He wanted to break. He wanted to push their lazy son Jaden into the brush and punch his wife right in the mouth.

But instead . . .

"Sure, my love," he said. "Let's go."

When he turned, a woman rounded a bend in the dark trail. She was thin, dressed in blue jeans and a black Ramones T-shirt, her red hair pulled back in a ponytail. Her eyes widened when she saw them.

"Oh," she said. "What a cute family."

[4]

The flow chart on Glenn's laptop didn't flow. Elvin Miller to his wife Jennifer, Carrie McMasters to her husband John, Bobby to Boyd and Emily, a child—the fucking monster in my squad car—to Boyd, Hiram's heifer to Jacob Jenkins, Rebekka Marshall to the monster again, her baby. Yeah. The monster did that. Sliced the baby from Rebekka's womb, eating the little boy's fingers and toes before leaving his tiny, naked, bleeding body in a cornfield. A goddammed cornfield.

Glenn dropped his face in his hands. The monster. The memory of the monster haunted him every night. Those wide, glaring eyes locked on his in the rearview mirror, the jagged slab of meat from Maddy's throat caught in its shark teeth, his deputy's blood smeared across its horror of a face. Glenn sat in the driver's seat, a Glock 9mm on his belt and a shotgun by his elbow, but instead of shooting the creature that murdered his deputy, he ran. He pitched out the door, scraping his palms across the gravel, and he ran.

It didn't matter that minutes later, Thomas Cavanaugh blew a hole in the monster's chest with the sheriff's own shotgun and she—Jillian by then—stitched herself back together and blew him a kiss.

"Glenn?" The voice, a man's voice, came from the open office door. He lifted his head; Thomas Cavanaugh stood in the doorway.

The sheriff motioned Thomas to sit; he stepped into Glenn's office and lowered himself onto a wooden seat. Glenn leaned back in his chair but changed his mind, scooting it close to the desk and resting his elbows on top.

"We've known each other for a long time," Thomas said.

The sheriff nodded. The first week Boyd had hired Glenn to the Sheriff's Department, he took Glenn to lunch with Kyle, and Thomas had come too. Tommy was a kid then, but smart, funny, asked good questions. Yeah, he'd known Tommy for a long time.

"And?"

Thomas straightened and pulled his cap from his head, laying it on his lap.

"There's something that happened in January with Jillian," he said.

Glenn's jaw clenched. "It's May, Tom. Why the hell are you telling me this now instead of then? You *know* she's wanted for kidnapping Jacob. And now—" His words caught. Glenn coughed into his hand and continued. "Now she's wanted for murder. She killed Maddy. I saw it with my own eyes."

Thomas's rough hand rubbed across the stubble on his face.

"Yeah, about that." He reached up a hand and scratched the back of his neck. "Can you try to suspend disbelief while I tell you this?"

Glenn eyeballed the door; no one was close. He leaned as far as he could across his desk.

"I saw those teeth, Tommy," he said, his voice low, soft. "I saw that beast's mouth. Then I watched as this, this *thing* turned into Jillian Robertson and survive a shotgun blast right to the chest. How much more disbelief do you want me to suspend?"

"A bit more."

"Will it help me bring a murderer to justice?" Glenn asked.

Thomas nodded. "I think it will."

The sheriff leaned back in his chair. "Then I'll believe anything you say."

[5]

Jacob stomped down the steps to the back deck and plopped his skinny butt on the bottom one, the taste of Mom's turkey meatloaf still on his tongue. She always used too much chili sauce and onion, at least for Jacob's taste, but he ate Mom's food, even though he liked it better when Thomas cooked. Thomas had left for his meeting in St. Joe after supper. Jacob didn't know what the meeting was for, but it must be important; Thomas went every week.

A shadow moved across the grass as he sat there staring at nothing. Looking up into the darkening cloudless sky, he saw a big black turkey vulture circling overhead. "*Those birds are scavengers,*" Thomas had told him last Saturday when he let Jacob ride in Grandpa Kyle's tractor while cultivating a soybean field. A wake of the big, black, greasy birds circled over a patch of trees. "*You know what that means?*"

Jacob nodded. He watched nature shows on the National Geographic channel. "It means they eat dead things."

Dead things. What was dead here?

He stood from the porch step and stretched out his arms, spinning across the backyard like the pretty nun lady on the mountain in that singing movie Mom liked. Thomas still hadn't asked her to marry him, not that he knew, but it was coming. He did know that. A life of school, baseball, and a mom and dad were coming. This awful Jillian nonsense had to end soon. It just had to. Jacob looked up as he spun, the vulture's circles tighter, compact. It spotted what it was after.

Jacob looked around, but just saw grass, the shed, and farmer Paulson's field full of volunteer corn, sunflowers, and Johnson grass.

The dead animal must be just inside the line of corn and weeds. Jacob grinned and ran toward it. He stopped at the edge of the field and tried to smell the animal. Death had a smell, and it was awful, but all that came to him was honeysuckle from the edge of the shed.

A tug almost pulled him off balance.

Jacob spun to find no one behind him, only an empty lawn. His eyes dropped to the ground, his feet at the edge of the fairy circle.

"Oh no," he whispered as a force grabbed his legs and dragged him toward it.

A hum came from everywhere. Jacob thrashed against the invisible power that held him, his hat flying from his head. Fear gripped him and he bellowed—the force blowing him away from the circle of fungi. He landed in the brush of Trent Parman's weed-filled field, his body tingling from electricity. A light-purple flame erupted from the circle. Jacob threw himself to his feet and spun to run away from this fairy ring and back to the safety of Thomas's house—*his* house—but the flame shot from inside the halo of mushrooms and wrapped itself around his legs. He coughed a "help" as the lavender chord pulled and threw him off balance, dragging him into the ring. His scream, buried in that hum, died when he looked at his legs buried to the knees in the lawn like he'd been planted.

Then the world flushed like a toilet.

[6]

Elizabeth sat low in her car, watching alcoholics and their Al-Anon partners enter the Delores Hadley Community Center. The damn Jesse James Days carnival blocking the streets downtown had made it hard to get there. She'd parked near the back of the lot and worn sunglasses, trying to stay off people's radar, but realized she'd probably look silly if anyone walked by and saw her dressed like a movie caricature of an undercover cop. But they wouldn't be looking at her while an enormous Ferris wheel loomed in the St. Joe skyline, she hoped.

Jerry pulled his old pickup closer to the front and stepped out, untucked himself from the seat like he had extra joints. At least Elizabeth thought the old man's name was Jerry, but it had been so long since she'd been to a meeting, she couldn't remember. The to-go cup in her hand smelled of vodka more than orange juice, so she knew she'd mixed the screwdriver too strong. Tough. She didn't have any more juice. Plenty of vodka, though. She needed it to get here to do what the fairy wanted.

The fairy. The damned fairy. When the tiny woman visited her in the night, it wouldn't let her breathe. It stood on her chin and leaned on her nose.

"You know Thomas Cavanaugh. It took me ever so long to find you," the little red-haired woman in the white dress said in the middle of the night. Then she stared deeply into Elizabeth's eyes and told her why she'd looked for Elizabeth in the first place. "I need you to kill Thomas Cavanaugh."

"What? Why?" she stuttered. "No. I'm a nurse. I heal people. I don't hurt them."

The fairy woman leaned into Elizabeth's nose, the pressure nearly enough to break it.

"I gave him my name—my actual name," the fairy said. "Names hold power, *Elizabeth Condon*." A slight grin melted into something painfully wide before it dropped into a flat line. "He holds my name, so he holds control over me. I cannot be the one to kill him, or I would destroy myself. You must do it for me."

From all Elizabeth could tell, Thomas was a good man. She started to open her mouth, but her jaw muscles wouldn't work.

"You heard what I said." The fairy's smile returned; this time it shone with glowing, white needle teeth. Elizabeth tried to scream, but the fairy held her mouth shut. "You *must* help me, Elizabeth. Then I will help you." The fairy disappeared, and in her place lay a bottle of Crystal Head Vodka, the transparent skull grinning like it knew something Elizabeth didn't.

So, fifteen hours later, Elizabeth sat outside the Delores Hadley Community Center, waiting for Thomas Cavanaugh like the fairy told her to.

Another truck pulled in; she caught it in her driver's-side mirror, red and covered with dirt. Elizabeth sank lower into the seat as it rolled past, the driver not giving her car as much as a glance. She knew that truck; she'd talked to Thomas after a meeting once, the man doing his best to escape into that truck before she mentioned Jacob Jenkins's name. That had stopped him.

The truck slowed and pulled into the spot next to Jerry's, or whatever his name was.

"Thomas Cavanaugh is a villain," the fairy had told her. "He killed my mother. Do you have a mother?"

Mother? Killed? Thomas didn't do that.

"My mother's dead," Elizabeth said when she was finally allowed to speak.

The little woman nodded. "Did Thomas Cavanaugh kill her?"

"No," she said, her voice cold. "Of course not."

"He will kill again," the fairy said. "And it will be me. You have to stop him."

A shiver shimmied across Elizabeth, the cold raising gooseflesh on her arms; her nipples tightened.

"I . . . I can't. I won't."

The fairy leaned closer, her eyes glowing lavender. "You will."

A calm brushed across Elizabeth, the kind of calm when she smoked weed in college. Everything was right. Then the calm began to melt away, and everything was wrong; hunger ate her hollow.

"Sure," she said through dark, cloudy thoughts. "When do you want me to do it?"

"After his meeting," the fairy said. "You know where that is. You're a drunk just like him."

Now, Thomas opened the truck door and stepped out, stretching his shoulders before locking his vehicle and turning toward the building.

"Kill him," echoed through her head.

Elizabeth slid the chef's blade she'd taken from the knife block in her kitchen before mixing a screwdriver and getting behind the wheel. He was there. Right there. The man the little fairy woman beckoned her to kill, willed her to kill.

A car pulled into the spot next to Thomas and a slight, older woman stepped out. Thomas smiled and spoke to her before he held out his arm and escorted her into the building.

"I can't," she whispered into the empty cab.

"Do it," the fairy's voice said aloud. Elizabeth jumped in her seat. "Or I'll do you."

The chef's knife fell to the seat, and Elizabeth guzzled the rest of her screwdriver. The meeting lasted an hour, only an hour.

[7]

The timing is all wrong, Pope thought. Why would this young woman, maybe twenty-five, be out in the woods alone at this time? The Daugherty family Subaru was the only vehicle in the parking spot. Where'd she come from?

Pope opened his mouth to speak, but Amanda beat him to it.

"I'm sorry, hon," Amanda said, moving herself in front of this strange woman, her children behind her. Olivia wiggled between her mother's body and arm, peeking out from beneath her armpit. "We're in a hurry."

The woman bent to eye level with Olivia and smiled. "Oh, you're a cute one. I bet you're tasty."

"Hey–" Pope started.

Amanda folded her arms across her chest. "Excuse me?"

Pope made a fist. I had this, Amanda.

A smile, like the grin of a fox, crossed the young woman's face as she rose and looked at Amanda.

"It's just a saying. I didn't mean anything by it." Her grin expanded as she looked up at Pope, teasing her bottom lip with an index finger. "I'll be going."

And with a hip-wag, the woman moved down the trail. Pope watched every step until Amanda slapped his arm.

"What was that all about?" she growled.

He shrugged and huffed. "I don't know. Well, kids, let's get on with this. Obviously our family needs fixed."

"Damn right," Amanda said, soft but not so soft the words didn't crawl into Pope's head brandishing knives.

Five minutes later, Pope pointed at a bend in the path. "The map I found online showed a pond up here, and willow trees love water."

"Why a willow tree, Dad?" Jaden asked.

"I'm happy you asked," Pope said, picking up his pace. "Willow trees grow fast and can take root if you slice off a limb and plant it. The Chinese believe they stand for renewal and immortality, which is exactly what I want for this family. I love you guys, and desperately want renewal."

"What's renewal mean, Daddy?" Olivia asked from behind him.

Pope felt good about this. The trip out here, the forest, the togetherness. Yes, today was a good day.

"It means—"

"Holy crap," Jaden shouted.

Everyone froze; Pope swung around to face his family.

"What is it, honey?" Amanda asked.

The boy stood, eyes wide, pointing off the trail into the forest. "The woman. That red-haired lady. She was sta— standing, right there, holding her finger over her lips."

Pope growled.

"Nobody," he said, "and I mean nobody is going to mess up our day. Our day." He stepped to the edge of the trail, the shovel handle in both hands; blood pounded in his temples.

"Hey, you," he shouted into the trees, the woman nowhere in sight. "I don't know who you are or what you think you're doing, but this isn't funny. Back off!"

"Pope," Amanda whispered.

"You hear me?"

Amanda rested a hand on his shoulder. "Pope. She's not there anymore, if she ever was." Pope's wife turned toward their son. "Was she?"

Jaden nodded, his eyes wide, his skin pale.

Pope nodded at the boy before turning back down the trail, the sky suddenly dark and heavy with clouds. His stomach sank; the shovel slipped from his hands and thumped on the well-worn dirt. The red-haired woman stood before him with a smile as wide as a pumpkin, jagged as a chainsaw. She grabbed Pope's shoulders and jerked him forward. He screamed as she pushed his head into her gaping, slathering mouth and slammed it closed.

[8]

Glenn sat in his office and fumed.

"Fairies," he said, loud enough to hear, but not loud enough for anyone else to. Not that anyone was around. Brittany Curtright walked through the front glass doors with a brown paper bag of something greasy, from Clem's, probably; Aaron was still out on traffic patrol, the rest had gone home. The night shift were on their way in, or they sure as heck better be if they wanted to have a job tomorrow.

"Fairies," he said again, and tried to laugh, but it wouldn't come.

An hour ago, Thomas had sat across the desk from him before he left for his AA meeting—a meeting Thomas was proud to attend every week—and told Glenn with a straight face that fairies existed. Fucking *fairies*. Thomas left with a warning, a warning about Norse fairies. Don't eat their food, don't give them your name.

So Glenn spent the past hour reading about them. Not the fairy-dust pixies, but the timeless worldwide phenomenon of little people not being good citizens. Curdling milk, tying cows' tails together, lying, stealing, kidnapping—especially children—destroying crops, murder. Disney sold the world a bill of goods with helpful sprites that weren't out to suck humanity's soul through a straw.

Glenn had seen what he now knew to be a fairy. He'd also read how to kill one.

"Sheriff," the 9-1-1 dispatcher shrieked over the radio, "S5 at Pigeon Hill Conservation Area. Multiple victims. Looks like a family."

A family? Damn it.

Glenn picked up his microphone and hit the button. "Night shift. ETA."

Hiss.

"Three minutes, boss," Sutherland said.

Followed by Kreiger. "Two."

Glenn looked into the squad room and found Brittany's eyes locked onto his, panic on her face. He rose, strode out of his office, and pulled his door closed behind him, pointing at his deputy, then himself.

"You're with me," he said. "First one?"

She nodded.

"You good to go?" Glenn asked.

Brittany nodded again and pushed her cap beneath her arm, moving away from her desk.

"Take your food, kiddo," he said. She grabbed the grease-stained bag and he took her arm, escorting her toward the door. "You've gotta have something to throw up."

[9]

The fairy returned, sitting on the dash of Elizabeth's Honda, this time in a pair of blue jeans and what looked to be a black Ramones T-shirt instead of a white dress. Which was a good thing, Elizabeth thought, because the blood that currently soaked her clothes would never have come out of the dress. The sticky red liquid dripped off the fairy, down the dash, and onto the car's carpet.

The fairy winked, and alcohol dragged sleep through Elizabeth, her head dipping forward and colliding with the steering wheel. When she opened her eyes, the fairy was gone, a bloody smear on the dash where she had been.

"The doors open any minute, Elizabeth," the fairy said from beside her.

"Wha?"

The fairy woman sat in the passenger seat, now a full-size horror splattered with blood and gore, what looked like bits of flesh stuck in her hair. The woman pulled open the fingers of Elizabeth's right hand and placed the handle of the chef's knife in hit, folding fingers into a tight grip. A lavender glow emanated from that hand and into Elizabeth's, heat traveling up her arm.

"You don't want to disappoint me," the fairy woman said.

"I don't want to disappoint you," Elizabeth repeated, her words as slurred in her brain as on her lips.

The fairy woman said nothing, the car's interior as quiet as an old cellar. Elizabeth looked back at the seat; except for the bloodstain it was empty.

"You won't disappoint me." The words came from nowhere.

"I won't disappoint you," Elizabeth said, sobriety creeping through her body.

The doors to the Delores Hadley Community Center opened, and people began to drift out, all sober and smiling. Elizabeth slowly opened her car door and pulled herself to unsteady feet, the knife behind her back. Thomas came from the building and approached his truck like he was in a hurry. She picked up her pace, the world around her in a fishbowl.

Thomas noticed her and smiled. "Well, Elizabeth," he said. "It's been a while."

She said nothing when she pulled the eight-inch cooking knife over her head and drove it into Thomas's chest.

CHAPTER TWELVE

A SHERIFF'S CRUISER and the evidence technician's van sat next to a Subaru Outback on a half-moon of a gravel parking spot at the head of a trail at Pigeon Hill. Given it was after 7 p.m., the deputy was probably Aaron, the forensic tech Alice Landry. Efficient, knows what she's doing, but is creepy as hell. Last Halloween she came to the office dressed as Wednesday Addams and nobody noticed. Glenn pulled his car to a stop, gravel popping beneath the tires. Brittany chewed on the last of her waffle fries and stepped out, patting her stomach.

"I'm not going to throw anything up, Sheriff," she said. "This thing is made of cast iron."

"If you say so," he said, adjusting his hat. "When you do, just make sure it's *before* you get back in my car."

His shoulder mic clicked as he grabbed it, stepping in front of the Subaru. "This is Sheriff Kirkhoff."

Static erupted from the speaker. "Murphy, sir."

"Run these plates for me, Bill." He squatted in front of the silver car, his knees popping. "K55-BR5."

He stood. Seconds passed before Murphy's voice came back over the speaker.

"It's a 2022 Subaru Outback registered to Pope Alexander Daugherty of St. Joe. No criminal record."

Pope? "Do a quick check on his family. Married? Children?"

"Just a sec."

In his head he pictured Bill Murphy hunched over his computer, punching keys. The deputy didn't realize Glenn knew half the man's computer time was spent shopping for a bass boat.

"Wife: Amanda, forty-two. Two children: Jaden, twelve, and Olivia, eight. Amanda works as a CPA at Miller and Associates. The boy attends Robidoux Middle School, the girl Pershing Elementary School."

"Nice work, Murphy," Glenn said, and signed off the call, turning toward Brittany. "Now we have names. Let's see the faces."

The trail meandered through 424 acres of hardwood forest, the loose surface of the path scarred by the weight of whatever Landry pulled out here in her spinner luggage.

"You prepared for a murder scene?" Glenn asked.

The young woman shook her head, her tight ponytail swung behind her. On another day, in civvies, Glenn thought this might be like a father taking his daughter for a nature walk. Today, it was going to be a mess that'd scar this poor kid for life.

"Dead bodies aren't fun," he said. "Especially children, and there may be two."

She stopped, ready for a quick response, maybe pithy—she was eager and sharp, a college graduate—but Glenn didn't stop walking. He just wanted to get this horrible day over with.

They approached a curve in the trail, the falling sun buried behind tops of trees, and Glenn could smell the death already: the combination of wet pennies and spoiled hamburger. He stopped; Brittany took a step ahead before turning toward him.

"Sheriff?"

Glenn remembered his first murder. John McMasters, his neck sliced wide by his wife, Carrie, the knife painted crimson. When he arrived, Carrie had eaten her plate of pot roast and vegetables even though it was covered with her husband's blood. She denied being angry with him or even remembering the attack. That didn't matter. What mattered, as Glenn took a step forward, was that the McMasterses' dining room smelled exactly like this.

"Get ready," he said to his deputy. "We're here."

Yellow police tape stretched across the path, separating it from a great red stain, like human bodies had simply exploded. Detective Landry knelt beside an unidentifiable piece of meat, picking at something with tweezers. Birds sang in the canopy, but the trail lay covered in pools of blood and chunks of flesh splattered across the foliage, along with bones and clothing. A line of sweat ran down Glenn's face as he lost feeling in his hands and feet, a numbness spreading throughout his body.

"Shit," he whispered and leaned toward the side of the path, hands dropping to his knees as coffee and the hamburger he had for lunch heaved into the bushes.

"No worries, boss," Landry said, not looking up from a piece of what had been a human. "Happens to the best of us."

She pulled out what she'd been tugging on and stood. He tried to focus on her black eyeshadow, her hair the color of crow.

"Sheriff?" she said, waving the tweezers at Glenn. "I know it looks like they went through a wood chipper, but it was an animal."

There weren't any animals in Northwest Missouri that could shred—*shred*—a human being, let alone two or three or four. Strips of flesh hung anywhere upward to twenty feet in the trees. The taste in Glenn's mouth was vile; he stood straight and hocked as much as he could off the trail.

"What could do this?" Brittany asked, her voice breathy. Glenn realized she was trying not to use her nose.

"We get a black-bear report up here every ten years or so," the sheriff said. "Sometimes people think they've seen a mountain lion, but a mountain lion wouldn't do this. It couldn't. What's your best guess?"

Landry took a few steps toward Glenn and held up the tweezers to him; from the chunk of flesh she'd pulled a long, wicked, curved tooth.

"By the shape and size of the thing, my closest guess is a saltwater crocodile," she said. "And one of those big aggressive Australian crocs, not a pussy Nile croc."

Brittany folded her arms. "That's impossible."

"I know that, and you know that," Landry said. "But these fine folks didn't."

Blood gleamed off the dangerous tooth, the tooth of a dinosaur. Glenn had seen ones like it before, and it sure didn't come from a crocodile.

It came from a little girl.

He turned toward the trees and opened his mouth. A greenish-yellow stream of bile splattered the underbrush.

[2]

The knife impacted like a punch. Elizabeth stood, her legs unsure beneath her, breathing vodka over Thomas, before she dropped to sit crisscross-applesauce on the pavement, pulling out the knife as she went. A spurt of blood sprayed her face.

What just happened? Thomas tried to take in the scene, but his mind, heavy with disbelief, couldn't register it.

A fierce tingle stung him, as if a sadistic farmer was grinding a cattle prod between his tits. The sting flooded his senses, then—oh, God—the heat of a stove ignited inside his chest. Thomas's chin fell; blood soaked his T-shirt.

"What did you do, Elizabeth?" Hot blood oozed between his fingers. He pressed a hand on the wound, trying to hold it in.

She didn't respond, at least to him. She sat on the cracked, oil-stained asphalt and rocked back and forth; mumbles spilled from her slack, drooling mouth.

"Thomas?" a man's voice called. Thomas's head turned toward the sound. Jerry shuffled to him as fast as he could, and more dry drunks followed closely. The meeting leader's eyes spread wide. "Holy shit. Elizabeth? What the hell?"

A woman—Thomas thought she might be named Sandra—pulled the mobile phone from her purse and poked the touch screen.

"Yes, I'd like to report a stabbing," she said into the phone.

Stabbing? Thomas pulled his hand from the wound; blood covered it in a paint-like sheen. The world began to spin and his eyes rolled back in his head. An arm wrapped around his waist and held him up against his truck door.

"Stay with me, buddy," Jerry said. Or was it? Are you Jerry?

His cloudy eyes fell downward. Elizabeth sat still, her hands on her knees, a kitchen knife on the pavement, the first inch or so red—with my blood.

"Why?" Thomas tried to say, but although his mouth moved, no sound came out.

Sandra—yes, Sandra—now stood in front of him, phone to her ear.

"At the Delores Hadley Community Center. The suspect is contained." She nodded fiercely. "I'll stay on the line." She cupped a hand over the bottom of the phone and said, "They're sending an ambulance," to Jerry.

A cluster of AA and Al-anon members formed a mob around them, many looming over Elizabeth to stop her in case she moved. Someone kicked the knife out of her reach. Thomas's senses returned just enough for pain to sear his chest. Oh, God. His knees buckled, but at some point Frank slipped his old-man arm around Thomas's back and helped keep him on his feet with strength impressive for the guy's age.

"Thanks," Thomas said, although it came out in a slow wheeze. "Remind me not to piss you off, Frank."

"Hush," Jerry snapped. "You're bleeding." He turned to Elizabeth. "Why did you do that?"

Sirens grew in the distance.

Elizabeth began to cry, mumbling beneath her breath as her thumbs fought each other.

"What?" Jerry shouted.

The nurse turned her chin toward Jerry, her eyes swollen and red, tears washing her cheeks.

"I don't know," she said. "The fairy told me to do it."

"*Fairy?*" Thomas tried to shout at her.

His arms thrashed, throwing himself out of Jerry's and Frank's grips. Fresh blood ran down his shirt, the pain like the knife plunged into him again.

Thomas dropped to one knee, his eyes even with Elizabeth's. He reached toward her, and she didn't move, her face a zombie's. Thomas grabbed her shoulders and shook; the tear from his wound shot deeper pain across his chest.

His world darkened before he could focus again.

"Was it Jillian?"

Jerry and Frank struggled to kneel beside him.

The sirens screamed closer. A St. Joe police vehicle screeched to a halt in the parking lot, an ambulance behind it. Two officers piled out of the cruiser and ran toward the cluster of AA regulars. Thomas was going to lose his chance.

"Did Jillian do this?" he shouted, his wound agonizing.

Elizabeth's chin moved; a line of drool dripped onto the pavement. "Yeth."

[3]

The stench of the blood and meat turned the forest trail into a noxious nightmare, the dimming day darkening the forest. Whatever had done this—whoever had done this—may still be out there watching, waiting. Aaron had continued past the murder scene before Glenn and Brittany arrived, cutting through the trees to avoid accidentally tampering with evidence. And evidence dripped everywhere.

"I went all the way to the shooting range at the south end of the woods," Aaron said as he got back, sweat stains under his arms. "I didn't see anything."

Glenn stood with his back to a tree, stomach under control. Brittany patted his shoulder.

"It's okay, Sheriff," she said, her voice calm, soothing, motherly, the voice of a person whose last meal stayed on the inside. "Nothing could have prepared us for that."

While Landry plucked at the remains of the Daugherty family, he and Brittany scoured the area for footprints, animal and human. The only prints not on the trail were from a pair of Vans, by the waffle treads, size 7 for a woman, size 5.5 for a man. The prints were still fresh, the edges sharp, crisp.

"So you're telling me a petite woman did this to a family of *four*?" Landry asked, her disbelief palpable.

Glenn's jaw clenched. "That's more believable than an Australian saltwater crocodile."

She raised her hands, palms up. "I never said a crocodile was the murder weapon," Landry said, Glenn trying to make solid eye contact through all that mascara. "I just said, given the tooth, given the injuries, that was my best guess."

"That's not good enough, La—" he started, but Brittany cut him off.

"Hey," she snapped, then dropped her volume. "I heard something."

"Well, wha—" Glenn stopped when she put her finger to her mouth. Landry stepped next to him.

They stood still, the rustle of leaves in the breeze, the jeer of a blue jay, the bark of a squirrel in the branches above—then he heard it. A voice. A small, high-pitched voice emanating from deeper in the trees.

"Mommy?"

[4]

The ER doctor pulled the curved needle and tied off the nylon suture with a needle holder. She snipped the remaining thread with tiny scissors and smiled at Thomas, who lay bare chested in an emergency-room bed, a heated blanket across his legs, green gripper socks on his feet.

Dr. Pangborn, by the name tag, placed her tools along with others she hadn't used but would be sterilized anyway, on a cloth-covered stainless-steel tray. A machine behind Thomas, attached to him with wires, beeped. A bag of saline fluid hung off an IV pole.

"You're lucky," the doctor said, snapping off her vinyl gloves and dropping them on the used tools. "The police officer patiently waiting for you outside the curtain said you were stabbed with an eight-inch chef's knife. If four inches of that had gone through your chest, we wouldn't be having this conversation."

A nurse, who introduced herself as Bonnie, painted the wound with Polysporin and pressed a large square bandage over the stitches.

"Because I'd be dead."

Dr. Pangborn nodded, her smile beginning to droop. "Yes. The lucky part is, a chef's knife is around one-and-a-half to two inches wide, which is a lot more than the 19.7 millimeters between the intercostal spaces." She stopped herself and grinned again. "That's the space between your ribs."

Thomas nodded. He liked this doctor; she translated her words into plain English. "How wide is 19.7 millimeters? I never had to learn metric."

"Around three-quarters of an inch," she said, holding up her index finger and thumb. "The angle of the blade, the force behind it, and the position of the strike had no chance of doing any more damage than it did, which is to penetrate your pectoral muscle. Now, if she'd come up under the ribs—"

Thomas raised his palm toward her and she stopped; pink rose in her cheeks.

"Oh, sorry," she said, taking a small step backward. "I'm happy you're all right."

"All right? As in, I can go home, all right?"

Dr. Pangborn nodded, the smile returning, the pink fading. "Yes. Just make sure you clean the wound with cold water and regular old soap, rub some Neosporin on it, and change the bandage twice a day. If it starts oozing, or the skin begins to turn red—especially if the redness snakes out from the wound—please see your primary-care physician." She stood, reaching behind her head and pulling her ponytail tight. "If everything goes fine, they can remove those stitches in two weeks. However, you might not want to lift anything heavy for a while."

"I work on a farm," he said.

She patted Thomas's arm. "Not for at least two weeks, you don't."

"Thanks, Doc," he said, and started to sit up.

She rested a hand on his shoulder to stop him. "I'll get you a scrub top. You can leave *after* the friendly officer has a few words with you."

Thomas knew if Elizabeth, a nurse, really wanted to kill him, she could have. Gone right up under the rib cage and pushed all eight inches of that blade into his heart. She didn't do this, at least not on her own, but as the shadow of the St. Joe cop rose behind the white curtain, then pulled it open, he knew he couldn't tell him a damn thing.

[5]

Shadows stretched long through the trees. The hoot of an owl just waking to hunt echoed in the canopy. Glenn pulled to a stop as he and Brittany broke into a clearing. On a great, wide oak in the center of prairie grass, a smile—*the* smile—painted with the Daugherty family's blood on its trunk, the words "Taka Farinn At Dagr" carved into the bark below. He tried to swallow the knot that gripped his throat.

"Find out what that gibberish means," Glenn said to Brittany before turning toward the forest. "Olivia?" he called. "This is Sheriff Kirkhoff. My deputies and I are here to help you."

Something tugged at his arm. He turned, expecting his sleeve caught on a branch, or that monster ready to eat his face, but it was Brittany. She shook her head at him.

"That might scare her, sir," she whispered. "Young children are sometimes afraid of authority, like they might have done something wrong. Please, let me."

"Yes," he mouthed, and she took a step in front of him, cupping hands to her face.

"Olivia. Sweetie, we know you're out here somewhere," she shouted, but not really. Her voice was loud, but soft, caring. "My name's Brittany. I'm here with some people who want to take care of you, baby girl. Please let us. It's getting dark, and I don't know about you, but I need French fries."

A squeak came from nearby. Glenn didn't realize it, but he'd been holding his breath.

"How do I know you're nice?" the little girl asked. "That other lady looked nice, but she wasn't. Not at all. She, she—she ate my daddy's head."

Glenn gritted his teeth and let out his breath. In another reality, that would be funny.

"Well, honey, that's awful. That's the awfullest thing I've ever heard," Brittany said, her hands now down at her sides. "But we're with the sheriff's department. It's our job to take care of kids who are lost out in the woods. If you come to my voice, we can put you in the sheriff's car and take you someplace safe, where you'll never see that other lady ever again."

A bird trilled, making Glenn jump. He leaned back, sticking his thumbs in his belt.

"What about the French fries?"

Brittany exhaled, a smile crawling up her cheeks.

"We'll stop at McDonald's on the way there."

A waif of a girl stepped from behind the wide oak, her clothes torn from brush, a cheek scratched, her knees stained with dirt. She sucked her thumb.

"How about a Happy Meal?" she asked around the digit.

This time Brittany laughed. "I'll buy it for you myself," she said, squatting to the child's eye level, knees popping from the movement.

Olivia stepped over tree roots and fallen branches; Brittany didn't stand or move toward her. She let the girl—this girl without a family—walk to her, and kept her hands down before Olivia wrapped her arms around Brittany's neck. Only then did the deputy fold her own arms over the girl and stand.

She looked toward Glenn, tears beginning to run down her cheeks. "You ready, boss?"

[6]

St. Joe Police Corporal Downs seemed polite enough when he stepped into Thomas's partitioned room, cap under his arm, interview notebook and pen in his hands. The man nodded to Thomas and asked if it was okay if he sat.

"So," Corporal Downs began. The man, tall but lanky and perched on the stool the doctor vacated, looked like a teen whose width hadn't caught up with his height. "Did you know the suspect?"

Thomas nodded. "Yeah. For a couple of years, actually. Not well, just casually."

Downs scratched Thomas's words in his notebook.

"What reasons might she have had for assaulting you? Bad blood? Jilted lover?"

"No, nothing like that." *There's a devil coming here.* "She, uh. Before I met her, she delivered my girlfriend's baby." *It smiled at me like it knew something. Like that demon baby knew something.* "I only know her because of AA meetings."

The officer's head cocked to the side. "But she was drunk at the time of the assault."

Thomas nodded, the movement sending a pain through his chest. Not bad, not even a flinch, but it was going to be tough pulling on that shirt.

"Relapses are common. I hadn't seen her for several months before tonight."

Downs wrote more into his notebook and flipped over the page. "Did she say anything? Such as why she attacked you?"

"*The fairy told me to do it.*"

Thomas shook his head. "No, sir," he lied. Jillian was behind the attack, she forced Elizabeth to try to murder him.

Although, if Jillian wanted me dead, why didn't she do it herself?

The nurse wasn't a killer, she was a healer. To Jillian, she was a tool, a puppet, a plaything; and if he explained this to Downs, the officer wouldn't understand a bit of it.

Thin paper rustled as Downs licked his thumb and went back in his notebook.

"During interviews with AA members Jerry Luftkin and Frank Gilbert, they both said after the attack, she sat on the pavement like she was waiting for the police, and that a 'fairy' instructed her to stab you." He flipped back to Thomas's interview. "What do you remember about this?"

A slight smile crossed Thomas's face and he motioned to his chest. "I was a little distracted at the time."

"Of course." When Downs looked up from his notebook, his face was flat, emotionless. "Mr. Cavanaugh, I know your past. I'm well aware of your stint in Sisters of Mercy, your involvement with the St. Joe Angel of Death Robert Garrett, your presence at his death; now you're dating his girlfriend."

Thomas's stomach began to pinch into a knot; the bed seemed to want to swallow him. This was wrong. The dressing over Thomas's wound rose and fell over his pounding heart. Downs leaned forward, his pointed elbows resting on his pointed knees. The colors of the man's eyes spun into a cartoon hypnotist's, the blacks and whites rotating until they stopped, nothing left but a black, oily sheen.

"It's all very suspicious." His breath smelled like a cornfield. A hand went to his holster, the click of his thumb unlatching the weapon nearly covered by the machine that went "beep."

"Tom," he said. "I can call you Tom, right? We're friends here. Now, Tom, what do you know about elves?"

Thomas's phone buzzed on the table beside his bed; it barely registered.

The curtain pulled back and a nurse in Disney princess-themed scrubs stepped in, a teal scrub top in one hand, a clipboard in the other. Thomas choked back a scream.

"Oh, I'm sorry," she said.

At the sound of her voice, Downs leaned back; confusion covered his face.

"No," Thomas said, the word soft, pained. "That's fine. I think we were finished here." Thomas glared at the demon cop, the man's eyes human again. "Isn't that right, Corporal Downs?"

Buzz.

The man glanced at Thomas, then the nurse, then at his fingers on the handle of the Glock. He jerked his hand away like it had been burned.

He doesn't know where he is, Thomas knew. *Jillian was in control of him. He was going to kill me.*

The nurse stepped up to Thomas and helped him sit, Thomas watching Corporal Downs over her shoulder, the pain only a backdrop to the insanity. She eased his arms into the shirt, then pulled it over his head.

Buzz.

"You don't have to return this, Mr. Cavanaugh," she said, the cheer in her voice a sharp contrast to the death that had hung over the room seconds before. "Consider it a souvenir of having survived."

Downs stood, arms stretching out to the sides to keep his balance, and failed. He dropped back onto the stool, the wheels scooting him into the wall.

The nurse dropped the clipboard on the bed and moved to him. "Are you all right, Officer?"

Buzz.

The man looked up, his eyes wide. "Y-yes," he stuttered. "Just a, uh, long day, ma'am." He used the wall to help him stand and said nothing more as he left the room.

"That was strange," the nurse said before picking up the clipboard and handing it to Thomas. "These are your discharge papers."

He ignored his phone and began to fill out the paperwork to get the hell out of there.

[7]

Word had come in that Elizabeth Condon, the drunk woman Glenn had driven home, stabbed Thomas Cavanaugh at an AA meeting in St. Joe. The same meeting Todd Marshall had once attended. Todd had been married to a woman both Thomas and Jillian knew from their stay at Sisters of Mercy. Too many coincidences, too many connections.

With Brittany and the girl, Olivia, finishing a Happy Meal at the deputy's desk, Glenn called for Elizabeth Condon to be placed in an interrogation room.

Deep inside the joint home for the Buchanan County Sheriff's Department and the St. Joseph Police Department, the brick-and-stone building spanning two city blocks, he stood and watched through the two-way glass. Elizabeth, in prison orange, sat at a scarred metal table, her restraints secured by a metal ring that kept her from attempting to run or jump her interrogator. As Glenn watched this broken woman, her forehead resting on her hands, he knew she wasn't going to try either. He popped a piece of peppermint gum before knocking on the door; his mouth still tasted like vomit. He handed a deputy his gun belt. No weapons around dangerous criminals, even when they looked like whipped pups; it was policy.

She didn't move when Glenn knocked and punched in the code to unlock the door; didn't register that another human was in the room, even after the sheriff pulled the metal chair across the worn tile, the bare tips of the legs screeching.

He sat and rested his elbows on the table. "Elizabeth?"

She still didn't move. He could smell the booze that clung to her from across the table.

"Elizabeth, it's Sheriff Kirkhoff."

The nurse lifted her head from the table, the hands it had rested on wet with tears. Her eyes, swollen and red.

"I already told the police officer, I did it. I took a knife from my kitchen, drove to the Delores Hadley Community Center, and drank vodka until Thomas Cavanaugh came out of his AA meeting." She paused and coughed; the cotton-mouth had gotten to her.

Glenn looked at the window, where he knew an officer stood, watching, waiting for this woman to do something stupid. He formed his hand to look like he held a cup and raised it to his mouth.

"Then I walked up to him and stabbed him in the chest." Her head lowered back into her hands. "It's as simple as that, Sheriff."

A beep signaled the door would open in a moment. A St. Joe police officer he didn't recognize, no more than a kid, handed him a paper cup with water. Glenn placed it in front of Elizabeth. Her head rose and she looked at it over her knuckles.

"Thanks," she said, and sat up, taking a long drink.

"What I'm confused about is why, Elizabeth?"

She crushed the empty cup in her hand; it bounced against the table. "I'm sorry, Sheriff, but you won't believe me."

The chair shrieked as he pushed it back far enough to cross his legs. Casually, he clasped his fingers behind his head.

"Try me. You have no idea what I'll believe." His eyes glared into hers; she didn't fidget like someone who was guilty, like someone lying. "For instance, there's blood in your car. It's a mess, frankly. Good thing you have vinyl seats." He paused for a reaction. There was none. "It's a mixture of the blood from three people slaughtered in the Pigeon Hill Conservation Area, south of town."

He dropped his leg to the floor and leaned forward. "They were fed through a food processor, by the looks of them."

"I didn't do that," she snapped, life coming back into her.

"I know," Glenn said, slowly moving back in his chair. "Closest estimate we have is those murders happened right before you stabbed Mr. Cavanaugh. You didn't have time to attack the Daugherty family and drive to the community center to stab Cavanaugh, let alone get as intoxicated as you were. So the question is, who did? And why were they in your car?"

Her eyes finally broke away; she looked at her hands in a bunch before her.

"That's the part you won't believe," she whispered.

"You keep saying that." Glenn pulled a toothpick from his uniform pocket and stuck it in his mouth. It wasn't a habit of his, but the friendly good-ol'-boy effect usually lightened people up. "But you don't know me very well, Elizabeth. In fact, this is only the second time we've met. The first time was—well, I suppose you might not remember. You were drunk as hell, swerving all over the road, and I pulled you over. I didn't arrest you, nope. I drove you home and tucked you in." He dropped a hand on the steel table, his index finger tapping a steady cadence.

"Now, who killed the Daugherty family, and why were they in your car?"

The table slid a few millimeters when Elizabeth sat back in her chair, her wrist restraints catching. Her head leaned back; she stared at the ceiling.

"Her name is—"

"Jillian," Glenn finished for her.

She jerked toward the table, hands pressed on its top, her red swollen eyes soaked with fear.

"I told you you'd have no idea what I'll believe." Glenn produced a notebook and pen, opening to a blank page. "You see, I've had Jillian in my car as well, disguised as a little girl, lost and wandering the back county roads. When she opened her mouth, it was big and wide, wider than a human mouth *could* be. It was full of crocodile teeth, Elizabeth. Have you seen those?"

Her head moved in a slow nod; she was on autopilot.

"Jillian ripped out my deputy's throat with those teeth." He scribbled the date, time, place, and their names at the top of the page, and stared into her eyes. "She just killed a family and, I believe, coerced you into trying to murder a man I've known since he was a boy. I need to stop her before any more bodies pile up, but I can't without more information. Will you help me?"

It took more than an hour, but Elizabeth told him everything.

CHAPTER THIRTEEN

[1]

THE MOBILE PHONE in Thomas's pocket vibrated as he approached his truck in the hospital parking lot. Jerry had driven Thomas's truck there from the community center—just another example of recovering drunks being the nicest people he'd ever met. He pulled out his phone. Fifteen missed calls and a dozen text messages, all but one from Marguerite. The other was from Mom; she and Dad were in Florida. They needed the break. Thomas figured he'd have to hire someone to do the farm chores until a doctor gave him a thumbs-up.

In the distance, the Ferris wheel at the Jesse James Days festival turned slowly and an empty car crested the top of the roller coaster, visible over the downtown buildings. No screams, just air wrenches grinding in the distance.

The carnival would be up and running soon enough. He grinned. Marguerite's going to shit when I tell her I'm taking Jacob to ride the roller coaster.

The phone vibrated again; it was Marguerite. He swiped his thumb.

"Hey," he said and unlocked the door.

"Oh my God, Thomas, where have you been?" Panic drenched her voice.

"Oh, wow, okay." Any thought of the past few hours gone. "What's wrong?"

She blew her nose on the other end of the call. "It's Jakie," she said. "He was, he was . . ."

No.

"Honey, what about Jacob? Is he hurt?"

She snorted, probably sucking back running snot.

"No, Thomas. I can't find him. He's gone." The tears she'd tried to hold back started to flow, the sobs choked her words.

Thomas took a deep breath, trying to calm his pounding heart. He slowly pulled himself into the driver's seat, the knife wound shooting pain through his chest.

"Don't get too worried. There's lots of places he can hide," he said through gritted teeth. Thomas had hidden at Uncle Boyd's place at Jacob's age, but Jillian was here; Jacob wasn't safe. "I'm on my way. Hey—" He paused and took a deep breath. "Everything's going to be okay. We'll find him."

But Thomas didn't believe that.

He started the truck and tore out of the lot.

[2]

Sedate gray on concrete painted Elizabeth's world. She lay on the bottom bunk in a seven by twelve-foot jail cell in the depths of the facility, the thin, bare mattress doing little to relax her. The image of the knife in her hand puncturing Thomas Cavanaugh's chest was burned into her consciousness. She knew it would be burned there forever, however long that was.

The springs of the upper bunk creaked as the occupant rolled over, but Elizabeth knew there was no one else in the room. A pair of legs in blue jeans dropped over the side of the bunk and dangled two feet from Elizabeth's face. She didn't flinch; the tendrils of fear she'd lived with since that demon Jenkins baby squeezed from his mother's womb were gone. She never thought she could be surprised again.

"What the hell do you want?" she asked, her voice flat, emotionless.

The upper springs gave one last squeak as the legs dropped, the flat Vans the person wore slapping the concrete. Jillian, the fairy woman, turned and sat cross-legged on the floor. Reaching behind her, she pulled a pint of vodka from her back pocket, the dim light from the corridor causing the invisible liquid to glow inside the clear plastic bottle. Or maybe the fairy did that. Jillian sat the bottle within Elizabeth's reach, then leaned back, holding her knees for balance.

"You tried, honey. Oh, yes, you tried to do what I asked, but you failed. Now you're here, useless to me." Lips, so gentle, so tender, so fragile, pulled across Jillian's face, stretching to her ears, like her face were made of rubber. "What, oh what, am I going to do with you?"

Elizabeth propped herself up on one elbow.

"I don't know. What *are* you going to do with me?"

Jillian's smile widened further, an occasional sharp, conical tooth popping from between her lips. She picked up the bottle and tossed it onto Elizabeth's bed.

"Keep you lubricated until I need you again."

The drink in her system had begun to fade; she pulled the bottle closer.

"What am I going to do when you come for me?" Elizabeth asked. "Walk through the bars?"

A black, oily sheen flowed across Jillian's eyes until it covered her sclera. She reached into the air and shuffled her fingers like a street magician. A key card appeared between her thumb and index finger. She held it out to Elizabeth.

"No. Walking through bars is *my* trick." Jillian pushed the card closer to the nurse. "Take it. You'll need it."

Elizabeth plucked it from Jillian's grip, not touching the fairy's skin.

"It won't do me any good. Guards do cell checks. They'll find it."

Jillian laughed, the cold, mirthless rhythm natural out of her jagged mouth.

"They're only human, my dear," Jillian said. "All they'll see is the three of clubs." Elizabeth opened her mouth, but the fairy woman pinched her fingers together in a Darth Vader Force choke, cutting off the nurse's words. "And your prison orange? I'll bring you some clothes that suit you better. You will—"

Oh shit.

Elizabeth scooted back until she was pressing against the cold concrete. Jillian's cold black eyes, as big as a cartoon character's, froze her to the jail-cell wall. The fairy's jaw fell, stretching until the chin hit her lap. Elizabeth's scream split the dimly lighted prison wing. Someone down the corridor shouted for her to shut the hell up.

"I have to go now," Jillian said, her face snapping back to human. "That little bastard finally stepped into my trap." She nodded at Elizabeth. "Don't go anywhere, honey."

The red-haired monster stood and walked toward the bars to Elizabeth's cell, her flesh absorbing the rolled steel bars as she stepped through to the other side, the bars remaining whole. The fairy's split flesh melded back into Jillian. She turned toward Elizabeth, who was propped up by the concrete wall, and blew her a kiss, vanishing in the dim light of the corridor.

Elizabeth unscrewed the pint of vodka with shaking hands and drank deeply.

[3]

The sheriff's cruiser sat at an angle on the wide shoulder of Interstate 29, its wheels turned toward the highway. Vehicles comically slowed when they noticed law enforcement, but Glenn wasn't interested in speeders. His hands shook too much; he needed to put some time between now and a short interview he'd had with Olivia Daugherty.

"We met a lady in the forest," she'd told him. "She said I looked tasty."

Tasty? It was as disturbing as it sounded.

"What did she look like?" Glenn asked, holding a pretend cup of tea, pinky out.

Red hair.

"Her hair was red, Sheriff man."

Pretty.

"And she was really pretty."

In jeans and a T-shirt.

"What did she wear, hon?" he asked.

"She wore a T-shirt with a band on it, I think. It looks like one Jaden wears, and she had jeans and shoes with black-and-white checkers."

"So, she stopped your family on the trail." Glenn swallowed hard. He did not want to ask the next question. "What did she do next?"

Olivia's gaze stared straight into Glenn's. "She ate my daddy's whole head in one bite."

The ring of Glenn's mobile phone on the passenger seat jerked him away from this memory. He fumbled with it, his hands still shaking, almost hanging up on the caller—Brittany. He finally slid his thumb across the screen and placed the device to his ear.

"Yes?"

"You okay, Sheriff?" his deputy asked.

"Yeah, of course," he said, knowing he did not at all feel okay. "What can I help you with?" He resisted calling her "kiddo."

"A couple of things, sir." A crunch sounded through Brittany's pause. "First, I got a return call from a dead languages professor at the university up in Maryville. Those words on the tree are apparently Old Norse, you know, the kind Vikings spoke. They mean, 'welcome to the end of days.'"

That's not at all ominous.

"What's number two?"

More crunches.

"I'm at the scene of the Daugherty family murder," she said. "It's weird. Everything here is dead."

Are you kidding me? "I was there, Deputy. I know that."

"No. Not the people. That's not what I mean." The crunching came closer to the mic. "You hear that? It's leaves."

"So? There are dead leaves in the woods."

"It's May, Sheriff," she said, "and I didn't pick them off the ground, although I could have. I pulled these leaves off an oak. All the trees, the underbrush at Pigeon Hill, they're, well, they're brown. It looks like October. And the creek's dried up. It's not the Daugherty family I'm talking about. The *forest* is dead, Sheriff."

What now?

"All except that big oak tree in the clearing, the one with the red smiley face with all the teeth and those strange words."

Yeah, I remember.

"We had one of those smiley faces when I worked up in Andrew County about, I don't know, six, eight years ago."

The phone slipped from Glenn's shaking hand.

[4]

Marguerite leaped from the porch steps and ran toward the truck when Thomas pulled under the big tree and clanked the steering column gear shift into park. He slid the door shut just as Marguerite threw herself into his arms. Pain tore through his stitched knife wound.

"Owwww," he hissed.

Marguerite slid off him, her arms still around his neck.

"What's wrong? And why are you wearing scrubs?"

The thought of keeping one more thing off her mind had crossed his own; Thomas was going to keep the attack quiet as long as possible, but she would find out soon enough. He pulled her hands from his neck and held them in his.

"I'm okay, honey. I, uh, um, I was stabbed in the chest after my meeting tonight."

Eyes, often soft, usually mischievous, were now wide with fear. "You were *what?*"

She yanked her hands from his and pulled at his shirt, revealing the bandage.

"It's okay, I'm fine, really. The knife was too big to fit between my ribs, so it didn't do anything but cut a coin slot in my boob."

The shirt dropped back into place. "Why the hell would anybody want to stab you?"

He scratched the back of his head and shrugged. He couldn't mention Jillian when Jacob was missing.

"That's the weird thing. It was the nurse in the birthing room when you had Jacob." Thomas put an arm around her waist and drew her close again, trying to hide his wince of pain. "Have you found Jacob yet?"

She shook her head.

"He's not in the house, and I've shouted and shouted out here. I've heard nothing." Her voice cracked at the last words. "Except coyotes, a few minutes before you pulled up. We've got to find him before dark."

Thomas leaned in and kissed her forehead, the salty tang of sweat on her skin.

"We will," he said. "I'll head out back. When I was a kid, I couldn't resist running loose in the fields."

As she kissed his cheek, he hoped he was right.

[5]

The bladed corn leaves scraped Jacob's face and arms as he walked down the row. The fairy circle. The fairy circle pulled him in, and the earth swallowed him before pooping him into this field. Stupid Jillian did this. The moment he materialized in the dirt between the cornrows, he knew. Jacob stood and walked, the corn on either side short, stunted.

A turkey vulture squawked and burst from the corn as Jacob stomped down the row toward a sun-bleached barn at the end of the field. The big greasy-feathered bird flapped clumsily like it didn't know how to fly; the ungainly wings beat until the creature gained air and lifted its bulk into the sky.

The burn of frustration ignited an urge to throw something at the bird but quickly vanished as if in a mist. A woman stood at the end of the rows, the barn looming over her. She wore jeans and a T-shirt, but it was her fiery hair that threw a fist into Jacob's chest. It was Jillian, of course.

He trudged toward her.

"Well, hello, honey bug," she said when he'd closed the gap between them. "It's been too long."

"No," he wanted to shout at her, but the anger got lost in the uttering. What came out was soft, weak. "It hasn't been long enough."

Jillian laughed, the sound of chimes on the wind.

"Oh, you've grown so much, little man, but something's different about you."

Jacob pushed his hands into his pockets. "Why did you bring me here?"

Another laugh escaped her mouth, the lips now stretched beyond their width, the sound not chimes but iron bells out of key.

"I want you." She paused to shake her head, her red mane flying free behind her. "No, that's a lie. I *need* you, Jacob."

A frown dragged across his face.

"What for?"

She stepped toward him, and Jacob stepped back. Once, he'd had no fear of her, he could do things she couldn't. Now his world seemed so much different. Jillian's slim hands grabbed his shoulders, and squeezed.

"Remember how you breathed life into my dead world?"

All the dust, the heat. Jacob remembered holding his arms to the sky, a warmth escaping him as grass sprouted from the scorched, cracked earth, and water fell from the sky, filling the basin of the sea. Then she made him (no she *didn't*—I kinda wanted to) drag people from Earth to the Alf place for her to kill, or capture, or whatever. The memory made his stomach hurt. All that power, the power to create and to kill, seemed an impossible memory. He didn't want to do anything like that ever again.

"I don't do things for you anymore," he said in a whisper.

She nodded, the motion slow, rhythmic, like a bobblehead.

"Sure you do, baby," she said. "I need you to transform something else."

His brow pinched. "What?"

Jillian's eyes grew—a dim light appeared deep inside her pupil and grew brighter.

"Everything."

[6]

The backyard shed sat quietly, its shadows looming like old movie monsters in the deep corners where the light couldn't reach. The rusty engine from a 1940s Model B Allis Chalmers tractor lay on a slab of concrete; beside it was a snow shovel once attached to a pickup Uncle Boyd hadn't had since Thomas was a kid. Thomas rarely ventured out here, not only because he didn't need to but also since the first time he stepped into this old building, with its thick layer of dust and bowing A-frame roof, it looked too much like the machine shed on Dad's farm. The shed where the little girl haunted him. Since then, Thomas had hated dusty corners in dark places.

"Jacob!" Marguerite's voice was soft and muffled by distance and the old shed between them.

"It's Jillian," Thomas said to no one. He slammed a fist into a rotting board; his hand went through the wall, and pain lanced his wound. "She took him. She had to."

He started toward the door, but a flicker in a dark corner froze his feet. Thomas pulled his fist from the hole and stepped toward the corner, blood welling from a dozen superficial cuts. The light flickered again, and he stepped closer; a dusty Lite-Brite sat on a rusty arc welder.

The toy flickered again, then the light stayed on. Thomas leaned over the Lite-Brite, a hand on either side. Pegs of blue, red, and yellow formed a sentence. A sentence written by—

"Jillian."

I HAVE THE BOY, it read.

The anger boiling inside Thomas almost threw the Lite-Brite across the shed, but he stopped. It was evidence.

"Jacob," he shouted. No voice returned.

He left the shed and approached Parman's field, behind his house, a field he would have played in for hours as a child. Something red lay at the end of the lawn. Thomas jogged toward it, but the knife wound sent sharp jabs into his chest. He stopped and lifted his shirt; blood soaked through the bandage.

"Jakie, baby," Marguerite called from the far side of the house, her voice now raw, mournful.

Thomas walked, grasping his wound, and stopped at the red lump. A St. Joe Mustangs cap; the one Jacob wore earlier when they'd played catch. It lay in the circle of mushrooms. Jillian's fairy circle.

"Goddamn it."

[7]

Jillian was wicked, Jacob knew, like Maleficent from that movie. She stood and held her arms up to the sky.

"I need you to transform this."

Jason Offutt

"No," Jacob said, with the voice of a child much younger. "I can't and I won't. Do it, do it yourself."

"Oh my, little one. You have changed so much," she said through her terror smile. "I am magic, but I have to feed to find that kind of power, to suck up so many of those tasty little souls, and that takes time, Jakie. So much time. What happened to you? You were a god. You could once transform this world with a blink of your eyes. Can you even do that anymore?"

She clenched her fists and a patch of stunted, green cornstalks withered into dried sticks.

A frown pulled at him. "I'm not going to help you."

She laughed, no humor in the sound.

"It was Daddy Tom, wasn't it? He's instilled some sense of right and wrong in the little devil boy." She snorted a laugh. "He's weak, you know? Nice people always are." She turned her head to stare at the sun for an uncomfortably long time before she waved him off. "I might eat him first."

Fear stabbed at Jacob. "No." He again tried to scream it, but there was no force behind the word.

Jillian shrugged, then cupped her hands together. Purple fire blazed from between her fingers.

"Suit yourself, weaky, weaky weaker," she said, and threw her arms forward. A ball of sizzling lilac flew at Jacob.

Those words had come out of Jacob's mouth as a younger child. They described Gramma, Mom, those Alf people he pulled into Jillian's world. Shame washed over him, pulling him down; she was right.

He did nothing to defend himself, and the ball struck him in the chest, knocking him backward onto the rough clods of dirt between the rows. His head bounced off the hard ground; pain erupted in an explosion.

"I guess I don't need you anymore," she said, her voice small and far away. "Goodbye, little one. Have fun being nothing."

(230)

A feeble cough came; it hurt his chest. He lay still, the jagged edges of clods jabbing the tender parts of his back. Tears stung his eyes as he stared into the cloudless blue sky; high above, the turkey vulture still soared through his line of vision, but his head didn't move to follow it. The tears broke free and ran silently, washing the dirt from his cheeks, because he knew Jillian was stronger than he was. He hadn't even had the will to try to protect himself with what little power he had left—if he could. And what if he couldn't?

Jacob didn't know how long he lay in the field, but when he finally stood, Jillian was gone. He ran.

[8]

Glenn pulled his patrol car onto M-31. The graying asphalt covered in a drunken spiderweb of cracks needed patching, and he knew the county didn't have the money to do it in their budget this year. The warm shadows of dusk, cast from tall patches of johnsongrass in the ugly cornfields, stood like markers in a graveyard. The gravel road south of US 36 and north of Easton would take him to his sister Kathy's house. She'd called on his way out to the parking lot saying she'd fixed too much stroganoff, and if he'd like he could swing by for supper and a couple of beers afterward with Roy while they caught the Royals game on TV.

He didn't know how much attention he'd pay to the game. A call to Bob Gonnor up in Andrew County filled in a blank. The monster who ate Maddy—Jillian—wasn't confined by geography. Calumet Cemetery was a short drive from Boyd's old house, where she'd been living. Every scrap of evidence on his laptop connected the smiley-faced murders to Jillian Robertson and Thomas Cavanaugh; some were loose connections, but they were there.

When the Andrew County Sheriff's Department arrived at the cemetery, they found the body of Trey Dawson spread across the hood of his 2016 Camaro, a ragged wound in his chest and his heart missing. The smiley face was painted on his front windshield.

"Gruesome," Bob had told him. "Went on the call myself. My nephew had just bought seed from him too."

Seed?

"Where'd he work?"

"Pioneer Seeds in St. Joe," Bob said. "He was an in-person salesman; drove around to farms cutting deals with farmers. He must have been pretty good at it, from the looks of his car."

He made a note to ask Thomas or Kyle where they bought their seed.

Glenn turned on South 14 East and cruised down the gravel road, a streak of dust traveling behind the car like a jet contrail.

The connections kept clicking into place around Thomas Cavanaugh, except Maddy—his jaws tensed—who was in the wrong place at the wrong time. Jillian must be trying to hurt Thomas one little piece at a time. The only part that really puzzled him were John and Carrie McMasters. Where did they fit?

He pulled the mic from its cradle and clicked the talk button.

"Kirkhoff here."

The radio hissed and a deputy came on. "Yes, Sheriff."

Aaron.

"I want you to contact the following to see if you can locate a photograph of Jillian Robertson." He paused to run a sleeve across his upper lip. He had no idea when he'd begun to sweat, but it came. His undershirt stuck to his skin. "The psych ward at Sisters of Mercy Hospital, Kyle and Debbie Cavanaugh, Thomas Cavanaugh. You got that?"

"Yes, sir," Aaron said. "What do I do when I find one?"

"Put out an APB on her. This woman is dangerous, Deputy. I believe she's responsible for the deaths of at least eleven people in Buchanan and Andrew Counties in the past eight to nine years."

A whistle came through the speaker. "What? A serial killer? We have a *serial* killer?"

"Arrrr!" Glenn shouted inside the cruiser, his thumb off the talk button. Why did I say that over the air? But—

He scratched his red chin stubble with the mic before clicking the button. The press would get this, but they needed to. Everyone needed to.

"Yes, we have a serial killer. Find that picture and get her face in front of everybody you can. And—" He stopped, his jaws clenched tight. "She's dangerous."

"I kind of got that, Sheriff," Aaron said, a hint of a grin in his voice. Damn it.

"She killed Maddy." What am I doing? He sucked in a deep breath; it seeped out in a slow hiss: "That night, Thomas Cavanaugh saved my life when he shot Jillian in the chest with my shotgun." It was too late in the game to keep playing like she was normal. The rules changed whenever Jillian showed she could change too. This woman wasn't a woman, she was a monster; it was time to treat her like one. "She walked away from that, Aaron. She walked away from a gaping chest wound. I saw it. It healed itself before she vanished."

Silence.

"Uh, Sheriff. Do you feel all right?" the deputy asked. "Boyd talked like this sometimes. He listened to that Cap Anderson UFO show almost every night. He—"

"Listen to me, Deputy." Glenn's voice was a low growl. "I don't give two shits if you believe me. What I do give two shits about is taking down Jillian Robertson. She is more dangerous than you can imagine, son. She's not human. If anyone finds her, shoot to kill."

The radio fell silent for what felt like minutes, but Glenn knew it was probably a few seconds.

"Sheriff? Are you serious?" Aaron asked.

I sound crazy. But I'm not. "Those are my orders. Follow them or get me somebody who will."

Aaron came back on immediately. "Yes, sir."

"And alert St. Joe PD and the Highway Patrol."

The mic clicked back into its holder; in the second it took for Glenn to look at the dash holder and back to the road, a child staggered from the cornfield into the road.

"What?" he snapped, his foot hitting the brake pedal. The big car slid toward the ditch before it skidded to a stop on the gravel; gray powder filled the air.

He sat as the dust swirled around the car, parts of the child appearing and disappearing in the cloud.

"Jillian?"

Jillian the fairy, Jillian the monster. His finger hit a button on the armrest, and the door locks clicked loudly, even over the hammering of Glenn's heart.

He sat, his knuckles aching on the steering wheel as the dust began to dissipate; sweat beaded on his face and soaked into his undershirt despite the air-conditioning blowing over him. Through the swirling cloud he saw the child was a boy of about seven or eight; the kid stood trying to wave the dust away from his face, his eyes pinched tight. He—

"Jacob?" Glenn wheezed, his chest tight.

A sudden burst of wind sent the dust over the field on the south side of the road, leaving Jacob Jenkins standing in the road, coughing. Glenn shifted the car into park and unlocked the driver's-side door, standing tall, his right foot still in the car, his right hand on his service weapon, piss ready to squirt down his leg at any second.

"Jacob?" he said, loud enough for the boy to hear over the purring engine. "Jacob Jenkins?"

The boy coughed into his right forearm, his shoulders slumped, his eyes on the road.

First piece of evidence: Jacob's right-handed.

"Yes." He coughed again; the word barely audible. "Yes, Sheriff Glenn."

Second piece, he always calls me Sheriff Glenn.

"What do I call your mom?"

The boy squinted at him before shoving his fingers through his dust-whitened hair and shaking his hand. When he was finished, his hair was more or less black again. He finally looked up at Glenn; the child's face was grim, like it held too heavy a burden for his age.

"Margie," the boy said. "But I don't know why. That's not her name."

Third. I call her Margie.

"What are you doing out here, Jacob?"

His hands found their way into his pockets.

"That stupid Jillian again," he said. "I wanna go home, Sheriff Glenn." He took a step toward the car, stopping when Glenn flinched. But when the child's eyes looked up into Glenn's, he saw pain and worry, a canvas void of hope.

"Can you take me home?" Jacob asked. "Mom and Daddy Tom are probably worried."

Glenn choked back his own tears.

Yeah. Daddy Tom. The warm evening air, carried by a breeze, suddenly felt good. This was Jacob Jenkins. Jillian would have no idea he called Thomas this.

"Sure, kiddo." Glenn nodded toward the passenger side. "Get in."

His thumb rubbed against an armrest button and the passenger side unlocked. Jacob opened the door and sat. Glenn tried to smile, but the boy's demeanor troubled him. Jacob pulled down his seat belt and fumbled the latch into the buckle. Dark, muddy lines streaked from his eyes. The boy had been crying for a while.

"Why did Jillian kidnap you this time?"

Jacob bit his bottom lip, then forced out little spits of dirt. "She wanted me to help her feed."

Glenn's stomach felt like it dropped to his toes.

"Feed? What . . . what does Jillian feed on?"

The little boy's deep, dark, mournful eyes seemed to swallow him as tears began to flow.

"Souls."

Steam rose into the cool May evening from the surface of the hot tub, the jet-driven water set at 102 degrees Fahrenheit. Dana Carroll sat a pitcher of margaritas on the deck next to the hot tub, the double-bowl glass and plastic container of margarita salt next to it. A lime to moisten the rim of the glass on the salt container.

She fixed a drink with hands that had done this many times before and slipped into the water slowly, sucking air through her teeth as the change in temperature confused her skin, just for a few seconds. She exhaled and stretched her arms to either edge of the tub and lay her head back on the section of pool noodle she used to protect her neck. The stars Sirius A and Polaris shone brightest in a sky turning from blue to black. Venus held up its end, shining in the west, just over her neighbor's trees. Dana took a long drink of margarita, the Roca Patrón tequila smooth, delicious. Not like the raw McCormick tequila she'd pounded with her sorority sisters in college. Too many headaches and too much vomit made her realize tequila with an Irish name might not be the best choice. But it was cheap.

She didn't have to be cheap anymore. Nurse Carroll had ruled the psych ward at Sisters of Mercy Hospital for the past thirty-one years, earned every dollar that bought this house in Mission Woods, and put up the six-foot-tall wooden privacy fence that separated her home from her brainless neighbors who wanted to talk. Pfft. If Dana wanted to talk, she'd initiate it, and she didn't—ever.

She tipped the stemmed glass and drained half of it before resting the drink back on the deck. Work today had been hell. The cops brought in a teen boy who'd stuck an ice pick through a classmate's temple. Ice pick? She didn't know those relics from the days of ice boxes still existed, but she looked it up. This wooden-handled murder weapon can be purchased online for $10. He sulked, then screamed, then collapsed enough that she could talk with him.

"A shadow follows me," he'd told her. His hands shook, his body twitched. "She's behind me at every step."

"She?" Dana asked the young man.

"*She.*" His hands flapped across his lap. "She, she, *she.* She told me her name. Oh GOD. She told me her name. It's Jillian." He wiped his hospital gown's sleeve across his nose. "Jillian is a nice name." The boy's eyes flared, his mouth pulled into a grimace. "But she's evil. The red-haired monster wants to kill us all. She told me. She . . . she said the next time I see her she'll drink my soul." He giggled. "She wants to eat us up, eat us all up."

Dana threw back the rest of the margarita, and ran the lime wedge across the edge of the glass before removing the lid of the container and grinding the glass's rim into the salt.

Red hair. Jillian.

She'd overseen a red-haired girl named Jillian at Sisters of Mercy years ago. The girl had, what? Why was she there?

Oh damn. She'd scrambled her stepfather's brains with a screwdriver.

A potted blanket flower fell off the deck rail and crashed onto the deck boards. Dana screamed; the margarita glass slipped from her hand and plopped into the water.

"Great," she hissed, and turned back around. Breath caught in her throat. A pair of legs that led up to emerald bikini bottoms stood at the edge of the hot tub. She followed the body up until her eyes reached the face. A pretty young girl of about fourteen stood in front of her, her hair bright red, the smile on her face hard, cold.

Oh dear God, that's Jillian Robertson.

"You haven't aged," stumbled from Dana's lips.

"Nurse Carroll, it's been a long time. Too long," Jillian said. "Let's catch up."

CHAPTER FOURTEEN

THE THIN RED-HAIRED girl dipped her toes into the water, then her whole foot, followed by the other. She lowered herself in up to her armpits and smiled at Dana; the face, the body were now those of a grown woman. Dana's mouth gaped. This was impossible—*she* was impossible.

"What are you?" she whispered.

A margarita glass materialized in Jillian's hand as the pitcher rose from the deck and flew toward her, pouring green liquid into it. Dana couldn't believe what she was seeing.

"Oh, I'm just your friendly neighborhood *álfr*," Jillian said and took a sip. "Oh, Nurse Carroll. This is tasty. You are quite the mixologist."

A shiver ran through Dana despite the 102-degree temperature of the water.

"What do you want from me?"

Jillian threw back the rest of the margarita in one gulp and tossed the glass into the yard.

"What, what, what. Can't I come over and get reacquainted with an old friend?" She swirled a finger in the churning water, a frown puddled in the corners of her lips. "It's a little chilly, don't you think? How hot does this thing get?"

One hundred-four degrees, Dana thought, the words dammed behind her lips.

"One hundred four?" Jillian shook her head. "Look at you, you're shivering."

"Go away," Dana said. "You're not supposed to be here."

Jillian leaned forward, her long red hair dragging through the water. Dana couldn't move.

"Go away. You're not—you're not supposed to be here?" Jillian wagged a finger at her. "Is that what you said to good ol' Robert Garrett when you signed him out of Sisters of Mercy and let him loose on the world?"

The shiver had gone; sweat now rolled down Dana's face. "I—"

"Shhh," Jillian hushed. "Bobby boy was special, I'll grant you that. He may have even controlled your thoughts long enough for you to write that letter to the judge. But in the end, it was your name that set Bobby free."

Dana found her feet and tried to stand, but her shaking legs wouldn't allow it.

"I don't have to explain myself to you," she said, her voice slight, weak.

"He killed hundreds of people." Jillian leaned back, a full margarita glass again in her hand. She took a drink. "And that's on you, honey."

No. No, it's not. You, you—

"You're a monster," Dana finally spit out through her dry mouth.

Jillian raised her margarita hand and placed her other over her chest, her face in mock sorrow.

"Oh, Nurse Carroll. If you prick us, do we not bleed? If I boil you, do you not cook?"

Pain, simply uncomfortable at first, began to attack Dana's skin, searing into her flesh. "The water's burning me." Tears ran down Dana's reddening face, her hair drenched in sweat. "Please. Please leave me alone. I've done *nothing*."

"Yes, you have," Jillian said. "You're a sadistic bitch and have emotionally wounded all those you were supposed to be healing."

Dana looked down at her arms, her breasts. Blisters grew on her skin.

"That's not true!" she moaned. "I only wanted to help my patients. I tried to help *you*. Please, please stop this."

Jillian waved a hand in front of her face, throwing off drops of water. "It's only 120 degrees Fahrenheit, you baby. Tough it out." She leaned back in the tub and stared up at the sky. "Lovely night tonight, isn't it? The moon's almost full. I love it when the moon's full, don't you? Of course, my world has two moons."

Dana's vision began to spin, her head light from the pain, the insufferable heat.

"You ever seen a blood moon? It's when the moon is in a total lunar eclipse." She sucked in cool air while her toes played footsie with Dana. "We're going to have one soon. The astronomers are going to shit themselves because it's not supposed to happen. Oh baby, I guarantee it."

Black spots swam in Dana's vision, her consciousness beginning to fade.

"You're killing me," she wheezed.

"I know. Nice weather for it," Jillian said as Dana's eyes shut and the nurse in charge of the mental health ward of Sisters of Mercy Hospital slid beneath the scalding water.

[2]

The sky hung heavy with night when the sheriff's cruiser pulled into Thomas and Marguerite's yard; the headlights sliced the darkness like a cutting torch. The car pulled to a stop next to Thomas's old pickup, and Marguerite launched herself off the deck, Thomas behind her. Glenn had called earlier, right after he picked up Jacob, and was pretty sure the boy wouldn't turn into some kind of monster and eat him before getting to Boyd's former house. The time he'd spent in the car with the boy nearly brought his own tears, but Glenn had never seen Boyd cry, and he sure as hell wasn't going to start. Something had happened to Jacob; the happy, confident kid he got to know after he and Margie moved in with Tom was gone. The kid cowering next to the car door reminded Glenn of a beaten dog.

"Jakie!" Marguerite shouted as she broke into a run. The boy stepped from the car; his mother swept him into her arms and spun him in circles. "Oh my God, baby. I was so scared."

A smile crossed Thomas's as Glenn approached, but it quickly faded. Jacob hadn't responded to his mother. He hung limp in her arms, a plushie that had lost its stuffing.

"We got problems, Tom," Glenn said.

Thomas nearly laughed.

"No shit, Sheriff." He shoved his hands into his jeans pockets and kicked at a rock that had gotten into his yard from the gravel road. He looked back up at Glenn. "Jillian took Jacob again."

"No. Not really," Glenn said. "He told me she tried, then just laughed at him and walked away, leaving him lying in the dirt."

"Laughed at him?"

The sheriff sucked in a long breath before continuing. Thomas wondered exactly what Glenn knew.

"My 'want to be reelected' stance would be to say bullshit to all of this." Glenn tipped his wide-brimmed hat back on his head and leaned backward against his car. Marguerite planted loud kisses on Jacob on the other side, the boy simply hanging onto her neck. "But I've seen enough. He told me there's some kind of portal in your backyard. A—"

"Fairy circle," Thomas finished for him.

Glenn nodded as Marguerite carried Jacob toward the house, her expression as she looked into Thomas's eyes one of worry, fear.

"I found Jake's ball cap in that circle," Thomas said, "and I found a Lite-Brite with a message on it from Jillian. I thought the worst."

Glenn took a quick look at Jacob's slack face and dead eyes, looking over his mother's shoulder at nothing.

What's going on? Glenn thought. "You know Elvin or Jennifer Miller?" he asked.

"Yeah, sure," Thomas said. "Elvin always seemed like a nice old guy, and Jen sometimes brought over cookies when I was a kid."

The nod from Glenn was more knowing than it should have been.

"Jillian know them?" he asked.

"Well," Thomas said. "She watched their dog sometimes when they were away, up until"—he stopped, the thoughts grinding away behind his eyes—"the dog died."

"How about Pope Daugherty?"

Thomas's face fell. "Pope Daugherty?"

Glenn squinted. "Yeah. You know him?"

Goddamn it.

"Yes. I know him." Thomas gritted his teeth before continuing. "What is this all about?"

Glenn nodded. "Him, his wife, and son. His little girl escaped, somehow. Out at Pigeon Hill. Our forensics expert said it looked like a saltwater crocodile tore through them."

Glenn's thumb scrolled through pictures on his smartphone until he held it up to Thomas.

"Jesus Christ, Glenn," Thomas said, pushing the phone away. The photo was of a conical bloodied tooth in the palm of a bloody latex-gloved hand. "My gut just dropped off a cliff."

"Look familiar?" Glenn asked.

"Yeah, it does."

Glenn slipped the mobile phone back into his uniform pocket, his brow as furrowed as a field.

"Jacob said . . ." He paused to swallow, not sure how Thomas would take what he had to say. He waited until Jacob was gone. "Uh, he said Jillian attacked him."

Pasty white filled in where color drained from Thomas's face.

"Hold on," Glenn said, raising a hand, his palm shaky. "He doesn't seem hurt, at least not physically." Unsure what to do with his hands, he shoved his thumbs in his belt. "But mentally? Emotionally? Jillian used some kind of magic, or ray gun, or whatever the hell she has."

"What happened?"

"Jacob only said, 'Jillian beat me. She's powerful.'"

Thomas swallowed a growing lump in his throat before dropping a hand on Glenn's shoulder. "You want a drink?"

The look on the sheriff's face said yes before he did. "You drinking again?"

Thomas shook his head as he coaxed Glenn toward the house. "Nope, but this stuff isn't mine. Marguerite has some wine in the house, and I have no desire to touch the stuff. It's in a box."

The slam of the screen door told Glenn Marguerite had taken Jacob into the house. The night sounds of insects and distant coyotes were silent for a moment.

"Not usually my first choice," Glenn admitted, "but right now, even that sounds good."

[3]

The lime-green roller coaster cars ratcheted up the lift hill toward the first drop.

Click.

Click.

Click.

The dragon head of the lead car topped the rise, its tooth-filled mouth open, a forked red tongue lolling to one side. Children in that car threw their arms in the air, probably screaming as the cars started streaming down the tracks. Elizabeth didn't know, though. Through the distance and concrete, she couldn't hear a thing. The clicking in her head was a memory of a child. She watched from her cell, the small square of wire-mesh safety glass offering her a narrow view of the carnival. Elizabeth had always hated the Jesse James Days festival.

Noise, artery-clogging bits of processed food that should never be fried, drug deals, concerts from bands people forgot forty years ago, and vomit. Lots of vomit. That's what happens when a stomach full of deep-fried butter meets a pendulum ride in the form of a Viking longship. The ER always filled during the festival, but that didn't matter to her anymore. She didn't work at the hospital. She didn't work anywhere. Elizabeth leaned her forehead against the window. Awaiting charges for attempted murder was something new, and she always loved a challenge.

"If Mom could only see me now," she whispered, her breath fogging the glass.

"What would she say?" Jillian's voice said from behind her.

Elizabeth spun to face the bitch of a fairy woman, her heart pummeling her rib cage. A trace of vodka still tickled her brain. Maybe she did still get scared after all. Jillian sat on the top bunk in a deep-green bikini; red stains streaked her face and torso.

"Would you please stop showing up covered in blood? It's becoming an inconvenience."

Jillian grinned and wiped her hand across her chest, flicking red droplets across Elizabeth's orange jumpsuit.

"Nobody's ruining my fun, sister." Jillian dropped to the floor, a bloody butt print on the bare mattress. "Now," she said, draping an arm around Elizabeth's shoulders, "it's time for me to play. I mean, really play."

Play?

The fairy's arm squeezed Elizabeth; her shoulders screamed in protest.

"Yes, play. You remember my black snow, don't you?" Jillian paused, hugging even harder. Elizabeth let out a yelp and the pressure relaxed. "It was working so beautifully until that brat told everybody how to treat it."

Fingers slipped beneath Elizabeth's chin, forcing her face toward Jillian's. Panic grabbed her, squeezing her chest, her bladder.

"You know him, don't you?" she asked. "Yes. You—" Her eyes rolled back until only the whites showed. "You helped bring that little nuisance into the world."

Urine, hot and wet, ran down both Elizabeth's legs, her breath too fleeting to catch. Jillian leaned closer and kissed Elizabeth's forehead, the fairy's lips rough as a cat's tongue.

"But he terrifies you, doesn't he, honey?" She didn't wait for a response. Jillian released Elizabeth and leaped effortlessly back onto the top bunk. "Let me tell you a secret. He used to terrify me too, but not anymore. He's gone soft, but he still pisses me off. So, you help me perform a seven-years-past-due abortion on the little monster, and I'll make your life heavenly. No addiction, no self-loathing, no job, no worries."

A lavender glow began at Jillian's palm and lasered into Elizabeth's chest. The pressure dissipated. Her breathing, her heartbeat, dropped to normal.

Oh Jesus.

"There," Jillian said. "Feel better?"

Elizabeth nodded.

"That's good. Now—" Jillian tossed an object Elizabeth didn't know she had. It hit her hands and bounced off her chest before she clumsily grabbed it. Another plastic pint of vodka. "This is your last drink, my friend. I need you pliable for what's about to happen."

The bottle felt unnaturally cold in Elizabeth's hands. She didn't want to want it. But she did. She wanted it so fucking bad.

"What do you need this time?" Elizabeth asked.

The smile that went too wide crossed Jillian's mouth and Elizabeth's bladder released again.

"Just wait for my signal," Jillian said. "You still have an important part to play in all this."

"All what?"

But Jillian had already dissolved like a night demon from some old story.

[4]

To Glenn, the wine tasted like something a mechanic might drain from a car, but then again, he wasn't partial to wine. It was too pretentious, too dry, too sweet, or too expensive. Except this wine. It was in the fridge looking to all the world like a juice box for adults. He took a sip and set the glass on the table, running a finger through a bead of condensation that trickled down the side.

"I gave the order to find Jillian," he said, lifting the glass to take another drink, grimacing as it went down, the crack of a Dr Pepper can opening loud in the kitchen.

"That's dangerous," Thomas said. "You don't know what she's capable of."

Glenn drained the rest of the cheap wine, shaking his head as he put down the glass.

"Don't I, Tommy?" His elbows hit the table as he gripped his hands in front of him. "Remember, I was there when she killed Maddy. I think I damn well know what Jillian's capable of."

Thomas held up a hand. "You're right. Sorry."

The chair legs squeaked across the tiled floor as Glenn pushed his chair back and stood, grabbing the wineglass and stalking toward the fridge. He turned.

"I'm not crazy, Tommy, and neither are you."

Thomas's chair groaned as he leaned back, a hand still on the soda can. "I know that better than anybody."

Glenn returned to the table with a glass full of crappy wine and sat.

"I—" he started before his mobile phone cut him off.

The caller ID read "Brittany." He answered.

"This is Glenn."

"Sheriff?" His deputy's voice was soft, shaky. "I, uh. Hey—"

"What's wrong?" Glenn asked, leaving out *now*.

Thomas shifted in his chair, the creak louder than it should be. Glenn motioned him to keep still. The television in the living room was loud with Bugs Bunny. Brittany stuttered as soft as Porky Pig.

"It's, uh. It's—It's . . ." She sniffed loudly on the phone. "We've got another body, sir. You'd better come. I'll text you the address."

Thomas reached across the table and touched Glenn's arm. "What is it?"

The sheriff lowered the phone from his ear, his eyes heavy, the marks beneath nearly as dark as the grease stripes athletes wear.

"She said 'another body.'" Glenn ran a hand through his hair and looked up at Thomas, his hair like he just woke. "I guess that means Jillian's still hungry."

He rose from the table and dropped his brown hat on his head.

"Thomas," he said, nodding, then turning toward the couch where Marguerite and Jacob watched him over the back. "Margie, Jake. I have to—"

"She won't stop," Jacob interrupted, his voice too small for him. "She's getting ready to go home. But before she does, she needs to eat enough to get full, and when she gets full, she can be queen."

Glenn rubbed a hand across his chin. "Queen? What do you mean?"

The boy stood and walked into the kitchen area, stopping in front of Glenn, his dark eyes hard black buoys in sea of worry.

"Jillian is getting ready to leave; she's almost powerful enough to go home and rule. And I can't stop her. She's, she's more powerful than me."

"Baby," Marguerite called, rushing to his side but stopping as if she'd hit an invisible wall.

"She's leaving?" Glenn sat back down, looking at Jacob eye-to-eye. "That's good, right?"

Jacob shook his head.

"No," the boy said. "She's still feeding. More people will die before she leaves. Lots more. She—she wants to hurt this world." He looked toward Thomas, tears running down his still-dirty face. "She wants to hurt Daddy Tom; she wants to hurt Mom. She wants to hurt me."

Marguerite moved, the invisible wall gone, and dropped to her knees next to Jacob, her arms hugging him tight.

"How do you know all this, baby?"

He leaned into her. "I can still feel her, and she's cold, like a brain freeze from ice cream, but I feel it all over."

Fatigue kneecapped Glenn as he looked into the little boy's solemn face.

"What do we need to do, Jake?" he asked, raising a hand to rub his temples.

"We need to kill her, Sheriff Glenn," he said. "We need to kill her dead. And we need to do it tonight."

[5]

The familiar knot—the one that visited Thomas's gut when he was frightened as a child—twisted itself into a ball. Jillian. "*We need to kill her, Sheriff Glenn.*" Those words hit hard. He looked from Jacob to Glenn, the two staring at each other like they were about to throw punches. Glenn exhaled and picked the boy up, setting him on his lap.

"I don't know how to find her, Jake," Glenn said.

The boy exhaled slowly before speaking. "I do."

"No," Marguerite snapped, pulling out a kitchen chair and sitting across from Glenn and her son, a full wine glass in her hand. "Absolutely not. You're not putting my boy anywhere near that monster. She's kidnapped him once, and tried to again. She obviously wants him for some reason."

Jacob leaned forward, his elbows thunking on the table, his chin resting in his hands.

"Not anymore, Mom," he said. "I'm not strong anymore." He looked at Thomas. "But you are. You have to get her before she goes home, or—"

"Or what, kiddo?" Thomas asked, lifting the boy's face toward his.

"Or she'll eat us all."

"Jesus Christ," Marguerite hissed before she drained her wineglass.

[6]

The flint grinder rolled under Tick Tick's thumb; sparks flew, but no flame erupted from the convenience store lighter, its plain white surface marred with Sharpie. He'd drawn a dick on it because, why not? Tick Tick slipped the filtered Pall Mall behind his ear and shook the cheap lighter.

"Mother farging bratch," he hissed, and tossed it toward the storm drain, giving that dumb Stephen King clown something to play with. The lighter hit the asphalt and clattered to a stop a good two feet from the hole.

Tick Tick's hands flinched, and he stuffed them in the front pockets of his oil-stained jeans to keep them still. His fingertips landed on his key ring and he wrapped it in a fist.

"Need a light?"

Tick Tick yelped and lurched away from the unexpected woman's voice, his forehead clanging against the steel strut support of the Dragon's Revenge roller coaster. The skinny man dropped to his knees, his hands pulled out to grab his head, and the keys fell from his grip and chimed on the asphalt.

"Mother whatin' dang it."

A touch, soft and light, rested on his skeletal, acne-scarred shoulder, most of it exposed from beneath the stained wife beater he wore.

"Hey," the woman said.

He flinched and dropped onto the pavement, his yellowing eyes wide.

"Are you okay?"

What the fudge knuckles? The woman who knelt next to him was beautiful. Through the acne scars and the black rot staining her teeth, Tick Tick saw a stone-cold fox in a Nirvana T-shirt.

"Uh, hey, baby," he said, his own voice as shaky as his hands. "Yeah. I need a light."

Tick Tick reached for the cigarette, but all he felt was greasy hair and grime behind his ear.

"Poopy diapers, man."

Smiling, the woman reached behind her ear and pulled out Tick Tick's Pall Mall.

His eyes bugged. "Are you like, a wizard or something?"

The woman's smile morphed into a tight grin, and her eyes glowed. "Yeah. Or something," she said, pinching the smoke between her lips. "Watch this."

The woman flicked her thumb across the inside of her index finger and a lavender fire erupted from the nail. She held it to the cigarette and sucked in the flame, then held the cancer stick out to Tick Tick and stuck the flaming thumb into her mouth, pulling it out wet.

"Wha?" came from him in a whisper.

A thin trail of smoke blew from between the woman's pursed lips.

"Take it," she said, pushing the cigarette close to his face.

Tick Tick reached for it, and his jittery hand finally plucked it from hers, his eyes lingering on her face and those iridescent eyes.

He found his mouth with the filter and sucked in deep, the smoke flooding his system with nicotine, his eyes never leaving hers. A light-purple glow grew in her pupils.

"Um, uh, thanks," he said through an exhale of smoke. "My lighter was like—"

"Out of fluid," she finished for him, "Norman." Her grin fell into a frown. The woman rested a warm hand on one of his, and the warmth spread up his arm and through his chest. Oh, dear Jesus.

"Hey," he said, but she pushed an index finger over his chapped lips.

"Shh, baby. I have a couple of questions for you. Then—*then*—I'm going to give you something amazing."

Tick Tick squinted. "Do I, like, know you?"

She shook her head, the greasy ponytail lifeless. "You're about to."

[7]

The dusty Ford accelerated to 62 mph on the rural highway. Marguerite sat with Jacob on her lap, her arms clamped around him, both buckled into the same seatbelt. Thomas didn't want to go too fast or too slow. It wasn't safe for them to sit like that, and it wasn't legal, but he knew he wouldn't win that battle with Marguerite.

"Why, Thomas?" she asked, not looking at him. He glanced over. Her chin was resting on the crown of Jacob's head. Her hair blew in the airstream of the open window.

His hands tightened on the wheel. "I should have discussed this with you before I agreed to anything with Glenn. I—"

"You're goddammed right. This is my son, and we're putting him in danger, Thomas. We're—"

"Mom?"

"—supposed to protect him from that witch, not hand him over to her."

"Mom."

She was right, Thomas knew. But—

"Momma."

"Not now, baby," Marguerite said. "The grown-ups need to talk."

The truck engine sputtered, then stalled. Thomas gripped the wheel harder as the power steering went out. A quick look into the rearview mirror revealed no farm truck barreling down on them. He hit the brakes and muscled the pickup to a stop on the shoulder, his wound screaming for him to stop.

"What now?" Thomas reached to his side, the click of the buckle release loud in the quiet car. He reached for the door handle, but the lock knob clicked down by itself.

Jacob cleared his throat.

"It's my turn," the boy said, at least some strength returning to his words. "I have to do this. I have to lead you to her before she feeds."

"But baby—"

He cleared his throat again.

"I *have* to do this. I can find Jillian. Sheriff Glenn can't, Daddy Tom can't, but I can. We're closer now—I can feel her anger." He paused. Marguerite opened her mouth to speak, but Jacob raised a hand and she stopped. "Jillian wanted me before I was born. Not me, but what's inside me. The reason I can do things nobody else can. She wanted my power." Air hissed from between pursed lips. "I guess I don't have that much power anymore, but I *can* find her for you."

Thomas slid a hand on the boy's shoulder and gave a slight squeeze. Tears wanted out of Jacob, Thomas could almost feel them.

"So she took me and made me do things, magic stuff to rebuild her fairy world because she wasn't strong enough to do it herself. Then she wanted me to suck all the life out of the Earth and give it to her, but I wouldn't do it."

Marguerite let out a choked gasp. "Can you do that?" wheezed from her.

Jacob nodded. "Yeah. No. I could back then, but she couldn't. I don't know what I can still do. All I know is she's been feeding a lot; I think she's almost strong enough to do everything herself."

"What's that mean, baby?" Marguerite asked, but Thomas already knew the answer.

"It means she's going to do something bad. Really big, and really bad."

Thomas released Jacob's shoulder and grabbed the key from the ignition. "Where is she, buddy?" he asked.

Jacob pointed out the windshield toward St. Joe.

The truck started before Thomas turned the key. He pressed the accelerator and drove, taking them closer to the monster. He didn't think they had a chance.

[8]

Yellow police tape already hung from the front door of Dana Carroll's house and across the gate in the six-foot privacy fence that probably kept the backyard safe from absolutely nothing.

Two deputy cruisers, Phil Rolfson's coroner van, and forensic tech Alice Landry's 1970 Dodge Dart took up Carroll's driveway and part of the yard. Glenn grabbed the handle and pushed the gate inward, ducking under the tape.

The sun, hanging low in the sky, cast a golden glow over the yard, the huge back deck with built-in stainless-steel grill and hot tub making it something out of a real-estate commercial. Glenn wondered, briefly, if Todd "I Sell Homes FAST" Marshall had been her agent. A folding aluminum gurney stood next to the tub. Glenn mounted wooden steps that led to the surface of the deck and the smell hit him. He stopped for a moment, his left foot on the deck flooring, his right still on a step. If someone offered him a thousand dollars to move that foot, he wasn't sure he would.

"Sheriff," Brittany called from over the railing next to the hot tub.

"Is it—?" he began, the stench forcing a cough.

"The smiley face again?" Her eyes told him all he needed.

The right boot, as heavy as if it were full of concrete, lifted and Glenn pushed himself onto the deck floor. Phil Rolfson, the county coroner, stood next to the hot tub in a pair of chest waders, arms folded across his chest, as Brittany tried not to look down. From the green tinge to Aaron's face, he might have already vomited.

Alice Landry leaned over the corpse of a woman floating in the water, just another day on the job. Glenn stepped closer and saw the tooth-filled smiling face carved into the woman's chest with something sharp.

"What happened?" he asked.

Brittany flipped through her notebook. "Dana L. Carroll, fifty-three, died sometime around—" She stopped and looked at Landry, who didn't return her gaze.

"Eight twenty p.m. yesterday," Landry said.

"The cause appears to be, well. She, uh. She—"

"She cooked," Landry said, pulling something from the cuts on the woman's chest with tweezers. She turned her head toward Glenn, grinning. "That's what you smell. It's crazy. When human muscle tissue is boiled, it releases an aroma similar to boiled beef."

Glenn raised a hand to stop her. It didn't work.

"So that's the smell. However, if she wasn't petite—say she was large, like that Hurley guy from that old show *Lost*—what you'd smell would be more like a nice fatty piece of pork. Now, if—"

"Landry," Glenn barked, then dropped his voice to little more than a whisper. "Thank you. You've really put this into perspective. What you're telling me is she cooked in her own hot tub."

The forensic tech nodded.

"But that would be 212 degrees Fahrenheit. How hot are these things supposed to get?"

Phil raised a hand. "On the older models, 104 degrees; 102 on these newer ones."

Glenn's brows nearly slammed together.

"I've been shopping for one," the coroner said. "So there's no way this happened. However, since it did, we're looking at the fact that Ms. Carroll got drunk on margaritas—"

Landry swept a hand over the pitcher and overturned margarita glass like a game show model.

"—and passed out at the most inopportune time. The tub's heater must have gone on the fritz."

Wrong. That's wrong. Anger began to burn deep inside Glenn. "No," he said. "Nothing malfunctioned here, Phil, Landry. She was murdered."

"We know, Sheriff," Landry said flatly. "The art project on her chest carved with a shattered margarita glass is a pretty big tip. What we *are* saying is that our toothy serial killer must have tampered with the heater in order for it to reach a temp that would cook this woman alive."

Glenn opened his mouth to speak but thought better of it.

"I have a repairman from the company that manufactured this model on her way here, Sheriff," Landry continued. "We know what happened, it's the how we're still working on."

A long exhale escaped him. Yes, these are smart people. Let them do their job. "Nice work, folks," he said. "What now?"

Landry stood, pulling her right latex glove off with a snap. "I'm finished with the body, Sheriff. Phil's up to the plate."

"Gentlemen," the coroner said, nodding toward the corpse in the discolored water. "Help me get her on the table?"

I can't do this anymore, ran through Glenn's head. But I have to. "Jesus, Phil," he said.

The coroner handed surgical gloves to Glenn and Aaron before snapping a pair on himself.

"One of us may have to get in the water," Phil said, then grinned.

Fucking coroners.

The man lowered himself into the tub and pushed his arms under the corpse. She rose slightly.

Glenn grabbed one arm, Aaron the other.

"Okay, gents," Phil said. "On the count of three. One, two, three."

Glenn pulled as Aaron did, Phil pushing from beneath. The Carroll woman's arms twisted in her shoulders, and the weight disappeared as the flesh pulled from the bone like she was a cooked chicken. The corpse splashed back into the hot tub; soiled water soaked Glenn's pant legs.

"Wow," Phil said. "You don't see that every day."

Glenn flopped the woman's cooked arm onto the coroner's table, turned, and walked to the steps, peeling off his gloves and dropping them onto the deck flooring. His boots stopped at the edge of the stairs and he breathed deeply, one, two, three times. He was going to kill Jillian, kill the hell out of her, then go fishing for the rest of his life.

"I'm going to the carnival," he said. "Send backup to the roller coaster or the Tilt-A-Whirl. I'll be at one of them. Make sure they bring the Remington 700 sniper rifle, shotguns, and flak jackets. Alert St. Joe PD too."

"Jesus, Glenn," Aaron said, the boneless flesh of Carroll's arm still hanging from his grip. "What do you think's going to happen?"

The sheriff started down the steps. "Everything," he said. "I thought we'd be used to that by now."

CHAPTER FIFTEEN

[1]

THE SCENT OF fresh popcorn brushed past Tick Tick, his spent cigarette crushed under his foot. The girl sat on the curb next to him, her glowing eyes causing his nut sack to tighten into a hard ball. What was she? He didn't know. Some sort of wizard, or demon, or cyborg. Cyborg? His fractured nervous system jerked his head in what felt like two ways at once. The Cyberdyne Systems Model 101 Terminator's eyes glowed too.

Fudge knuckles.

"Something wrong, baby?" she asked.

He sat up straight, ever-quivering hands gripping the curb. "No, no. Nothing wrong." He stuck a hand in his pocket looking for his crumpled pack of cigarettes. It wasn't there. "Who, um, who are you?"

An easy, damaged smile forced its way to the surface as she rocked back and forth on the curb. "My name's Jillian, silly. Didn't I tell you?"

Did she? Is she messing with me?

"That's a, a pretty name," he mumbled. No girl had given him more than a half-assed conversation since Becky McNamara, the ride monkey at the Haunted Hotel, got baked as hell and blew him in the Hall of Mirrors. She hadn't talked to him since.

Jillian dropped a hand over his and squeezed. Her hand was warm and soft. "Thanks, Norman." She took her hand back and turned to face him. "Now, I need you to answer a question."

Okay, okay, okay, ran through his scrambled head. I can do this. Then, then maybe we can go to the Hall of Mirrors.

"Sure. Yeah, yeah, yeah." Oh poop. Oh poop, Normy.

He sucked in a slow breath; his abused lungs threw him into a coughing fit. When it subsided, he wiped tears from his eyes and continued like it never happened, because in his short-term memory, it didn't.

Her eyes blazed now, the lavender light masking her face. "When is the carnival the busiest?"

His eyes pinched tight and he shook his head, trying to dislodge something. When he opened his eyes again, the glow was gone.

That was me. I'm fried, man. I'm seeing stuff.

"Norman?"

"Uh, yeah, yeah, yeah. Busy, busy, busy. It starts getting busy at dusk. That's when all the parents with little kids start to go home and all the teenagers come out."

Jillian's smile spread wider than her face. Did it? Her black-toothed smile was now normal. I'm such a burnout. Her smile grew again, all the way across her face and past her ears.

Jillian held out a hand; the palm held crystal meth. It glowed lavender.

"You ready to get glassed?"

[2]

The flutter in Jacob's chest started slight and sleepy, like a moth waking from a nap; now the moth beat against the window, trying to get to the light inside the house. He squirmed on his mother's lap.

"What's a matter, baby?" she asked.

"It's Jillian, isn't it?" Daddy Tom asked, never taking his eyes from the St. Joseph streets.

"Yeah." Jillian didn't make that feeling, not on purpose. She didn't want him to find her. Not now. Not since she was so near to what she wanted. "We're super close."

The Ford pulled into the lot of the Delores Hadley Community Center. Daddy Tom killed the engine, and they got out of the truck. A new flutter, this time in Jacob's stomach, had nothing to do with Jillian. As they left the truck, Jacob counted only two open spots left. A press of people, a wall of flesh and Axe Body Spray, filled the air; Jacob wasn't close enough to see them, but claustrophobia squeezed him tight.

Mom knelt to eye level. "You okay?" she asked.

Jacob nodded, although he wasn't. Pressure built in downtown St. Joe and it swallowed him; he waited for the pressure to blow like when Mom made tea in the kettle. He took Daddy Tom's hand in one of his, Mom's in the other, and they began to walk; with each move of the feet on his shaking legs, Jacob came one step closer to hearing the whistle blow.

A kettle of turkey vultures passed overhead in the waning daylight. Jacob's eyes watched the black, greasy birds begin to circle in the sky above the carnival as they marched toward the roar of the rides and the laughter of teenagers. Jacob's breath caught as more birds joined them. He didn't like the look of those buzzards. He didn't like it at all.

[3]

The sheriff stopped his cruiser at a long, orange sawhorse blocking a street and got out. A lot about the job had driven Glenn to drinking more than he used to, and pushed him to the brink of kissing the Sheriff's Department bye-bye. He didn't like that feeling. He pulled on his flak jacket, but it wouldn't buckle. Glenn sucked in and pulled it tight, the snaps clicking into place.

"Geez," he wheezed, the manganese steel plates inside the ballistic nylon vest hugging his torso. "This what happened to you, Boyd?"

Boyd. He'd never wanted the former sheriff back more than that minute. Boyd would know what to do, how to handle things, when to pull the trigger, and if he didn't know, he'd at least look like he did.

Glenn pulled the shotgun from the mount between the seats and held it at rest position. Best not to scare the hell out of everyone.

The top hill of the roller coaster rose above the Delores Hadley Community Center. He nudged the car door shut and started walking.

[4]

The Jillian girl's hand held steady, the shards of purple crystals still as a prayer in church, a halo around the small pile of rocks. Tick Tick had seen blue meth, pink meth, meth that could have been cubic zirconia. But purple?

"Why is it glowing, man?"

That smile, that too-wide smile started to freak him the heck out. "This is the best shit you've ever had, baby," she said, her voice soothing.

The tension melted from his tight, stringy shoulder muscles and he smiled back. "Is it magic?"

The smile widened; tips of pointy monster teeth peeked from behind her lips. Tick Tick exhaled. He didn't care anymore.

"You bet your ass," she said.

Don't do this, poked around in his noggin. Not yet.

Tick Tick shook his head, greasy hair matted to his scalp. "I, uh. No." That's it, man. That's it. "I, I can't. If I tweak while I'm working again, Bonny Donny will have my ass, and I need to get paid, dude."

The smile faded. Tick Tick liked this less than the teeth. "Your boss?"

He nodded.

Her smile returned and a man's brief scream came from the midway.

"Bonny Donny is no longer your problem." The glow of the crystals flared; Tick Tick flinched. "You ready for the ride of your life?"

Ready? Fart knocking heck poop. "Yeah, I'm ready." He fumbled in his pocket and pulled out a tweak pipe, the clear glass bulb stained by the fire of past highs.

"No." She clenched her fist, and when she opened her hand, the crystals were now ground to powder.

"Whoa," Tick Tick wheezed. "You *are* a wizard."

"Damn right," Jillian said, and pulled a butterfly knife from somewhere, flicking it until the blade rested parallel to her palm. She scraped some glowing meth onto the blade and held it out to Tick Tick. "Up the nose is where it's at, baby."

Heck yes, heck yes, heck yes.

Rocking back and forth, Tick Tick tried to hold in his excitement. He leaned forward, a finger on his left nostril, and snorted. He went up and never wanted to come down.

[5]

The Dragon's Revenge rose four stories into the St. Joe skyline, the paint-chipped metal frame held together with bolts and hitch pins. It vibrated as the lime-green dragon cars rolled up the camelback hills and roared down the other side. Jacob flinched as the cars screamed down the final hill and rumbled past them before stopping at the loading platform.

Thomas held out a string of tickets to Marguerite.

"Wait. You're serious? There's some kind of monster out there that could attack these people at any time and you want me to go on a *carnival ride?*"

He shrugged. "I promised him."

"We don't have to," Jacob said, head bowed, staring at his feet. "But it'll be easier for me to see Jillian if I'm up high."

An unspoken apology passed between Thomas and Marguerite. She huffed before grabbing a handful of Thomas's shirt and pulling his face close to hers. He stagger-stepped to keep from tripping.

"This is your butt, mister. And there's only one thing I want you to promise." She leaned in and pressed her lips to his. Her warmth, the sweet smell of her skin engulfed him. "And the roller coaster is *not* it." Marguerite released Thomas and walked Jacob toward the back of the line to the Dragon's Revenge, the boy's shoes scraping the pavement.

I'm going to do it. When this is over, we're getting married. He'd already planned in his head how to ask her, and he was going to say *hitched*.

They approached the line, Marguerite cutting off a group of pimply junior-high kids too busy trying to out-cool each other to notice. She turned and blew Thomas a nervous kiss. Jacob never looked back.

Thomas felt a body step close behind him. He froze, muscles tight as strings.

"I hope this isn't a mistake," the person said.

It was Glenn.

Thomas pivoted in slow motion to find the sheriff behind him dressed like he was about to save the president's daughter from terrorists, a shotgun strapped to his back.

"Come on. Don't sneak up on people. I almost crapped myself."

Glenn nodded, his smile hard as granite. "Sorry, Tommy. I'm wound tight; I feel like my spring might snap any second."

The line to the Dragon's Revenge shuffled forward as another group locked into the cars. A kid in a Def Leppard T-shirt pushed Jacob from behind, and the boy disappeared in the mass of oily bodies. Thomas lurched forward, but Glenn grabbed his arm as they watched Marguerite slap the Def Leppard kid on the back of the head. The boy moved to the rear of his pack.

"So are you, Tom."

In through the nose, out through the mouth. In through the nose, out through the mouth. "Yeah. Jacob knows Jillian's somewhere nearby. I don't know how this works, but he *felt* her presence." Thomas scanned the flowing crowd for red hair, but there were too many people to single out one. "Do you remember the Day St. Joseph Died?"

A laugh came from a nearby booth; a teenager in a backward ball cap won a prize for his girlfriend.

"Everybody does," Glenn said. "It was hell."

"I was in the middle of it. Me and Marguerite and Jillian." Thomas stopped and looked behind him, the mention of her name raising hair on his arms. "Jillian caused all of it."

"No." Glenn shook his head. "It was Robert Garrett, the Angel of Death. That's what—"

"*That's* what Jillian led everybody to believe." The roller coaster cars rattled past, and the rush of air mussed Thomas's hair. "I didn't remember anything until Jillian disappeared. Her—I don't know—her spell wore off, but I was there in the hospital parking lot, she was there, and Marguerite was there, pregnant with Jacob."

The sheriff held up a hand. "I know all this. What are you getting at?"

The cars came to a hard stop, and laughing riders stepped off. Marguerite and Jacob stepped into the now-empty front car; the boy's body language was like he'd lost his favorite Pokémon card.

"I'm getting at the fact that after I pushed a hunk of sharp plastic through Dauðr's eye and the monster poofed into so much ash, Jillian searched through the remains."

"For what?"

Thomas's hands found his front pockets and buried themselves. "I didn't know for the longest time because she wouldn't let me know, but now I do. Jacob. She was looking for Jacob."

The cars began to *tick-tick-tick* their way up the hill, and some kids already had their arms in the air.

"But—"

"Let me finish. I think the monster had something special inside it, something powerful Jillian doesn't have. Dauðr put that something powerful inside Marguerite's womb and it *became* Jacob."

A sheriff's deputy, dressed in the same type of bulletproof vest as Glenn, strolled by, nodding at the sheriff as he did.

"You know how that sounds?" Glenn said.

The shrug felt like a lie. "Yeah, I do, but I also know you've seen things that shoved your worldview into a blender. She took Jacob because she needed him. She needed his power."

The Dragon's Revenge cars started down from the hill; screams and laughter cut the night.

"According to Jacob, she doesn't need him anymore."

"Damn," Glenn wheezed.

"You're telling me."

[6]

Adrenaline and dopamine flooded what was left of Tick Tick's brain. He shot to his feet and hooted to the sky.

"Whoa!" Fists flying at an invisible boxer, Tick Tick skittered across the asphalt, tripping over a bound clump of power cables and crashed face-first into the dusty street. He popped up and ran to Jillian, the blood rushing from his nose painting his smile red. "I feel like freaking Superman!"

He raised his arms over his head and ran in circles making *sssssshh-hhhh-sssssshhhhhh* sounds.

Gravity seemed to vanish as Jillian rose from the curb, a human-shaped balloon.

"Norman," she said, the word calm, friendly.

Tick Tick began spinning in tight circles like he was Julie freaking Andrews.

"Norman?"

"The hills are alive, baby," he shouted.

A faint lavender glow grew from Jillian's palm and wrapped around Tick Tick; he stopped twirling, grinning like an idiot through the wet, glistening blood.

"I need you to do something for me, Norman."

Involuntary muscle movements jerked the man's body beneath the binding light. "Yeah. Yeah. Anything you say, baby cakes. Anything you say."

This time when she smiled, all Tick Tick could see was teeth, and he didn't care.

"Good," she said, sliding the handle of the butterfly knife into his palm and closing his fingers around it. He whimpered a puppy whimper before she unwrapped the purple light and set him free.

Tick Tick hooted and sprinted from the shadows toward the midway.

[7]

Blood pounded in Jacob's ears as the car climbed the first hill. The ticking of the chain built tension better than any chase scene on *Scooby-Doo*. His hands gripped the metal bar that crossed his and his mom's laps, although he knew most of the kids behind him were waving their arms.

"You ready for this, baby?" Mom asked, leaning close enough he could hear her over the ticks.

Yes, I am.

After seven years of knowing more than anyone his age, being able to do things no one else could do, being ignored by his classmates after he turned Sophia Cumberland's glue stick into a mouse, this was normal. He felt as normal as Daddy Tom treated him. Jacob wasn't sure he could turn Sophia Cumberland's glue stick into anything anymore. Killing Daddy Tom's truck was one thing—engines were easy—but transforming a glue stick into a living creature was a talent of a god. A wiggle deep in his memories told him Jillian had called him that once. The car reached the top. Mom's lips brushed his ear.

"The first drop is a doozy. You ready to scream?" She didn't try to mask the excitement in her voice.

Hey, he realized. She's having fun.

Then their lead car dropped over the edge and gravity tried to pull Jacob's stomach from his body. Breath struggled to find his lungs until the cars reached the second hill and everything fell back into place.

"Yahoooooo!" he shouted, gripping the metal bar tighter, the terror of the day momentarily forgotten. Mom laughed beside him.

Down it dropped again, and screamed sideways around a corner, the back side of the roller coaster running parallel with a darkened street. A lavender light ahead in the shadows drew his attention, and the car climbed another hill. A red-haired woman stood holding what looked like a glowing purple rope.

Oh no.

He leaned into his mother.

"Momma," he shouted over the rush of wind and the screams of the passengers. "I found Jillian."

[8]

The guy seemed to come out of nowhere.

"Sheriff," Aaron's voice snapped over the radio clipped to Glenn's shoulder. "Seven o'clock, NOW."

Glenn spun, Thomas slightly behind him. A too-thin man in an oil-stained T-shirt and jeans ran at Glenn, his wild, greasy hair streaming behind him, eyes wide—meth eyes—a knife in his right hand, his face covered in blood. The shotgun strapped to Glenn's back forgotten, his thumb popped the snap on his side holster, but the man was too close, running too fast.

Glenn didn't have time to draw his sidearm.

Thomas dove in front of Glenn and into the legs of the Meth Man. The knife went flying as the bag of bones went down, face colliding with an elbow Glenn threw up to protect himself. Meth Man bounced off Glenn and hit the pavement.

"Sheriff?" a woman said.

Meth Man lay at Glenn's feet, his arms and legs cranking like he was still running. Brittany appeared next to them, yanking Meth Man onto his stomach, her knee in his back as she zipped flex cuffs tight over his scabby wrists.

"Hey, hey, hey," Meth Man barked through the bloody mess of his nose.

A few milling teenagers stopped to stare, others ignored the scene. Just another day in St. Joe.

Thomas held out a hand for Glenn to help him up. The sheriff took it, then turned to Brittany. "Deputy, remind me to give you a promotion."

The roller coaster whooshed past on its second trip around the track.

Brittany pointed at Thomas. "You're my witness."

"Jah-Jah-Jah," Meth Man spat as he tried to get a word out.

Brittany's hand in the man's back pocket produced a green camo wallet held together with ragged duct tape.

"We're not getting anything out of him, Sheriff," Brittany said. Glenn knew she was right; he'd dealt with meth users before. She peeled an expired library card, three dollar bills, and a driver's license from the wallet and handed it all to the sheriff.

"Norman Albert VanBrockton, twenty-four years of age, Hattiesburg, Mississippi. Hmm. Carney, probably." The photo was of a healthy young man with close-cropped hair, clear skin, and about thirty pounds heavier. He handed the ID back to Brittany. "The past few years have been hard on Norman."

"But why did he come at you, Glenn?" Thomas asked.

His eyes felt heavy. "Meth doesn't do anyone any favors." He clicked the radio mic on his shoulder. "Aaron. Brittany and I are at the roller coaster. Get a couple of uniforms down here. A friendly fella who likes to experiment with chemistry tried to give me a little kiss."

"Jesus, Glenn. You okay?"

"Yeah. Little help from my friends." He released the button and nodded at Thomas before clicking it again. "Any sighting of our red-head?"

The Dragon's Revenge cars squealed as the coaster came to a stop.

"Negative, Sheriff. We'll keep looking. Marquez and Sullivan from St. Joe PD are on their way."

"Daddy Tom, Daddy Tom!"

Thomas knelt as Jacob came running to him from the roller coaster exit, the boy's eyes stretched wide with fear. He slammed into Thomas, sobbing. Margie stopped behind her son, hands on her knees, and out of breath.

Glenn knelt next to Thomas and rested a hand on Jacob's head.

Norman Albert VanBrockton, the Meth Man, thrashed on the street like a beetle on its back, unable to find his way up.

"Jah-Jah-Jah-Jillian," he shrieked.

Jacob lifted his head from Thomas's shoulder and met Glenn's green eyes with his dark ones. "He's right. Jillian did this to him."

Jesus, kid.

"Don't 'Jesus, kid' me, Sheriff Glenn," Jacob said, the boy's voice low and flat. "I *saw* her."

A tight, arid pull spread down Glenn's throat. "Did you just read my m—"

Lightning cracked. A lilac bolt shot from black, swirling clouds that hadn't existed seconds before. It struck the dome on the Buchanan County Courthouse; shattered glass exploded outward, raining over the carnival. The crowd screamed and scattered for shelter.

What's happening?

Glenn almost pitched off balance when Jacob grabbed the top of his flak jacket and yanked him forward.

"She's here."

[9]

Hard-soled shoes slapped in the distance. Elizabeth pulled a scrubs top over her head. Jillian had done this, left a stack of clothes on the top bunk far enough away from the bloody spot she'd imprinted on the mattress that Elizabeth wouldn't obviously stick out as a murderer. The scrubs were a nice touch, she thought. Nurses are the kind of people no one thinks twice about because they're supposed to be places. In a building like this, with hundreds of people—police and prisoners alike—of course there was room for a nurse to be about anywhere at any time.

She pulled on the pants and stuffed her orange jumpsuit beneath the bottom mattress for someone to figure out later. The FIGS/New Balance shoes the elf lady included with her outfit showed she'd done her homework about the medical profession's footwear preferences.

The slapping got louder. Elizabeth draped the stethoscope Jillian had included over her shoulders and approached the door, key card in hand. She vaguely remembered where she got the key card—that wicked fairy thing must have given it to her. Elizabeth didn't know; she'd already finished the vodka. Wait, she thought, pulling the bottle from a pocket. The bottle was full again.

"That's pretty nifty," she said as a prison guard ran by, radio in hand, the fat man sweating and cursing.

He's going to have a heart attack, she thought, reaching through the bars and swiping the card through the electric lock. It clicked and she slid the door open. Another guard sprinted by, taking no notice of her open cell.

Jason Offutt

"Cool," she said, and stepped onto the concourse. Prisoners hooted and hollered, waving arms and middle fingers between the bars. An alarm sounded somewhere inside the sprawling building that held the county prison and the sheriff and police departments.

Elizabeth followed a flashing red light at the end of the concourse. Her key card opened the door of metal bars there too. The guard at the station, watching monitors and listening to the chatter over the radio, nodded as she passed.

Damn right. I'm a nurse. I'm supposed to be here.

Ten minutes later, Elizabeth reached the front doors of the long brick building, all but invisible to the officers running and shouting.

[10]

Asperitas clouds churned across the St. Joseph sky, an angry ocean in the heavens. Lightning flashed and crackled, the lilac bursts as unnatural as the clouds. Wind churned in the distance, and the carnival sat silent; the ride monkeys hit the emergency off buttons except on the Dragon's Revenge, which still roared down its tracks. The crowd cowered beneath benches, behind food stands, anywhere they could find shelter. Even Norman lay as still as he could, his meth-addled body twitching as if jolted by electricity. Brittany stood next to the sheriff, shotgun at low ready.

Thomas lifted Jacob from the street and held him close; Marguerite threw her arms around them. "Anybody looking for her, Glenn?" he said, the question loud in the silent pocket of the carnival.

"Yeah," the sheriff said. "We got deputies, uniformed and not, all over the place, and there's a sniper on top of the Civic Arena."

A sniper? Wow.

Glenn clicked his mic. "Who's up top?" he said, the question even, calm, the sheriff in full-professional mode.

The speaker hissed, then squalled with feedback.

"Bridger here, Sheriff."

"Any sign of our target?"

"Not yet sir. I—" Then the radio fell dead along with the carnival, the crowd.

A weeping teen bolted from behind the hot-dog stand and down the midway. Thomas never saw her again.

Jacob pressed his face close, his breath hot in Thomas's ear.

"I can feel her," the boy whispered. "It's like ants are crawling all over me. You can't stop her with guns."

Thomas pulled back far enough to see the boy. Tears stained Jacob's cheeks.

"I know, buddy."

The black figure that had posed as his father rushed through Thomas's memory, a memory suppressed by Jillian for years. He destroyed the monster with a talisman—the snake head from Skeletor's Snake Mountain play set—and with strength from Jillian to kill her mother. They killed her mother because Jillian wanted power, but she didn't get it then.

Thomas had no "talisman" now, and he had no Jillian to help him. All he had was anger and a little boy.

"But we'll win this," he said.

Small hands cupped Thomas's cheeks. "How do you know?"

"Because," Marguerite said, pulling them both tighter to her, "we don't have a choice."

[11]

A crack-pop split the silence. Thomas and Marguerite ducked, Brittany's weapon snapped to high ready, Glenn didn't flinch.

"Bridger," he said into his mic. "Bridger, come in."

The radio hung like a brick from his belt, the mic on his shoulder useless. He turned to Brittany.

"She's here somewhere, Deputy," he said, nodding toward the roof of the Civic Arena. "He wouldn't have fired at nothing. Keep your eyes open for anything. A red-haired woman, a red-haired little girl, a goddamned red-haired Sasquatch. I don't know. She can look like anything."

"Anything?" Brittany asked. "You mean like a disguise? Or—"

"Anything," Thomas snapped. "Absolutely anything. She's not human."

She shook her head. "Oh, come on. What is she? A goblin? A sorcerer?"

"She's a monster, Deputy," Glenn cut in. "You saw what she did to the Daugherty family. No human could do that without running them through a combine."

"But—"

"Sheriff Glenn?" Jacob said.

"—there has to be a rational explanation."

A tug on his sleeve broke him off the argument. Jacob stood next to him, pointing into the sky.

"Look."

Norman shuddered. "She's flying."

Jillian floated from the darkness over the tallest hill of Dragon's Revenge, arms outstretched, face to the heavens, her red hair flowing around her head as if gravity couldn't affect it. Purple cracks of lightning framed her body as she rose over the midway.

"What the hell?" Brittany whispered.

The floating figure raised her face even higher and began to spin, the clouds above her moving as she did, the blanket of gray rage churning into a whirlpool sucking in clouds as far as Glenn could see. The dark, swirling mist stretched into a cone, surrounding the carnival. Lightning danced between the churning walls, their world an enormous plasma globe.

"We told you, Deputy," Glenn said. "She's not human."

Sirens blared in the evening air. Elizabeth took in a deep breath as the glass doors to the front of the Buchanan County Law Enforcement building slid silently shut behind her. She reached into the wide front pocket of her scrubs top, pulled out the bottle of vodka and took a swig.

Hmm, she thought, holding it up to the light of a streetlamp. That crazy fairy bitch underestimated me.

She tucked the bottle away, turning west onto the sidewalk and walking toward the carnival. Something in the back of her head, a thought, a command, a hypnotic suggestion, told her that's what Jillian meant when she said, "Just wait for my signal. You still have an important part to play in all this." The cops running around all crazy was the signal. Probably. Well, maybe.

But what's my part?

As if a finger snapped, the world around her became silent, followed by streaks of lilac lightning forking across the cloud-covered sky.

"Whoa."

The sky hanging over St. Joe didn't look like aerial phenomena; it looked like a world beneath the sea. She'd read about these clouds, and they were rare, low-lying, and undulating like ocean waves. Lightning flashed purple again.

"That's not right," she whispered.

The clouds began to rotate, not like a tornado, which Elizabeth would have liked better. Maybe it would whip her to Oz. She'd always wanted to know where the yellow-brick road ended. The churning clouds spun faster and faster, lightning spitting into the sky; then they dropped into a cone, swallowing the Fortieth Annual Jesse James Days carnival.

She pointed herself toward the Delores Hadley Community Center. With any luck, her car would be in the parking lot, Jillian's bloody elf-butt stain still on the dash.

The cops had left her car in the rear of the western parking lot of the community building, a key left in a magnetic key holder her father had given her twenty years ago because, "You never know when you're going to lose your keys. It may sound stupid, but, baby girl, I'm not going to be around forever to come to your rescue."

Cotton Condon died of a massive heart attack two days later. Elizabeth never lost her car keys until right now, but they weren't really lost, were they? Cotton never considered that the St. Joseph Police Department would confiscate her keys after she tried to murder someone.

"Glad you didn't call that one, Pop," she said as she knelt beside the rear passenger tire and felt until her fingers touched the rusty old box. "But thanks for this."

The door clicked when she pushed the unlock fob button. When Elizabeth turned to climb into the car, the storm was almost upon her.

Hurry, Elizabeth. Hurry.

Black-and-slate clouds churned and groaned, spitting blades of purple lightning into the sky and crashing them into buildings; concrete and glass exploded into the street. The maelstrom swelled, spinning papers, tree limbs, and a bicycle in its twisting malevolence. A maroon Mini Cooper parked on the street began to skitter across the asphalt before the storm reached it and shot it through the front window of . 3 Wishes bakery.

The storm seemed to burp before lurching closer to the Delores Hadley building. Elizabeth gripped the door and roof of her car, wind threatening to pull her off her feet.

Move, Elizabeth. Move.

She fell into the car and stabbed the key at the ignition switch until it found its way in. The old Honda fired up and she slammed it into reverse. The storm reached Delores Hadley, peeling the metal roof off as if it were an apple skin.

"No, no, no," came out in a whisper.

The car spun in a tight doughnut, the tail end clipping a stupidly big SUV as she pushed the Honda away from the storm. The right front tire dropped over the curb when she turned too hard to hit Felix Street, the thundering storm swallowing the building in her rearview mirror; bricks flew like a bomb went off. The car whined when she downshifted and whipped through a red light, skidding south on Third Street.

A dumpster rolled across the road, dragging a scream from down deep; Elizabeth swerved and zipped around it. The grinding clouds loomed over the car, crumbling the city as it rolled after her. Sweat ran down her neck; she tried to swallow but couldn't. She didn't recognize her own face reflected in the window.

Charles Street came with a shriek of tires, the passenger side of the Honda lifting off the ground. Elizabeth straightened the tires and tore up the Interstate 229 on-ramp, the calamity behind her ripping into the street, tossing chunks of asphalt to the side. Utility poles snapped and splintered on the ground.

"No, no, no."

The taste of heat and iron filled her mouth. Elizabeth wiped her forearm across her bloody lip; she'd bitten down too hard.

The car sped past a 45 mph sign at 70 and hit an empty I-229. Elizabeth's foot bore down on the accelerator. The churning storm crawled onto the interstate, and the raised highway crumbled behind her.

I'm going to die. I'm going to *die.*

A glance into the rearview. The storm's crawling clouds threw out tentacles that grabbed the sides of the highway, jerking itself forward like a Lovecraftian beast. Elizabeth screamed again, the sound pitiful inside the car. Between the arms of the storm, a circle squirmed to life, twisting and writhing until it formed a face and—

Oh, Jesus. The face was Jillian.

Elizabeth punched the clutch and ground the car into fifth gear, coaxing more speed out of it as she approached the US 36 intersection. The storm struck the rear of the Honda; Elizabeth gripped the wheel harder. The Jillian tempest smashed against the Honda again, sending it into a spin. Jillian's cloud-face grinned into the windshield and the storm reached a hand to grab the car, but Cotton Condon taught Elizabeth how to drive, and Cotton Condon was a badass.

She cranked the wheel and straightened the vehicle, hitting the Pony Express Bridge at 110 mph. As the Honda screamed over the Missouri to the Kansas side of the river, she looked back. The Jillian storm froze at the water's edge and moved no closer. Elizabeth reached up to give her the finger, but Jillian screamed, and the sound pushed the car harder. Its windows shattered, the Honda sprinkling glass onto the highway as it crossed over into Kansas.

CHAPTER SIXTEEN

[1]

THE CLOUDS ROSE and fell as if they breathed. Lightning splintered around Jillian floating dead center above Thomas, the sky around her a bloodshot eye. The Dragon's Revenge didn't stop, the riders locked into a screaming loop that might never end. A metal-wrenching screech tore through the howl of the wind; the Tilt-A-Whirl snapped from its base, torn power cables spitting like July Fourth sparklers. The metal death trap, people strapped into its wheel, rolled down the midway and crashed into the carousel. Restraints released on impact, throwing bodies up toward the clouds; some disappeared into the spinning wind, others crashed into concession booths.

The screams of a man in his thirties ended when he landed face-first onto the street fifteen or twenty yards from Thomas, the sound like a dropped a bag of custard.

The street moved, asphalt quivered and cracked; chunks popped out and scattered. The trestles that supported the Dragon's Revenge groaned and pitched to the side. Steel ground on steel shrieked as the structure buckled and crashed onto the writhing midway. The flashing colored lights of the carnival flickered and died, leaving the midway bathed in pale purple light.

Hands grasped Thomas's shoulders and turned him around. Marguerite's face was inches from his. "What the hell is happening?"

His arms slid around her waist as he buried his face in her hair. "She's going home, and she's taking St. Joe with her."

"What?"

He kissed Marguerite's hair and released her before leaning close to Glenn. "We've got to do something," he said.

The sheriff didn't move.

"Jesus. Give me that."

Thomas reached for the shotgun on the sheriff's shoulder. Glenn whipped the 12-gauge Mossberg into his hand and pushed the weapon toward him.

"It didn't help the first time," Glenn said, holding the stock as Thomas took the weapon.

Thomas nodded toward the boy who stood pressed against him and Marguerite. "*He* wasn't with us the first time."

Thomas slammed the pump action, the *ca-chick* of the chamber loading dulled by the storm. A tug on his pants pulled his attention to Jacob. The boy's dark eyes were wide.

Jacob shook his head. "No," he mouthed.

"Why?" Thomas asked, his voice weak over the storm. Another wave cascaded through the asphalt; a pipe burst, spewing water into the air.

Because I can't help you, Jacob said inside Thomas's mind. Cold shivered throughout his body. Jillian used to speak with him that way.

Thomas nodded and lowered the weapon, kneeling in front of Jacob. "Why not, son?"

Jacob's face looked skyward before answering. "She's taking us to her world. If she drops us or we fall off the side, we'll be lost."

"Lost?"

"Lost everywhere, and nowhere," Jacob said, his words flat. The swirling dizziness, the heat, the disorientation as Jillian dropped him onto the dusty, dead land, rushed back to Thomas. "We're going to hell, Daddy Tom."

Marguerite dropped to the pavement and wrapped them both in her arms.

"I love you." She planted a long, wet kiss on Jacob's forehead, then stared into Thomas's eyes before pressing her lips into his. "Please," she said, breaking off. "Don't do anything stupid."

[2]

"Fu-u-u-dge."

The roller coaster frame twisted and crashed to the ground. Ground? Wasn't the ground supposed to stay in one place? Why was it moving? Tick Tick jerked and wrestled with his tightly bound hands and feet, flopping onto his back. Purple lightning struck a nearby building, and a wall of windows exploded behind him.

"Oh, wow, man. Wow, man. Wow, man," burbled from between his blackened, ruined teeth. Then he shouted, "Hey, hey, hey."

The chick cop knelt beside him, gripping a Taser. She dropped a hand onto the shaking pavement to hold herself upright.

"No, no, no, no, no. Don't tase me. I did-d-dn-dn-d-d-dn-dn-dn't do nothin'. But—but listen, listen. That Jillian lady. Oh man. She gave me the stuff. Purple stuff. It glo-o-o-owed."

"What are you talking about?" the lady cop asked.

Oh man. Is she real? Is this cop even *real*?

"The crystal meth. It was like a glow stick you could snort."

She doesn't get it, man. She doesn't get it.

"Did you suh-see her teeth?" Tick Tick stuttered. "She looks like a fracking shark, man. She's gonna eat us." Oh, yeah, she is going to eat us. She's going to flippin' *eat us*. "I'm tellin' you, she's not human."

The deputy pointed to the sky.

"She's not human? Don't you think I can see that? She's *flying*."

The cop lady pointed to the floating woman in the storm before holding the Taser over Tick Tick's face. His wide eyes reflected the lightning. "Now, keep your face shut, Norman, and stay out of the way. The grown-ups have work to do."

Grown-ups? Whatever. The cop chick stepped over him, and he rolled away from her, away from the sheriff man and the weird family. Jerking himself to sitting, he bit down on the excess line of the zip tie around his wrists and yanked it tight before hauling his jittery arms over his head and slamming them forward into his lap. The plastic line snapped, just like he saw on that YouTube video.

His ratty, oil-stained tennis shoes flopped noiselessly onto the street as he wriggled his feet free of the tie and scrambled to standing before he took off in a lumbering gait, thrashing his way over the undulating street and in between the kiosks, vanishing from sight.

[3]

The salt and oil on his mother's skin clung to Jacob's lips after he kissed her cheek.

"I love you too," he whispered in her ear and stepped away. Her hands tried to hold on, to pull him tight, but her fingers couldn't grasp hold.

Wind died as if by a switch; detritus fell to the ground, papers fluttered; cans and bricks crashed into the stands and kiosks surrounding the Midway. A lavender dome covered the sky. A teenage boy, as tall as Daddy Tom but skinny, stumbled toward Sheriff Glenn, tears running down his face. A gash in his left leg gushed blood.

"Help. Help me," he said, his voice quivering. He dropped to the rippling, crumbling asphalt at Sheriff Glenn's feet, blood oozing onto the street.

The sheriff rested a hand on the teen's sweaty head. "Just stay here, son," he said.

Jacob didn't know how Mom's friend could sound so calm when hell gurgled at the edge of their world, but he did.

"Well, hello, folks," Jillian said in the now dead silence of the carnival, lowering herself to the pavement, something like Supergirl if Supergirl were evil and crazy. "Long time, no see."

Screams and sobs came from people hiding where they could became a drumbeat in the night, undercut by the rumble of the puckering asphalt. A four-story building outside the carnival leaned wildly before straightening and then collapsing onto itself. This was a bad place.

Jacob stood and walked toward the bleeding teenager, whose eyes were wide and streaked red from tears. Jacob sat beside him.

The crack-pop of a gun echoed from somewhere on the midway. Jillian's right hand rose and caught something in midair. She opened that hand and dropped a bullet onto the ground.

"Hi," Jacob said.

The teen looked at him, sweat, tears, and snot glistening on his face.

"Jillian," Daddy Tom shouted over Jacob's head, the grown-ups inhabiting an entirely different atmospheric layer. "This is over. Send everyone home."

Jacob held his hands up palms first. I can't do it. I can't do it. I know I can't do it. "I'm going to try and do something to your leg. I don't think it will hurt."

The teen broke into sobs.

"It's nice to see you've finally figured out what courage is, baby, but it's too late for that," Jillian said to Daddy Tom. She didn't shout. She didn't have to. "We're almost in Ālfheimr."

Jacob chanced a peek at Jillian as the teenage boy cried and bled. A purple web spun itself around the fairy woman; an inward glow melted the web away. The glow remained and Jillian stood in a gossamer gown of lilac, a crown of purple flowers in her hair.

"This is my kingdom," she continued, "and my people, and there are so, so many of them."

The teen winced as Jacob concentrated on his leg, pushing his negative thoughts away to maintain focus. Then it came; a cold energy pushed outward through Jacob, thick and viscous; Jacob thought it felt like electric pudding, if that could be a thing. The older boy sucked in a breath through clenched teeth, then let it hiss out. Jacob raised his head; the gash had disappeared.

"How?" the teen wheezed.

Jacob ignored him and stood to face Jillian. He'd healed the older boy, but didn't know how.

"No," Mom said, standing between him and the bad fairy lady.

"Let him go." Jillian cackled. "It doesn't matter anyway. My people are here."

There was an explosion, and Jillian flew backward, landing on the street, a bloody hole ripped through her chest; Thomas loaded another shell into the shotgun's chamber. Jillian dusted herself off and stood. A screaming young mom, visible through the hole in the elf-monster's midsection, stood behind her, her baby crying in its stroller. The mother and baby disappeared as Jillian's flesh and organs folded themselves back together.

"That wasn't very nice, lover," she said to Thomas through a horrifying wide mouth of needle teeth, humor gone from her tone. "I liked my pretty dress."

Thomas cocked the shotgun. "It wasn't your color."

[4]

The world thudded to a stop beneath Glenn's feet; the collision threw him and those clustered around him to their knees. The sudden drop wrenched a half dozen cars from the arms of the Octopus ride, screams of the riders silenced when the chrome green cradles crashed into the pavement. The ground lurched one last time, and the central axis of the off-balance Octopus snapped, the top of the ride rolling into the food kiosks. People scattered; splintered lumber and nachos rained over them, the wood clattering onto the street. This is too goddammed far.

"Jillian!" Glenn shouted, rising to his feet, service weapon in his fist. He never wanted to shoot anyone. Not as a rookie, not in his years as Boyd's second-in-command, and he sure as hell didn't want to shoot anyone as sheriff. Until now. "This ends. You have the right to remain silent—"

Jillian's cackle echoed in the night.

"—anything you say—" he continued.

She stepped toward them, her glowing gown flowing as if she was walking through water.

"Are you giving me a Miranda warning, Sheriff?" Another laugh escaped her, lighter, merrier, pitying. "You do know my world is a bit out of your jurisdiction, right?"

"—*may* cause me to fucking shoot you," he finished, cocking his pistol. There was no other way he knew to stop her. This was it. This *had* to be it.

Her arms drifted into the sky and she rose again, the lilac glow growing, hurting his eyes, but he never turned away.

"You're not going to shoot me, Sheriff," she said. "But you're so cute standing there with that little popgun."

Tears welled in his eyes. He'd never signed up for this.

"You killed my friend." His words hard as iron. "Her name was Maddy. She was a good person, a good deputy. You ate her neck."

The glowing fairy queen continued to rise, slower than the carnival rides but just as high.

"I have a bad memory for species, Sheriff. Besides, I eat a lot of things." She pulled her arms in, her hands clasping at her breast. "Now, I'd like you to meet those who are going to greet you as guests and treat you as kindly as you want to treat me. The warriors of Ālfheimr."

Howls of surprise, anger, shock, and terror erupted from outside the midway. Carnival goers ran into the purple light, some police officers and members of Glenn's own department among them. A man in a charcoal suit, his red tie hanging like a panting tongue, walked among them, his attention solely on Jillian.

"Jesus," Brittany whispered. Glenn didn't know when she'd gotten so close to him, but she was there. "It's the mayor. He was supposed to announce the winners of the Little Mr. and Ms. Jesse James Days tonight."

The mayor? No.

"Hello," the man called toward the woman in the sky. "Hey. Hello."

Jillian's face tipped toward the crowd; she spotted him forcing his way through people who were quickly losing their grip on reality.

"And who are you?" she asked, drifting closer to him.

He stopped and straightened his tie.

"Stop," Glenn barked at him, and started to move, but Thomas wrapped his arms around the sheriff's waist, holding him back.

"I'm Paul Burnett, mayor of St. Joseph, Missouri. What have you done with us? What have you done with our city?"

"Don't." Thomas's breath was hot on the side of Glenn's face.

A grin tugged at one side of Jillian's mouth as she moved even closer.

"Your city is now mine, Paul Burnett, mayor of St. Joseph, Missouri, as is the whole corner of your sad little state. I've taken it; it's now the ugliest part of my beautiful world."

A moan rippled through the people.

"Oh, don't be sad. It's not like I've brought you here for no reason. You have a noble purpose in the land of elves."

She sank to eye level with Paul, her feet hovering half a foot above the ground. The mayor leaned toward her.

"We already have a purpose. We're alive. We're free. We're able to choose for ourselves, to care for ourselves, to care for others who need us. Our purpose is to be human."

Jillian's hands clapped and she squealed.

No, Mayor. Get away. Run.

The fairy queen spun, spraying purple sparks over the terrified mass of people. "Oh, my." A finger rose and tapped her lips. "Do you know what I think of humans?"

Paul opened his mouth to speak, but his jaw dropped.

Goddamn it, no, no, no.

Glenn pushed against Thomas's grasp. "Let me go!" he screamed.

The shark's mouth opened as Jillian's guise became distorted, the smile splitting her face. "I think they're delicious."

The mayor's head snapped off in her teeth, blood shooting from the hole in his neck as the body fell to the ground.

[5]

Thomas held Glenn as the sheriff's muscles, tight as a pair of eighties jeans, relaxed after the mayor's headless body dropped to the street. He slumped in Thomas's arms for a second, only a second, before shaking him off. Hundreds of people screamed and tried to scatter, bouncing off each other, stumbling, falling.

"You couldn't help him. He w—"

Glenn's fist caught Thomas in front of his right ear and dropped him to the pavement. The shotgun flew from Thomas's hands and clattered against the asphalt. Pain ripped through his head, and the world around him spun as he dropped, the stitches screaming when he hit the ground.

The warmth of fresh blood leaked onto his chest.

"You son of a bitch," Glenn grumbled, his right fist pulled back to hit Thomas again if he stood. "I could have stopped it."

Thomas pushed himself to sitting, pain lancing his breast.

"How, Glenn? How?" he said, squinting, the words whispered as if speaking too loud would hurt worse. "She would have killed you."

"You don't know th—"

Jacob stood beside the sheriff, Glenn's breath coming too damn hard.

Goddamn, Thomas thought. That hurt. Jacob tugged at Glenn's shirt.

"She would have, Sheriff Glenn. She would have eaten your head instead of that man's."

Jacob reached to help Thomas up, but Glenn grabbed his arm first, hefting Thomas to his feet. Thomas yelled, the spot of blood on his chest spreading. Glenn couldn't meet his eyes.

"I'm sorry, Tom. It was emotional. Knee-jerk."

A woman ran by them, a stuffed unicorn in her arms. A teenaged couple followed. Jillian floated above the crowd, rising, nearing the top of the tilting Barnstormer ride.

A shout and the throng of carnival goers backed into the midway, trying to stay out of reach of people who marched in wearing bowl-like helmets and armor of chainmail, lamellar, and hardened leather, swords and spears in their hands.

A murmur mumbled beneath the undercurrent of whispers until theses Renaissance-fair rejects pushed their way through the crowd, snapping chains onto the fairgoers' wrists and ankles. As the soldiers marched toward them, they chanted words Thomas couldn't under-stand. Something about a *dróttning*.

"They're herding us," he whispered before leaning into Glenn's face. "They're *herding* us."

Thomas grabbed the shotgun from the street before wrapping an arm around Marguerite's waist, pulling her close, stifling another scream. An angry woman/elf/fairy at the vanguard pointed her sword toward them, the polished blade glowing lavender in the distant, waning light of Jillian.

Thomas waved Brittany to him. "We're leaving," he said.

Marguerite grabbed his chin and turned it to face her. "Where are we supposed to go? They're everywhere."

A small hand wrapped itself into Thomas's big, calloused one, another folded into Marguerite's.

"Sheriff Glenn knows where we need to go," Jacob said calmly as people began to scream around them. "Let's follow him."

"Glenn?" Thomas asked. The sheriff stood as still as a rock, his mouth open. "Jesus, dude. Get your shit together."

The sheriff shook his head, and he turned to Thomas, his face blank. "We need to get to the station," he said, the sentence as slow as pancake syrup.

A spear flew. It missed by yards, clattering to the broken pavement.

"Now," Thomas said.

No one argued with him.

[6]

They ran, Brittany and Marguerite dragging Glenn along as Thomas clutched his wounded chest, the sheriff mumbling to himself. The sky—storm clouds now all but gone—let through bright pinpricks of stars. A moon rose above the crumbling skyline of downtown St. Joseph, too large, too close to be Luna.

A second, smaller moon hung by its side.

"How?" Glenn asked.

Soldiers in ancient battle gear pulled the circle tighter; people in chains, screaming, fell to the street before them. A giant, at least seven feet tall, brandishing an iron sword, stepped from the ranks in their way. Brittany fired her Glock 22, the bullet wide. The giant grinned and sprinted toward them.

Thomas pulled up, releasing Glenn's arm to fire his shotgun.

"Get behind me, baby," Marguerite said, corralling Jacob with her hands.

Thomas raised the weapon and aimed low before firing, the blast echoing in the night. The giant soldier's eyes widened as his right shin disappeared in a splatter of blood and bone. He crashed into the line of elven warriors, tumbling them into the wreckage of the stands and food kiosks.

Thomas grabbed Jacob and Marguerite's shoulders. "Hurry."

[7]

The hot dog was still warm. Tick Tick pulled the foil-wrapped redneck taco from the wreckage of a food stand and ate it in three bites as lines of dudes in breastplates holding swords—*effing* swords—marched from the shadows. He watched them as he chewed.

Oh poop. Am I chewing too loud?

A leather boot kicked a chunk of split lumber; the wood skittered over the asphalt until it thunked to a stop less than a foot from Tick Tick's twitching head. That glowing purple stuff was *the* stuff.

The boots kept moving forward, and Tick Tick realized he'd stopped breathing. He thought a moment or two before he decided he should start again.

Those warrior dudes kept moving toward the midway, rounding up people like livestock. They said nothing, made no sound as they walked, tossing spectral chains around arms and legs, pushing their prisoners to the ground.

Tick Tick knew what he had to do. Hands pushed through the dust and rubble around him, finding a scattering of change, somebody's arm, a pair of tongs.

When he brought his hands out again, one held another foil-wrapped hot dog, the other a handful of mustard packets. Tick Tick wasn't hungry; he was a stress eater.

The glow from the bad flying lady began to dim as she rose higher than the carnival, but he could see well enough from the light of the moons.

Moons?

A huge armor-and-sword dude lifted off his feet and blew backward, bowling over the guys behind him like, hmm. Like he was a bowling ball. Tick Tick flinched, squishing the half-eaten hot dog in his hand.

"Huh? Wha?"

A boy stood behind his parents, or whoever they were, the dad guy holding a shotgun. The cops flanked them, although the sheriff man looked sick. Tick Tick shoved the rest of the hot dog into his mouth, pushing it into his cheek.

"You're running *toward* the cops, dude," Tick Tick thought he whispered before he moved. He had no idea if he'd said anything aloud. "Toward the *cops*." The past couple of years, the sight of a cop had sent fear dancing across the few parts of his brain that still worked right. Now? Fart.

Sucking in a deep breath around the sting of cheap mustard, he pushed himself to his knees. His bare feet tingled as he stood, bumping his head on the bottom of the shattered bleachers the freaky purple storm had sent crashing into the food stands.

"Fudge knuckles," he said at some volume. High, low, whatever.

Leaning away from the bleachers, he stood and shoved his hands in the air. He'd had enough run-ins with the law to know they liked to see everyone's hands, and Tick Tick was not going to disappoint anyone.

"Hey, man," he said. "Can I come with?"

The little boy turned toward him first. Fear and exhaustion hung on his face. The big farm boy-looking dad and the hot mom stepped on either side of the kid.

"It's okay, baby," the hot mom said to the boy. "He's not going to hurt anybody, not now." She glared at Tick Tick. "Are you?"

Tick Tick's muscles jittered as he stood, arms and legs flinching in a drug-filled confusion of neurological misconnections. I need you, he thought. Please.

"Take me home, Mom, Dad," tripped over his tongue. "Norman just wants to go home."

The lilac glow in the sky vanished behind the law enforcement building, the full white glow of the two moons nearly as bright as a sun.

Thomas released Glenn and jogged up the steps to the front entrance. The glass doors were shattered, but whether from the trip from Earth or the warriors dressed like Vikings, he couldn't tell.

He lowered his weapon to waist high and stopped just outside the door frame.

"It's from the inside." The sentence came from Glenn, soft, shaky.

Thomas turned back to his family, his friends, and the guy obviously on meth. "What?"

Glenn ran a hand through his hair and tried to straighten his tie, but most of it was pinned beneath his flak jacket.

"I said the glass is from the inside," he said, stopping to swallow. The words began to come out stronger. "It's scattered on the stairs, so whatever happened to shatter it didn't go in, it came out."

Thomas looked at his feet.

Glenn was right.

"Okay." Thomas tried to grin at the sheriff, but grins weren't happening. "Glad you're back with us. You said we needed to come here. What are we after?"

Glenn held up a hand and ticked items off on his fingers. "Uh, riot gear, like body armor, and shields, and helmets." He stopped, his jaw muscles bunched for a moment before he started again. "We have two AR Five Sevens we took from some rednecks with a meth lab down by De Kalb. Those are in the evidence room. I think we'll, um, we'll need some bolt cutters and some water."

"Oh, yeah, man," Norman said. "We gotta stay hydrated."

They headed inside and hoped it was at least a little safer than the chaos surrounding them.

Men and women, teenagers, children, all in chains, marched down the midway, pushed into motion by leather-and-metal-clad warriors with the butts of their spears. Jacob sat on a squeaky chair in the sheriff's department squad room watching the parade through a hole in a crumbled concrete wall; the moans and cries of those captured crawled their way inside.

Tears wanted to come, but Jacob didn't think he had any more; his eyes hurt from crying. The lights of the midway flickered and popped on, the rides that still stood groaned back to life.

"This is messed up, man," the person Brittany arrested whined as he paced the room, occasionally stopping to stare out the hole in the wall for an uncomfortably long time. Jacob didn't know what was wrong with the man, but his body jerked and twitched. He reminded Jacob of a squirrel. "I mean, seriously messed up."

The man stopped pacing; his hands flittered like birds.

"Shut up, Norman," Brittany said.

Mom and Daddy Tom sat at a table across from Sheriff Glenn and Deputy Brittany, bulletproof jackets strapped tight across their chests. Weapons from rifles to pistols to police batons lay on the table between them.

Norman threw his twitchy hands over his head. "She flippin' flew, man, and I don't know what she did, but there are two moons out there. Two gosh-darned moons. It's like she pulled us into a different plane of existence or something." He stopped talking, his face drawn tight as he scratched the back of his head. "Like, you know, when Kirk totally effed up negotiations with the Halkans and tried beaming the away team back to the *Enterprise* during an ion storm and they ended up in the mirror dimension."

Jacob flinched when Sheriff Glenn slammed his fist onto the table. "What the fuck are you talking about?"

"Glenn." Mom glared at the sheriff before she turned toward the twitchy man. "I don't think there were two moons on that episode," she said.

"No, but, but Spock had a beard."

Calliope music, soft at first, came through the wall. As Jacob focused on the crumbling land beyond the hole, the music grew louder.

"For the love of—"

Mom shoved a palm toward Sheriff Glenn and he shut his mouth.

Why are grown-ups so stupid? Jacob wondered.

The chair groaned as the boy slowly turned it away from the hole.

"He's saying—" Jacob's words slow, pained. "That we're here, the carnival is here, the city is here, but here is different. Here's not here anymore."

"You're saying we're in a different dimension, baby?" Mom asked. "That Jillian moved the entire *city?*"

Jacob shook his head.

"No. She moved more than that." Jacob could feel the emptiness, the loss wavering in his soul, his connection to home tenuous, but still there—for the moment. Jillian stripped the northwest corner of the state clean. All that was left back home was dirt, the patch of bare earth a scab.

"Then," Sheriff Glenn said, "how do we get back?"

Daddy Tom lifted a shotgun from the table and lay it across his lap.

"We don't," he said. "Not yet. If we don't end this, Jillian will suck every bit of life from what she's stolen, then go back for more."

Jacob's chair stopped squeaking. Everyone faced him.

"You can't kill her with guns," he said, frustrated. "I told you that. Are grown-up people this dumb? You've already tried."

Mom grabbed his arm. "Do you know how we can stop her, baby?"

He shook his head, and straight black hair fell over his right eye. He didn't smooth it back into place. Tears rolled down Marguerite's cheeks.

"Okay," Sheriff Glenn said. "I don't know what any of this means, but I've seen enough not to ask any questions. Guns are all we got. Now all we have to do is find her and unload everything."

"I don't think that's going to be a problem, Glenn," Daddy Tom said.

Sheriff Glenn stood and approached the hole, gazing out at the limping carnival, the captives gone, dragged away by long-dead elfin and Viking warriors. Soft purple glowed from windows and cracks in the walls of a horror funhouse, the Pixie Brothers' Haunted Hotel. He pushed his sheriff's hat back on his head and exhaled.

"You gotta be kidding me."

CHAPTER SEVENTEEN

[1]

THE MOANS FROM the calliope's compressed air shooting through its brass whistles dominated the night when the power flickered back on and the carnival thrashed to life. The volume increased when they stepped through the hole in the wall of the squad room and out into the strange, otherworldly night. The recorded organ sounds were as haunting as a Doors song.

Thomas lifted Jacob over the remains of the wall, the too-large bulletproof vest hanging off the boy's shoulders like a heavily armored sundress. After he lowered Jacob to the ground, Marguerite's fingers laced through Thomas's and pulled him back up.

When he stood straight, her eyes met his. He'd seen those eyes reflect drunk, happy, horny, sad, momma bear, and shock. They'd never looked at him this way.

Not once.

Marguerite was terrified for him.

"Hey," Thomas said, cupping his other hand on her cheek. "We're going to do this, okay?"

A tear, only one, broke dam and trickled from her right eye. She didn't admit it was there.

"Jacob's right, isn't he?" she said, rather than asked, her words solid. The warmth he felt for her filled him; her voice didn't quiver, no matter how scared she was.

"About what?"

"Tom," Glenn hissed, waving him toward himself and Brittany. Jacob stood between them, looking back at his mother, his little hands in fists.

The boy was ready, no matter how uncertain he sounded.

Thomas ignored the sheriff.

"He told me you were going to ask me to marry you."

As Thomas stood on the ruins of a section of the Buchanan County Law Enforcement Building, the destroyed carnival background their music for the night, the flush in his cheeks seemed wrong.

"One hundred percent, lady," he said. "You're the person I've needed my whole life. You're my One Ring."

The corners of her mouth Mona Lisa'd.

"Do you read, ever? The One Ring was evil," she said, releasing his hand and grabbing the front of his shirt in both of hers. "The whole story was about small people destroying evil." She pulled his face closer to hers.

"Like now?" he said.

Glenn appeared beside them.

"Are you two kidding me?" he said, an arm pointing toward the Haunted Hotel, with the lilac light still pushing through its cracks. "We're on a different fucking planet getting ready to fight a monster, and you two are discussing wedding plans?"

Thomas started to respond, but Marguerite beat him to it.

"You're right, Glenn," she told him. "But this was important. And anyway, I've decided my son and I are going to stay in the squad room. You three can go do whatever shooty thing you have to do to stop Jillian, but I'm not risking my boy."

"Hey—" Thomas began before Jacob stepped toward his mother.

"No, Mom," he said, his tone older and more serious than a seven-years-old's should ever be. "I have to go. She can't surprise us that way."

Thomas grabbed Marguerite's shoulders, but she shook him off and knelt to look into Jacob's face. He was right.

[2]

The rides Tick Tick had helped tear down and put back up—the Dragon's Revenge, the Sizzler, the Tilt-A-Whirl, the Octopus—were all damaged or ready to collapse. The carousel was Downtown Tony's, and Tick Tick kept the hell away from it because Downtown Tony was freaking nuts, but that merry-go-round lay crushed, bodies tossed around it on the broken street. The Pixie Brothers' Haunted Hotel was the only exhibit he'd helped build left standing.

Recorded calliope music moaned, and a hint of Twizzlers drifted by on the breeze.

"Are we ready?" the sheriff asked.

Tick Tick flinched. Am I a part of a team? Are we like the Scooby gang, or the Losers Club, or the Power Rangers? He stood as tall as his five-foot-eight frame could and faced the sheriff.

"Do I get a gun?" he asked.

"Seriously?" Glenn grumbled as he turned toward the Haunted Hotel and started walking. "It's like a goddammed sitcom here."

Thomas held Marguerite's hand as the six of them marched across the short debris-filled lawn behind the cop shop and into the street, lavender light spilling from the Haunted Hotel forming the face of a sentient, malevolent jack-o'-lantern. The weight of the moment dragged at him. The Haunted Hotel, with its orange Howard Johnson's roof, its skeleton valet, its cheesy recorded screams, was their sewers of Derry, their Mount Doom, their Death Star. Pennywise was there, and Sauron, and Darth Vader. Terror hit him as a child, but Thomas had never been this frightened in his life.

He leaned close to Marguerite. "I can't risk you getting hurt," he said. "When we get there, I want you to stay outside."

She squeezed his hand. "You're not risking anything, baby. I am." She never turned to look at him, she simply tightened her grip on the shotgun she'd taken from the sheriff's office. "And do you really think that outdated 1950s misogynistic attitude will work on me?"

"Look," he said. "I'm just—"

"Worried," she finished for him. "I know. We all are, but that monster stole my son. She *stole* him. I'm happy you put on your man pants this morning, but"—Marguerite dropped his hand, the slap on his butt making him jump—"save it for later."

The Haunted Hotel loomed over them, its two stories leaning awkwardly.

Glenn reached out an arm and everyone stopped.

"Norman," he said. A recorded wolf howl wailed from a speaker above the door. "How many entrances?"

The carney stood, fidgety hands shoved deep into his front pockets, the young man's bleached face ghostly pale in the dancing carnival lights.

"Two," he said. "One in the front, and one in the back. It's like, you know, a house."

Thomas didn't need any more information to tell him Norman had encountered Jillian. Even high, the guy was scared too.

"Then Brittany and me are going in the front." Glenn motioned to Thomas. "The rest of you go through the back door. Then—"

The sheriff stopped when Norman tugged his sleeve.

"What?"

"Well," Norman said, his voice weak. "On the second floor, in the bedroom, when the people get really scared, the floor of the back hallway drops and they go down this slide. That's the back door."

"So there's no way in the back door?" Thomas said. "Looks like we're all going in together."

As they stood, bathed in the soft purple escaping through the cracks, the light faded and finally disappeared. They stood in silence.

"What do you think that means?" Marguerite asked.

Thomas stared at the front door, expecting it to open. It didn't.

"This was a bug light," he said, opening the door. "It means she knows we're here."

[3]

The grown-ups went in first. Jacob didn't know why—he'd told them, and more than once, he was the only person who could find the fairy lady, but Sheriff Glenn stuck him in the back with the shaking man Jacob was pretty sure took drugs. He looked like the "after" pictures the deputy showed his class when the sheriff's department came to his school.

Daddy Tom grabbed the door handle and pulled, the action triggering a recorded "Muh-wah-hah-ha."

"Geez," Sheriff Glenn hissed. "If she didn't know we were here before, she does now."

Jacob could feel Jillian's presence on the second floor, so he figured she could feel where he was too. She always knew.

Daddy Tom took the door from Sheriff Glenn and they walked inside. The sheriff, the deputy, Daddy Tom, Mom, the shaker, and Jacob.

The door snapped shut as the druggy man let go of it. No more recorded sounds barked out their location. The only noise came from speakers scattered around the building—moans and screaming. A stuffed black bear, the fur old and dusty, stood by a plastic palm tree across the room from a reception counter. Behind that, wooden mailboxes, some with envelopes, others with diamond-shaped key fobs. Cobwebs hung from the ceiling.

"Hey," the shaky man whispered over the recording. "There's like this motion sensor on the bear. Don't get too close."

It would be fun to make the bear move, Jacob thought, but followed the grown-ups when they scooted along the wall to the counter and all but tiptoed to the doorway; the *tink-tink-tink* noises of *Scooby-Doo* characters tiptoeing sounded in his head.

They entered the next room. An old-fashioned rug lay in the center of the floor, a bookshelf covered one wall, and two chairs separated by a lamp held skeletons wearing glasses and reading books.

"Hey, there's a—" the shaky man started before Glenn's foot landed on the rug and a closed cabinet flew open; a vampire lurched toward the sheriff.

A scream shot out of him before a shotgun went off, the noise deafening in the small room. The vampire exploded into red chunks.

Jacob slapped his hands over his ears.

"Margie," Sheriff Glenn said. "Damn it. You could have shot me."

"Sorry," she said through clenched teeth. "I got spooked."

Daddy Tom threw his weapon strap around his shoulder and swept Jacob into his arms; a strong, calloused hand covered his eyes. But Jacob had seen enough. The vampire was a real person and the wall was splattered red.

[4]

Glenn dropped to one knee. The body of a man dressed as Count Dracula lay in the center of the room, his blood soaking into the filthy rug beneath him. He turned the body over and the corpse's plastic vampire teeth fell out. He touched the man's face; it was cold.

"Oh my God!" Margie's arms wrapped around Jacob and Thomas, her face buried in Tom's chest. "I killed somebody. I—I—I killed somebody, honey."

"Margie." Glenn stood and rested a hand on her shoulder. She was shaking; so was he. "The body's cold. You didn't kill anyone. He's been dead for at least twelve hours."

She peeled her face from Thomas's shirt, her eyes red, her cheeks wet.

"You're sure?" she asked.

"Unfortunately, dead bodies are something I know about." He slid his hand off her shoulder and held the assault rifle tight. "We should hurry. Norman?"

The drug-addled kid didn't move.

"Norman?" Glenn said louder.

Norman shook his head like he'd just gotten up from a nap. "Wha?"

Glenn grabbed Norman's thin forearm and pulled him closer. "You know where these traps are," he said. "You're in front."

[5]

Oh crap. Oh crap. Oh crap.

The sheriff guy pushed Tick Tick into gear; his legs stumbled him into the next room. Motion-sensor lights flared to life, the yellow glow of tungsten bulbs reflecting off every surface.

"You've got to be kidding me," the sheriff said.

They'd reached the hall of mirrors.

"What hotel has a room like this?" The sheriff reached out and touched the surface of a mirror that extended from floor to ceiling. "None. No hotel has a room like this."

"Norman?" the pretty lady asked. "Can you get us through this?"

Can I get you *through* this? Ha!

"Sure. No prob," he said.

The room became quiet, hushed. Quieter than a room with two cops and two armed civilians with a kid should be. Maybe it was just him. The reflections in the glass nearly wrenched a scream from him at every turn through the mirrored maze. A left, five steps, then a right, then an immediate right. He stopped for a moment at the spot where

Becky McNamara had given him head baked out of her gourd, Tick Tick taking it all in, watching dozens of him and dozens of her get it on in overlapping reflections.

"This is a damned horror movie," the farm boy said, the shotgun off his arm and gripped in both hands.

Tick Tick took another step.

Wait. Is it three steps here? Or five? He took another, and another, and another, his face bumping against a cool, smooth mirrored surface. Four. It was four. He turned right and a stairway appeared, the rickety wooden boards going one way—up.

"We're, like, here, man," Tick Tick said as the sheriff dude stepped next to him, their combined shoulders filling most of the skinny hallway.

"What's next?" the sheriff asked.

"Um—" Next. Next. "The stairs and, uh, a T to two hallways. The one on the left goes to the Haunted Hotel's banquet room, where anima—anima—anima—robot mummies and the Frankenstein monster play in a polka band and a ghost in chains drops from the ceiling. The right goes to the bedroom where there's usually a woman—a real woman—dressed as Elvira, Mistress of the Dark. Oh, and that's where the slide trap is."

The sheriff man slid the bolt back on his assault rifle. The lady cop did the same.

"Anything going to jump out at me?"

Tick Tick shook his head. "Not unless it's Jillian."

[6]

Thomas pushed in behind Glenn and his deputy, Marguerite and Jacob close behind him. The stairway was so cramped he didn't know if good ol' Norman followed them. Thomas tried to keep his cool—at least look like he did—but the knot in his stomach kept threatening to expose him.

The upper hall, lit by fixtures that resembled candles, hugged claus-trophobically around them, the ceiling not taller than six feet. Thomas bent his knees to keep from hitting his head.

Glenn pointed down the left hall. "Tommy, you and Margie and Jacob go that way," he said, his stern in-control voice wavering as he spoke. "Brittany and I are going to the right. If you see Jillian, light her up."

Thomas wanted to speak, to protest; thinning their forces was a stupid idea. Jacob beat him to it.

"We're not splitting up," the boy said, standing next to his mother.

Glenn leaned over him. "Why not?"

"Because," he said. "Shaggy and Scooby always get in trouble when the gang splits up."

Thomas smiled. We *have* to make it out of here. For him.

"Besides," Jacob said, pointing to the right. "Jillian's that way."

"But—" Glenn began.

"He's right, Glenn." Marguerite wrapped her other arm around her son's shoulders and hugged him. "We do this together."

The sheriff's knuckles on the hand gripping his assault rifle turned white. Thomas realized Glenn was as scared as the rest of them.

"Okay," Glenn said, "but Brittany and I go first." He nodded to his deputy and they crept down the hall.

[7]

The electric candles ended after about ten feet; the already dim yellow glow faded as soon as they filed by. Jacob didn't need light to know where he was going. He'd already felt Jillian, and now he was close, very close. He closed his eyes and a woman's hand wrapped itself over his right one. Mom walked on his left side, and on his right was a wall. The hand squeezed gently once, twice.

Hey, kiddo, Jillian's voice said inside his mind.

Go away. I don't want to hold your hand.

The hand tightened, and this time it stayed tight.

No way, Jakie. We're buds. I'm going to swallow the souls of the law, but your mom and Thomas? No way. I'm going to keep them around for a long time. You get to help me play with them.

Anger flamed in his chest. Jacob was tired of this. Jillian took him away, she took him from his mother, and when he came home, it was years later. She threatened Mom and Daddy Tom. She stole a whole city. His mind screamed and the grip on his hand flew off. A solid thud struck the wall and the group stopped.

"What was that?" Sheriff Glenn asked.

In the darkness, Mom knelt next to Jacob, her hands finding his shoulders.

"Was it Jillian?" she asked.

"Yes," Jacob said. And I pushed her away. *I* pushed *her*. But how? "We're close. We have to get to the bedroom."

"I know, but—"

Jacob stomped his foot, and the thump echoed on the cheap plywood flooring. "She's evil. She's always been evil. She—" He inhaled deeply and let it out slowly, trying to calm himself like Mom when she did yoga. "She destroys things. That's what she does. If we don't stop her, she'll—she'll destroy our whole planet just to feed herself."

Mom became silent, but he knew she was frowning. Sass mouth, sass mouth, sass mouth.

That was rude, Jakie, Jillian's voice echoed inside his head. *Don't force me out. That doesn't make me happy.*

He pushed his mind forward into the Haunted Hotel bedroom. Jillian stared at him, her eyes boring into his brain. Pointed needle teeth flooded his thoughts.

Really, buddy boy? Here's what happens when I'm not happy.

A rush of thoughts knocked him to the floor. Mom screamed and tried to hold him, but her arms flew back, sending her crashing into the opposite wall; her shotgun thumped to the floor. A shout from Daddy Tom came from somewhere above him, but the word was muddled, as if spoken through water.

A red light ignited deep down in his memories, dim at first, but as he stared at it, the light grew brighter, and a rhythmic *thub, thub, thub* pumped somewhere inside. A soothing warmth spread over his body, engulfing him. His fear had gone, his worries, his doubt, his desire to destroy Jillian vanished. Somewhere far off, a voice came to him. A soft, soothing voice. He focused and words became clear.

"I call you on the phone, but you're not the-re," a woman sang off-key. She was somewhere nearby. Where? "I sit at home alone and won-der whe-re."

I've heard that song bef—

Then he knew. Mom had sung that song in the garden when he was little. An involuntary muscle movement threw his fist out. It connected with a wall, soft but tight, smooth but strong. His leg was next, pushing forward; the wall moved as if he pushed against the surface of a balloon.

"Whoa, little man." The muffled voice stopped singing. Something large and strong moved against the other side of the pliable wall, steering his leg away from it. "You're kicking Mommy to death, here."

Kicking? Mommy? His hand dropped to his stomach; a cord, like a flesh rope, emerged from his belly and snaked through a fluid that he now knew surrounded him.

I'm not born yet. I'm—

The red around him swirled, and his world became dark. The fluid drained from around him, but warmth still surrounded him. His hand remained on his belly, but the cord had disappeared. The rubbery walls narrowed as he began to move, muscles pinched him and forced him down a tunnel. Then light. Ow, light. Enormous hands suddenly held him. A man, a large man.

"Hey, I know you. You're the Mentos doctor," he tried to say, but his mouth couldn't make the words.

A rush of anger raged through him, followed by a need. A need to feed, to eat this doctor's life, then the nurse who backed away from him, seeing him as what he really was—the spirit of the monster called Dauðr.

This is your true self, Jakie, Jillian said. *Embrace it.*

No. Jacob's eyes popped open, his surroundings in darkness, Mom's arms once again wrapped around him. "Jakie. Wake up, baby," she said, her voice pleading.

"I'm awake," he said, trying to process everything he'd seen and felt and—oh, wow. "It was Jillian, Mom. I think she's scared."

[8]

Thomas had only seen Jillian scared once; the day he told her he'd delivered a sandwich to Bobby. The terror she'd felt had been real and she packed up and disappeared from his life hours later.

"If she's scared," Thomas said. "We can beat her."

Glenn huffed. "Don't you mean, if she's scared, she's dangerous?"

Thomas's frown deepened, although no one saw it in the darkened hallway.

"She was already dangerous, Glenn, but maybe now she'll make a mistake." The tension in the hallway thick as Missouri summer humidity. "We should take advantage of it."

Cautious. We're being too cautious, Thomas thought. There was no surprise, not with Jillian. There couldn't be. She knew who they were, she knew where they were, she knew what they could do. A cheap door ahead in the darkness was all that separated them from the monster he saw all those years ago in the passenger seat of his car behind his apartment, a sign bolted to the outside brick wall reading, "Private Lot. Violators Will Be Towed." He challenged her and she turned on him, her face stretching into a caricature of Jillian if she were a shark. Then she hid his memory.

"Norman," Thomas said. "You still with us?"

"Yes," came through the darkness in more of a whimper than an actual word.

"Is there anything we should know about between here and there?"

Bare feet tapped on the plywood flooring.

"Uh, a spot in the wall for people to jump out of. Most of the monsters and ghosts are just people in costume." He stopped and his feet shuffled again. "This place is all jump scares. You know, like the vampire."

Marguerite groaned beside him, and Thomas wanted to take a swing at the meth kid.

"It's here," Brittany said from farther down the hall. "Empty."

Lucky.

"Then let's move." The sheriff tried to sound stern, but his voice wavered. "Brittany opens the door and goes left. I go right. Tommy, left, Margie, right, and Jacob. Stay exactly where you are. You don't need to see this."

Glenn, Thomas thought. You have no idea what you're doing.

Then, the door to the bedroom—the last scare in The Pixie Brothers' Haunted Hotel—slammed against the cheap panel wall, weak lamplight creeping into the hallway. Brittany rushed in, weapon at high ready; she disappeared around the corner. Glenn followed, turning right.

Thomas's mouth felt dry and tacky. The bed, a cheap hotel bed, sat against the back wall of the room. A painting of a sailing ship hung over the headboard—the same painting from Jillian's room at the Starlight Motel, the motel where Rodney lived, the motel that had crumbled beneath his feet. Jillian sat on the edge of the bed waiting for them, her elegant dress replaced by jeans and a black Ramones T-shirt with a shotgun scatter pattern.

An elbow struck his chest.

"Come on," Marguerite hissed.

Adrenaline flooded his veins, his heart pounded like a paint mixer. This was it. Thomas's feet moved before he realized, and he followed the officers into the room; his breath came hard. Marguerite stepped into the room and stood beside him, her shotgun leveled at Jillian.

Jillian's eyes narrowed to slits, her smile barely registering. "Hey, lover," she said.

"I want to see your hands," Glenn barked, the butt of the assault rifle pressed into his shoulder. "Now!"

A giggle echoed through the room, and Jillian lifted both hands from her lap, middle fingers up. "Whatever you say, Sheriff," she said, her voice ice-cream smooth.

"Did you, Jillian Robertson, murder in cold blood one Loraine Miller?" Glenn shouted, his words loud in the small room.

"No," she said. "Elvin Miller did, I just gave him a nudge."

"Did you, Jillian Robertson, murder in cold blood one John Mc-Masters?" The sheriff ground his teeth.

"No," she said. "His loving wife, Carrie, did. Again, I gave her a push. Just a little. They weren't as happy as they seemed, Sheriff, baby."

"Sheriff Boyd Donally and Kristiansen?"

Thomas's fingers ached, his chest tight. Where are you going with this, Glenn?

A laugh escaped Jillian. "Oh, goodness no. That was Robert Garrett, pure and simple. He was a naughty boy, you know?"

Glenn winced but continued. "The poisoning of the Rolling Meadows Shopping Mall?"

"Nope."

"The Day St. Joe Died?"

"Uh-uh. Still Bobby."

"Then." Glenn stopped to clear his throat. "Did you take the lives of Rebekka Marshall of St. Joseph and her unborn son, Todd Marshall?"

"Now we're getting somewhere. Yep. Sure did. Yummy, yummy, yummy, I had toes in my tummy."

Brittany took a step forward, but a hand motion from Glenn jerked her to a stop.

"The Daugherty family?"

Jillian ticked off three fingers and nodded. "Most of them. I think I missed one."

Fear welled, Thomas's chest tight as a drum skin. This was wrong. He couldn't take it anymore. "Glenn?"

The sheriff didn't respond.

"Trey Dawson?" Glenn asked.

Long, red hair bobbed as Jillian nodded.

"Glenn," Thomas growled. "Stick with the plan."

"Dana Carroll? Mayor Burnett?" He paused, the anger in his voice deadly. "Deputy Maddy Glines?" A quiver ran through those words.

Jillian leaned forward. Her eyes hard, joyless. "One hundred percent."

"And did you," Glenn continued, stepping closer to the bed, his heavy cop boots loud on the cheap wooden floor, "kidnap Jacob Jenkins?"

"Oh, Sheriff." Her tongue pushed from her mouth and slowly wetted her lips. "Give it to me. Oh, yeah. I did, honey. I did it all."

"Sheriff Kirkhoff!" Thomas shouted, his body flush with heat. Glenn didn't move.

"Then," Glenn said, resting the rifle on his shoulder and pulling the handcuffs from his belt. "With the power vested in me by the voters of Buchanan County, I'm going to have to ask you to come with us."

Jillian's eyes locked with Thomas's, the once-emerald irises now black, as if they were injected with ink.

A knot formed in his stomach.

She clapped her hands together. "This is wonderful," she all but sang. "He's trying to arrest me again, honey. Wanna be cuffed with me? Grrrrrr."

Glenn stood still and silent. A trickle of drool hung from the sheriff's lower lip before it broke and dropped to the floor.

"Sheriff?" Brittany asked.

"It's Jillian, Deputy," Thomas said. "She's got him."

The monster's face puckered into a pout. "Oh, Thomas," she whined. "You never were any fun."

"Let him go, Jillian."

"Pfft." Her arms crossed her chest. "Or what? You going to shoot me again? You see how well that worked last time." The pout crept into a smile. "But that was in your world, and I was weak, oh so weak. But now, here we are. I'm home and strong. I don't need you anymore, Thomas, or your little buddy."

A nudge poked Thomas's leg, and a body pushed past. Jacob stepped before him, his hands in fists at his sides.

Marguerite jumped in front of her son faster than Thomas could react. Jillian's eyes widened as Marguerite's fist flew. It popped against Jillian's jaw and the monster's head snapped to the side; her body followed and she tumbled off the bed, landing with a thump.

"Leave my boy alo—"

Marguerite's words were cut off. Her body lurched backward and lifted off the floor, feet dangling as her hands moved to her throat. Jillian stood, eyes no longer black, but blazing purple.

Good God. Thomas stood slack-jawed, the shotgun in his hands forgotten.

"Don't hurt my mom!" Jacob screamed, throwing his hands toward Jillian.

A whoosh filled the room and Jillian flew backward, the cheap pressboard splintering as she crashed through the wall and disappeared into the night. Marguerite fell to the floor, sucking in breath.

Thomas dropped beside her; Jacob was already there.

"Honey? Are you, you know?" he asked.

A cough. "I'm okay." She blinked and stretched her neck. "If that's your bedside manner, mister, having you wait on me is going to suck if I ever get pregnant."

"Is that it?" Brittany asked. "Is this over?"

A woman's shriek pierced the night and violet light streamed through the hole in the wall.

"Nope," Thomas said. "Not by a long shot."

CHAPTER EIGHTEEN

[1]

THE TRACTOR TRAILER that once powered the carnival lay over-turned, the enormous generator on its flatbed cracked, a mixture of oil, coolant, and fuel spreading across the pavement below, soaking into the great fissures that cobwebbed the asphalt. The lights that had illuminat-ed the carnival were now dark, the calliope silent, the world still—the carnival finally dead.

Thomas spilled from the Haunted Hotel, his feet kicking open the door at the bottom of the slide. He rolled away from the building as Marguerite, holding Jacob, slid out directly behind him. Brittany and Glenn followed.

Norman didn't come down.

Thomas pulled Marguerite to him; his lips pressed against her fore-head.

"That was dangerous as hell," he said. "*Never* do it again."

She stretched upward, and her lips met his, the kiss long and warm. When she broke it off, her face was solid as stone. "Don't tell me what to do."

A hand landed on Thomas's shoulder and Glenn pointed to a lav-ender light that sparked deep inside the destroyed generator.

"We have to move while she's down," the sheriff said. "We have to flank her. Tom, you—"

A scream burst from across the ruined midway; the industrial generator exploded in a shower of steel plating and copper wire. The remains clanked across the broken asphalt. Jillian emerged from the wreckage bathed in purple fire.

The storm that faded between worlds, revealing the deep night sky and two moons of Jillian's world, swirled back to life above her. Lightning crashed to the ground beside Jillian, moving with her, 300 million volts blasting ruts into the ruined pavement.

"Get behind me," a small voice said.

Thomas looked down at Jacob. The weak, frightened boy was gone. Jacob's eyes flared in anger.

"I can't," Thomas said, trying to move but unable.

Jacob's tender jaw was set, his eyes black orbs, the dead eyes of a predator.

"No!" Marguerite knelt in front of her son and grabbed his shoulders. She gasped and fell backward.

"Sorry, Mom, Daddy Tom," Jacob said, his words calm. "You don't have a choice."

[2]

Power surged through Jacob's thin frame. He didn't know where the energy came from; it hid somewhere deep inside him. It had lain dormant, like cicadas, until the perfect conditions emerged for it to come out. Sometimes when he was happy, sometimes when he was sad, but always when he was angry. The power had left his control, he thought, when Jillian knocked him down in the cornfield, but it hadn't. Not really.

It had always been there—waiting.

Jillian's fiery form rose into the air, bright against the backdrop of the storm. Lightning flew from her fingertips.

"Jacob." His name came from her mouth in a boom. She flew toward him, her feet crashing into the pavement. Dust and chunks of dried oil and rock flew from the impact. A smile split her face, her teeth long and sharp.

The deputy lady behind Jacob screamed.

Oh, little man, Jillian's voice hissed in his head. *You still know a trick or two, don't you?*

The power, the fire that burned inside Jacob when Jillian hurt his mother, flickered for a moment; panic began to seep in.

"I'm—"

"You're weak, boy," she said aloud, cutting off his words. "And Thomas and your Mommy will suffer for that." The lightning from her fingers crackled.

Jacob felt Daddy Tom move behind him. His muscles pushed against the force Jacob used to keep him back.

No, his mind screamed at Thomas.

"I'll take care of Mommy first, while you watch, of course." Jillian's eyes blazed; purple fire leaped out in a stream. "Oh, the lady who hit me—with a fist? A *fist*? I'll enjoy taking her apart."

Jacob sensed movement behind him, but it wasn't Daddy Tom. It wasn't Mom. Sheriff Glenn and his deputy had backed away toward the Haunted Hotel and disappeared into the shadows.

"Run away, Sheriff," Jillian shouted. "You're good at that!" Her laughter sliced the night.

[3]

Glenn slid to a stop behind a stack of overturned bleachers, breath coming in shallow wheezes. Too much fatty food, too much time behind his desk. *My own damn fault.* As he stood, sweat soaking his undershirt, he just hoped he'd live long enough to change his diet. Brittany pulled up beside him, the young deputy not even breathing hard.

"What are we doing, Sheriff?" she asked.

Running away.

"No," he hissed under his breath.

"Sheriff?"

"We—" He coughed his throat clear. "We're"—*wheeze*—"going to surround her." *Wheeze.* "You stay here. I'll—" *Wheeze.* Geez, my chest hurts. "I'll go to the west of the—the. Whoo. The wrecked generator truck. Then—"

He stopped, his heaving breath slowing.

"Are you okay?" Brittany asked.

Glenn shook his head. "Old. Outta shape." Holy shit. How am I not having a heart attack? "Scratch that. I'll stay here, you go to the west of the truck."

Glancing between the shattered benches of the stands, Jillian rose into the air; lightning shot from her fingers, setting fire to a piece of the Octopus and a crushed food kiosk.

The boy remained still, shoulders back, a far cry from the whipped pup who had ridden in Glenn's patrol car. Tom and Margie were frozen.

"Watch for me," Glenn said. "While they"—*wheeze*—"while they keep that thing distracted, we'll come in from the sides. Stay in the shadows."

Brittany nodded. "Classic pincer movement?"

Glenn managed a slight smile. She was smart as hell. "Damn straight."

A section of lumber that had splintered from the stands clattered against the pavement and Glenn spun, weapon to his shoulder. Norman stumbled in the darkness. When he stopped, a slice of purple light cutting through the space between the ruins of the bleachers shone across his face.

The only thing that kept the addict from falling face-first onto the broken street was the Nordic spear in his right hand, the butt pressed against the ground.

"What about me?" the young man asked, his voice high-pitched and shaky.

"Norman," Glenn said, lowering his weapon. "You may have just given us a better chance."

[4]

Thomas moved as if he were slogging through Jell-O. Jacob held them back, he knew, keeping them away from Jillian. She moved closer as he was all but frozen in place, moving only millimeters at a time.

Come on, kid. I have a shot.

The monster Jillian, the shark Jillian, approached Jacob; the boy seemed tiny before that gaping maw, but he didn't budge. He stood before the oncoming killer like Rocky Balboa before Ivan Drago, David before Goliath.

This wasn't the boy he played catch with. The other kid was back.

Jillian spread her arms wide, and protesting groans of metal tore through the night; roller coaster tracks twisted into the air. She wailed as the pretzeled metal slammed down, encircling them in a gnarled fence. She easily leaped it.

"Now, little man," she hissed from her spiked grin. "Let's play with Mommy."

No. *Nooo*, Thomas tried to shout, but his mouth wouldn't open.

"Don't touch her," the boy said, the voice cold as winter.

The monster laughed again, this time the sound low; the vibrations pressed into Thomas's ears.

"Oh, you're so sweet, Jakie, but you can't do anything about it."

A snap, the crack of a twig in the forest, popped beside Thomas, and Marguerite screamed, her right index finger leaning unnaturally to one side. Marguerite's middle finger bent backward; another snap, another scream.

"Stop it!" Jacob shouted at Jillian, who laughed.

Thomas waited to see any amount of damage done to Jillian, but nothing happened. His heart raced out of control.

Another finger broke, and another. Then Thomas was free. Marguerite groaned as she grasped her hand, her broken fingers bent like pipe cleaners.

Terror rose in Thomas, filling his chest. Jacob was wrong. He couldn't stop her.

"Leave my mother ALONE!" Jacob screamed.

The monster laughed again.

"Jake," Thomas tried to say, but his jaws wouldn't move. Jillian was the strong one. They were going to die.

The fence of tangled rails flew over their heads and spiraled over Jillian, the steel twisted into a ball around her. The metal crinkled and popped as it tightened, then purple fire flared, and globs of orange molten steel fell to the street, hissing as they melted into the broken asphalt below. Jillian's laugh ruled the night.

The invisible grip that held Thomas released him, and he nearly stumbled onto the ground.

Marguerite moaned beside him. Thomas threw the shotgun sling over his shoulder and took her in his arms. Jesus Christ, her fingers; Jillian snapped them like toothpicks.

"Are you okay?"

"Am I okay?" she shouted. "Are you shitting me? *Shoot her.*"

[5]

Ohpoopohpoopohpoopohpoop.

Tick Tick sprinted around the perimeter of Jillian's purple glow, the spear over his head like he didn't know how to hold one, which he didn't. His feet slipped on gravel as he rounded a corner, almost spilling him onto a pile of broken concrete and spiked rebar.

"Sheest," he hissed, catching his balance and sliding to a stop behind the destroyed generator truck, his heart slamming so hard his churned brain wondered if it could bruise his ribs.

An orange liquid splattered against the frame of the overturned generator trailer and crawled down its steel frame onto a wooden plank. The wood hissed, and fire burst to life. Tick Tick cocked his head to the side as he gawked stupidly at the fire.

More drops struck around him; one hit his forearm. Pain burned through the effects of the drugs he'd taken.

"Ow, fudge!" he screamed, and dropped to the ground in a twitching mess. The smell of a backyard barbecue touched his nose.

Hello, Norman, the fairy lady's voice said in his head.

His gaze shot to the ball of spitting orange metal as she floated over the midway, facing away from him. "How do you know it's me?"

Because no one is as stupid as you, Norman.

The voice in his head stopped just as the metal ball snapped and flew from her in chunks. One struck the trailer and skipped over his head.

The heat left behind the smell of singed hair. *Now, my friend. If you want more of my magic purple powder, kill the sheriff, or his deputy. I don't care. Kill somebody, Normy, baby.*

No.

He stood, holding the shaft of the spear in his right hand. She's a liar, she's a cheat, she's a monster, ping-ponged around his skull. "Norman," the sheriff guy had said. "*You may have just given us a better chance.*"

A better chance at stopping this jagwad. Frickin' A.

Debris tumbled as he knocked against the tangles of the Dragon's Revenge, the ruins of the roller coaster a vertical maze. A woman screamed and he looked up; his feet caught on rusty steel and he fell. Drug-dulled pain shot through his head as his nose exploded blood over the pavement. The weapon he carried clacked when it hit the asphalt, but his grip on it never faltered.

The pricks of Jillian's howl stabbed him deeper than the throb of his broken nose. He pushed himself to his knees and spat on the asphalt, the bloody mess glowing in Jillian's light. She stood so close to him he could steal her purse, if she had one; her back was to him, all attention on the kid.

"*You're a fuckup*," his father had said the last day he'd ever gotten angry, the day Tick Tick got behind the sun-stained wheel of his rusty 1992 Geo Prizm, with a factory-installed cassette player, and drove the hell out of Hattiesburg, Mississippi, toward Florida, "Highway to Hell" in the tape player. Florida, the land of Disney, unlimited potential, alligators, and drugs. Lots and lots of drugs.

He'd made it as far as twenty miles outside Pensacola on Interstate 10 when the Prizm's radiator blew and he left it on the highway. When an eighteen-wheeler with "The Pixie Brothers' World Famous Carnival" on the door pulled to the side of the interstate and the driver, Mike, offered him a ride, then a job as a carnival ride monkey, he knew he wasn't a fuckup. Not really. Fuckups didn't have jobs. Mike fired up a bowl of gak for them both when the carnival caravan stopped for the night in downtown Niceville, Florida, where they'd set up in the morning.

Niceville. That was its freakin' name, like a town in a satirical movie. Tick Tick had felt nice that night. Real nice. So nice he didn't sleep for three days and learned what it was like to really be a fuckup.

His shoulders tensed as the storm overhead shot that purple lightning in a spiderweb across the sky, the bolts crashing into whatever height remained in the crumbling buildings that surrounded what was once the Pixie Brothers' World Famous Carnival. His head snapped back to the demon fairy woman dripping molten steel from her body as she laughed at the boy and his mom and dad.

The breath he sucked in tasted of smoke, hot metal, and oil. He gripped the spear like Gandalf's staff and forced himself to his feet.

"I'm not a fuckup, Dad," he mumbled, hands shaking. Tick Tick—*no*, Norman Albert VanBrockton, damn it. This is it, dude. Your retributt-ton, retred-beauty-on, retribution. Frick this beach. Norman pulled his arm behind his melon and hurled the spear.

[6]

Glenn leaned against the wrecked bleachers, his breath back, the assault rifle tight in his hands. Gravel rained from a nearby lightning strike, thumping his shoulder; concrete dust fell like snow. The radio on his shoulder crackled. If Jillian heard the radio spit static, she didn't show it.

"Sheriff?" Brittany's voice came through high and thin. The radios didn't seem to work well here, wherever that was.

Glenn clicked the call button. "Here. You in place?"

"Yes, sir."

Good. The plan played in his head. He'd radio "Now" to his deputy, and they'd fire at Jillian at a sixty-degree angle so they wouldn't shoot each other, or Glenn's friends, in the crossfire. The plan didn't hinge on Norman doing something stupid, but Glenn knew it would help.

Jillian's laugh cut through the roars and crackles of lightning. She hovered over the street. Jacob had wrapped the ruined roller coaster rails around her, and she flew, bursting into flames, the metal dripping in molten tears as she cackled. In a moment, her melting bonds would be gone.

Now would be good, Norman.

The radio hissed when he hit the button.

"Now," he said.

As if on cue, a spear flew from behind the twisted mass of the roller coaster, wobbling. Glenn pushed the butt of the assault rifle into his shoulder, leveled it to his eye and, on the count of three, he fired.

[7]

A spear appeared from the darkness and clattered onto the pavement. Jillian looked at it, and the ancient weapon burst into flames. The *rat-tat-tat* of automatic rifles filled the air, drowning out the roar of the storm above. Bullets pummeled Jillian; her body shook as the final specks of melted steel dropped from her, and she collapsed to the pavement, her purple fire extinguished.

Smoke rose from her still body as it lay motionless in the ruins of downtown St. Joseph, Missouri, the carnival a mass of metal, wires, and splintered pine lumber.

Jacob spread his arms wide, pulling Thomas and his mother to him. They were going to see if Jillian was really dead, and he couldn't allow it. That was dumb. Not dumb, it was foolish. The dead villains always—*always*—sat back up.

"Let us go, Jacob," Daddy Tom said, his voice low, like that time Jacob played in the pickup and knocked it out of gear. This was different. Everything was different.

"No," was all he said.

Jillian sat up, like Jacob knew she would. Blood oozed from the bullet wounds that littered her torso.

"You made a mistake, Sheriff," she shouted, rising to her feet without using her arms or legs. "A bad mistake. I am not amused."

Sheriff Glenn and the nice deputy lady rose from behind the shelter of ruins, their rifles dropping to the ground as they floated toward Jillian. Jacob's insides bunched. This was bad.

Watch me rip them to shreds, baby cakes. Jillian spoke into his head. *Then I'll get back to the people you love.*

"You will not!" Jacob screamed as Sheriff Glenn and the deputy sped to the evil fairy woman, suspended in the air on either side.

"I missed you so much, Glenny," Jillian said. "But you've been naughty."

Anger welled inside Jacob. This was it. The time. The final time. He had to kill Jillian, and he had to do it now. His teeth gritted, and sweat ran down his temples as he focused on Jillian, focused all his anger, and—

Nothing happened.

A scream, raw and savage, burst from the sheriff. Jacob winced. He'd never heard a grown-up man scream like that before.

I told you you were weak, baby boy.

Sheriff Glenn's right arm ripped from his body, and the limb flew across the storm-darkened sky; a trail of spurting blood followed. Jillian flicked a hand and he fell. She discarded him like a piece of trash.

"No, Jillian!" Jacob tried to shout at the dark fairy, but he didn't have the strength.

The sheriff slammed into a pile of mangled metal, and jagged points burst through his chest armor. Jacob dropped to the ground and hid his eyes.

[8]

Thomas's world rushed into full speed, the force Jacob used to keep him rooted gone. Glenn. Not Glenn. The sheriff lay limp on the remains of the Octopus, impaled on the wreckage. Jillian had already turned from him, her attention on the deputy. She brought Brittany near her, turning the terrified woman in the air. The deputy flinched as the devil poked her with invisible fingers as casually as if picking out a piece of fruit at the market.

Not for the first time, Thomas wished he'd never met Jillian. Never fallen for her spell. Never followed her. Never allowed the monster into his home.

But it was way too late.

"Jillian," he bellowed. Holding the shotgun to his shoulder, he ran toward her and stopped next to Jacob. Brittany began to wail.

The fairy's eyes, once soft, kind, looked down on him, the glow gone, replaced with inky blackness.

"Hey, baby," she said, the words dripping with poison.

"Let her go," Thomas said.

She laughed. "And what fun would that be?"

He raised the shotgun. "Now."

Jacob lay on the pavement, curled into a ball; Marguerite, cradling her injured hand, tried to comfort him with the other.

What the hell was happening?

"Jake?" Thomas couldn't see much of the boy, the fetal position and his mother swallowing him. "Buddy, it's time."

What he could see of Jacob didn't move.

"Jakie," Marguerite said. "Get up, honey."

His voice, slight and beaten, said, "I can't," over the crackling energy around them.

No. No, no.

The scream from Brittany pierced the night.

"Jacob," Thomas said, kneeling beside the boy, his mother trying to rock him. He looked up and met Thomas's gaze. His eyes told Thomas the end of the story: they were defeated.

Tears fell down the boy's face. "I can't do it, Daddy Tom," Jacob said. "I can't help. I can't do anything. She's too powerful."

He dropped a strong hand on Jacob's shoulder and squeezed, just slightly. "You're wr—"

An invisible force struck Thomas, sending him flying. His body skipped across the pavement like a stone. Stitches ripped in his chest wound, the pain as if the stabbing happened all over again.

"Tom!" Marguerite shrieked as she was lifted off the ground, anything else she might say choked off by Jillian's lavender fist.

Thomas struggled to move, his elbows ripped open by the pavement, his shirt soaking from the knife wound. It was over. Jacob, Marguerite, him, everything. Over.

Jesus Christ, we're all going to—

The world shifted.

The heavy black clouds overhead dissipated before vanishing in the upper wind currents; the temperature fell off a cliff, misty breath heaving from Thomas's mouth.

The boy pushed himself to his feet, his hands balled into fists, the hank of untamable black hair drooping over one eye. His visible eye glowed with a piercing yellow light. Mist pushed from his nostrils like a dragon.

What the hell? Jacob moved closer to Jillian's floating form.

"Never"–the growl from the boy was raw, primal–"*ever*, touch my mother!"

The sound of an enormous pair of shears sliced through the air; Marguerite and Brittany fell, slowing before they touched the pavement.

"No!" Jillian screeched.

That shriek, that plaintive cry. Thomas knew she was losing control.

Jacob moved beneath Jillian, the purple blaze that engulfed her now nothing more than a match flame.

"Jakie," she said. "Jakie, honey. What are you doing?"

He looked up at her–his hair back now, both fiery eyes cutting into her–but didn't speak.

[9]

I asked what you were doing, you little shit.

Hate filled Jacob's heart, black and oily. Jillian, the fairy, the evil fairy, hovered in the air, some kind of stupid balloon. He wanted nothing more than to cut her string.

I'm not afraid of you. The words slow, strong.

A scream ripped from Jillian, her face now that of a shark. *Then you're as fucking weak and stupid as your mother!*

The anger flared hotter; he imagined a giant fist wrapping its fingers around Jillian, then slammed her to the ground. A cloud of dust and debris exploded from the dirty pavement. A moan escaped her.

"Enough," she said, fear in her voice. She pushed herself to her feet and stood on wobbly legs.

There was no more fear in Jacob, no doubt, no worry. Jillian was wrong; he wasn't weak. He was strong, stronger than her, and he would show her.

You're wrong, Jakie. This is my world. This is my kingdom. You're not welcome here anymore. I can make you—

He imagined the fist flinging that stupid Jillian, and it did. She squealed as her arms clamped against her sides, and she flew screaming across what was once the carnival midway. Cheap lumber shattered into splinters as she crashed into the Pixie Brothers' Haunted Hotel and disappeared through a wall. A weak groan of nails ripping from wood grew in the air and the fragile building collapsed on top of her.

A moment passed, then two.

"Is she—" Daddy Tom started to ask before words stabbed into Jacob's brain.

You can't get rid of me, Jakie boy. The ruins of the haunted hotel exploded into the sky, detritus slamming to the pavement in scattered chunks. Lavender fire burst to life around Jillian and she rose into the night. Storm clouds again rolled overhead, the two moons hidden behind them. *And I'm tired of playing.*

Jacob swallowed, a knot in his dry throat. *You're old and tired, Jillian,* he pushed toward her. She simply laughed.

A weight fell on him, pushing him to his knees. Mom and Daddy Tom dropped beside him.

"Jakie!" Mom yelled. Jillian had forced her to kneel beside him, but Mom sounded far away.

You're pathetic, you little parasite.

The weight he couldn't see grew heavier; he dropped onto his hands.

Don't expect Mommy and Tommy to be there for you when you really need them. The purple glow grew stronger; Jillian must be closer. Mom's hand landed into his narrow line of vision, the broken fingers making it resemble a squashed spider. *They won't be, will they, pumpkin? They weren't when you started school, remember?* continued Jillian. The darkness swirled and grew brighter, the lavender faded away. The ruined carnival was gone. Daylight, golden and warm, streamed through the high windows in the old rural school. Jacob stood in the back of the room, shelves of backpacks and lunch boxes, and empty coat hooks before him. He looked down, an empty green pocket folder and the textbook *History of Our Planet* in his hands.

Why am I here? He remembered that day, the day he went to public school, a small public school near Daddy Tom's house. The children in class didn't smile, and they didn't say hi. He was the new kid. They looked at him like he had a disease.

An elbow shoved his shoulder and the items he held dropped to the floor; a chorus of laughter erupted from behind him.

A boy he'd soon find out was Mike Tyrance appeared in Jacob's periphery. He was a year older and at least twenty pounds heavier. A grin twisted on Mike's fat, stupid face.

"Dummy," Mike said, then leaned close to whisper, "Do you stay after school for Panther Time, or are you going to ride the bus?"

Did I answer? Jacob wondered, but Mike interrupted the thought by shoving him into the coat hooks, one of the old brass fixtures digging into his bicep. A shout formed on his lips, but didn't make it any further. Mike leaned closer.

"It doesn't matter," he said, his hot breath reeking of peanut butter Cap'n Crunch. "I'm going to beat the snot out of you sometime. You just wait."

Why did he do it?

Why does Mike hate me? Jacob remembered wondering, but he never discovered the answer. All the kids hated him. It was Mike he took it out on; he gave the big dumb bully a shove at the top of the stairs on the way to the lunchroom. Mike Tyrance screamed like a baby as he dropped, his body flopping as badly as one of those dummies dropped off a cliff in an old TV show. But instead of him standing up and walking away after the fall, Mike's legs snapped, and his head slammed into the brick wall.

No one talked to Jacob after that. He had to change schools.

A tear trickled from his right eye as the memory ground shattered glass through his brain. *Everyone hated me.* More tears built up and threatened to erupt. *Everyone—*

Wait. The memory drained, and Jacob's head cleared. *That didn't happen.* The force holding him down broke with the realization.

He pushed himself to his feet, anger pounding in his temples. He snatched Jillian with the invisible hand, and she pushed, trying to fight back, but—*you can't.* The purple light dimmed even more as Jacob twisted the huge hand and shook; the evil fairy bobblehead flopped. He yanked the hand back, but he lost his grip and Jillian flew through the night air, blood dripping from dozens of small cuts across her face and arms.

The calliope erupted again in its insane rhythm. The dying lavender flame erupted around the fairy and she caught herself before she catapulted into the jagged ruins of the Tilt-A-Whirl.

A howl ripped from Jillian's lungs and nearly pushed Jacob to his knees. Her fury was thick enough to reach out and grab. A deep purple flame grew between her hands as she cupped them just as she had in the cornfield.

A hot stab of fear shot through him. *She beat me in that cornfield,* he thought. *Knocked me down.*

Weakness grabbed his knees as doubt crept back into his head, burrowing like a parasite. The smile on Jillian's face—the razor-toothed smile of a T. rex—pushed him back a step, then two.

"Jakie, baby," came from beside him.

He turned toward the sound; Mom and Daddy Tom were on their hands and knees, blood running from their nostrils.

You hurt my mother. You hurt my mother!

Rage exploded.

Jillian's hands began to open, the violet glow blinding.

"JACOB!" she screamed.

"I *told* you. Never hurt my *mother!*" His voice was low, strength returning to his legs.

A ball of red flame burst from Jacob's body and struck Jillian before she could attack; the monster shot into the wreckage of the great generator, slamming into the machine's engine. A metal rod jutted from her side.

"Honey," Mom eked out, finally free from Jillian's hold.

He swung toward his mother and Daddy Tom, still on hands and knees, a line of snot dangling from Jacob's flared nostrils, his eyes blazing yellow. The pinched pain on Mom's face made his stomach clench.

"Momma," he whispered, wiping his nose with the short sleeve of his T-shirt.

Her smile radiated pain. "You did good, baby," she said.

I'm not weak, he thought, his inner voice small, four years old again. Tears he thought were used up grew in his sore eyes. Jacob's mind reached out, and his mother sucked in air as her fingers, one by one, snapped back into place, the bones knitting in seconds.

Daddy Tom's thick hand mussed Jacob's hair, then his eyes shot to something behind Jacob.

The only thing behind me is—

"Jacob Jenkins!"

He turned; Jillian stood on the pavement, a hand cupped over the wound left when she pulled her body from the metal rod. Her hair hung in sweat-soaked ribbons over her face.

She's not healing.

"Ja-cob Jen-kins!"

A hand, warm and soft, rested on his shoulder. "I love you, baby," his mother said, her power surging through him.

She's helping me, Jacob realized. He could leech power from Momma and Daddy Tom.

Jacob smiled. His invisible hand, joined by a second, wrapped thick fingers around the fairy's torso and legs. Jillian's own hands shot to her head, grabbing handfuls of red hair as her screams filled every corner of the night. Jacob pulled, a cracking and stretching squeaking through the air, sounding like when Daddy Tom deboned a rotisserie chicken.

The fairy's middle showed, her belly button ripping up and down, spilling intestines and abdominal fluid over the pavement. Jacob didn't stop. He grunted as he tugged, his hair drenched in sweat.

Finally, the lightning crisscrossing the darkness emitted one last burst, then died. The storm stopped writhing and disappeared; the wet rip ended Jillian's screams, her body bisected, held together only by a strip of intestine.

Marguerite slid beside Jacob and threw her arms around him, her sobs louder than Jillian's death.

"It's okay, Mom, Daddy Tom," Jacob said. "She can't hurt us anymore."

"Oh, Jacob, baby," Marguerite moaned. "Are you sure?"

"It's over," he said.

Daddy Tom rose on wobbly knees. The two moons lit the rubble that was once downtown St. Joe. Jillian's ruined body lay in two halves, her face to the heavens.

"I'm proud of you, kiddo," Daddy Tom said as he walked toward the fairy, the monster. "Goodbye, Jillian," he said. "Nobody will miss you."

He held the barrel of the Mossberg up to her face and fired.

CHAPTER NINETEEN

THEY BURIED GLENN when the sun came up, the wide green berm off US 36 pretty enough in the warm morning light. Marguerite, her hand healed by her son's magic, said a few words about the sheriff; she'd known him the longest. Jacob floated a granite boulder used as decoration in a nearby yard and placed it at the head of the grave, carving "Sheriff Glenn Kirkhoff" into the rock with his recovered powers, which appeared to be even stronger than before. The boy stopped a few times to make sure he got the spelling right, then they were off in Thomas's pickup.

The old Ford had a flat tire from the voyage between worlds, but Thomas had it changed fast enough. They'd driven around what remained of St. Joseph, honking the truck's horn and shouting for survivors, but found only five or six people. The rest apparently had fled or were taken by Jillian's guards.

By the time Thomas pointed the nose of the pickup toward the country east of town, he'd left plenty of messages for those they were leaving behind.

"Honey," Marguerite said from the passenger seat, Jacob between them, and Brittany and Norman in the back. "It's been five miles."

Five miles. Yes, it had been. Thomas turned on his blinker out of habit and pulled to the side of the road. There wasn't a vehicle moving as far as he could see. There were people, though. Whether St. Joe residents or Jillian's fairy people, Thomas couldn't tell, but Jacob told him nearly half of St. Joe's 72,000 residents survived. That wasn't nearly enough. He'd stopped a few times to talk to those five or six on the road, but no one looked at him, their eyes far away. Shock, he guessed.

Thomas hopped from the cab of the truck.

"Here you go, boss," Norman said.

Thomas was happy Norman made it; he had plans for him. Norman handed Thomas a can of red spray paint from the mostly full case of them in the bed of the truck. That was Jacob's idea. He'd sent out a message with whatever magic he had, telling the survivors there was a way home. It was Thomas's job to make sure they knew where to go.

"Thanks." He took the can and walked into the middle of the highway.

The can rattled as Thomas shook it, the small metal ball bearing inside mixing the paint. He pressed the spray valve and a red mist left words on the shattered asphalt.

HUMANS.

FOLLOW US

TO GET HOME.

↑

"Humans? Really?" Marguerite asked.

Thomas stood and walked back to the truck, handing the can to Norman.

"There are more people here than just humans, you know?" he said.

She huffed. "I know that, mister. It just sounds. Well, I don't know. A little racist."

Brittany pulled open the sliding back windows of the truck cab.

"You do remember one of the denizens of this place destroyed a city of almost eighty thousand people, murdered my boss, and tried to kill the rest of us, right?" she said through the open window, her face growing pink.

"Denizens?" Norman repeated.

"Yeah," she said. "I read a lot."

"Come on, guys." Thomas patted the roof of the cab and smiled at a drug addict and what might be the only member of the Buchanan County Sheriff's Department left alive. "Let's play nice."

As he drove toward the country, he lay on his horn. If there were people here, alive, he wanted them to follow him home.

Five miles later, he sprayed another message.

[2]

The old farmhouse grew in the truck's windshield, home to Uncle Boyd, and before that Boyd's parents, who died before Thomas was born. Thomas had lived there the past seven years, most of it with Jillian.

That thought ground into his heart like metal shards. He parked the truck on the rural highway for just a moment to paint a red arrow turning onto the gravel lane, then got back in the truck.

The porch steps were intact, but the porch itself had lost enough decking planks that Thomas went first to make sure it was safe. A few things he wanted to take with him were inside, and he wasn't going to let them go. Marguerite and Jacob followed in his footsteps close behind.

"Don't worry, Mom," Jacob said as Thomas stepped carefully around the gaping holes in the flooring. "I won't let you fall."

This was the kid who had scared the hell out of his own mother, the one who reminded Thomas of Billy Mumy from that episode of *The*

Twilight Zone; one false move and Jacob might send him out into the corn and no one would see him again. The front door fell when Thomas grabbed the knob and pushed inward. Dust erupted into the air; the interior of the house seemed layered with it.

"What's the plan?" he asked. "I'm going for the photo albums in the hall closet."

Marguerite pointed toward the kitchen. "The box of index cards with all Gramma's recipes."

Jacob nodded toward the hall that led to the bedrooms and the back door. "I wanna get our baseball gloves."

A warm flush grew over Thomas. *He's my boy too.* "We'll meet you out back, son," he said.

Jacob smiled at him and jogged down the hallway. Marguerite leaned into Thomas and kissed his cheek.

"He loves you, you know?"

"Yeah," Thomas said, cradling her cheeks in his thick hands. "I know."

He leaned forward and pressed his lips to hers. When he broke off, tears swam in his eyes. "I want to ask—"

She shook her head. "Nope, mister. Not now. Take me home."

[3]

THE WAY HOME

BACKYARD

←

Four whacks with a hammer put two nails into the sheet of plywood, securing it to the old elm tree next to the gravel road. Thomas crossed his arms, the orange handle of the Craftsman tight in his grip.

It's over. She's gone.

We're heading home.

They were all back there, along with the Martins, a family from St. Joe who'd followed Thomas's spray-painted directions. Thomas hoped there would be more—many more.

Norman leaned against another sign, the last sign Thomas had made and tied to a metal fence post with baling wire. It simply pointed at the ring of mushrooms and read:

STAND

IN THE

CIRCLE

↓

"How is this supposed to work?" Chris Martin asked, his arm around his wife's waist. Claire held their infant son; their four-year-old stood between them. "It's a mushroom circle."

"It's a fairy circle," Thomas said.

"Oh, come on. I'm an educated man. I know how these circles are formed, and it has nothing to do with fairies."

His world literally moved under his feet, and he doesn't see it.

"Then," Thomas said, picking the photo album up off the ground and sticking it under his arm, "how do you explain this?"

He didn't step gingerly into the circle; he hopped. Marguerite gasped, Jacob giggled. Nothing changed.

"Was something supposed to happen?" Chris asked. "Because it didn't."

Thomas crushed his eyes closed, but when he opened them, he was still in his yard.

A sigh pushed through Marguerite's lips. "But I don't want to stay here."

A gasp escaped Claire. Wha—?

The air around Thomas grew heavy, clinging to him, grabbing, twirling. He began to spin, and seconds later he was somewhere else.

It took ten minutes for everyone to come through.

Jacob next, then Marguerite, Norman, and the Martins. Brittany came last.

They stood on a vast plane in the darkness, the dry, raw earth lit by a mostly full moon.

One moon.

Their moon.

"We're home," Thomas said, holding Marguerite.

She leaned into him. "It doesn't look like home."

"What happened?" Claire asked.

It was Jacob who spoke. "She happened," he said. "Jillian, the bad fairy. She took St. Joe, took our farm, took everything to Ālfheimr."

"Ālfheimr?" Chris asked.

"Land of the Elves."

Chris barked a laugh. "Oh, come on."

There was a crackle and hiss as Brittany's radio came to life.

"Echo Base, this is Patrol Bravo Five; we have a 10-37 in grid niner. Repeat. We have a 10-37 in grid niner."

Thomas turned to Brittany. "What's that mean?"

"Bravo Five, proceed with caution. Bring them in," a different voice responded.

"It means we're not supposed to be here," Brittany said before clicking the push-to-talk button. "Echo Base and Patrol Bravo Five, this is Deputy Brittany Curtright of the Buchanan County, Missouri, Sheriff's Department. I'm accompanied by eight civilians. We're unarmed, except for my service weapon. Please respond."

Crackle.

"This is Bravo Five. I suspect you have a story to tell, Deputy. We're on our way."

[5]
2026, Florida

The United States Army established a base in the Northwest Wasteland in 2024 for scientists to study the storm that stripped Northwest Missouri of every trace of life, leaving behind a vast scar of subsoil. The scientists were on the wrong track, Thomas knew, but they wouldn't believe a word he said. In the end, it didn't matter. The military transported all of them to various destinations: the Martins to Kansas City, Missouri—that hadn't escaped all of the destruction; Brittany to Columbia, Missouri—the Boone County Sheriff's Department had offered her a job; and Thomas, Marguerite, and Jacob to Panama City Beach, to be close to Marguerite's mother. Thomas's parents, Kyle and Debbie, were just two hours away, in Pensacola. They visited once a month. Thomas took Norman to Florida with them and put him in a rehabilitation facility. He planned to drive Norman home to Mississippi when he got out. It was the least he could do.

On a Friday night, maybe two months after the government settled them in Florida, Marguerite stepped onto their front porch; Jacob was already in bed. She sat in a deck chair next to Thomas as she had back home in Northwest Missouri and slipped a hand into his. The Gulf of Mexico was three blocks away; the smell of salt came on the breeze.

"Jakie asked about school," she said. "I told him I could get him enrolled this week. It'll be August before we know it."

Thomas turned in his chair, slipping his other hand into Marguerite's. "I love you, you know?" he said.

"I'd hope so. You say it enough." She laughed. "I love you too."

A cough, the sound of Thomas clearing his throat: "Honey, I—I need to ask you something." He paused to swallow, his throat suddenly tight. "Will you marry me?"

"Well, Thomas Cavanaugh," she said, releasing his hands to pull him closer. "It's about goddamn time."

It took a week for Thomas to realize he hadn't said *hitched*.

[6]
Arizona

The car pulled to a stop at the southwestern end of Boynton Canyon Road, the town of Sedona behind it in all but its city limits. The temperature had already started to drop, the ninety-degree day now down to the low sixties. Elizabeth Condon opened the door, the mechanical click and warning buzz out of place in this world of beauty.

The red sandstone of an ancient shoreline made up the walls of the box canyon; the layered rock was obvious, but the color had begun to fade in the waning light of day, although the dusk made up for it. Pink, yellow, and orange pastels painted the western sky. Crucifixion thorn and desert willow dotted the landscape between the car and the canyon, the tree trunks twisted from what the new-age hippy types claimed were energy vortices that connected dimensions.

If Elizabeth really had a part to play in the fate of the world as that fairy said, it would be here.

She grabbed a twelve-pack of beer and a bag of chips from the passenger seat and stepped from the car, shutting the door behind her. The air here was clean and dry and smelled of sweetgrass and coumarin, of dry mesquite and desert sand. The front of her old Honda dipped slightly as Elizabeth climbed onto the hood and sat, the beer box beside her. She pulled out a Tim Binnall Burlington IPA and popped it open with the church key she kept on her key ring.

After escaping the Jillian storm over the Missouri River Bridge and into Kansas, she got her car windows fixed; Cotton Condon had also taught her to sew extra cash into the floor of the vehicle under the seat, just in case. Badass extraordinaire.

Then she took two detours: west of Lebanon to stand on the geographic center of the United States, then down to Cawker City, a town of less than five hundred people, to see the world's largest ball of twine. When in Kansas . . .

But she didn't know where she was going; Elizabeth simply followed the road before her.

Sixteen more hours through Colorado to New Mexico, she stopped in Albuquerque to throw a pizza on the roof of the house from *Breaking Bad.* The owner ran onto the lawn yelling for her to "get that pizza off my house before I call the cops." Elizabeth gave him the finger and drove off.

Catching a few hours' sleep in the parking lot of the Fire Rock Navajo Casino, she made it to Sedona by mid-afternoon. During the trip, whatever national news she could pick up on the radio from a network mentioned the devastation of the carnival in St. Joe with words like *total destruction, natural disaster,* and *EF-5 tornado.*

"Bullshit," she said into the interior of the car when the news first broke at the top of some damn hour on KSKU out of Sterling, Kansas. When she'd walked out of the station in St. Joe in scrubs, police and sheriff's department officers running here and there ignoring her, what she saw wasn't a tornado. Purple electricity shot through the sky like a mad scientist was trying to bring a monster to life; a vortex roared around the carnival. It wasn't an EF-5 tornado, but it had a name. The storm was called Jillian.

The scent of pine and citrus caressed her nose as she brought the IPA to her lips and tipped it back, the taste as good as the smell.

"What the hell are we doing here, Elizabeth?" she said over the lip of the brown bottle.

A barn owl hooted from its perch in a nearby juniper tree, its moony face haunting in the early night. Elizabeth raised the bottle in salute.

"And a happy Tim Binnall evening to you too," she said.

That round white face turned to consider her, then the bird stretched its wings and pushed itself into the sky, the only thing in the night air. Insects lay silent, pastel clouds condemned to the horizon.

She'd never seen a sky without contrails, the white exhaust lines from jet airliners as common in American skies as nannies with umbrellas in England. Maybe. Elizabeth had never been to England.

Elizabeth pushed herself back on the hood until her back found the windshield. She tipped back another swig; an *aaah* stretched out as she lay the back of her head on the roof of the car, stars beginning to twinkle in the growing darkness.

She'd come out here every night since arriving in Sedona, and nothing happened. She wondered how many nights she'd do this. The yips of coyotes were nice, but—

Elizabeth brushed across her ears.

She raised her head and looked into the desert, the trees and the distant canyon still and quiet.

"Hey," she said into the darkness. "Show yourself."

I'm right here, the voice said, but as she sat up and crossed her legs, she couldn't see anyone. The voice may have come from the trees, but the words were almost in her head.

Almost?

No. They were. Elizabeth slid back down to the end of the hood, dropping her heels onto the bumper.

"Where are you, Jillian?" she asked. "I thought I was finished with you."

"No, my dear." A light popped on in the shadows beneath the trees and moved closer, bobbing as if it had trouble moving. "I need your help."

"Ha!" Elizabeth watched the rising and dipping fairy light as it flew closer. "After what you've put me through? Fat-ass chance."

The light limped toward her face until she made out the figure inside, a small human form with diaphanous wings that beat out of time. Yes, it was Jillian. Her red hair hung limply across her scarred and ragged face; Jillian could have been an extra from *The Walking Dead*. Her arms dangled helplessly beside her. The sight of the fairy's lower half caught Elizabeth's next sip in her throat. She coughed, spewing the beer across Jillian. The spray pushed the fairy backward, her offbeat wings dropping her below the grill. Elizabeth reached down and pinched Jillian's shoulders between her finger and thumb. The fairy's waist and lifeless legs dangled from her torso, hanging by what could only be her tiny intestines.

"What happened to you?" Elizabeth asked.

"Jacob," she said, no power behind the word. "And Thomas Cavanaugh. They wounded me. Please, Elizabeth. Oh, please. You're a healer, heal me."

"Healer? Yeah, I'm a healer, all right." She took a long drink of beer and sat the empty on the car hood behind the beer box so it wouldn't roll off. No littering in a national park. "When you covered the Kansas City area in black snow, do you know who healed the people you poisoned?"

"Jacob." The word came out like her mouth was filled with gravel.

She pulled Jillian closer to her face.

"He gave me the cure," she said, pinching Jillian a little tighter, "but I'm the one who told the CDC, and they told the press. I helped piss on your party."

The fairy struggled beneath Elizabeth's grip but didn't have the strength to escape.

"Oh, I'm sorry. Are you uncomfortable?" Elizabeth moved her hand, Jillian's lower torso a part of a broken toy. "I'm sorry, hon. How about I set you down so you can relax?"

Using her left hand to prop up Jillian's lower bits, she lay the tiny broken body on the hood of the car, and pushed the halves closer together. Jillian let out a screech of pain.

A sense of peace spread through Elizabeth.

"Now, why did you come to me? Don't you have some kind of elf magic that can stitch you back together?"

A cough rattled Jillian; a spray of blood burst from her mouth.

"No. Sew me or tape me. Spray me with something. I've never been like this. I—I can't heal."

A fresh bottle of Tim Binnall Burlington IPA clinked against another as Elizabeth pulled it from the box. She didn't open it, not yet.

"Sure, I'll help you," she said. "But I want to know something first. What happened to all those people you whisked away with the carnival, from Northwest Missouri? What happened to Jacob? To Thomas? To Jacob's mother? I assume she was there. Are they alive?"

The nod from the fairy, weak and minute, was still visible in her slight glow.

"That's nice to hear," Elizabeth said. "Because I hope they live good, long lives, even Jacob the demon boy, because he opposed you. That means he's probably growing into a good person."

"Elizabeth?" Jillian said, the word barely audible.

"And you never were."

Elizabeth raised the bottle and brought it down hard on the fairy, crushing Jillian's skull; brains and blood sprayed across the car hood. Elizabeth ground the bottom of the bottle in circles across the monster's body before cracking open the top and taking a long, slow drink. After finishing her beer she planned to scrape up as much of Jillian as she could find, pile it atop a nest of dead leaves and sticks, and set fire to the fucking thing.

Then she'd go into town for a prickly-pear cheesecake at the Mariposa. Yelp reviews said it was delicious.

ACKNOWLEDGMENTS

I'M SITTING IN my downstairs office. That sounds more romantic than it is. By "downstairs," I mean basement, and by "office," I mean whatever small, cluttered room there was no previous use for other than being small and cluttered. This is exactly the type of setting many authors consider their "office."

Author's Office [Awe-thors awe-fis] *noun*
1. Wherever an author can hide for a few hours a day and peck at a keyboard.
2. The toilet.

I consider myself lucky for being able to do this here (and the toilet stuff there), and I imagine other authors do as well. I'm also listening to AC/DC as I write this. That doesn't really matter, although it does, because I dedicated this book to them. AC/DC is the first band I latched on to as a freshman in high school when I was attempting to discover my identity as a person. Music often does that. High school for me was in the early 1980s, and I still crank that band. I find "Highway to Hell" is great to write fight scenes to. So, now. People to thank. Damn.

A lot. Writing a book is a solitary process, but seeing it grow from an idea on a computer screen to a volume on a bookshelf takes a lot of help.

First up, my family. They're cool with my disappearing into that basement office to do what Daddy does.

The rest:

Travis Kline and Gary Darling, the best beta readers around. Love you guys. You've made each of my novels better.

Editor Christie Stratos, who was both bitchen and awesome in pointing out all the issues I needed to fix. For those about to rock? That's you, Christie.

Helga Schier, editorial director of CamCat Publishing, who gave *The Boy from Two Worlds* the go-ahead.

Maryann Appel, CamCat's art director, who rocks at design.

I mention Kris Ketz in Chapter 6 of *The Boy From Two Worlds*. Kris is an Emmy-award winning anchor and investigative reporter at KM-BC-TV9. He's worked at Channel 9 from July 4, 1983, until the publication of this book (and, I hope, beyond). I was an intern at KMBC in 1986, and during a stifling-hot remote shoot in downtown Kansas City, Missouri, Kris walked over to a street vendor and bought me a Bomb Pop. Kris Ketz isn't just an Emmy award-winning news anchor, he's a Jason award-winning human being. Thanks, man.

And last is Tim Binnall (I know I've forgotten a ton of people. Sorry, y'all. Every one of you is totally awesome). Tim is a longtime compadre, podcaster, and news editor for *Coast to Coast* AM who refers to himself as a "sublime scoundrel of the paranormal," and "professional lunatic." When my first novel was published, Tim asked if I'd include him in every one of my future novels. I have. He's been a street (Tim Binnall Boulevard), a victim of a car theft, and here he's a beer—Tim Binnall's Burlington IPA. Cheers to you, Tim.

Thanks for reading, folks. Until next time.

Jason Offutt, June 22, 2023, Maryville, Missouri

ABOUT THE AUTHOR

JASON OFFUTT ATTENDED college in the 1980s, earning a BS in Bitchen and a minor in Gnarly. He'd always wanted to be an author, although his parents strongly encouraged him to become something lucrative, like an accountant, despite the fact that he was (and still is) deplorable at math. Since then, he has published seventeen well-received books, such as the first book in this duology, the 2022 and 2023 IBPA Benjamin Franklin Gold Award-winning *The Girl in the Corn*, the humorous sci-fi romp *So You Had to Build a Time Machine* (the Shelf Unbound Best Indie Book Competition's 2020 Top Notable 100 Books, and the American Book Fest's best books of 2020), and, well, uh, some more.

He lives in Northwest Missouri where he teaches university journalism, cooks for his beautiful, supportive family, and will get around to tiling the downstairs bathroom one of these days, honey. He promises.

If you'd like to reach Jason, check out his website: *www.jasonoffutt.com*. He's also on Twitter, Instagram, and Threads as *@TheJasonOffutt*, and Facebook as *TheJasonOffuttAuthor*. If you'd like to reach Jason, and actually know how to tile a bathroom, that would be awesome. Thanks.

If you've enjoyed reading
Jason Offutt's *The Boy From Two Worlds*,
consider leaving a review
to help our authors.

And check out
The Building That Wasn't
by Abigail Miles.

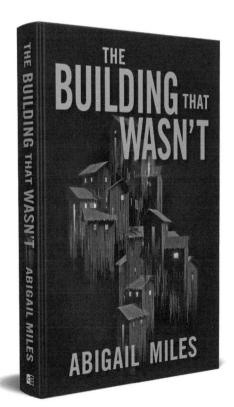

1

❧❧

T HE ROOM WAS WHITE—almost blindingly so, with surfaces that had been scrubbed to a shine, so that by staring at the floor or a wall it was nearly possible to see one's own reflection. It was clean and fresh and sterile. The perfect canvas.

The most beautiful aspect of the white room was how stark contrasting shapes and colors appeared on the initial blankness. This was an aesthetic quality that the man found particularly pleasing to explore, and so he did as such extensively, to a near-compulsive rate. He fancied himself an artist, with the borders of the room providing the ideal location to bring his masterpiece to life.

Keeping that in mind and aiming for the truest form of artistic perfection he could conjure, the man gripped the tool in his hand—his paintbrush of choice—and hefted it before him. His arm dropped in an almost graceful fashion as he completed a full swoop, similar in form to that of a baseball player setting up to bat. Then, pausing once to allow the moment to settle in its resplendent glory, the man slowly lowered his arm, tool in hand, and looked around at what he had created.

The white backdrop truly was perfect, he thought. It made the red look so much fresher, sharper and more potent. And the shapes the droplets formed, the pattern they enacted across the room. Perfect. The man admired the final product and couldn't help but think that this may have been some of his finest work yet.

Not to mention the added pleasure derived from the screaming.

While some find the sound of a human scream to be unpleasant, the man found it to be more precious than music—a chorus of varying pitches and volumes coming together in a resounding crescendo at the final moment. He would do it all for that, for the symphony that was forged as a result of the fear, the excitement. The pain.

That's why he was there, after all. To create such a stupendous pain in the people they supplied.

Well, that was not technically true. Technically he was there for many, many more reasons. Glorified kidnapper being one, rubber duck watcher another.

But the pain. That was his favorite.

Though usually the pain was accompanied by a distinct factor of more—the unraveling of the universe and all that.

Not this time. This was only an ordinary body, with no spark of the otherworldly in sight.

The man didn't care.

Maybe others would, but he found purpose enough for himself in the beauty of what he could fashion there, with or without the ulterior motive. In some ways, one could say that having a secondary reason for the pain only tarnished it, whereas this belonged solely to him. This moment, right here.

The man took a deep breath, savoring the complete ambiance of the space he was in, before he turned back to his subject and assessed his options. Settling on a different, more precise tool—one with a much sharper edge—the man once more lifted his arm and continued with his ordained task.

From a different room, a set of eyes casually observed on a screen as the man set to work on his masterpiece, nodding once in approval before turning away. The screen left on displayed the white walls, no longer pristine, which echoed back the horrendous chorus the man's work produced.

THERE WAS AN ELDERLY MAN Everly had never seen
before standing behind all the black-clad patrons, and his
eyes had been focused on her for the duration of the service.

She blinked and realized that wasn't quite right. There was an elderly man Everly recognized, as if from a dream, as if from a memory,
lodged deep and low down in the recesses of her brain. She squinted at
him, because if she could just . . .

She blinked again, and of course she knew him, why wouldn't she
know him, why would she ever not recognize—

Blink. Everly shook her head. The man was still there, and she
didn't know why a second before she had recognized him, because she
did not, though she felt oddly unsettled by the memory of recognizing
the man. Not as unsettled as she was, however, by his mere presence or
by the fact of his staring at her.

He was too far away for her to actually see his eyes, to know for sure,
but she could feel his attention pierced on her like a dagger through her
spleen. The sensation was disconcerting, but in a strange way she appre-
ciated the man and the mystery he presented. It gave her something to
focus on. Something to puzzle over.

Someone to look at other than the form in the coffin on the elevated platform in front of her.

The man wore a bowler hat over his tufted gray hair, and a brown tweed coat, which worked even further to set him apart from the sea of faces that encircled him—the rest of whom were all adorned in shades of black or blackish blue, all at least a little familiar to Everly. The friends, the coworkers, the distant acquaintances and associates.

But not the family. She had no other family. None but her.

The preacher had finished speaking, Everly realized with a start, and was gesturing for her to step forward. She didn't want to. She wanted to go back to pondering the peculiar man in the bowler hat, trying to work out how he had found his way there, and why, but they were all staring at her, so she stood, refusing to breathe as she crossed the distance between her chair and the platform ahead of her. A sharp pang flashed through her skull when she reached the front. Everly grit her teeth, resisting the urge to lift a hand to the side of her temple.

She couldn't look at the body. They had asked if she wanted to beforehand, to make sure he looked okay—like himself, she supposed—but she knew it would be no use. He would never look like himself. Never again.

A car accident had led her here, to that raised platform, in front of all the vaguely familiar forms in black and the solitary strange one in brown. Or at least, that is what they had told her, when it was already too late for the cause to even matter.

But according to them, it had been a car accident, and so he hadn't been quite right. Or his body hadn't been. They told her it would be okay if she didn't want an open coffin, but she wasn't able to stand the thought of locking him up in there any sooner than she needed to. So even though she refused now to look, she kept him out in the open. She kept him free.

Afterward, Everly was ushered to a dimly lit reception room, where she had scarcely a moment to herself before the other mourners came flooding in to report how very sorry they were, how devastating of a loss it must be, how much she would be kept in their prayers. Everly hardly heard any of them. She leaned against one of the whitewashed walls of the hall and rubbed her temple, trying not to close her eyes, though she wanted nothing more than to shut out everything and everyone around her. She wanted them all to go back, to their lives and their families and their homes. She wanted to go back.

But back to what, she couldn't help but ask herself. Back to the empty house with too many rooms and the life that she wasn't sure she could picture any longer in his absence.

Her father's absence.

She was too young, all of Everly's neighbors had tried to claim. Too young to be all alone. But at twenty-four, she was hardly a child anymore, and really, what would anyone have done anyway? Where would she have gone?

She had nowhere else to go, no one else to go to, and they knew it as well as she did.

She was on her own.

Everly considered leaving. She thought better of it a moment later, looking around at all the people who had come out to celebrate her father's life, but an instant after that she realized she didn't even care. None of them had truly known him anyhow. They had only come for the cake, which was now set out on a plastic folding table by the door, the words Our Most Sincere Condolences traced out in poorly scripted black icing across the center of the buttercream sheet. They probably wouldn't even notice if she left, Everly thought, and even if they did, she could see no reason why she should care. No reason at all.

Everly stood up from the wall to leave, trying to appear as nonchalant as possible as she walked between the well-wishers, making her way toward the doors of the reception hall.

As she stepped out into the deepening evening air just beyond the doors, she caught sight of a blur of brown fabric far ahead of her.

Straining her eyes against the dusk that was swiftly descending, Everly could just make out the shape of the strange man from before—the one she remembered and knew yet was certain she had never met—as he strode off into the night, the shadow of his curved bowler hat protruding distinctly above his head as he left without so much as an insincere commiseration offered her way.

༓༓༓

I T WAS HIS OWN FAULT, and he knew it. Luca shouldn't have
told Jamie that he'd take on the second shift, but he hadn't been
able to resist. It had felt like the right decision at the time, and
like all the worst decisions, it was only through the harsh lens of retro-
spect that he could see how little he had thought this through. After
nearly a full twenty-four hours in front of the screens set up around the
cramped surveillance room, Luca's eyes had more than glazed over, and
he was becoming afraid they'd get stuck that way if he stayed in there
much longer: frozen in a state of half-awareness.

Struggling—failing—to suppress a yawn, Luca leaned back in his
chair and looked over the screens again, searching for anything he
might have missed the past thousand times he had scanned the camera feeds. It was proving to be an unusually dull shift—doubly so, for
the added hours of monotony. Despite the long hours and unending
boredom, it was almost worth it for the chance to be alone, if only for
a little while.

To be the eyes instead of the watched.

(As far as he was aware, at least.)

And to use his eyes for his own purposes.

If only he could stay awake to use them. Luca could feel himself fading, and every few seconds he had to jerk his head up to prevent himself from collapsing from exhaustion. If only something interesting would happen, he thought. Something to wake him up.

Unbidden, his mind began to drift, in a half-conscious state, to the dreams that haunted him during the night—not the only reason, but certainly one of the reasons that had driven him to make the ill-guided decision to stay awake through the night in front of those awful screens.

Though, perhaps haunt wasn't the right word. Haunting implied ghosts from a past lived through and regretted. If anything, Luca's dreams hinted at something that hadn't yet come to pass, if he was feeling high-minded enough to label himself as being prophetic.

And really, would he have been that far off?

He was never able to place a finger on what it was about his night-time visions that unsettled him so, but more often than not, Luca would jerk awake during the night, drenched in sweat and with fleeting images filling his head, then vanishing moments later. He didn't ever retain much from them—mostly just a feeling of dread—but occasionally he would find something tangible to hang on to, something that he thought he could remember, if only for that brief instant.

Sometimes he saw her. She was always different: sometimes a child, with strawberry-blond pigtails and a lopsided grin; sometimes older, with a sharp chin and mouth perpetually turned down on the ends; most of the time she was a young woman in her twenties, around his age—fierce, tall, defiant.

Always she burned.

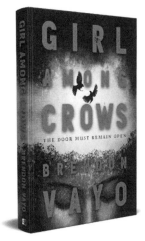

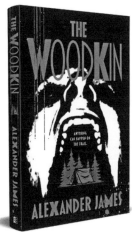

CamCat
Books

VISIT US ONLINE FOR MORE BOOKS TO LIVE IN:
CAMCATBOOKS.COM

SIGN UP FOR CAMCAT'S FICTION NEWSLETTER FOR
COVER REVEALS, EBOOK DEALS, AND MORE EXCLUSIVE CONTENT.

CamCatBooks   @CamCatBooks   @CamCat_Books   @CamCatBooks